The CHILD of the HOLY GRAIL

The CHILD of the HOLY GRAIL

The Third of the Guenevere Novels

ROSALIND MILES

CROWN PUBLISHERS
NEW YORK

3 4858 00286 5799

Copyright © 2001 by Rosalind Miles
Map copyright © 1998 by Rodica Prato

Published by Crown Publishers, New York, New York. Member of the Crown
Publishing Group.

Random House, Inc. New York, Toronto, London, Sydney, Auckland
www.randomhouse.com

Crown is a trademark and the Crown colophon is a registered trademark of
Random House, Inc.

Originally published in Great Britain by Simon & Schuster in 2000.

Printed in the United States of America

Design by Nancy Kenmore and Lauren Dong

Library of Congress Cataloging-in-Publication Data
Miles, Rosalind.
        The child of the Holy Grail / by Rosalind Miles.—1st ed.
        Sequel to: Knight of the sacred lake.
        1. Guenevere, Queen (Legendary character)—Fiction.   2. Arthur, King—Fiction.
    3. Lancelot (Legendary character)—Fiction.   4. Grail—Fiction.   5. Arthurian
    romances—Adaptations.   I. Title.
PR6063.I319 C48   2001
823'.914—dc21   00-064487

ISBN 0-609-60624-7

10 9 8 7 6 5 4 3 2 I

First American Edition

For the One
Who Hears
the Silence of the Stars

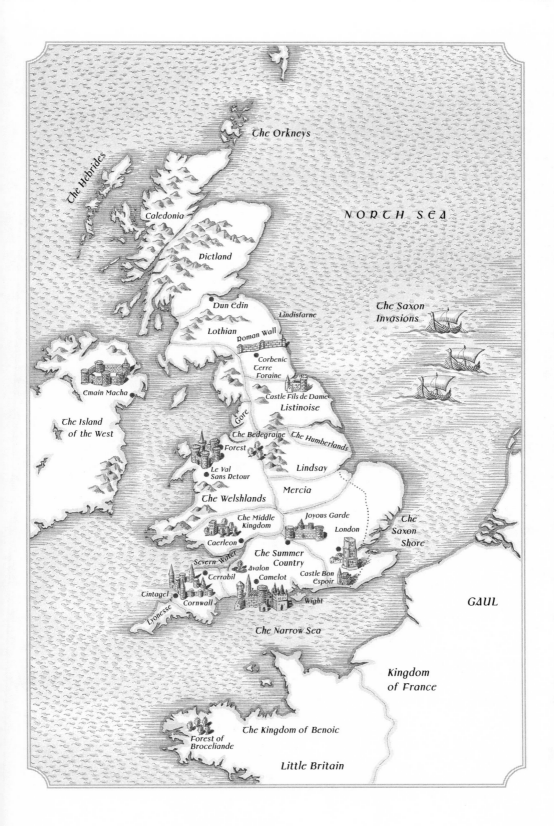

The Orkneys

The Hebrides

NORTH SEA

Caledonia

Pictland

Dun Edin

Lindisfarne

The Saxon
Invasions

Lothian

Roman Wall

Corbenic
Terre
Foraine

Emain Macha

Castle Fils de Dame

Gore

Listinoise

The Island
of the West

The Bedegraine
Forest

The Humberlands

Le Val
Sans Retour

Lindsay

The Welshlands

Mercia

The Middle
Kingdom

Joyous Garde

London

The
Saxon
Shore

Caerleon

The Summer
Country

Severn Water

Avalon

Castle Bon
Espoir

Terrabil

Camelot

GAUL

Tintagel

Cornwall

Wight

Lyonesse

The Narrow Sea

Kingdom
of France

The Kingdom of Benoic

Forest of
Broceliande

Little Britain

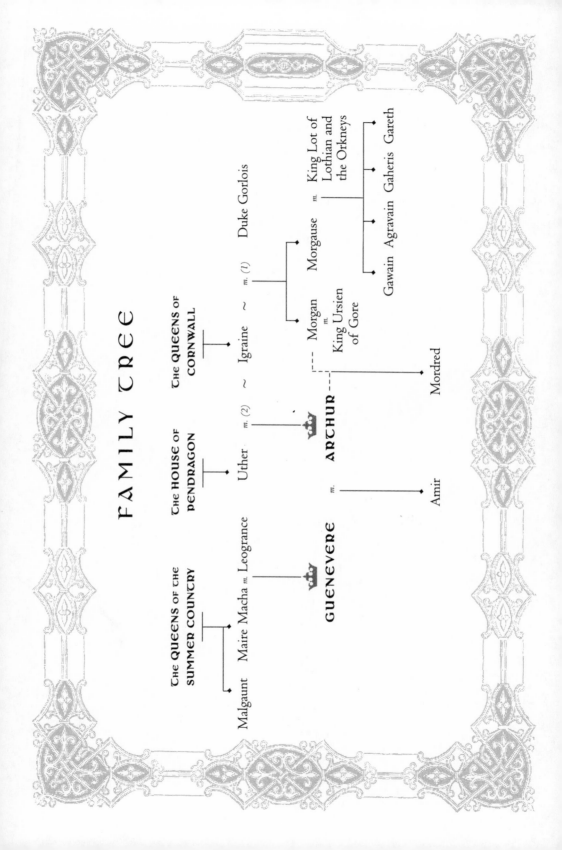

FAMILY TREE

THE QUEENS OF THE SUMMER COUNTRY

Malgaunt   Maire Macha *m.* Leogrance

GUENEVERE

THE HOUSE OF PENDRAGON

Uther *m. (2)*

ARTHUR

Amir *m.*

THE QUEENS OF CORNWALL

Igraine ~ ~ *m. (1)* Duke Gorlois

Morgan   Morgause *m.* King Lot of Lothian and the Orkneys
m.
King Ursien of Gore

Gawain Agravain Gaheris Gareth

Mordred

The Child of the Holy Grail

IT BEFELL IN THE DAYS *of Uther*

Pendragon, King of all England, that he loved the Queen of Cornwall, a fair lady by the name of Igraine. So he slew Igraine's husband, Duke Gorlois, and Merlin brought him to Igraine in her castle at Tintagel, and Uther lay with her and begat on her the child called Arthur.

Then Uther took Queen Igraine as his wife, and disposed of her two daughters according to his will. The elder, Morgause, he wedded to King Lot of Lothian and the Orkneys, and the younger he put to a nunnery, because he would have it so. And for she learned much of necromancy there, the people called her Morgan Le Fay.

And when the Queen was delivered of her child, the infant Arthur was given to Merlin to nourish as his own. But within two years King Uther fell sick and died, and his enemies usurped upon his kingdom and overtook his lands. And after many years, Merlin called all the people to London to show who should be rightwise king of the realm, and Arthur drew the sword out of the stone.

And when Arthur was King, it befell that he would take him a wife. He said to Merlin, "I love Guenevere of Camelot, that hath in her house the Round Table, and she is the most valiant fair lady alive." And Merlin said, "Sir, if you loved her not so well, I should find you a damsel that should please you more."

And Merlin warned the King privily that Sir Lancelot should love Guenevere, and she him again, but the King's heart was set.

So they were wedded, and ruled together with good cheer. And a son was born to them that Arthur took to war, and the boy perished because he was too young.

Then the King cast great love to his sister on the mother's side, Morgan Le Fay, and lay with her and begat on her a son called Mordred. When she was found with child, Arthur gave her to King Ursien of Gore to wife. And when she was delivered, Arthur ordered all the young infants of that age to be put in a ship and cast out to sea. And the ship was wrecked and the children drowned and their bodies cast up, save that the boy Mordred was never found.

And Sir Lancelot of the Lake, son of King Ban of Benoic in Little Britain, came to court, and in all tournaments and feats of arms, he passed all other men. Wherefore the Queen held him in high favor, and Sir Lancelot loved the Queen above all other ladies of his life.

Yet for the love they had of Arthur they might not partake of their pleasure, nor dishonour the noble fellowship of knights. So the Queen said to Lancelot, "Fair sweet friend, break my heart, but I must desire you to leave."

Then rode Sir Lancelot adventuring high and low, and the Queen betook herself again to the love of the King. But ever and anon the false enchantress Morgan Le Fay lay in wait for King Arthur, to do him wrong.

Yet ever the King strove to have peace with his kin, and desired both his sisters to be at peace with him. To this end he favored the four sons of his sister Queen Morgause, Sir Gawain, Sir Agravain, Sir Gaheris, and Sir Gareth, above all other knights of the Table Round. Yet for all this, Sir Agravain nourished evil in his heart, and he slew Sir Lamorak, the queen his mother's champion of the Orkneys, at the which Queen Morgause tore her face and hair and so died. Then was Sir Agravain banished from the realm for the rest of his natural life.

And for all the love between Guenevere and the King, yet never again did she quicken with child. Then Merlin bethought him of the lost son of Arthur, and went about to find the boy Mordred, so that the house of Pendragon might endure.

So traveled Sir Lancelot also, till he came to a place called Astolat, where dwelt a fair maid who cast such love to him that she would either marry or die for his love. At the which the Queen fell into a great jealousy, and there was much misery before the truth was seen.

And then the love between them might no longer be contained. Much loving sweetness passed between the Queen and her knight, and either made great joy of the other, beyond compare. Yet always was the love in their hearts that each held toward Arthur the King.

Then it fell out that the Lady of the Lake feared for the Hallows of Avalon, that they would be stolen away. So Guenevere swore to find a place where they might have safe concealment, and Sir Lancelot undertook this quest. And the quest was long, and the Hallows were lost, and never the Queen knew where her knight laid his head, or where he might be found.

So did Merlin also go about his quest, and he found the boy Mordred, and brought him back to King Arthur, and the King took him as his own. And the years passed, and Mordred grew to manhood, and Queen Guenevere was ware of a stirring in the land...

MORTE D'ARTHUR

CHAPTER I

The bitter rains of March beat on the hillside overhead. But deep in the heart of the rock, it was warm and dry. Inside the high-domed underground dwelling-place, the light from many candles played over walls swagged in blood-red velvet, looped and tied back with ropes of silver-gilt. Bright rugs from the East covered the stony floor in amber and indigo, garnet, rose, and black.

A low fire glowed and murmured on the hearth, its slender plume of smoke lost in the void above.

In the center of the chamber, Merlin lay on a curiously made couch, staring at the ceiling through tightly closed eyes. A wand of golden yew lay within reach, humming softly to itself in a high, beelike whine. His hands lay loosely at his sides, palms upward, fingers reaching, ready to catch his dreams as they came down. A ring of candles shone around his head. The flames quivered and changed color, and he knew the time was near.

"Yes, yes," he muttered tensely. "I am ready—come—"

Suddenly his thumbs began to itch. For a second his mind turned to milk, warding off the ancient sign of impending evil and danger ahead. He crushed his thumbs in his fists to drive it away. The itching intensified.

"No!" he moaned.

No, he was Merlin still; it could not be. Feverishly he composed himself again for waking sleep, the magic sleep of the Druids he had learned long ago, preparing to send his spirit from his body as he always did. Once he had made the long hard leap of faith, his spirit self would walk the astral plane, gathering the secrets of the Otherworld. When he had to return, when his roaming soul submitted to his body's chain, he would know how to deal with what was to come.

"Come to me! Come!"

Yesss—

He could feel his soul straining at the leash, hungry for the void. Any moment now, yes, yesss—

Merlin, Merlin, attend—

A series of stabbing pains shot through his thumbs. Moaning, the old enchanter opened his eyes and forced himself to sit up. There was no avoiding it. There could be no flight of the spirit while this loomed. Evil impending? Where did the danger lie?

Throwing his skinny feet to the floor, he struggled upright and began to pace his cave dwelling, blind to the dark beauty of the place and the books and treasures he had brought there over the years. Mumbling and twitching, he came to rest at last before a silk curtain hanging on the wall. Behind it was an oddly shaped piece of glass in a deep frame. In its clouded depths, he saw a reflection stir and forced himself to interrogate the shadowy shape within.

"Danger then?" he ground out.

Danger, the answer came.

"To Arthur?"

Arthur.

Merlin gasped in fear. How could it be? He had left Arthur well and happy, not three moons ago. To be sure, Arthur was not as young as he was, and the old man detested the lines deepening on the face he loved, and the gray spreading through his former pupil's glistening fair hair. But for a knight in his forties, Arthur was in his prime. His massive frame was almost unscathed by tournaments and battles, his fine face had lost none of its warmth, and his gray eyes were as kindly as ever, and much wiser now.

Arthur—

With another stab to the heart, Merlin remembered the boy Arthur once had been. Never had a fairer youth trodden the earth, except for Uther Pendragon, Arthur's father, Merlin's kinsman and dear liege lord. Merlin paused, ambushed by bitter memories again. Well, Uther had long gone down to the Underworld. Gone, all gone, all the Pendragon kings. No grieving or pining would call them back now.

But Arthur—

Merlin turned back to the shadow in the mirror and tore his long gray locks.

"How can Arthur be in distress?" he wailed. "He has what his heart desired! I found him the child!"

The child? quibbled the image in the glass.

"Yes, yes, child no longer, I know," Merlin retorted feverishly. "He's a grown man. But how can the danger lie there? Arthur loves the boy! Why, Mordred is everything to him now—"

But still the smoky shape wavered in the glass. *The child, the child, the child*—

"Gods above!" Merlin struck his head. Twenty years had passed since the boy Mordred could be called a child. If he was not the child, then it must mean another child to come.

A child of Guenevere's?

Merlin tore himself from the mirror and flung himself down on his couch. The Queen had indeed been childless for many years. But she was still within her childbearing years. Many a woman in her forties still gave birth, let alone one like Guenevere, tall and well formed, blessed in life and love. Could the child his spirit was warning him of be *hers?*

Gods above! Around his head the candles danced blue and yellow, mocking his distress. Guenevere, yes, he might have known!

Guenevere!

The old enchanter gave full rein to his spleen. If only Arthur had taken another bride! He could have married a princess of the Christians, a sweet silent thing, tame as a caged bird to his ruling hand. But instead he chose a queen with her own kingdom, one born into the way of women's rule. Time and again, Guenevere had taken Arthur by surprise. And this would not be the last.

"How long, ye gods, how long?" Merlin wailed, beating his breast. When would he be free of his eternal task of saving the house of Pendragon, keeping it alive till its name was fixed forever in the stars? He had found the lost son, and had given Arthur an heir. Another child now would lead to confusion, and worse. A boy would encourage rebellion and bring rogue lords and disaffected kings to challenge Mordred as the rightful heir.

And a girl—

Worse, much worse. Merlin clasped his head. The Summer Country followed the rule of queens. Guenevere was the last in a line going back to the Great One Herself, the Goddess who had mothered the whole world. To those of the old faith, a girl child would inherit the Mother-right, she would be born to take command. Guenevere's daughter could prevail over Arthur's son. And Pendragon then would be swept away, no more than a blink in the long eye of time.

"No!"

Merlin scrambled round his cave, cursing and weeping his fill. All his life, all his many lives, he had fought for Pendragon, only to see his great work threatened every time. Now he must leave his warm, secure refuge and take to the road. He must close up the hidden door in the hillside with strong spells so that no one would disturb his mountain lair. The harsh winds would scour his unprotected flanks and make a tangled mat of his long hair, the iron-gray locks that he groomed and perfumed each day with such care. The wild rain would be his only clothing now, the cold highway his lonely habitation, as he lived at one with the hare and the midnight owl, and no man could tell when he would be home again.

But it would all be for Arthur.

And for Arthur's child.

The child.

A spark of hope flared in the old man's wizened heart. Guenevere might bear a child such as Arthur had once been, sturdy and well made, with hair of bright gold and eyes of heartbreaking truth. And perhaps he, old Merlin, might get the child for himself, wrest it from Guenevere as he had taken Arthur from the arms of his mother, Igraine. Then the future of Pendragon would be secure. And he, Merlin, would have the rearing of a new High King—

"Yes!"

The old man leaped to his feet in ecstasy. Throwing back his head, he emitted a soundless hail. The white mule grazing on the mountainside above would hear the cry, he knew, and amble to his door. Call the mule, change into his traveling dress, assemble his few effects—soon, soon, he would be on his way and gone.

Gone—

His old heart revived as he looked ahead. Out in the open air, wearing the woodland green with his wand in his hand, he would be part of the wild wood again, one with the forest creatures who had always taken him as their own. And already he could feel the call of the road. The highways were not as good as they had been when the Roman legions marched away, but they would serve. And no one alive, no, not even the Old Ones who made the world, knew the lesser tracks and hidden greenways as Merlin did.

"On your way, then, old fool!" he chided himself. "Leave your fireside, go!" There was no time to waste if his thumbs were to be believed—if he was to search out the evil now threatening Arthur and come once again to the rescue of the King—if he was to discover what the warning meant and find the child.

Find the child.

Yes, that was what he must do.

With a racing pulse, Merlin began to prepare.

AVALON, AVALON, *sacred island, home—*

The mist clung to the hillside like a living thing. The muffled figure went carefully downhill, though she had trodden the path a thousand times. When day broke, the towering pines and silver apple trees on the slopes would be easier to see. But now, in the darkness before dawn, she had to trust to her feet, not her eyes, to find the way.

Ahead of her the still waters of the Lake gleamed blackly in the darkness, ageless, impenetrable, pulsing with life. To her right a solitary lantern marked a stone jetty where two boatmen waited with their rough-headed lad, looking up in awe at the veiled figure as she drew near.

The boatmen came to meet her, squinting a silent greeting through thick fringes of black hair. Shyly they handed her into the boat and set off with a will, one rowing, the other poling from the stern, while the boy scrambled nimbly around, casting off and stowing the mooring rope. Then he doused the lantern, and the mist of night took them in its dank embrace.

The low barge drove onward through the dark. The only sounds were the steady plash of the oars and the faraway wailing of a waterfowl. The woman sat in the prow, digesting the rich damp smell of the living water, looking forward without fear. Unwary travelers were often lost on the Lake, circling the watery darkness till the Great One took pity on them and turned them into marsh fowl forever lamenting their plight. But these men knew the waters like the wildfowl themselves.

At the back of the boat a silver spray of water feathered the darkness as the taller of the two boatmen drew up his long pole. His small black eyes were fixed on her, damp but friendly, like a water vole's. She met his gaze.

"The Lady has sent you?" he asked, in the rough tongue of the Old Ones.

"To the Queen," she confirmed. Her voice, too, had the rusty cadence of one who rarely spoke.

Crouched in the foot of the boat, the boy stared at her, radiant with desire. "You go to Camelot?"

In her mind's eye she saw the great castle bright with many flags, its white citadel and slender spires, its towers roofed with gold. She nodded. "Yes."

On the far shore, another lantern beckoned them to land. There a young girl clad in water pelts stood holding a pony, a dappled mare with huge soft eyes. It was the finest thing the people had, she knew. But for the Lady's messenger, nothing was too good. She mounted and took up the reins. The little mare turned her head trustingly, asking without words, Where are we to go? The rider reached down to stroke the smooth, warm neck. All the way, came the silent command, all the way, my dear.

One by one the Lake dwellers faded into the breaking dawn. For a moment the traveler sat, taking leave of the still lake of shining water, the green island floating in the mist, rich with apple blossoms and the song of birds.

Farewell, Avalon: the words breathed from her like a charm. Then she turned the horse's head into the dawn as the silver mist enfolded her like a lover and hid her from sight.

CHAPTER 2

I t was time. Praise the Lord, it was here. King Pelles raised his head from his clasped hands and gazed in blind ecstasy into the breaking dawn. Three days of fasting and three nights of prayer had brought the word at last—the word of God, the revelation of what he had to do.

Through the chamber window, a weeping sky loured above the castle, with the promise of sleet before the day wore on. The weather was harsh for spring, but King Pelles never heeded what the skies might do. It was always cold in the kingdom of Terre Foraine, even in the rare hot summers when the sun scorched the gold off the scrubby gorse and fleetingly warmed this wind-burned northern land.

And the castle of Corbenic was colder indoors than out. A clammy chill hung in the old stone walls, even up here in the ivy-mantled belfry where the king had his eyrie and kept the world at bay. Down below, where those the king hated were stowed, the dungeon holes were green with spreading slime, and water ran down the sides of the living rock. There, in a world that never saw the sun, bottomless wells served the living and the dead, keeping the castle fed with springs of sweet water to outlast the longest siege, and lapping the bodies of the damned in a merciful last embrace.

High above the unheard cries and groans, King Pelles often prayed for the sinful souls whose refusal to accept the Lord God had forced him to put them there. But this morning, they were not in his thoughts. Praying, brooding, transported by the mystical union of self-starvation and the lack of sleep, the king had had the vision he had so long sought. After all these years, it was time.

He sprang up with the vigor of a man of half his age, and turned to the other occupant of the room. His skeletal frame was twitching with renewed force, and his eyes glowed in the sockets of his bony face. "Theophilus!" he cried.

The monk drowsing on a bench against the wall stumbled to his feet. "Sire?"

"A letter, Theophilus," the king said feverishly. "I have seen what must be done. We are going to court—I must send to King Arthur at once. Have the fastest galloper standing by in the stable yard."

"My lord."

With a bow, the monk took his leave, and the slapping of sandaled feet died away on the stairs. Pelles stood transfixed, pressing his clammy temples with both hands. O Lord, he prayed, shall we now see Your dawn?

Hastening to the table, he took up quill and parchment, heedless that the ink clotted blackly on his pen and that every quill he took up frayed worse than the last. At length the letter lay finished in his hand. "So," he breathed. "So—"

There was a light sound outside the door. Pelles knew the footstep before he heard the voice. "Come in, my dear."

"Father—"

Always, always the fretful note in what she said, King Pelles noted for the thousandth time—well, she would lose that when they came to court. "Yes, Elaine?"

A pale, pointed face came round the door, and a young woman entered, clad in sober gray. She had her father's height and was framed like him too, strong-boned but lean, her breasts high and hard, and her hips as flat as if she had none at all. But above the collar of her nunlike gown, she had features to blind a saint, eyes like twilight filled with dreams, pearly skin, and tendrils of hair at her temples as soft and blond as a child's. As always, his heart bounded and sank again at the sight of her. Her mother would never die while Elaine was alive.

Her mother.

Well, it was too late to weep for that now.

"You wanted me, Father."

"Yes." He gestured to the paper in his hand. "It is time."

Dear God, was it here at last, the moment she had been waiting for all her life? Elaine's eyes flared with shock, but she did not speak.

Pelles reached for the sealing wax, then slipped the royal seal off his fleshless hand. "Have you spoken to the child?"

"No." She shook her tightly wimpled head. "But he is ready. He has always known." A slow light lit her face. "We go? When?" Feverishly she began ticking off the tasks. "I must—"

"You must do nothing," he said quietly.

She did not hear, her mind and her tongue running on. "He will need new armor," she said, almost to herself, "and a better horse. The gray has done well enough, but he'll need something finer for King Arthur's court—" She laughed unpleasantly. "And for Queen Guenevere. The Queen will see—"

"Daughter, attend my words—"

Instantly she fell silent and dropped her eyes. There was no mistaking the menace in his tone. She could still remember the locked doors of her childhood and the muffled cries and prayers. Her mother was confined for her health, she was told, never having recovered from childbirth when Elaine was born. But one day the tears and pleadings were no more. Child though she was, Elaine had understood that her mother had died because she did not want to live.

Then her father had taken her into the chapel where her mother lay, and forced her up to the thing lying in the box. Pressing both her hands against the stone-cold face, he had told her that her mother had failed the Lord God, and he had made her promise never to do the same. Hoarse with weeping, he had pressed her body to his, and whispered that God had called her to take her mother's place.

Since then, God had called her through her father many times. Soon after her mother died, the king, weeping and fasting in a night of visions, foresaw a great destiny for her, if she would only submit. That was her mother's sin, he impressed on her, the failure to yield to the will of God.

From then on, he had ruled her night and day. She must never leave the castle, he insisted, for she was destined for one man alone and the chosen of the Lord must be pure. She slept in a chamber to which he had the only key, and was woken every dawn to fast and pray for her sins. She hungered for her mother and in her sleep she fleetingly felt a soft touch, a kiss, but her father said she must not trust evil dreams. She must obey his word and submit herself to him, for he alone could call her to her destiny and interpret the will of God. And it was only right that he should, she told herself querulously, trying to fill the ever-present hollow in her heart. All Corbenic knew, and all the kingdom of Listinoise around, that King Pelles had been chosen of the Lord.

And she had been chosen too, when her time came, to bear the holy child. And now he too was the vessel of God's will. The time had come! Her heart soared. "Command me, Father!" She curtsied and bowed her head.

He gave a fleeting nod of acknowledgment. "Call Dame Brisein."

There was a dry cough from the door. "I am here, sire."

An old woman made her way into the room. She was withered with age, and her thick black gown and shawl hid a crooked frame. But her movements suggested that her long body had once been as lean and supple as a snake, and her sloe-black eyes still burned with a hidden fire. When she spoke, her voice had a vigor quite at odds with her crabbed appearance and old-fashioned garb. "I was down in the courtyard when Brother Theophilus came. He told me of your purpose."

"My purpose?" cried the king in a passion. "Not mine, Brisein, the Lord's! You have been with my daughter all her life. You above all know she was chosen to bear the holy child!"

The black eyes roamed like leeches over Elaine. "And I nursed him too," continued the old woman in her strange, compelling voice. "God's will made flesh on earth."

"Yes, yes!" mouthed Pelles, his eyes as pale as his lips. "And God Him-self directs our efforts now. The truth came to me last night after the drink you brought me to break my fast."

Something stirred in the depths of the midnight eyes. "It was only lemongrass water, lord, nothing more." She paused. "With an herb or two to taste."

"My good Brisein, it opened my inner eye!" Pelles cried. "Your faithful Christian service brought me the watchword of Our Lord."

Dame Brisein threw up her hands in humble joy. "Blessings on you, sire!"

Watching closely, Elaine wondered why her old nurse did not seem surprised. But both she and my father know the ways of God, she lamented in the depths of her small soul. They are truly among the chosen of the Lord, while I am ignorant and sinful, as Father always says. That is why I have had to expiate my sin to him all these unhappy years.

But now—now—!

Her lovely eyes lit with a dull new hope. Soon I shall be among the chosen too. When we bring the child to the Queen, all the world will know who chose me for his own. Then they will see that the Queen is not the only woman who has had her knight.

My child—

My knight—

Fearfully she choked back the proud, sinful thoughts and tried to still the hunger in her soul. Till then, I must bend my body to the will of the Lord, as Father insists. But when we come to the Queen—

"Elaine!"

"Yes, sire?"

"Hear me, girl, and obey!"

"I do, my lord, I do." Falling to her knees, Elaine veiled her fragile hopes, and bowed herself again to her father's will.

CHAPTER 3

The sun rose late in Camelot, weltering in blood. A baleful light played over the ancient citadel of the Summer Country, reddening the white walls looking down on the valley below. A spiteful wind ran peeking here and there, driving the dead leaves into whispering heaps. Hurrying through the castle, the servants agreed that the omens were not good. If Sir Gawain and his brothers thought they'd get round the Queen, they'd better think again.

"The King, maybe," opined the Captain of the Guard at the end of the night watch, taking a deep warming pull on his morning ale. "They might get round the King. They're his kin, after all, and the King has always favored Sir Gawain. But the Queen—"

He broke off. Standing beside the brazier in a raw red dawn, the young soldiers of the guard listened, and hoped to learn. The King—the Queen—these were names of mystery and awe to them. A tall, shapely woman drifting in white and gold, a great bear of a man in royal red and blue, this was all they knew. But the Captain knew more, and seemed ready to tell them now.

"The Queen—?" prompted the boldest of the band.

"Queen Guenevere?"

Smiling, the Captain warmed his hands on his mulled ale, unaware that the glow he felt was coming from his heart. "Five thousand years and more we've had queens here in the Summer Country, and she's been the best of the lot. Twenty years she's ruled in Camelot—since before you were born," he added, eyeing the newest of the recruits, a youth still devoid of a beard.

The lad blushed to find the attention focused on him. "What about Sir Gawain then?" he wondered. "Where does he fit in?"

"Oh, he's all right." The Captain chuckled knowingly. "A bit of a rough one, especially with women, but as loyal as the day. Him and his brothers too."

A silence fell as they all recalled the three mighty figures riding into court through the early-morning mist.

"But if they're loyal to the King," puzzled the young guard, "what'll they want from him that he won't give?"

The Captain's face darkened. "Don't ask, lad," he said sourly. "Don't ask."

GUENEVERE STOOD IN the window gazing out on the blood-red sun. Far below, the fields and woodlands still slumbered in the chilly mist, and the little town huddled round the walls of the great castle to keep itself warm. Behind her came the footfall of her maid, as soft and familiar as a cat. "I've looked out a heavier robe, my lady, the Audience Chamber will be cold today."

"Thank you, Ina."

Guenevere stepped back into the low, whitewashed chamber, the private quarters of the Queens of the Summer Country since time began. Now a table by the wall gleamed with her perfumes and lotions, lavender, patchouli, and sweet almond oil. A massive bed stood in the shadows at the back, swathed in royal red and gold. A great cloudy mirror rested against the wall, and an applewood fire filled the air with spring.

In the center of the room Ina was holding a long robe of gold with a white fur collar and sleeves falling to the floor. Watching Guenevere approach, the maid marveled to herself. Was there any other woman of the Queen's age who still boasted the same body as when she was young? Tall and inclining to fullness in the breasts and hips, Guenevere had not lost the small waist King Arthur had loved when they met. To look at her, you'd never know she'd borne a child.

Borne, and lost. And the Queen was approaching the time when there would be no more. Was that why she was looking so sad today? Or was it this awful business with Sir Gawain?

A fierce possessive love seized Ina's heart. How did the big knight dare? And why did the Gods permit it? Well, no use complaining about what the Great Ones did. Briskly Ina slipped the robe onto Guenevere's shoulders and tugged sharply at the sleeves.

Guenevere felt Ina's devotion in the flurry of brisk touches and gave her a quick smile. For herself, she was not much interested in the image now before her in the glass, a tall figure in a red silk robe and an overgown of white and gold, gold at her neck and wrists and on the long fingers of each hand. She knew that her face told the story of her life, and that the lines round her eyes showed each of her forty-odd years. But for one who had borne all she had, she told herself, she looked well enough.

"The crown now, madam?" Ina inquired. Standing behind her, the maid reached up and placed a deep circle of gold and moonstone on Guenevere's head. "There!" she breathed, entranced. Her small face clenched like a fist. "I wish you well, lady, in the audience ahead. They're bad blood, all the sons of Lot."

"Not all of them," Guenevere said with a frown. "Gawain was the King's first companion and he swears he'll be the last. And Gaheris and Gareth are men of honor too."

Ina shook her head. "They are Orkneyans, lady," she said simply, "Men of blood. And you know what Sir Gawain wants now."

Guenevere's soul darkened. "Yes, Ina," she breathed. "I do."

THE AUDIENCE CHAMBER had been slowly filling all morning, as the word spread through the court of what was afoot. Now, as the raw spring day moved toward noon, the lofty hall was crowded with furs and velvets brushing against soft whispering silks and shining silver mail. Between the bright lords and ladies were scattered the harsh black habits of many monks, drifting together like clouds on a sunny day.

At the far end of the room, three massive figures stood with their backs to the crowd, facing the dais with its empty thrones. Sir Gawain and his brothers were waiting for the King and Queen in a silence like the tomb. At their head, Gawain shifted from foot to foot, stifling an inner groan. Gods, make it right, he prayed fervently. Let me not be wrong!

Yet how could he be? His big face knotted in an angry frown. Blood was blood. There had always been four princes of the Orkneys, four sons of Lot. For ten years now there had been only three. It was time to repair the breach in the Orkney ranks.

Not that the other two agreed with him. Gawain sighed and cast a swift glance at Gaheris, standing by his side. In Gaheris, the third of the clan, the tawny coloring of their mother had come out as true red. Her fair skin had become his milky pallor, and his blue eyes were as pale as the rain-washed morning sky. But now his face was set in a grim stare. For his brother thought he was mad, Gawain knew.

"Why rake it all up again?" Gaheris had cried. "Agravain's well enough where he is, why not leave him there? He'll only cause trouble if you bring him back."

And Gareth, too, the baby of them all, had shaken his great blond head with the same fearful regard and begged Gawain to think again. "He was born to make mischief, brother, you know that."

Yet damn them both, Gawain muttered darkly in his heart, I am still their elder brother and the head of the clan. We are the sons of Lot, and King Lot always had his way. Gawain's laboring brain returned to where it had begun. Blood was blood. Why all the argument, then?

At the entrance to the hall, reflected in the great bronze double doors, a pair of shifting shadows appeared in a blur of red and gold.

"Attend there, all attend!" The sharp cry of the Chamberlain broke through noise of the crowd. "The King and Queen! Make way for the King and Queen!"

So many people—

Gripping Arthur's large and comforting hand, Guenevere moved forward with him into the crowded hall.

Lords, knights, and ladies pressed in on all sides, with mighty land-owners and petty kings bowing before them. She smiled and nodded greetings, noting the familiar faces in the buzzing throng.

She threw a glance at Arthur, always glad on these occasions to have him at her side. He caught her gaze and smiled, and there it was again, the old uprush of love for him, the same catch in her heart. *Thank the Gods,* she thought, *the years have treated him well.* The sorrow in his eyes would always be with him now, and the bright hope of youth had long ago left his face. But his keen gaze had lost none of its force, and the crown of Pendragon sat lightly on a head only brushed with gray. His great broad frame carried off the bright scarlet tunic and flowing cloak of gold as it always did, and the ancient sword of state swung from a waist no thicker than in his boyhood days. He still led his troops in battle and was undefeated at the joust. Of all the men in the hall, there was no doubt which was the King.

In the body of the hall, a cluster of black monkish gowns caught her eye. *And the Christians too, how numerous they are.* She suppressed a frisson of distaste. When the men of Christ had first brought their faith from the East, they had had only one meager church in London and huddled together in its crypt to keep warm. Now those few beginners were leaders of their Church, spreading the word of their God throughout the misty isles. London, York, and Canterbury were their strongholds now, and whole kingdoms knelt to the Father God.

But here in the Summer Country, the Goddess still held sway. Here the people worshiped the Old Ones, who had made the world, and the Great One, who was the Mother of them all. The Summer Country traced its line of Queens from Her, and kept the Mother-right. This was a land where women were born to rule. The Christians loudly preached the rule of men, but for years now they had not troubled Guenevere. In truth, she hardly noticed them at all. They comforted Arthur, and that was enough.

They moved on down the hall. Ahead of them the angry sun was pouring through the far window, washing the Orkney brothers in streaks of red. Waiting by Arthur's throne were the King's three companion knights, Sir Kay, Sir Bedivere, and Sir Lucan, their keen glances showing their sense of what lay ahead. Behind them Guenevere caught the white heads of two older knights who had once served her mother, Sir Niamh and Sir Lovell, always known as the Bold. They were the last of the dead queen's knights still alive. In their midst was a tall, smiling young man, cutting a striking figure in royal blue and gold, and with something Otherworldly in his air.

Arthur's eye lit up at the sight of the handsome face. "Mordred!" he cried.

Mordred stepped forward jauntily and made a deep bow. If he wanted to show he was the son of the King, Guenevere thought sardonically, he had done that. His short cloak and well-made tunic set off a lean, well-muscled frame and long, horseman's legs. Wide gold bangles hung on his wrists, and a gold coronet held back his thick, blue-black hair. His eyes had the same hyacinthine glint, and his wide, white smile touched every heart at court.

Except one. Guenevere drew a ragged breath. She had never warmed to Mordred, and she would not now. The young man was a living reminder of Arthur's betrayal, when her husband had yielded to his half-sister Morgan, seduced to her bed by strong spells. Mordred had been the result, a child of lust. Guenevere had lived through her anger long ago, and had vowed to accept the boy for Arthur's sake. So for years she had smiled and held her peace, while Mordred had grown to become Arthur's delight. But she had never trusted the son of Morgan Le Fay.

Yet what had Mordred done to deserve her mistrust? She caught herself up. *He has done nothing, remember? He is not the cause of your present fear.*

They mounted the steps to the dais and took their thrones. Arthur leaned over and fondly touched her hand. "Never fear, my love. Nothing will be done against your wish, even for my own blood kin."

She inclined her head. "Thank you, sir."

Arthur signaled to the Chamberlain. "Begin."

Gawain approached the throne. "Ten years ago, sire," he began, breathing heavily, "you banished my brother Agravain. We have come to ask you to allow him back to court."

"Reprieve Agravain?" said Arthur sternly. A ripple had run through the court at the sound of the name.

"Yes, sire." The color rushed to Gawain's face. "He has paid his blood-debt. For years now he has wandered overseas. And he longs to tread on his native land again."

"Gawain, your brother killed a knight of the Round Table, and for that the penalty is death." Arthur nodded somberly to Guenevere. "It was only because of the Queen that he escaped with banishment."

Guenevere clenched her fists. *And that did not mean that ten years later he would be welcome back. Only a lifetime can pay for another life.*

"Sire, he came upon Lamorak in the dead of night," said Gawain doggedly. "He killed in self-defense."

In self-defense? Guenevere gripped the cool bronze arms of her throne. *Lies, all lies, Gawain, and you know it. Well, say on.*

"And Sir Lamorak's death is not the only burden that Agravain must carry till he dies." Arthur's voice was heavy with remembered pain. "Have you forgotten the death of your mother the queen? Mourning for Lamorak, she lost her own life too."

Gawain's beefy face turned an angrier shade of red. "Our mother concealed her love for her knight from us. Agravain never meant to kill her chosen one. I swear he should not be paying for her death!"

He paused, holding the moment with unconscious power. In all the court, not a soul moved.

"As for Sir Lamorak——" Gawain heaved a furious sigh. "Sire, all the world knows his father killed my father long ago. Our brother saw a blood-feud, a just debt. And all this was ten years ago and more. The dead are sleeping quietly in their graves. We beg you, let my brother return and live. He longs for nothing more than to serve you now."

Guenevere leaned forward. *He wants his brother back, that I understand. But that's not all.* She pressed Arthur's hand. *Arthur, Arthur, attend.*

"Sir Gawain," she said clearly, "you have told us why you think your brother should return." She paused for emphasis. "But why now? What makes this the moment he should return?"

In spite of himself Gawain's eyes slid toward Mordred, standing at the side of Arthur's throne. Guenevere nodded to herself. *As I thought.*

Now Arthur was frowning too. He let go Guenevere's hand. "You heard the Queen, Gawain," he said stiffly. "Why now?"

Gawain took a breath. "My lord, all the world knows that Prince Mordred is to be knighted at Pentecost. When I was young, I swore my allegiance to you and in twenty years I have never broken faith." For a moment, a searing shaft of love made Gawain's big face almost beautiful. "I ask no more than to swear the same oath to Prince Mordred your son. And I pray that my banished brother may do so too."

Oh, this is clever, Gawain. Guenevere sat still and allowed her thoughts to run. *At Mordred's knighting, everyone knows that the King will name him as his heir. Is it you, Gawain, or your dark-scheming brother who wants to be there to greet the rising sun? Do you even plan, perhaps, to help the new sun arise?*

She watched Gawain's eyes as they flickered over Mordred, then returned to Arthur again. *No, Gawain loves Arthur. He has no desire to see Mordred in his place. If any man dreams of evil, it is Agravain. He must not return.*

She leaned across toward the neighboring throne. "Arthur—" she said urgently.

But Arthur's eyes were filling with tears of joy. He reached out for Mordred's hand. "Take these good knights to your heart, my son," he cried out. "They are our kin. We shall never have any more."

Cold certainty gripped Guenevere like a claw. *Arthur means to reprieve Agravain.* She seized his arm. "Arthur, wait—think what he has done—"

Without warning a dark sickness filled her sight. Through it she saw Agravain advancing with his familiar storklike stride, casting around like a hunter for his prey. He was armed for close combat with a vicious stabbing sword, daggers at his belt, and a shield on his left arm. Soundlessly he slipped through the palace corridors, pale and grinning like an avenging ghost. Behind him she could see a band of knights, all armed for the kill and smiling like him too. Suddenly she knew they were making for the Queen's apartments, they were approaching, *they were here*—

"Guenevere!"

She came to herself with a violent, shuddering start. Arthur was frowning at her with angry concern. Mordred leaned forward anxiously. "Oh madam," he said, "thank the Gods—we thought you were ill."

She waved him away. "Arthur—" she began hoarsely.

He shook his head. "The time has come for forgiveness, Guenevere." He leaned toward her throne. "If Gawain can forgive the death of his mother, so can we."

Arthur, beware. The Orkneys love no man but themselves. Already they are looking toward your heir. Agravain will court Mordred, and you will be cast aside— She drew a breath. "I don't trust them, Arthur." Another sudden tremor gripped her heart. *Agravain above all*—

But Arthur was already patting her hand. "Don't worry, Guenevere," he said reassuringly. "What is it I've so often heard you say? 'We must seek love and understanding, not anger and hate?'"

"It's what the Lady teaches on Avalon," Guenevere said numbly. "'Religion should be kindness. Faith should be love.'"

"And so it is," chuckled Arthur. "And Agravain should come back." A smile from long ago lit his fine-featured face. "Chamberlain, bear witness to our royal decree," he called. "Our kinsman Agravain, banished ten years ago, is now reprieved—"

Arthur, oh Arthur—

Guenevere sat in silence as the sonorous sentences rolled on. Sir Gawain embraced his brothers, and all three wept for joy, leaning on each other's necks. Arthur beamed on them, and on all the court, rejoicing in his power of dispensing goodwill.

Outside the sun broke through the watery clouds and poured into the chamber in shafts of gold. In spite of herself, a sliver of hope warmed her heart. *All may be well. All may yet be well.*

But as the court rose, she slipped a ring from her finger and called Ina to her side, pressing it into the hollow of the maid's hand. Ina's eyebrows flickered a question they both understood.

"Yes," Guenevere breathed. "Send for Sir Lancelot."

CHAPTER 4

A mackerel sky overhead, oily and yellow, clouds scudding and torn by a wind from the west, and no trace of the sun. Sighing and shaking his head, Bors made his way into the courtyard with a heavy step. He did not need to look round the well-tended cobbled square, the sturdy towers and lofty battlements, to know that he loved this place like his life. Joyous Garde was the nearest thing he had to a home. Why did they have to leave?

Across the courtyard a tall, lean figure was coming toward him with a sleepy morning smile. As always, Bors' heart lifted at the sight of his brother, though he often jested darkly that he should have drowned Lionel at birth. From their earliest days, the younger boy had been the taller and handsomer of the two and a better fighter to boot. Beside the smiling, easy, fair-haired Lionel, Bors had had little regard. But Bors knew he was valued by the few he cared about. And he looked on Lionel with deep devotion and a fierce pride.

None of which was evident in his terse greeting and frowning gaze. "So, brother." He paused and cast an eye at the flurried sky. "Where's Lancelot?"

Lionel paused. He knew that Bors would not like what he had to say. "He says we're to ride out without him—he may catch up with us later on." He fixed his eyes on the sky. "He's thinking about the Queen. He wants to get back to Camelot earlier than we'd planned."

"Then we shan't see him today." Bors' face tightened. He swung round on his heel. "Well, let's be off."

Why was Bors angry? Lionel wondered unhappily as they moved away. Lancelot had loved the Queen for years. It would not change.

And he knew why. No other woman had that air of spring in January, that ever-bubbling fount of love and hope. Even her age became her nowadays, the tiny tracks of sorrow round her eyes, the lines that gave her looks their haunting depths. To be with her was to feel the dance of the rain in the wind, see the golden eye of a midsummer dawn, share the feast of hungry souls in the Great Hall at night, with the candles blooming over the last of the wine. To talk with her was akin to unfolding a rose. An inner warmth lit Lionel like a smile. Yes, he knew why Lancelot loved Guenevere.

None of this, he knew, Bors would ever understand. To Bors, Guenevere had bewitched Lancelot, taking advantage of a younger man. Whoever Bors would have chosen as a lover for their cousin, it would not have been this enchanting, terrible Queen.

Side by side they pressed on over the slippery cobbles to the lower court. The whole of the castle was astir, knights and servants greeting them as they strode along. At last Bors broke the silence, as Lionel knew he would. "Why does Lancelot want to leave early, did he say?"

"No. But you know the Queen's anxious about Mordred and the knighthood ceremony. He's probably concerned about that."

"She's just jealous of Mordred and the hold he has on the King," Bors burst out. "He's going to be knighted, we're all commanded to attend, and what in the name of the Gods can Lancelot do about that?"

Lionel made a soft demurring sound. "Nothing, brother." He knew Bors was unhappy at leaving Joyous Garde, and Lionel was not going to inflame him by defending Guenevere. "Now, where do we ride today?"

In the lower court twenty-odd bright-eyed horses hung their heads eagerly over their stable doors, breathing, "Take me!" Pink and white clouds hung above the lofty battlements, and the castle walls glowed in the morning light. Bors had to smile. Had they ever dreamed when they first came from France that Lancelot would own such a fine castle, such a great estate? But Joyous Garde was his through his courage and strength, won by the code of knighthood and the rules of war.

"Ready, brother?" Lionel was nodding across the yard. Under the watchful eye of the Horse Master, the grooms were leading out two horses for the ride, a snarling black stallion and a sweet-faced, doe-eyed mare.

"The big stallion's a handful, there's no denying that," the Horse Master said heartily. "He's only a youngster, and Sir Lancelot wants him uncut. But he needs exercise." He gave them a hopeful look. "And he'll surely give one of you an interesting ride."

Bors burst out laughing and felt his spirits rise. "That black brute's yours, brother, I'll take the little mare." He looked up at the sky. The early winds had ceased their tormented chase, and a fine spring sun was peering through the clouds. Bors glanced at Lionel, taking heart from his brother's smile. All might be well. Things might yet be well.

❖   ❖

AGRAVAIN REPEALED?

Her head pounding, Guenevere processed with Arthur out of the Audience Chamber, through the tightly packed crowd. Already she could see Gawain and his brothers breaking away, heading for the courtyard with long, impatient strides. Now she heard horses galloping out, their hooves slipping on the cobbles in their riders' haste. Soon they would reach the coast, and soon be with Agravain, wherever he lurked. *So, Gawain, you had already given orders to depart. Even before the audience, you knew that Arthur would grant your request, no matter what I said.*

The pounding in her head intensified, and the air in the courtyard was sweet to her burning skin. The bloodshot dawn had given way to a perfect noon, with little white clouds blooming in a forget-me-not sky.

Arthur grinned. "It's a sin to waste a glorious day like this." He pressed her hand. "By your leave, Guenevere, I plan to hunt the southern chase, then follow the game into the Deep Wood."

But before she could answer, Kay's sharp voice broke in.

"But, sire—surely we'll return tonight?"

"Come now, Kay!" Arthur burst out laughing at the sight of Kay's frown. "We slept out often enough when we were boys. Surely we aren't too old for it now?"

"Never, sire," murmured the loyal Bedivere, the light lilt in his voice betraying his birth in the Welshlands, even after all these years.

Laughing, Lucan threw back his red-gold hair and stepped up to the King. Both he and Bedivere knew how Kay still suffered from the wound in his leg, taken years ago, and knew too that Kay would never protest of his own accord. But knights supported each other at times like this. "Sire, Pentecost is at hand." He nodded at Mordred, standing at Arthur's side. "When your son the Prince becomes a knight. Surely Kay should come back after the hunt to check on progress here."

"For the ceremony, you mean? Yes, you're right," Arthur cried. "I want everything in order for my son."

He turned to Mordred with an adoring gaze. "For my son," he repeated, almost below his breath. His air of wonder cut Guenevere to the heart. *Arthur,* she wanted to say, *remember Amir. We had a son too. Oh, my dear, don't go out hunting, stay with me—*

Arthur took her hand and brought it to his lips. "Truly I am blessed," he beamed, "in such a son, such knights, and such a queen. Farewell!" He flourished a bow, and was gone.

AGRAVAIN REPEALED—

And Arthur says, My son Mordred, my only son—

Guenevere strode into the Queen's apartments in furious thought. As she entered, Ina's voice reached her from far away. "Madam, there is a messenger from Avalon."

She stopped in her tracks. "Who?"

"It's the chief Maiden of the Lady, the priestess Nemue."

"Where is she?"

"By the river, she said. She will attend you there."

OUTSIDE THE CASTLE, the winding road ran down through the town and broadened out onto the plain below. In the water meadows, kingcups and lady-smocks dotted the long grass as Guenevere made her way to the riverside.

The rolling surface of the water lay smooth and smiling in the midday sun. On the far bank, two swans were wrapping their long white necks round each other to bill and coo. *Swans mate for life,* she thought, *and pine when they are parted, as lovers do.* She drew a deep breath of the living water, and the familiar pain leaped up around her heart. *Oh, Lancelot—*

Along the bank, willows hung weeping over the water, their long green fingers rippling the slow-moving stream. Almost invisible in the shelter of the grove, the priestess stood gazing out at the river, lost in thought. She was lightly robed in shifting green and gray, the veil that normally covered her head thrown back, her features transfigured by the dappled light. Her skin had the luminous pallor of those who live much underground, and her eyes were as clear as the waters of the Lake. Guenevere paused. How long had it been since her girlhood days on Avalon, when Nemue was the first of the Maidens there? The years fell away as Guenevere saw again the slight, upright form clad in shimmering silk, the bright hair falling like water down to the golden applewood wand she held in her hand.

Guenevere hurried forward. "You are far from Avalon. But we are glad to welcome you here."

The priestess gestured toward the river and held her in a steady gaze. "All waters flow to Avalon in the end."

Her voice was as cool as breaking water, and each word fell like rain-drops on the ear. Guenevere nodded, struggling with a growing unease. The chief of the Maidens was taller than Guenevere remembered, and her look of luminous sweetness was deeper too. Soon, soon, Nemue would have to cover her face when her power, her beauty became too much to bear. Guenevere caught her breath. Was Nemue growing into the Lady's place?

The priestess read her thoughts. "The Lady is herself," she said gently. "That is not our concern."

Another concern flashed into Guenevere's mind. "Is it the Christians?"

"Yes." Nemue looked away. "They are planning to build again on Avalon."

"Gods above!" Guenevere gasped. "They have their cells, their store-houses, their church—what more do they want?"

"A great new church of stone, to shout their glory to the skies."

"Where?"

Nemue's water-lily face set like a stone. "On top of the Tor."

Goddess, Mother, no— On the body of the Mother as she lay asleep, their dull gray stones desecrating her green flanks? Guenevere choked back her rage. "Are they cutting down the apple trees?"

Nemue shook her head, a world of ancient sadness in her face. "The blossom is fading on Avalon. The trees are dying, and soon the apple orchards will be no more." She paused. "The Lady speaks of drawing down Avalon to the world between the worlds. But the spirit of the Mother will never leave the Sacred Isle." Nemue's voice grew stronger as she spoke. "A thousand years from now they will know of the Lady and the Great One she served. Our faith of love and truth will never die. But I say again, Guenevere, that is not your concern."

Guenevere struggled to obey the priestess's will. "I hear you. Speak."

Nemue turned her head away. "When did you last see your knight?"

"Lancelot?" Whatever she had been expecting, it was not this. "It's been a long time—" she whispered at last.

"He is at Joyous Garde?"

Guenevere nodded. "He'll be coming here at Pentecost for the feast of the knights, to attend Mordred's knight-making and celebrate with him." Guenevere closed her eyes. "But until then—for love of the King—"

She could not go on. *For the love we bear to Arthur, our lives must lie apart. Our love would shame him in the open court. So Lancelot takes to his estate to keep his honor bright. And when we come together, our love burns brighter still.*

"Why do you ask?" Dread stirred in her heart. "Has the Lady foreseen danger for him?"

"Perhaps." Nemue fixed her eyes on Guenevere's face. "The Lady has heard that the Hallows are about again."

The Hallows—

Guenevere could hardly breathe. Through tightly closed eyes she saw again the ancient treasures of the Goddess, the sacred objects of Her worship since time began. In her girlhood on Avalon, Guenevere had been one of the favored few to see the four massive pieces of antique gold hidden deep in their secret cave: the great dish of plenty, the two-handled loving cup, the sword of power, and the spear of defense.

"The Hallows—" She collected herself. "Have they been found?"

"No. But the Lady has sent me to say, Speak to your knight, and beware."

"Speak about what? He told us all he knew."

Nemue looked at her oddly. "All he thought he knew." She reached for a small velvet pouch at her waist. "The Lady sent you this. You must have a seeing. Use it when Lancelot comes."

Guenevere took the crumpled object without looking and paced wildly to and fro. "What can he tell us now, after all this time? It was ten years ago—no, twelve, maybe more. You know how long he spent searching for the Hallows when they were lost. Every trace of them must be dead and buried by now."

"On the contrary."

Before Guenevere's eyes, the figure of Nemue began to shimmer and expand, and her glow darkened the sky. "In twelve years, many things grow tall, and long-dead secrets meet the light of day." She raised her arm, and her pointing finger added weight to every word. "Speak to your knight. Find out what seed he planted, and what has grown that he knows nothing of. He will be here at Pentecost, you say? Speak to Lancelot then."

CHAPTER 5

Shadowed by yews and drenched by a sudden spring shower, the churchyard lay neat and gleaming in the morning sun. The young monk made his way carefully over the slippery stones and entered the Abbot's cell on silent feet.

In the confined space, the air was sour with toil. The hunched, black-clad figure had been at his desk since vespers, the monk knew. The tallow lamps had burned late into the night, and their rancid stink hung about the Father Abbot still. When did he sleep? the monk wondered, then put the thought away. While others prayed, their leader worked, without respite.

The monk coughed softly. "The emissary from Rome has arrived, Father. He's at the guest house now."

"Thank you."

The Abbot raised his aching head from his papers and passed a bemused hand across his eyes. Rome? He had been laboring for so long in these damp and chilly islands that he had almost forgotten the beloved city of the Mother Church, her shadowy alleys and her sun-baked squares. "The Papal Legate? Tell him I will attend him there at once."

"Yes, sir." The monk bowed, and padded away.

The Abbot sat for a moment composing his thoughts. Domenico here? God be praised, the Pope's adviser could not have come at a better time.

Outside, the grass in the graveyard was fresh and green and raindrops hung like crystals from every tree. Hurrying from his cell, the Abbot breathed deeply and gave heartfelt thanks. It was always good to get out of the cramped stone cell and come up into the light of God's good day. Ahead of him the whitewashed abbey guest house stood low and welcoming in the shadow of the church. The new arrival was surrounded by younger monks unloading his pack mule and helping him down from his horse. The Abbot lengthened his stride. Yes, it was good to have his old friend here.

Yet friend or adversary—what had he been in truth? For decades now they had worked together in the service of God, but the views of London and Rome did not always coincide. And Domenico was the very voice of Rome, the papal whisper from the throne of Saint Peter itself. For years the Abbot had resisted Rome's attempts to move him from London to York or Canterbury, setting him in one of the high places of the land. Was his old jousting partner here on the same errand again?

The Abbot hurried forward to make his greetings, conscious that he and Domenico made an ill-matched pair. The little man clambering stiffly to the ground had the leathery skin of a peasant and a fringe of sun-frizzled hair, topped by a pair of innocent blue eyes and a childlike smile. In contrast, the Abbot's own lean height, the pale and austere face, the lofty forehead, and the burning gaze proclaimed him as one of God's elect and a prince of the church.

Yet the Papal Legate was the prince of their faith, not he. Oh, Domenico still affected the humble black robe of their order, and had no taste for the silk and purple of his rank. But a careful observer would note that the little man's habit, though simple, was of the finest wool and the rope round his waist was made of woven silk. His friendly smile hid a mind like a mantrap, and his guileless gaze was a lake with untold depths.

"God be with you, Father," called the newcomer merrily.

The Abbot shook his hand with some warmth. "It was good of you to come."

Domenico favored him with an artless stare. "Your mission is significant, no? It was thought in Rome that you needed some support."

"It's true," the Abbot replied, his voice darkening with every word. "The Pentecost feast is no great thing in itself. But this time, when Arthur is expected to name the Prince as his heir—"

Domenico's round head bobbed in agreement. "Yes, we should be there." He raked the Abbot with a questioning gaze. "No sign of issue then from Arthur's Queen?"

"Guenevere?" Never could the Abbot accept Arthur's pagan consort as a rightful Queen. "The concubine, yes. She is barren. God has dried up her womb."

"And what of Merlin?" Domenico probed. "Does he have the King's ear? They say Arthur loves him still."

"He does. But the old enchanter has not been seen for years." The Abbot gave a contemptuous shrug. "They say he slumbers under a Welsh mountain, in his hollow cave. He may sleep till Doomsday for all we care."

Domenico chuckled, then his face grew grave. "Mordred—the Prince, the heir—can we count on him? Is he one of us?"

The Abbot drew a long, reflective breath. "He's Arthur's son, and Arthur loves him, even dotes on him, we hear. They hunt together, eat together, and pass their days together, so naturally they go to church together and Prince Mordred prays at Arthur's side."

Domenico nodded shrewdly. "But who knows how far the young man's faith truly goes?"

"Who indeed?"

Domenico paused for thought. "How old is he?"

"Twenty-five or so—twenty-six."

"And married? Betrothed?"

The Abbot shook his head. "Nor likely to be."

Domenico's sky-blue eyes grew opaque. "Does he not care for women?"

"On the contrary." A thin laugh broke from the Abbot's lips. "Half the ladies at court are mad for his fine, dark eyes."

"Why then is he neither wedded nor promised yet?"

"His father will not have it," the Abbot said simply. "Arthur wants to be sure of everything he does. There is so much at stake."

Domenico concurred. "Many kingdoms now call Arthur their High King."

"Yes indeed." The Abbot's pale eyes looked back into the past. "Who would have thought that the raw youth proclaimed here in this churchyard would have stood the test of time? That Arthur would live to become the greatest of our Christian kings?"

"And all on the back of a most un-Christian fraud!" Domenico laughed heartily. He nodded across the yard. "That was it, wasn't it, the so-called miracle?"

The Abbot followed his gaze and nodded somberly. "The very same."

In silence they appraised a great block of stone squatting like a living thing just inside the churchyard gates. Dank with moss, it sprouted a vivid trail of lichen from a slit in the top. The Abbot gave a short laugh. "Merlin needed a miracle to make Arthur king. The old fool had nothing except his mad belief that Pendragon would come again."

Domenico chuckled. "Well, he gave them one. Twenty years on, all the world knows that Arthur pulled the sword out of that stone."

The Abbot shrugged. "It's no more than a trick of the Welshlands, where Merlin was born. The young men harden their swords for battle on stones, trees, anything. The strongest can find the vein of weakness in any rock, to drive the weapon in."

Domenico chortled with delight. "Then of course, only those who know how the sword went in can draw it out?"

"And there's your miracle."

"And it made him King." Domenico fixed the Father Abbot with his bright-eyed gaze. "And from those benighted beginnings, you have spread the kingdom of God. Because you supported Arthur, there are great churches and abbeys flourishing here now, where only the blackest bogs of ignorance languished before."

A pale fire lit the Abbot's deep-set eyes. "Wherever the worship of their Great Mother was to be found. Their Great Whore!" His lip curled in a livid sneer. "The so-called Goddess followed by Guenevere herself. The spirit they think inhabits lakes and woods. The rule of the Mother, which they think gives women the right of thigh-freedom, to choose men at will."

Domenico gave the Abbot a quizzical eye. "Yet your work there comes to fruition, no?"

The Abbot shook his head. "We have a church now on the Sacred Isle. And the Lady hides, and dares not show her head. But so much remains to be done—"

"But not all by you, here in this place." The Legate paused. "You may not always resist the will of God," he said gently.

The Abbot tensed. "Where will you send me? Canterbury, or York?"

Domenico spread his hands. "First one, then the other, in the way of things." He gave a glimmering smile. "Unless the Holy Pontiff hears from God that you should overleap the lesser see and go straight to Canterbury to lead from there."

The Abbot stilled his soul. Lord, let me not depart, I am not finished here. He nerved himself for the leap. "Hear this, I beg of you, then tell me if my work here is done. We have had word of something we thought dead and gone—another miracle, if it is true—"

The Legate's eyes widened. "What is it?"

"The so-called Hallows are about again."

"So?" Domenico gave a barking laugh of disbelief. "After all these years?"

"We have a chance to win the Holy Grail." The Abbot paused. "If we can get these Goddess relics, turn them to our holy use—"

"We must." Domenico needed no long rigmarole. "Let us think," he said feverishly, "where they will be revealed."

The Abbot smiled. He had had time to work this out. "Where but in Camelot at Pentecost?"

"Where you and I shall be present too—"

"—for the knighting of Mordred—"

"—as a Christian Prince—"

"—if Mordred ever can be such a thing."

"And if he cannot—"

"Yes. We shall know what to do."

"And in the meantime—"

"—we shall find the Grail."

The two men hardly knew who spoke and who responded, their minds were so closely locked on the same desire. Domenico was the first to step back and smile. "So we are agreed," he said softly.

"We are indeed," replied the Abbot fervently. "We go to Camelot to seek the Grail ourselves."

The Legate laughed. "No Canterbury or York for you now, I can see that," he said cheerfully. "But how am I to refuse His Holiness again?" He stroked down his sun-frizzled hair. "Still, I think he will forgive us if we win the Holy Grail."

CHAPTER 6

"Madame?"

"Lancelot—!"

"You got the ring?"

"I was already on my way."

She had not thought he could be here so soon. Finding him waiting in the Queen's apartments when she returned from her ride left her breathless with joy.

Oh my love—

They came together as they always did, in a cloud of little kisses and soft shining tears. Later there would be time for the hard, hungry embraces they both craved, the fond, frantic attempts to ease the longing that never went away. But whenever fate brought them back to each other's arms, the first moments were silent and tender and touching every time.

Oh, the feel of him— Guenevere clung to the long, lean frame, drinking in the smoothness of his leather jerkin and the outdoor scents on his cloak and hair. The gold torque of knighthood round his neck was his only ornament, and he had ridden hard to come to her, she knew. She knew too that he had chosen the fine green tunic he wore because she loved woodland colors against his brown skin and chestnut hair. From the shelter of his arms, she traced every loved plane and angle of his handsome face. *His smile—the way his eyes light up—the lift of his head—* Every time they were reunited she mourned the betrayal of weak memory. *His strength, the wonder of him, how could I forget?*

"Oh, my love—" She trembled at his touch. "Ohh—"

"Hush, my Queen."

For the moment it was enough to hold her, cradling her head in the hollow beneath his chin that ached so much for her when she was not there. Then his hands moved on down the body he had loved for so long and he pressed the center of her body into his. She wore a loose chamber gown the color of red wine, and its silken feel was wondrous to his hand. He stroked his way up her back, caressing her spine like a string of pearls, till his fingers found the tender top of her neck. Then he took her face between his hands and drew her to him for a lingering kiss.

"Ohhhh—" She sighed with longing, then abruptly broke away. "Agravain is repealed," she cried, "did you know that?"

He was too familiar with her lightning changes of mood to take offense. "No, madame," he said patiently, stifling his desire. "Is that why you sent for me?"

"Yes!" She sprang to her feet, the skirts of her gown whispering *yess, yessss.* "He hates me because I counseled Arthur to banish him. But that's not what I'm afraid of now."

"Tell me," he said.

She rounded on him, her face pale and set. "You know Arthur's chosen Mordred as the next King. But Agravain could still disrupt all that. All the Orkneys are the sons of Arthur's sister, and for those who follow the Goddess, that gives them a claim to the throne. Agravain could overthrow Arthur's wishes and try to claim the Mother-right."

"But madame—" He tried to soften the truth, then gave up the pretense. "Prince Mordred is the son of the King and of his sister too. That gives him a claim on the mother's and the father's side."

"I know that!" Tears sprang to her eyes and she turned furiously away.

With a couple of strides, he had her in his arms. "My lady—oh my Queen—" He covered her face in kisses, stroking her hair. "Is it Amir? Your son should be King?"

"No," she wept. But he knew that in her secret heart, the answer would be *yes.*

He had never loved her more than he did now. "What then, lady?" he asked tenderly.

"It's Mordred himself," she brought out through her tears.

"You do not trust him."

"He is Morgan's son!"

"It is Morgan you fear?" White-faced, sheathed in red, she looked like a lily drowning in her own blood. He stroked her hand, and softly plaited her fingers in and out. "There has been no word of the King's sister for years."

Her eyes flamed. "Morgan will never abandon her revenge!"

"But the wrong she suffered was a lifetime ago."

"And it's not paid for yet!" Guenevere cried. "It was her life, remember, that Uther destroyed. And she did not suffer alone. She wants to avenge her mother and her sister too. She'll use Mordred against Arthur, she'll hunt him to death."

"Has she been seen?" He shook his head doubtfully. "Do you have any reason to think she's about?"

"No, but think of it—Uther raped her mother and killed her father to bring Arthur into the world. Then Arthur turned against her and took her son. Tell me she doesn't have reason for revenge!"

He stroked her cheek. "Madame, Queen Morgan's quarrel may be over now that her son will be King."

"He will indeed! He'll have Arthur's kingdom and mine too, let alone all the petty kingdoms that call us High King and Queen!" Guenevere gave a sardonic laugh. "My mother and I were poor breeding stock. I have no daughter to inherit the Mother-right, and she left no kin but me. Oh, Cornwall still follows the rule of queens, but Arthur's mother is in the winter of her years. She won't leave her kingdom to take over the Summer Country if I die. So Mordred will be High King after me!"

He pressed her hand. "Take comfort, then. Queen Morgan has no reason to persecute you now."

She drew away, suddenly cold. "What reason does she need?"

He knew at once she was on another track. "What is it, madame?" he demanded roughly.

Speak to your knight, and beware.

Nemue's voice was throbbing in her ears. "The Lady has heard that the Hallows have been found. We must have a seeing. She has sent what we need."

Lancelot closed his eyes and felt a wind from the Otherworld brush his cheek. What will be is written in the stars.

He pressed the hands he held dearer than his own. "Do it, my Queen," he said huskily. And his soul added, Whatever it may cost.

CHAPTER 7

Guenevere rose from the couch. Outside, a dusk as soft as a peach was shadowing the land with unborn hopes and dreams. Lancelot's face was stark and wan in the fading light. She took his hand, and drew him toward the fire. On the hearth lay a worn, faded velvet pouch, embroidered in broken letters and gilt thread. She picked it up, twisting it about to read aloud the ancient runes:

I am the eyes you seek.

Feed me to the flames, that your blind gaze may see.

Lancelot felt a shadow clutch at his heart. "What are we to do?"

"Go back to the past. When the Hallows were lost."

He groaned and threw back his head. "I told you all I knew."

All you thought you knew. "Tell me again."

He wanted to weep, but he forced himself to embark on the well-worn tale. "Ten years ago now, when the Christians first decided they wanted the Hallows—"

"It's twelve, almost thirteen."

He gasped. "Is it so?"

"Go on. When they launched their great onslaught on Avalon—?"

"They tried to claim the Hallows were their Holy Grail. The Lady asked us to help her get the treasures away. It was my task to take them off the Sacred Isle and find a safe place to hide."

She nodded. "I saw you off on the quest." Her tears rose again at the memory of that desolate morning, the great box containing the Hallows loaded between two mules, and Lancelot holding her as they said good-bye. Then his white stallion had vanished into the dawn and all that was left was the cold kiss of the mist.

His voice wound on. "And then I rode for many days, lying up by day and moving only at night. In all that time, I never lay in a bed but slept with the Hallows like my only child."

"Go on."

"At last I was passing through a strange northern land. The going was hard, and it grew colder every day. I saw no houses, not even a cottage where I could buy food. I had not eaten for days, and when I came to the castle, I thought it was safe enough to crave shelter for the night…"

IT HAD BEEN late when he saw the castle through the trees. All day the forest had grown deeper with every step, till he thought, I could die here. As the night thickened he lost track of time, and hunger was robbing him of the power of thought. When he saw the light glimmering ahead, he took it for a sign of the Fair Ones, or a will-o'-the-wisp.

He would have fallen back then, unwilling to disturb the woodland dwellers in their nighttime rites. But his horse pressed forward as if drawn toward the place by some unseen force. At last the dense forest thinned out, and he came to a level plain where a huge castle reared up on a rocky mount. Low, dark, and sprawling, its ugly bulk spread over the crest of rock like a mountain keep. Its walls were falling down, the ragged battlements gaped like broken teeth, and a lone bell tower brooded over all.

At the postern gate, an old woman in black looked out as soon as he approached, bright-eyed and wakeful despite the lateness of the hour. She had once been tall but now was bent with age, and her pallor showed that she never saw the sun. But her full purple mouth hinted at the woman she once had been, and her manner was that of one accustomed to command. Before he could say who he was, she had ordered the guard to throw wide the gates and welcomed him in.

"This way, sir," she said, bobbing a crooked curtsy and fixing him with her piercing blackbird stare. In a trice she had the Hallows unloaded from the mules and brought by a pair of laboring servants as they went along. She led him to a chamber where a basin of warm, scented water stood ready to clean off the dust and grime of the long ride. She stood by as he watched the precious box safely set down, checked all its cords and knots, then he took the key as they left, and locked it in. Then she took him down to a Great Hall, where a hundred candles bloomed in the dead of night. There at a long table laden with food for a multitude sat an aged king and a beautiful young girl.

The old woman led him forward to meet the king. He saw a shriveled old man on a massive carved throne, his heavy gold crown almost too much for him to bear. He was gaunt to the point of starvation, the image of living death. But a wild gleam haunted the ancient's sunken eyes, and he twitched with the energy frozen in his veins. He beckoned Lancelot forward, nodding to the old woman who had been his guide.

"I see you have met Dame Brisein," the old man said, in a high, cracked voice like the sound of breaking rock. *"She is the governess of my daughter here, and indeed of our whole house. Welcome to Castle Corbenic, stranger knight."* He paused. *"Yet no stranger to us. You are Sir Lancelot of the Lake."* He waved to the maiden sitting at his side. *"This is my daughter, Elaine. And I am Pelles, king of Terre Foraine."*

The maiden had risen unsteadily to her feet. She was tall like her father, but seemed cowed by him and dropped her gaze. The gown she wore called up memories of bluebells in a wood lifting their face to a sunshiny dawn, and it clung to her breasts and hips like a second skin. But her face would have drawn any eye on earth. A perfect oval of tender, luminous flesh, it glowed with inner light. A pale flush colored her rounded cheeks, and blond curls of baby-fine hair chased each other across her forehead in sweet disarray.

"You are welcome, sir." She curtsied to him and, rising, shyly met his eyes. The force of her glance passed through him like a thunderbolt, and for a moment he saw a raw, lustful longing light up her face. The next second he dismissed the idea with shame. The girl was a virgin pure. Woe to a man who entertained such thoughts!

The feast wore on. He found himself lapped in fine food and wine, his senses slowly sated one by one. It troubled him that they were dining so late at night, and that they seemed to expect him—no, to know him before he came. But he took these for disordered thoughts brought on by hunger and solitude and lack of sleep.

Afterward he could not say what the king spoke of, though he knew the old man had held them all night in thrall, tossing his unkempt white locks and fixing him with his rambling, glittering eye. He knew that Elaine spoke little, but her low voice had an unexpected power, and he felt her eyes on him at every turn. As the candles burned down, he saw that she too was pale and incandescent, staring like her father, though she always dropped her gaze when she saw she had caught his eye. *What do you want of me, maiden?* he was yearning to ask, but did not dare.

At length the meal was over, and he could seek his rest. He was sent off with feverish good wishes from his ancient host.

"God give you the best of nights, Sir Lancelot," he caroled wildly, *"and may He answer all our prayers."* He gripped his daughter with an iron hand and pushed her toward Lancelot. *"Daughter, bid good repose to your knight, and tell him you will match your prayers to his."*

A dull flush mottled Elaine's face and neck. *"I may not call Sir Lancelot my knight,"* she said in a voice sharp with pain.

"Go, fool, call him what you will!" hissed King Pelles. *"But you may not stand against the will of God!"*

"Sire," Lancelot cried, *"let the maiden say what she likes. All the world knows that I serve*

Queen Guenevere, and I am her knight till I die. But if I can help another lady, I am hers to command."

The old man recovered his composure with a laugh. "Forgive me, sir," he shrilled. "I forget myself." With a pounce he rounded on Dame Brisein as the old woman stood patiently by the door. "Pray conduct this weary knight to his bed. Tomorrow at dawn we shall break our fast."

"Very good, sir." Dame Brisein curtsied and hobbled from the room.

Thankfully Lancelot made his adieus, and followed her. The corridors now seemed longer than when they came. For the first time he noticed the moth-eaten hangings on the walls, the sour cobwebs in every corner, and the ratlike scurrying shapes of black and brown. His ears caught fleeting moans of horror too, distant cries that came from far below the ground. But it must be only the old castle creaking and feeling its age, he told himself, bemoaning its glories lost.

He reached his chamber at last with a sigh of relief. As Dame Brisein stood by, he unlocked the massive door.

"I'll bring you your night draught, sir," she said, and hobbled off.

Inside the room he went at once to the box, which lay corded on the floor. He knew at once that the knots had not been tampered with. Still, he would check the Hallows before he slept.

Dame Brisein returned with a steaming flagon in her hands. "The nights are cold in Corbenic," she announced, setting it down on the table beside the bed. "Best drink it while it's hot. It will help you to sleep."

"Thank you, good lady," said Lancelot, firmly shepherding her through the door and turning the key. Then he uncorded the rough outer box, and opened the box within. Made of finely turned thornwood, it was black and knotty and as hard as stone. Inside, the precious Hallows lay wrapped in silk and bedded deep in straw.

One by one he checked the great round dish of the Goddess, the two-handled loving cup, the sword of justice, and the spear of defense. The gold glowed in the midnight chamber, and his sad heart drew in a little warmth. He sat for a long while thinking of Guenevere. Then, length by length, knot by intricate knot, he corded the box again just as it had been before. All was well, he told himself valiantly. All might yet be well.

He was bitterly weary and sharp bone aches were stabbing him in every joint. He reached for the nightcap old Brisein had brought and drained its contents down.

The thick, sweet liquid warmed his throat and rejoiced his heart. As he lay down with the Hallows, a dozen little joyful winged thoughts made their way into his brain. He saw Guenevere when he first met her, radiant by moonlight in the heart of the wood. He saw her look at him with eyes of wild desire, and then with languid bliss when they were lovers riding a tide of joy. He saw his beloved cousins Bors and Lionel riding through the woods at Joyous Garde to welcome him whenever he came home.

Then Joyous Garde unfolded itself to his eyes, the wide, shining moat alive with silver-white swans, the gardens, the fountains, and the bright flags and banners flying over all. Now he was walking with Guenevere at Joyous Garde, drawing her aside into an arbor for a kiss sweeter than the honeysuckle round their heads. He dreamed that Guenevere was his at last, his true love, his wife, in his own house and home, and all he could want in the world was in his arms. Stretched out on the stone-cold floor, with nothing but the rough wood box of the Hallows by his side, Lancelot was as happy as he had been in his life.

He never knew when the waking dreams ended and he drifted off to sleep. But he woke cold and shaking in the dead hour before dawn. The chamber smelled like a she-cat's lair, and his skin was clammy with dew. He felt hollow, as if the life had been sucked out of him, and his stomach was gripped with a sickness near to death.

Ahead of him an open window flapped against the wall. Even through the mists of sleep, he knew that he had closed the casement before he slept. Stumbling awake, he leaped first to check the door, and then the precious box. The door was locked, and the key was still in his belt. The knots in the ropes of the box were just as he had tied them last night. But still his heart was threatening to burst in his breast. Feverishly he struggled to untie the cording, and threw back the lid.

At first his eyes refused to believe what he saw. The box was empty. There was nothing there. Madly he pulled out the wrappings till the inside lay bare. The Hallows had disappeared. And nothing to show how or where they had gone.

CHAPTER 8

"*G*oddess, Mother, no!*"

His scream brought the sleepy castle stumbling to his aid. First through the door was Dame Brisein, her black headdress firmly in place, her gown neat, her shawl around her shoulders, bright awake despite the untimely hour. She roused the guard and, with Lancelot at their head, they scoured the castle from the King's eyrie in the bell tower down to the grisly depths of the fortress below. There the torches flared into cavernous holes that had never seen the light, bringing blind skeletal creatures stumbling to their feet in the hope of release, only to redouble their cries as the clanging door plunged them back into darkness again.

What he saw sickened Lancelot to his soul. Now he saw King Pelles for what he was, and understood the fear in his daughter's face. And nowhere were the Hallows to be found. At last he had to end the pointless search and return to the Great Hall, where the king waited with his retinue. In courtesy he could not demand the release of the prisoners, or even question their treatment at Pelles's hands. And Pelles was quite beside himself that day, weeping and laughing by turns, and cackling maniacally as he spoke of his fury at the Hallows' loss. But Lancelot took the briefest leave he could before turning to the princess Elaine at her father's side.

The girl was paler than ever and seemed stricken to death to see him go. Gasping, she dropped her eyes and whispered, "Farewell, my lord" in a voice full of tears. But like her father, she had something oddly exalted in her air. When he made his good-bye, she pressed his hand and breathed, "Till we meet again." Never, he swore in the silence of his soul as he galloped away. But a voice sounded from the Otherworld: *Never is too long a word to say.*

From the first town he came to he sent word to Guenevere: "I have failed you and the Hallows are lost." Then for a twelvemonth, he searched for them. Too late he learned that the blighted greenwood where he had lost his way was the Wounded Forest of Terre Foraine. But he scoured every clearing, turned over every leaf. That done, he rode the length and breadth of

Corbenic. In that time he met many honest and decent folk, whose only weakness was that they lived in fear of their king. But nowhere did he have sight nor light of the Hallows of the Great One, the lost treasures of Avalon. The relics of the Goddess had vanished as if they had never been.

"AND ALL THIS you know," Lancelot concluded hollowly, half hoarse from his lengthy tale. He passed a hand over his face and felt the dust of the road and the gritty stubble he had not had time to shave. I am a wretch, he thought in misery too deep for tears. I failed the Lady and I failed my love.

Goddess, Mother, help us—

Guenevere stared at him. The dusk had thickened as he told his tale and the last rays of light made him look trapped, almost feral, to her eyes. *There is more,* Nemue had said. She nerved herself to the question she had not asked before. "Did you tell me everything about that night?"

She knew the answer at once. Anger and shame inflamed his handsome features, and he leaped to his feet and plunged away into the gloom.

"Tell me," she said.

He looked away. His voice was rough and raw. "When I woke that morning," he said raggedly, "I was lying on the bed."

"Not on the floor where you went to sleep?"

He gave a curt nod. "Yes." He hesitated. "And there was a foul smell in the room—like a cat in heat." He drew a shallow breath. "And something else, it was hard to believe—"

"What?"

He gave a hopeless shrug. "Judge for yourself. When I woke on the bed, the sheets were gone."

"Gone—where?"

Another shrug. "Who knows? When the Hallows were gone too, I did not think of the sheets."

But there is some grubby secret here he did not probe. There is more. I know there is more.

"Go on," she said implacably.

"That night I dreamed—"

"You told me—that I was with you at Joyous Garde—" Then she understood. *He dreamed of her.*

A raging shaft of pain shot through her heart. "Tell me what you dreamed!"

His voice was level and low. "It was nothing, madame. There is no reason to recall it now."

"Tell me!"

He clenched his fists. "At your command then, lady!" he ground out. "And on your head be it, if you make me speak!"

The purple twilight deepened in the west. He began again in a voice she did not know.

"I dreamed I lay watching the door and saw the handle turn till it opened without the key. Then the old dame of the castle brought the maiden into the room. Stitch by stitch she divested her of her clothes till she was mother-naked. Then Dame Brisein put her into the bed, with many strong spells. And I, lying on the floor—"

"You went to her." She could hardly speak. "You got into the bed with Elaine."

His face was a mask. The slightest nod was all he gave.

"And you took her—?"

He groaned and threw back his head. "Only in the dream."

"You knew her." The pain was unimaginable. "You made love to another woman—"

"Never!" he cried. "Some evil put that dream into my brain. She was a virgin—I would not take her maidenhead!" He seized her hands. "And how could I desire her? I love you!"

"But in your sleep you knew her!" She could not help herself. *"Was she good?"*

"Madame!"

You must have— Was her body young and firm—? A riot of youthful flesh flooded her mind. She saw the madness of biting embraces, kisses that tore out souls, and strong limbs blissfully intertwined.

"You loved her, Lancelot!"

He gripped her wrists to keep her hands from his face. "Enough!"

A new pain seized her. "Why did you never tell me this before?"

"Because of this!" He gave a furious laugh. "Your jealousy—which cost us both so much. You thought I betrayed you with the maid of Astolat. You nearly broke both our hearts before you saw you were wrong. And since then, you see rivals everywhere!"

"No!"

But she knew he was right. Always she saw women lying in wait for him, watching the greed and desire growing in their eyes. Always she feared that he would tire of her and choose a younger woman, one he could call his own. Yet how could she protest if he did? She was still tied to Arthur, who shared her bed. She cried out in distress. "Oh, Lancelot—is this all?"

"I've told you all I know!" His sigh of fury almost split her soul. But above it she heard the voice of Nemue, as clear and cold as water over stones.

In twelve years, many things grow tall, and long-dead secrets meet the light of day. Find out what seed your knight planted, and what has grown that he knows nothing of.

She leaped to her feet. "The Lady said there was more! That's why she sent us this." She reached for the pouch lying on the hearth and drew out a handful of tiny broken gemstones, flashes of rainbow light in the dark room. Drawing Lancelot down beside her, she tossed the glittering splinters onto the fire. There was a sigh as the fire itself exhaled, and a piercing sweetness filled the dusky air. The fire settled, and strange shapes shone in its glowing heart.

The first was a dark castle squatting on a rock. Lancelot recoiled. "Corbenic!" he spat.

Guenevere pressed his hand. "Hush!"

On the battlements of the castle stood King Pelles, tall and wasted, raving at the moon. Beside him was a young woman dressed in nunlike gray, her head wimpled against men's gaze. She wore sorrow like a veil, but her wounded eyes were triumphant too. *Elaine. But why is she so glad?*

Now a knight came into view in the nighttime forest below. Behind him plodded a pair of pack mules laden with a heavy box. The knight made his way to the castle gate as the king and his daughter looked down.

"It is just as I told you," Lancelot breathed. "I came to this place in the dark. I did not know they saw me from above."

"Hush!" hissed Guenevere. "Watch, and see!"

The castle slumbered in the bright moonlight. The portcullis was down, every window shuttered, and the postern gate barred. Then a door at the top of the gate flew open as a woman's head popped out. The moon picked out every detail of Dame Brisein's features, the long pale face, the large, bright black eyes, the full mulberry mouth.

"Welcome, Sir Lancelot," she said.

"No!"

Guenevere surged choking to her feet. "No!" she screamed again.

CHAPTER 9

Mordred stepped out into the dawn and made his way across the courtyard with a purposeful air. The sun was on his back, the smell of haymaking was wafting in from the fields, and the cloudless sky promised a perfect day. Yes, life was good.

Already the castle was humming like a hive of bees. But the busiest servants had time to greet the Prince.

"Good day, my lord!"

"Good dawning to you, sir!"

"And you—and you." With a ready smile, Mordred acknowledged each of the greetings as he went along.

"Oh, sir—!"

Struggling out of a side passage, a little laundry maid almost dropped her heavy basket at the sight of him. Mordred winked at her encouragingly and strode on, unconsciously reviewing her charms. Short and pink, but agreeably fluttered at the sight of him, and her figure was full enough for any man—

Shame on you, Mordred! He caught himself up with an embarrassed laugh. What, eyeing up the servants, how princely is that? He was used to receiving attention as the son of the King. But he had to admit that the excitement had been greater, the smiles and bows more fulsome and pronounced, since everyone knew that he was Arthur's heir.

Mordred's handsome features crinkled into a smile. Of course he was, who else could it be? He had never doubted that this moment would come.

So now, get to the King's apartments, he thought contentedly, to be there as always when Arthur awoke. Then to the stables—Arthur would want to try out the new gallopers—and, after that, most likely to the hunt; there were any number of things that Arthur might want to do. Putting them all in order in his mind, Mordred crossed the cobbled courtyard with a firm step.

Ahead of him, the white walls of the royal apartments beckoned in the rosy dawn. He was almost on the threshold when four lofty figures entering the courtyard caught his eye. Clad in red and black, they were shouldering through the gates of the castle, weary and travel-worn from the road. The Orkney colors, noted Mordred with sharp interest. The return of the banished brother, the wicked son.

"Prince Mordred," Gawain called, "will you greet my brother Agravain, back from the East?"

Coming forward was a tall, lean, watchful figure, moving like a heron about to strike. He had to be less than forty, as Gawain was, but his face was deeply wrinkled from years in the sun. His hair too, a thick mane prematurely white, suggested an older man. Only the raven-bright eyes, watchful and alert, proclaimed that this was one of the Orkney brothers, not the father of their line.

"Welcome, sir," said Mordred graciously. But the gaunt stranger merely gave a careless nod. Mordred's interest was piqued. "From the East, sir?" he inquired.

The newcomer nodded again. "The Holy Land."

Mordred's spirit of adventure gave him a sudden pang. "Fighting the Saracens?"

Agravain shrugged. "In their most sacred citadels—which we took from them by force of arms, and made our own."

Mordred fought down his envy. "I hear they are worthy enemies for our swords."

Agravain's eyes wandered over a handsome page just crossing the courtyard ahead, a pink-cheeked youth on the turn between boy and man. "They have—unusual ways." A strange gleam lit his eye and then was gone. "There is much to learn from them, if a man desires."

Gawain shifted his bulk from foot to foot. "You were not always with the Saracens, brother," he said, rather too heartily.

"True." Agravain gave a harsh, cawing laugh. "I lived in the desert for a while." He turned his dark eyes on Mordred. "One of a fellowship of like-minded men."

Mordred stared. "You joined a monastery?"

Another harsh burst of mirth. "No, indeed. We were mendicants, I had to beg my bread." His eyes snapped like snakes. "They were harsh times indeed. But I learned what a man will do to buy his life. That came in useful in the Holy Land. It is a lesson that all men should know."

A furious burst of rivalry seized Mordred's soul. "You are fortunate, sir.

You have seen things we can never know from here." He looked away, mastering the conflict between resentment and despair.

So! Agravain smiled softly to himself. The young Prince dreams of action and longs to blood his sword. Meanwhile the King keeps him here at court, facing nothing fiercer than the wild boar in the hunt. And Gawain has said he has yet to be made a knight. Yes, there is something I can work with here.

"Your knight-making is approaching, Prince, or so I am told," he said carefully.

Mordred's eyes flared. "Not before time."

Agravain worked his eyebrows sympathetically. "And do all the novices still keep vigil beforehand, as we did?"

Mordred gave a careless laugh. "Fasting the night in church, you mean, to purify our souls? Oh, yes, the Church insists on that."

"You'll do well, Prince, as my brothers did," Gawain put in firmly. "It's no more than you'll do on the road when you're a knight."

"If I ever leave court," Mordred burst out in spite of himself. He cast a dark gaze on Agravain, half admiring, half resentful by turns. "If my father ever lets me travel and do as you did."

Again the bony shoulders worked their offhand shrug. "I can teach you, Prince, if you wish to learn."

Mordred started. "Teach me what?"

"Oh, moves in combat, new feints and turns. A Saracen is the slipperiest fighter on earth."

Gawain's alarm could no longer be contained. "Brother, we don't want those scurvy tricks back here! We follow chivalry at Arthur's court."

Agravain's lip curled. "No tricks, I promise you," he said smoothly. "Nothing but weaponry, brother, skill with a blade." He flicked his eyes at Mordred. "Call on me if you will."

"Tomorrow," said Mordred boldly. "After noon, when the King goes to his rest. I shall see you then." He gave a hasty bow to the four big knights. "I must attend the King. Good day to you, sirs."

With narrowed eyes Agravain watched Mordred's retreating form, the long, lithe body with its springing step, the swinging mane of shining blue-black hair. Gawain looked at the hunched figure still intently watching Mordred, following his every move.

"Agravain?" he called suspiciously.

Agravain's brow cleared, and he gave a winning smile. "Coming, brother," he replied.

"MORGAN! MORGAN! MORGAN!"

"Hush, lady! Hush, my love."

Lancelot cradled Guenevere in his arms, stroking her hair and raining kisses on her face. But she shuddered with dread as the vision of Morgan burned through her mind.

Morgan!

Disguised as a crooked old woman, pretending to be King Pelles's devoted Dame Brisein. But Morgan, Morgan from her fatal eyes.

Now back to haunt us, after all these years—

She struggled to sit up. "It was Morgan at the castle all along," she cried hoarsely. "Didn't you recognize her? She hasn't changed!"

"I've never met her!" Lancelot ran a hand through his hair. "By the time I came to court, she was long gone."

Guenevere stared at him. It was true. Lancelot had been part of her for so long that she could not remember a time when he had not been there. But he had never seen Morgan. How would he know her face?

"So she tricked me." Lancelot was following his own train of thought. "She wanted the Hallows. But why?"

"Morgan grew up in Cornwall, where they follow the Mother-right," said Guenevere unsteadily. "She was a child of the Goddess. It was said she would be the Lady one day." She drew a breath. "If the Hallows were at large, Morgan would take them for her own."

Lancelot's mind darkened. "Could she have given them to King Pelles? Or to his daughter—to foster their Christian plan?"

Guenevere gave a savage laugh. "Morgan hates the Christians! King Uther put her in a nunnery as a child and she was starved and whipped for almost twenty years. She'd never let the Hallows go to them."

May the Great Ones make that true, Lancelot prayed.

Guenevere surged to her feet. "But she might try to use them against Arthur, to get her revenge."

"For the sin of his father?"

"And for his own!" she cried. "King Uther was the first to break into her life. But Arthur loved her and his love turned to hate. Then he took Mordred from her and wanted him dead. He ordered all the babies cast away. The Gods only know how Mordred survived."

Lancelot bowed his head. "Queen Morgan has borne griefs beyond her power to forgive—"

She cut across him, a new frenzy in her tone. "Lancelot, what really happened at Corbenic?"

He held on to his temper. "I told you—many times."

"I don't believe you!" she cried. "Remember the strange atmosphere in the room—and the sheets that vanished from the bed? Someone was with you that night!"

"Not Elaine!" He tried to take her hands. "It was only a dream, I told you—"

She tore herself away. "The old woman brought you a drink that night, you said," she muttered, her eyes glittering. "That means you were drugged into an enchanted sleep. You wouldn't have known—"

"Not know a woman I had in my bed?" He was almost too angry to speak.

"Lancelot—"

"You doubted me before, when you thought the Fair Maid of Astolat came into my bed," he said in a voice she had learned to fear. "You spoke daggers, and banished me from court. You were faithless then, and I was true to you."

He could see from her white face that he had struck home. "And we both suffered," he went on, breathing heavily. "I tell you, madame, it must not happen again. I have never been false to you. I will go back to Corbenic tonight to find out the truth."

"But you have to be here for Mordred's knighting. You are one of his supporters, Arthur's depending on you—"

He nodded heavily. "If I ride hard enough, I shall get back."

She paused and found her strength. "Go then," she said steadily, "if you must." She gave him one of her old smiles. "And till then—"

"Madame!" He kissed her neck, stroking the satin hollow at the base of her throat. She quickened instantly and reached out for him.

"Ah, lady!" As always, he felt himself responding to her caress. With a practiced hand he unlaced the front of her gown and bent his lips to her breasts as he freed them from the confining silk. That he loved her was his life's greatest grace—that she loved him was a burden and a mystery beyond compare.

"My love—"

He loves me—

Guenevere heard the feeling in his harsh, indrawn breath, and her soul soared. Her spine arched to meet his fleeting touch. Swiftly he shrugged his way out of his clothes, and drew off her gown. *"Ma belle!"* he murmured in his throat. *"Mon amour!"*

Naked, she suffered a vision of the young Elaine, her pure virgin body unmarked by childbirth or age. Then she felt his hard hands round her waist, his thumbs finding the hollows of her hips. Lovingly she traced his familiar wounds, the long ragged scar on his thigh, the pale puckered weals on his shoulders and arms. Ten years of adoring him naked had not diminished her appetite for his lean and supple toughness, his long, strong sex.

Love me, love me now. Moaning, she drew him toward her, crying out for the joy she knew would come. And suddenly she was laden with the grief that must come too, the harsh dawns after wakeful, hungry nights, the dull ache of lonely days.

In all these years we have never shared a bed, never known what is was to lie down and wake up in peace as true lovers do. Tears flowed from her overburdened soul and poured down her face. In a passion, Lancelot roughly kissed her tears away, then drove into her with a force that would not be assuaged.

In a second, her grief had given way to a panting joy. She drew him to her with a flurry of little kisses and cries. Together they crested the pleasure so near to pain, then the mounting wave broke over their heads and carried them to the shore.

Sated, they lay together in a love closer than their skin, meeting in the secret places of their soul. At last they stirred without speech. He helped her on with her gown, and in every touch she felt the love that bound them together without end. She wanted to shout his faithfulness from the house-tops. How could she have doubted him?

Now, when he left, it was harder every time.

"Lancelot—"

"No words."

He laid his finger on her lips and went quietly through the door. On the far horizon, the evening star was spreading its gentle radiance through the dusk. Soon she would have to go down to the Great Hall, and talk and behave as if nothing was amiss. She moved to the window to light the candle standing there. *Goddess, Great One, shine on my love,* she prayed, *guard him on the long, hard ride ahead, and bring him safely back.*

His last words were ringing in her ears: *I have never been false to you, my lady, my love.* The thought gave her a little wintry comfort now he was gone. Then the gleam in Elaine's eye came back to her like a haunting, and fear filled her heart.

CHAPTER 10

Merlin rode through the wood, tapping the ends of his fingers together and singing in a high, beelike drone. From time to time he bit the tips of his thumbs. Moodily he watched the creatures of the woodland come and go. Ordinarily he would have been in communion with them, but he had no heart for it now. What was the threat that was darkening Arthur's days?

Above his head the blazing sun roofed all the forest with fire. Under the trees, small shimmering clouds of mayflies danced madly toward the summer day, when they would mate and die. The broken pattern of sunlight falling through the leaves made the path melt and dissolve, till it seemed that the world was slipping away beneath his feet. This journey was taking him into unknown realms, lands even he had not traveled before.

He closed his eyes. He had been there when the first Pendragon swam out of the mists of time. He had crisscrossed these misty isles unnumbered times, in the endless service of that troubled house. He had put aside his own longings, his love, his life, to keep Pendragon safe. And still there was work to be done.

His love—his life—

He tugged at his long gray locks with a muttered curse. He would not think of the spirit woman now. She came to him only in the darkness of his soul. And he needed no darkness greater than that he faced.

Arthur—the danger—the child—

Fretfully his mind returned to the well-worn path. Weeks of brooding had brought no light at all and only deepened the twilight of his heart.

Arthur—

The child—

A deep miasma settled on his soul. To divert himself, he made the trees on either side of the path lean into each other like lovers, and kiss and caress. The silver birches were as coy as silly virgins, rustling and shrinking from the ash trees' five-fingered embrace. But the thorn was the tree of the

Goddess, and she turned to the oak with an open, raw delight, offering her lusty partner her white blossoms as he reached out for her, groaning to his roots.

A sharp bolt of memory passed through Merlin's frame. He saw himself as a young Druid, transfixed with love for the Goddess and blind with desire. He was groaning to be taken and possessed by Her, broken and made again new and whole. Yet though he had fasted and studied and gone to the wilderness in pursuit of his goal, he had never become one of Her chosen, as others were.

And then the Christians had come, and the whole world had tilted on its frame, making all its inhabitants move in different tracks. All that had been many lives ago. But he still remembered the pang of love never satisfied, the groaning soul. He restored the trees to themselves again with a deeper sense of gloom.

The woodland was thinning now as the hidden greenway began its descent to the high road to Camelot. Reluctant to leave the green shade, Merlin kept his mule under the shelter of the trees. As he rode past a hawthorn, a strand of creamy woodbine brushed his face. "Take heart," a soft voice murmured. "You are nearing your goal."

Merlin pricked up his ears. From his earliest days he had heard the low whispering of glowworms in the night, and the busy ants ordering their well-trained ranks. Now he caught a faint hum from afar and the slow rhythmic trudge of horses' hooves. A yellow flame of triumph lit his eye.

"Thank you, old Mother!" he breathed.

He was Merlin still. He had had the word.

Whoever these travelers were, they were the people he sought. And wherever they were, they were in his hands.

The next second he felt the stabbing in his thumbs. *Beware, Merlin!* his inner voice cried out. But he could not hold back now. Recklessly he tugged at his joints without mercy, cracking the knuckles beyond the point of pain, and spurred on his mule.

BUT ANOTHER DAY was to pass before he caught up with them. The hidden greenway was running down to the high road before he saw in the distance an aged man, two women, and a youth, laden with more baggage than they could surely need and attended by a well-armed band of men.

At the head the old man rode alone, lost in thought and seemingly without a care for those riding behind. Two women followed on low palfreys, the younger the old man's daughter by her neglected look, the older just as plainly her maid. But the rider in the rear was set apart from them all. At the sight of him, Merlin's blood growled in his veins.

He had the air of one who had never been young, born with a lifetime already on his back. He burned with a pallid, ferocious flame of inner fire, and his large-eyed stare seemed to come from another world. Yet this old soul was lodged in the body of a boy, tall and reed-slim, a youth with the promise of a marvelous man. His eyes were pale and wide-set like a child's and his straight fair hair fell in a page-boy crop. He wore a tunic of white and a coat of silver mail, and the morning sun bathed him in living gold.

Against him, the old lady-in-waiting seemed only half alive. Seated sidesaddle on an ancient nag, the crooked figure clinging to the pommel was little more than a bag of bones and cloth. Her narrow shoulders drooped with weariness, and her empty eyes were fixed vacantly on the ground. Merlin dismissed her with a cursory glance. She was a shell, no more, of what she once had been.

The younger woman on the white palfrey was dressed like a nun, in simple white and gray. Her head was veiled above a pale face and downcast eyes, and her mouth, too, drooped in discontent. She did not seem to notice what Merlin's eyes could not miss: the reverent adoration of the boy. But one sight of her exquisite features, the blond wisps of escaping hair and the eyes shining midway between dusk and dawn, told Merlin where the fair youth had got his looks. He was her son for sure.

And yet—

Merlin caught his breath. The boy was not like his mother but recalled someone else, someone once as young and ardent as this boy was now.

Who?

Merlin rode up, struggling to pin down a memory as fragile as a fleeting dream. It would come, he knew.

Soon, soon.

Merlin's whole body stirred, and his skin began to crawl. And suddenly there it was again, the pricking in his thumbs. But this beautiful child could never be a threat. Merlin rode up to the leader, undeterred.

At close quarters now, the old man was no dreaming graybeard, but a figure at war with himself and all the world. The hawklike swivel of his head, the stabbing gaze were those of one who saw enemies on all sides. What can he fear? Merlin thought irritably. Yet something, to be sure.

"Sir!" he cried.

"Who calls?" the old man shrilled with a dangerous glare.

At the rear of the little column, the pale youth smiled. "This is Merlin, sire, no enemy." He bowed to the old enchanter courteously. "You grace our party with your presence, sir."

Merlin nodded, deeply gratified to be recognized. "You go to Camelot?"

"We do," the old man said. He gave a preening smile. "I am Pelles, king of Terre Foraine."

Odd flakes of memory drifted through Merlin's mind. Terre Foraine, on the far northern shore—a Christian king, for twenty years nursing a rumored daughter of destiny, the living fulfillment of a prophecy—

Merlin bared his teeth in a smile. "I know you, sir."

King Pelles struggled to pull round his horse's head. "And this is my daughter the princess Elaine, and her waiting-gentlewoman, Dame Brisein. I am taking my grandson to King Arthur's court." A hectic flush rose up his sallow cheeks. "His name is Galahad. He is the finest knight in all the world!"

So!

Merlin heard his own voice through this mists of time. *Remember to make a seat at the Round Table for the knight who is to come. He will be the son of the most peerless knight in the world, and he is destined for the highest adventure of all. Call his seat the Siege Perilous, for he will face many dangers and defy them all. In his time too he will be the most peerless knight, and when he comes, the Table will be complete.*

He had prophesied thus to Guenevere from his crystal cave, all those lives ago.

And then the prophecy of Merlin will be fulfilled—

Merlin's flesh crawled. Was this the boy—this child—destined to complete the Round Table, fill the Siege Perilous as he had dreamed so many lives before?

His mind was a hornets' nest of stinging fears. He forced himself to speak. "Finer than Lancelot? Or Arthur the King?"

An unintelligible light flashed over the young woman's face. "Finer than all of them!" she cried. "My son is pure!"

A virgin, and a knight? Merlin turned to the boy. "Sir Galahad already, young man?" he asked. "May I guess your age?"

The youth gracefully inclined his head. "I am young for the honor, it is true," he said modestly.

"Tush, man, what's that?" cried Pelles furiously. "I knighted him myself at Easter last. Arthur must make him one of the Round Table Knights. He will take his seat at the feast of Pentecost."

"Which is almost upon us. Prince Mordred will be keeping his vigil even now." Merlin looked at Galahad. "The Round Table, eh, boy? You'll be one of a mighty fellowship." Again something fretted the edge of a memory of long ago. Who did the boy remind him of? *Who?*

No matter. It would come. Out of the corner of his eye he noted the king surreptitiously signaling the men-at-arms. "You are well guarded, sir." Merlin's yellow eyes emitted a sulfurous glare. "But King Arthur has rid the land of lawless men. What do you fear?"

The old king's face took on a crazy gleam. "The enemies of Christ are everywhere."

A thunder of hooves reached them from the high road below. A rider was heading north at a reckless pace, riding helter-skelter, careless of his neck.

Merlin craned his neck at the white plume of dust. The knight wore Lancelot's colors, he noted idly, and the long-striding gray he rode was like Lancelot's too. "Well, that knight will not trouble you, for sure. And I myself will see you safe to Camelot."

King Pelles stared at him triumphantly. "Our Lord Himself sent Merlin to take care of us!" he cried, grinning like a loon.

"Perhaps," agreed Merlin, cackling too. Yes, he would bring them in, the mad old king, his unhappy daughter, and the marvelous boy, even the hollow husk of the old dame. Arthur would be glad to see the prophecy fulfilled.

But Guenevere—no, she would not be pleased!

Merlin gasped with mirth till the tears stood in his eyes. Queen Guenevere would not welcome this motley crew. For now Merlin saw it all. Suddenly he had remembered whose face the boy wore.

HIGH IN THE BRANCHES above, the spirit laughed too. All around her the tender leaves shriveled in her scorching breath. That only made her cackle and wither them more. Let whole forests fall, let the birds drop from the trees and the sun run backward into night! All nature should stand in awe of Morgan Le Fay.

With a sensual relish she coiled her long length around the nearest trunk and laughed from her belly to the back of her sharp white teeth. Yes, Merlin was right, as he so often was, and Guenevere's pride was due for a painful fall. So what if the Summer Country's Queen had suffered from Arthur's betrayal, and suffered for Amir? The spirit snorted, pawing the rough bark, and writhed with rage. Guenevere could never suffer enough!

But Merlin was right only as far as he could see. And those sharp golden eyes had to be kept in the dark. When the darkness descended on him, he was no longer a lord of light, only a man of sorrows working out his pain. Yesss! Sorrow and pain—that was Merlin's due. For Merlin too had sins to expiate.

Morgan sighed and soared and returned to her perch. Soon, soon she would enter Dame Brisein's old body again. Shriveled though it was and lopsided like a crooked tree, it would serve her turn. And Merlin had dismissed old Brisein as an empty husk? What fools men were! No man could see her body hidden inside Brisein's, not even Merlin, though he had sported with every inch of her often enough.

Yesss, Merlin, yessss, you have loved me to madness and wanted no woman else when your darkness came down—

The wolf in the cave far below picked up her scent and greedily gulped up her heat. Eyes flaring, she fondled her long, white breasts and stroked her sinuous flanks. Well, Merlin had been her familiar in many lives. It was too soon to say she had finished with him now. He had taught her much and pleasured her much in the past. And the past was the future as the wheel of time went round.

For she still had to have her revenge. Uther and Arthur must pay.

And still—her howl blighted the meadows and made cows cast their calves—still, still she needed to know her son.

So then! seethed her restless, tormented soul. Let Merlin bring Galahad to Camelot and events will take their course. Even the old enchanter could not turn back that wheel. And then—*Mordred, Mordred, it will be your time! Your time and mine!* She hissed with glee again.

The sound of hooves on the high road sent her yelping with joy. Far below a knight was spurring his horse as straight as an arrow up the Great North Way. Behind him, King Pelles's party was slowly emerging from the shelter of the trees to make its way down to Camelot. Farewell, Lancelot. Ride on to Corbenic in vain!

All in vain.

The spirit hissed with delight. A cloud of vapor poisoned the roosting birds and drifted on, downwind toward Camelot.

All their efforts would be in vain, for she would have her way.

CHAPTER 11

Not yet dawn. But surely the vigil could not be much longer now. Chilled to the bone, Kay huddled wretchedly inside his cloak and wished himself anywhere but here. The courtyard before the chapel was mantled with a fine drizzle that drifted into every nook of the cloisters where he sheltered with Lucan and Bedivere. The night they had passed felt more like November than June, and the louring remains of the clouds threatened a rainy day. Had it been as wretched as this when Arthur and he were made knights?

No—but that had been another world. Briskly Kay pushed aside the memories of those endless boyhood days of blue and gold with his great rawboned companion, a youth always gentle and never afraid. But that was before they knew Arthur was a king. And long, long before Arthur had had a son.

A son who was now on his vigil to be made a knight. More, on his way to becoming Arthur's successor, the heir to the throne. So it was only right that other Round Table knights should keep vigil with him, outside the church where he and the other novices fasted the night away. Arthur had wanted all this, everyone knew. It was good to know that Mordred was fulfilling Arthur's will.

Good, yes. Kay heaved a sigh so deep that his bowels quaked. Why then did he hate all this so much? He ought to rejoice with Arthur and be glad that he had a son. But instead— Kay sighed again. Gods above, where would all this lead?

Standing next to Kay's small, shrunken form and doing his best to protect him from the mizzling rain, Bedivere heard the sigh, and threw a meaning glance at Lucan, waiting nearby. Lucan yawned and straightened up, eyeing the sky. The first faint glow of dawn was bathing the east. Casually he clapped Kay on the shoulders and rubbed the back of his old friend's cold, damp neck.

"Soon over now," he said warmly, "and then we'll see how Mordred has endured." He nodded ahead. "At least he has friends in support."

Beside the church door, still shrouded in half-dark, Mordred's squires and pages were waiting for their lord. All round the courtyard farther off clustered small groups of knights, their attention focused on the chapel ahead. The rising light picked out the glint of swords and the gleam of silver mail.

"Who's there?" demanded Kay with interest, craning to see.

Bedivere smiled softly. "Knights who were old when Arthur was a boy." He indicated two white heads close together, deep in talk. "Sir Niamh was here when we came to Camelot."

"And Sir Lovell too," said Kay, with a sharp laugh. "He was the Queen's champion, remember? They called him Lovell the Bold." He looked around, picking out another group. "And there's Sagramore and Dinant with Helin and Erec, and who's that behind?"

"It's Tor," said Lucan, peering through the rising gloom at a tall, battle-hardened figure, heavily armed. "The King has ordered him back from the Saxon shore. There's not much danger from the Norsemen these days, and he wanted all the knights here when Mordred is made up."

Kay's questioning gaze swept the courtyard from side to side. "There's Ladinas talking to Griflet and the terrible twins."

"What, Balin and Balan?" Lucan laughed. "Are they talking to each other? They're usually fighting these days."

Kay grunted. "Well, it seems the Round Table is out in force." He gave a sour grin. "Even the babes in arms."

Lounging near the church door were half a dozen young knights, their talk and laughter swelling as others joined their ranks. Unscarred, unlined, and snapping at each other's heels like whelps newly fledged, they were all no older than their twenties, and some indeed hardly out of their teens. Their bright tunics and unfleshed swords caught the first rays of the sun striking the dawn courtyard, to the cruel disadvantage of the older knights. For the first time Kay was aware of Tor's battle-scarred face and thinning hair, and Sagramore's ample, drooping paunch.

"Great Gods!" he swore to himself in disbelief. "Are we getting old?"

"Ha!" Lucan's face hardened. "Mordred's followers." He pointed to a sharp-featured, lean figure roughly greeting another youth strutting toward him like a turkey-cock. "And their fine ringleaders, Vullian and Ozark. Well, let's hope he can lick them into shape."

Bedivere shook his head. The quiet Welsh lilt of his birthplace only heightened the force of his words. "They do not care for chivalry as we did."

"Then it's up to us to teach them," snapped Kay, "if the world Mordred inherits is to be no worse than ours."

"Gods above, Kay," cried Lucan, "never say that!" He laughed, and tossed back his still shining hair. "We aren't finished yet. And neither are they." He waved a hand. "The Orkneys, gentlemen."

Coming toward them were four great figures all in variants of black and red. But where Gawain and his two younger brothers sported tunics of crimson and scarlet and dark breeches with flecks of bright red, the lean, sunburned form stalking behind Gawain was clad from head to foot in shades of coal. Only a blood-red sash across his breast paid tribute to the colors of his house.

"It's Agravain!" said Kay with sharp interest. "Well, let's greet the returning son." Cursing the pain in his leg, he hobbled nimbly over the slippery cobbles to stop the Orkney brothers in their tracks. "Greetings to you all, good sirs," he cried sardonically. "And Agravain—well, you're back with us, by all that's wonderful."

Agravain smiled faintly, and returned a glance as sardonic as Kay's. "Greetings, Kay," he said in his harsh, braying voice. "You have not changed. Still, I am glad to have your welcome."

"You're hardly welcome at this knighting, dressed like that," Kay put in sourly, gesturing at Agravain's dark dress. "You look as if you're burying a friend."

Agravain gave another distant smile. "In the East, men die from too much sun. I have worn these garments now for ten years of my life, and I do not think to put them off for you."

"Like Kay, some things don't change, Agravain," said Lucan, coming up behind with a measured smile. "Still your old self, I see."

Agravain nodded. "Indeed, it is the only self I have. Yet I have changed." He raised his head, and for a second his black eyes flashed fire. "I have done my penance, Lucan."

"As the King himself has acknowledged, by calling you back," said the gentle voice of Bedivere. He stepped forward, his liquid brown eyes fixed on

Agravain, and offered his hand. "And you are welcome back amongst us once again."

Gawain thumped his dark-faced brother in the small of the back. "There you are, Agravain," he said heartily, "you are one of the Round Table again."

As long as you kill no more of Arthur's knights, Kay wanted to say, but refrained. He contented himself with one final barb. "And you are back in very good time," he said, pointing to the church. "How lucky that you are here to greet our new knight, as he is about to be named the King's heir, too. Prince Mordred will doubtless reward your loyalty."

Agravain turned his eyes in the direction of Kay's pointing hand. Couched in the shadow of the keep, the low stone church winked in the rising sun. Through the round window over the carved oak doors, the eternal flame glowed red above the altar like a dragon's eye. As they watched, it lowered and dipped, then flared up again.

"It's finished," said Gawain grimly. "Now we'll see how Mordred endured."

Behind him Gareth let out a raw sigh. He glanced at Gaheris with a question in his eyes: Remember, brother?

"Yes, I remember," said Gaheris harshly. His milky skin had flushed to the roots of his hair. "Ten hours on my knees, till the very flagstones of the floor felt like knives piercing my bones—how could I forget?"

"But you came through it, brother," said Gawain, frowning. "We all did." His outsize face was set in an expression only a hair's breadth from annoyance: why must these two complain?

"Truly, brother?" interjected Agravain with interest. "And I thought the knighthood ceremony was ordained only after you joined Arthur, after he became King. I never knew you'd undergone a vigil as well."

Gawain turned color. Trust Agravain, he thought venomously. He cleared his throat.

"It is true," he said with difficulty, "that when I took my knighthood oath, knights were sworn only to their lord. We offered our faith and our swords, and our liege masters pledged themselves to take care of us. But with so many lawless knights and evil lords at loose in the kingdom when Arthur came in, he decided to bring knighthood under the sway of the church."

Lucan laughed and rolled his eyes at Gaheris and Gareth. "So the

Christians set up a vigil for all knights-to-be, to purge you all of your sins. You had to do penance all night in your virgin white shifts, if you wanted to be knights of Christ on the next day. Whereas we hopeless sinners, when we became knights"—his white grin embraced Kay, Gawain, and Bedivere— "all we had was the gold torque of knighthood clasped about our necks, our oath to the death, and Arthur's solemn pledge to be our lord."

An uneasy silence fell among the younger knights. Lucan's wide smile vanished as swiftly as summer snow. "And I wonder who will die first for him—you, or we?"

"Now, Lucan," growled Gawain uneasily, "no need for that. We are here to honor Prince Mordred—"

"—and here he comes," said Bedivere's soft voice.

The doors of the church cracked open with an iron groan. Two shaven-headed monks, straining against the weight of the ancient oak, came into view pushing them back on their tracks. Behind the first two stalked row upon row of their colleagues, all bearing lighted candles as they raised their voices in the first office of the day. *"Beatus vir, qui non abiit…"*

Blessed is the man who walks not in the counsels of the ungodly, Kay translated silently as the monks sang on. Is this for Mordred? Will he be free of evil, a blessed man?

Please, God, let it be—

A sharp tug on his sleeve accompanied Lucan's voice. "There he is!"

Behind the solid phalanx of chanting monks trudged a column of their beetle-black companions singing the descant. Caught between them, like a creature trapped in amber, Mordred hovered into view. His eyes stared like those of one who had come from hell. The dull light of early morning played over his pain-washed face and frozen limbs, his jerky movements like those of the risen dead. But he was on his feet. He had suffered and endured. He had passed the test.

A roar of appreciation swelled up from the crowd. With the shadow of a smile, Mordred raised a pale hand in homage, before his squires and attendants swooped down to bear him away.

"So!" Gawain squinted at the sun. "Now he can reap his reward. They've got an hour or so to give him a warm bath and all the reviving cordials, and make him fine. Then we shall meet again in the Great Hall."

"Having made ourselves fine as well, I would hope, to honor the King," said Kay with asperity, eyeing Agravain's dark robes. But as he spoke he shivered with the dank cold. The mists of nights had struck him to the bones.

"Here, let me help you, Kay," said Agravain solicitously. He came forward and took Kay's arm with a gentle smile. "These night watches will be too much for you. If you aren't careful, you're going to catch your death."

"MY LADY! We were not expecting you. His Majesty is still making his morning devotions—"

"No matter." Guenevere stepped in the King's apartments with a reassuring smile. "I will wait."

Through an open door she could see Arthur on his knees, his head bent, his hands clasped in prayer. Above his head, as if ready to tear himself from the cross, hung an eye-rolling, writhing Christ, and from Arthur's working face it was clear that he was wrestling with his soul.

She watched him on his knees, sorrowing inside. *Oh, Arthur, Arthur, why do you grovel to this failed prophet, this God-king from the East? You yourself were born a king among men, and you were always a God to me. When I met you, it was like breaking through from water to red wine. You made me a woman, and I made you a man. And together we brought peace to the land, and created between us the most beautiful child on earth.*

The sunlight falling through the window lit Arthur's graying head. She thought of the years when his dusty fair hair had outglinted the sun, and she longed to stroke his troubled face and smooth down his tangled locks. Her heart contracted with the old familiar ache. *Oh, Arthur, Arthur—*

He was her husband still. And with that thought came another ache of years.

Oh, Lancelot—

The sun in the chamber was full of dancing motes. In the slanting shaft of liquid golden light, she saw a faraway figure on a galloping horse heading into the setting sun. She closed her eyes. The race to Corbenic seemed like madness now, with the knight-making here. Lancelot would never get back in time. And if Morgan was in Corbenic as they feared, he might not return at all. She closed her eyes. *May the Goddess go with you, my love, and speed you home.*

"Guenevere?"

Arthur was standing before her, surprise on his face. "What brings you here?"

"Oh—" She hastened to collect herself. "I came to greet you, Arthur.

On formal occasions, you always wait on me. But you deserve to be honored on this special day."

"Bless you, Guenevere. You are good to me."

Arthur took her hand and drew her into the great chamber, waving away the servants coming forward with wine and sweetmeats to break his fast.

"Now we shall be alone," he said jovially, pressing her hand fondly all the while. But he was very pale, she noticed, and the smile on his lips did not reach his eyes. He was moving awkwardly too, and the thought she always wanted to avoid snaked into her mind. *How long is it since he called me to his bed?*

Too long for him, although not mourned by me, she realized with a frisson of fear. *His old wound has awakened again. It has to be that.*

Gods above, how long was it since he took the wound between his legs that had threatened his manhood on and off for years? Guenevere tensed, wishing she could thrust the memory away. That had been one of the worst of Morgan's cruel tricks, when she had turned one of Arthur's own knights against him in a fight to the death. Sir Accolon had been so loyal to Arthur that he had been specially trusted to guard Arthur's scheming half-sister when her evil came to light. But Morgan had taken the young knight as her lover, inflaming him to kill the King, and the battle between them had cost Arthur dear. With his final stroke, Accolon had driven his sword deep into Arthur's groin, and the King had barely escaped then with his life. He had had the best of the Druid doctors, and they had healed him at last. But in times of strain it returned to haunt him again.

She raised her hand to the crease between his brows. "You are troubled," she said.

He looked away. "Today, Guenevere, when Mordred is made a knight—you remember, we agreed—"

"Yes." She steadied herself with a long, indrawn breath. "Arthur, I know when you bring him to the Round Table, you will place him in—" *No, don't say Amir's seat, my beloved boy is gone—*

"—in the Siege Perilous," Arthur said brusquely, hurrying on. "Yes, and today I'll be naming him as my heir too—"

Guenevere raised her hand. "Arthur, let me speak. I've known this would happen for years, ever since Mordred came, and all Camelot is expecting it now. And he loves you, he wants to be a good son. He showed his faith, remember, when he brought back your scabbard and gave it back to you unharmed?"

"My scabbard?" Arthur gave an awkward laugh. "Your mother's, you mean."

"It was yours from the time I gave it to you on our wedding day. I wanted it to protect you as it had protected her."

She fell silent, unwilling to go on. Memories and reproaches were crowding her mind. *My mother's scabbard, yes. You knew it had the power from ancient days to protect the wearer against loss of blood. And Morgan knew that too. That's why she stole it from you to hurt us both. She gave it to Mordred, and Mordred brought it back as his passport to your love. All this came about because you loved your half-sister Morgan when you were married to me. And if Mordred loves you now, it's more than you deserve.*

Enough! her heart scolded. Aloud she said, "Why are you concerned?"

"Concerned? Oh, I'm not," Arthur laughed. Yet still he would not meet her eyes. And it came to her with silent certainty: *He is afraid that Mordred will not prove worthy of the Pendragon name. He has seen that no one knows what Mordred is. And he must be asking, Does Mordred know himself?*

Oh, Arthur—oh my love—

"They are saying on all sides that Arthur's son will prove a noble king," she said gently. She fixed her eyes on him. "But are you beginning to doubt—?"

As she spoke, a wave of doubt almost drowned her too. Was it only because of her jealous mind that she always saw something mocking in the depths of Mordred's guileless gaze? That she felt his sharp intelligence kept his true feelings in check? She took a deep breath. "Arthur, have you thought—or feared—?"

"No, Guenevere." Arthur sharply cut her off. "And I will not waver now. The day is here, the feast ordained, and the guests have come from as far away as Rome. Did you know that the Pope has sent his own Legate along with the Father Abbot to honor us?" He turned his gaze sternly on her. "But more than all that, Mordred is destined to succeed. He is a Pendragon. He bears the sign."

"He does indeed." Guenevere closed her eyes. *Yes, he bears the Pendragon tattoo, which you and Merlin wear around your wrists, and Mordred has concealed in his blue-black hair. A pair of dragons in the same blue-black, locked in combat to the death, each one attacking and swallowing the other's tail, both tearing and devouring their own flesh.*

Stop this, stop it at once! protested her inner voice. *Mordred was only a baby when Morgan set the Pendragon mark on her son. A child must not be blamed for his mother's acts.*

Arthur was still speaking. "It is the will of God," she heard him say. "Mordred is the only son of our house, and my only heir."

Only because our son Amir was lost.

Somehow she found her voice. "It's true, Mordred is your natural heir. There is no other son to follow you."

Her mind was roaming in a waste of pain. *Nor a daughter, to succeed me, after the way of queens. My mother was called Battle Raven, and the Lady of Light. But I am barren, and her line dies with me. Yet I am still the daughter of Maire Macha, and while I live, her spirit lives on!*

A new, strange tone came into Arthur's voice. "The Romans too favored the rule of men. They built a mighty empire on men's backs."

"The Romans built an empire?" She was startled out of her reverie. "Do you dream of doing that?"

His strained laugh told her that she had struck home. "Is that so foolish, then?"

"An empire? What, for yourself or for Mordred?"

Arthur frowned. "The Romans reached out from Italy to these misty isles, and conquered all the land that lay between." She could see him mastering his irritation as he spoke. "Surely a great leader of the Britons could follow their lead, and strike back along their tracks they left behind?"

"Arthur, think—"

"No, Guenevere!" His eyes began to shine. "The roads are already in place for others to tread. We could build an empire all the way to Rome. Especially with friends in Lancelot's kingdom of Little Britain, ancient allies from my father's time."

Guenevere struck her head. "Arthur!" she cried in anguish. "What madness is this? When you came to the throne, every man made war for himself, and the widows and orphans suffered in vain and starved. We ended all that, and our people live free from fear. But you have to be here if you want to keep the peace. It's still too fragile to abandon now."

Arthur stirred resentfully, then turned away. "Surely not, Guenevere?"

She gave a savage laugh. "Arthur, you know how Celts fight among themselves!" A darkness came over her eyes, and she heard her voice take on a raven's croak. "Leave these shores, and I prophesy that all your lands and people will drown in blood!"

"Enough!" He spoke calmly, but flurries of anger chased across his face.

"I won't have you talking like this! You'll put an ill wish on Mordred's hopes before they begin."

Mordred's hopes—who knows what they are?

"Arthur—about Mordred—we should never forget that he is Morgan's child—"

"No more words." Arthur drew himself up and gave her a deathly stare. "Whoever his mother was, he is my son." He drew a ragged breath. "And I have made my choice."

Her heart plunged. "Tread carefully, Arthur, I beg."

He reached for her hands. "Always the dark side, Guenevere!" He tried for a smile. "Believe me, my love, you have no need to fear." Then his lips tightened, and he threw back his head. "Today I plan to name Mordred as my heir. And he will surprise us all, I'll swear to that."

CHAPTER 12

n the Great Hall, every beam was hung with green. The fresh
scent of the open woodland filled the air, each tender branch
weeping out its summer sap. Between the mighty timbers of the
roof the knights' banners hung down in a forest of red, blue, silver, white, and black. High overhead, the red dragon reared and
snarled, as the standard of Pendragon vaunted over them all.

In the center of the great, cool flagstoned space, the Round
Table stood ready for the gathering of the knights, murmuring and humming to itself of what was to come. Its wide, round surface, gleaming like
the moon, rested firmly on many pairs of trestles set beneath. All round
stood the great carved high-backed sieges of the knights, each with its
wooden canopy painted in gilt letters with the occupant's name.

Beneath the vaulted roof of living green, the knights were assembling by
the Round Table, talking quietly as they waited for the ceremony to begin.
Looking up at the names all around, Lucan was ambushed by a sudden sense
of loss. *Sir Mador of the Meads* and *Sir Patrise*—golden lads both, those brothers, and seen no more these days. Lucan gritted his teeth and swallowed down
a sigh. Too many of the knights whose names were inscribed in gold would
never come again. Well, a knight's life was short. Unconsciously he raised the
soldier's prayer: Gods, let me die standing. And let me see my death.

"In ill thoughts, brother?"

Familiar as it was, the soft singsong voice of Bedivere made Lucan start.
"Don't be a fool!" he growled defensively. "What do I have to be concerned
about?"

"Nothing at all," snapped Kay, limping up behind. Nothing but our
land, our King, and our royal house, he bit back in a sudden fit of rage.
Today would change the future for them all. He threw a glance round the
tops of the chairs. *"Sir Niamh,"* he read under his breath, *"Sir Lovell, Sir Dinant,
Sir Tor"*—they were all there, all the names he had known for the last twenty
years. So! No canopy named for Mordred. Kay drew in his breath. Only one
place then where the new knight could sit.

But could Arthur truly mean to try his son there? A sideways glance at Lucan and Bedivere told Kay that the other companions were having the same thought. Three pairs of eyes turned to the one chair that had no name, the Seat of Danger, with its warning inscribed above in flaming gold:

Here Is the Siege Perilous, for the Knight Who Is to Come.

He Will Be the Most Peerless Knight in All the World,

and When He Comes, the Prophecy of Merlin Will Be Fulfilled.

Could it be Mordred? Kay asked himself, his mind savagely twisting between hope and dread. He could still remember when Merlin's vision had led to the seat being named, and the deep belief Arthur and Guenevere shared then that it must mean Amir. For Arthur's sake, he implored the Old Ones, let it be Mordred now, let it be.

"So!" breathed Lucan. "Mordred is to be the peerless knight?"

"Yes, and more." Bedivere gave a significant nod toward the dais at the end of the hall, where a third throne had been placed alongside those of the King and Queen. It was smaller than the massive matched pair of bronze thrones from which the Queens of the Summer Country and their consorts had ruled since time began. But once the King had set Mordred on his throne, there would be a new power in the land. The Prince would rule along with the King and Queen.

Lucan glared. "Ha! So it's true."

"More than true," Kay said in furious trepidation, though he could not have given a reason for his fear. "And that's not all."

He waved a hand down the hall, where the other knights were standing near the door. Sagramore and his followers, busily chaffing the veteran Sir Niamh and Lovell the Bold; Dinant quizzing Tor about his adventures against the Saxons; Griflet arguing with Ladinas; Helin, Balin, and Balan, all were falling silent as they found their attention drawn to an incomer who, for his part, showed no interest in them. None could say how it happened, for he came in with his brothers quietly enough, but all saw Agravain the moment he entered the great space.

In the dusk of the morning courtyard, Sagramore had missed the much talked of newcomer earlier that day and did not intend to lose the opportunity now. Flushed already from the excitement of the event, the well-fleshed knight pounced on the four tall brethren as they made their way silently into the hall.

"Agravain!" he cried ebulliently. "So you're back! I hear you're planning to take the Prince to the tiltyard, and teach him some of your dirty Eastern tricks."

Gawain's big face bunched like a fighting fist. "Look here, Sagramore—" he began dangerously.

But Agravain was calm. "Prince Mordred has nothing to learn from me. He's as good a fighter as any man alive."

"He's his father's son," chuckled Sagramore in delight. He gestured down the hall toward the dais, where the new throne stood beside those of the King and Queen. "And we'll be proud to serve him when he becomes our King."

When Mordred becomes King—

That would mean that Arthur was no more.

What had Sagramore said? A fear as black as bats' breath hung in the air, and a sense of something unspeakable seized the knights. No one spoke.

Agravain quietly assessed them all. When Arthur departed, would Mordred be High King? Or could these weaklings be led another way? A look too brief to read mantled his face and was gone. He nodded warmly to Sagramore. "You are right, sir. Prince Mordred truly is his father's son."

MORDRED HIGH KING—?

The son of Morgan Le Fay in his father's seat?

High in the rafters of the hall, the spirit let out her braying laugh, knowing that the clay ears of earthlings could not hear. It was as she had willed it all along. No man could stand against her and her plans, ripening so happily to fulfillment now.

Nowwwww—noooowwwwww— she mewed like a cat.

Which one should she choose?

Hungrily she eyed the bodies thronging below, as the knights gathered at the Round Table in twos and threes. There was old Sir Niamh, smiling cheerfully, but now so aged and spent that no one would notice if a whole army of spirits usurped his ancient corpse. Or his comrade-in-arms, old Sir Lovell, another living husk. Or Dinant, no stranger to lechery and lies, who would never miss his soul.

Which one should she enter to see her son made a knight?

❖   ❖

THE GREAT HALL had filled with a joyful, buzzing throng. But the silver sound of the trumpets silenced them all.

"The King and Queen!" cried the Chamberlain.

A cascade of trumpets took up the clarion call. Smiling and bowing, Guenevere made her way with Arthur into the hall. As always, Arthur's monks blighted the bright gathering with their huddles of black, and prominent in the forefront was her old antagonist, the Abbot of London, with a small sun-browned man, richly habited, who must be the Papal Legate Arthur had mentioned, newly come from Rome. Beyond them, she could see through the parting crowd the Round Table lying in their path ahead. Above the Siege Perilous, its gilt lettering pulsed and glowed. *For the Knight Who Is to Come. He Will Be the Most Peerless Knight in All the World...*

Could this be Mordred? Soon, soon it would be, for Arthur had chosen, and she had to accept it, for his sake alone. She had not loved and supported him all these years to abandon him now.

Arthur—

As they mounted the dais, she looked up at him, squeezing his hand, and was rewarded with a warm answering pressure on her own. Arthur was clad in a knightly robe of white, with the red dragon blazoned across his breast. He wore a royal red cloak with fine black breeches and boots, and the gold torque of knighthood around his neck. His wide belt and armlets were inlaid with gold, and Excalibur swung at his side in its precious gold sheath, the scabbard of the Queens of the Summer Country in its rightful home. Above it all gleamed the ancient crown of King Uther, surmounted by the beast of Pendragon, picked out in vivid emeralds, with ruby eyes.

Arthur himself stared out over the heads of the crowd with an air of exaltation she had not seen before. He looked pale and strained, but shining and transcendent too, no longer a mortal man but a being out of time, one who walked with the Gods. Guenevere drew a deep breath. Today would be a rite of passage for Arthur too, as much as for his son.

The brazen-throated trumpets snarled again.

"The Prince!" the heralds fluted. "Welcome the Prince, the Prince, the Prince!"

Framed by the great golden-bronze doors, a figure in white appeared at the end of the hall. With a knight on either side, he began the long, slow progress to the royal dais. One of his supporters was Gawain, unmistakable from his massive height and bulk. But the other, though tall, was lither and leaner by far—*Lancelot!* Guenevere's heart turned over in her breast. He had done what he promised, he had returned in time.

Raw tears surged to her eyes, and she forced them down. He met her gaze for an instant, and she could see from the dark depths of his somber stare that his race up to Corbenic had been in vain. She ran her eyes over him only long enough to see that he was white with exhaustion from the dreadful ride, then turned her face away. She must not look at him; this was Arthur's day.

And Mordred's too. Still stiff after the ordeal of the vigil, walking like a man risen from the dead, Mordred was moving toward them down the central aisle. Behind him came the Novice Master of the young knights and a small procession of his pages and squires, each loaded with the accoutrements of knighthood: sword, weapons, harness, and spurs. On the breast of Mordred's snow-white tunic, the red dragon blazed like blood. His face was as blanched as his robe, but a curious grin of triumph twisted his mouth. His eyes were pools of Otherworldly fire as he stared straight ahead, and to Guenevere, the thought in them was plain: *Nothing can keep me from the kingdom now.*

"Approach, Prince Mordred!" the Chamberlain cried. "Draw near and make your vow."

Together Mordred and the Novice Master climbed the steps to the dais. Mordred's eyes were very bright, his face transfigured with hope. *I was wrong,* thought Guenevere with a surge of love. *Mordred looks humble, thankful, even scared. He will be loyal to Arthur, he will be true.*

The ancient knighthood ritual began its course. Mordred fell to his knees and crossed his arms on his chest. With murmured words of love, Arthur leaned forward to bless the dark, bowed head.

"My son." The words were so faint that only Guenevere and Mordred could hear.

Mordred's heart swelled. He knew he was at the high point of his life. Arthur had acknowledged him before all the court. *My son.* Mordred rolled the words joyfully around his soul.

And then they came again, inside his head. *My son.* The voice was hardly more than a soft hiss, but it seemed to Mordred that he knew it from a long time ago. It came back to him now from the dawn of his life on earth, and a joy he had forgotten flowed through his veins.

Mordred took Arthur's hand and kissed the rough knuckles with their silver scars. "My liege lord," he said huskily. "From this time forth, this life of mine is yours."

Arthur could hardly speak. "You are mine, sir," he whispered. "Nothing but death will cancel out this bond."

In the plangent silence a sigh echoed from Avalon and winged its way across the astral plane. Above it rose the high ethereal call of Excalibur singing in its scabbard at Arthur's side. Arthur drew the great sword from its sheath, and it flashed through the air. Once, twice, the blade of Excalibur lightly buffeted Mordred's left shoulder, and then his right. At the third blow, Mordred raised his face to his father, wet with tears.

"Arise, Sir Mordred!" cried the Chamberlain, and all the court saw that Arthur was weeping too.

Mordred rose to his feet, and fell into Arthur's arms. The two men held each other in a close embrace and wept without restraint. At length Arthur disengaged himself and gave Guenevere a husky smile. "The Queen will arm you, sir."

"Sir Mordred—"

Guenevere stepped forward, taking the sword and buckler from the Novice Master's hand. Mordred turned toward her, looking lost, pain and fatigue suddenly darkening his eyes.

She waved him toward her. "By your leave, good sir."

"Majesty—" Mordred bowed his head.

She reached up to pass the gilt strap of the harness over his shoulder, then clasped the heavy sword belt around his waist. On her right, a squire held up a tasseled cushion bearing a pair of dragon-handled daggers with emerald eyes. Another knelt at Mordred's feet with a set of gold spurs.

Guenevere slid the daggers into their gilt holders at his belt, and signaled to the squire to strap on the golden spurs. Then she gave him her hand, smiling into his eyes. "Welcome, Sir Mordred of Pendragon, to the Round Table fellowship of knights!"

"Welcome!" cried all the knights at the table in one full-throated roar.

Arthur took Mordred's hand and turned him to face the crowd. "I give you Sir Mordred!" he cried. "My loving son. The house of Pendragon comes to fruition in him. It is time that our destiny was fulfilled."

A hum of excitement began to run round the hall. Raising Mordred's hand, Arthur led him down from the dais, with Gawain and Lancelot following behind. Passing by the chairs of the other knights, they came to a halt beside the Perilous Seat. A sudden silence descended like a cloud. Arthur's voice echoed as in a tomb.

Sonorously Arthur read out the words scrolled above. "'Here Is the Siege Perilous for the Knight Who Is to Come…'"

Was Mordred ordained to take Amir's seat? Could he truly be the most peerless of all? Guenevere caught her breath. Then a surge of love for Arthur broke over her head. *Goddess, Mother, for Arthur's sake, let it be—*

From the dais, she could see over all the hall. Surrounded by a hushed crowd of knights and their ladies, monks and Druids, lords and vassal kings, the Round Table knights waited tensely for Mordred to take his seat. Kay, Bedivere, and Lucan stood by their chairs, next to the reverent ancients, Sir Niamh and Sir Lovell the Bold. Sir Niamh looked unusually bright-eyed, Guenevere noticed, and the fierce frown he wore was strange and new. But others too like Gaheris and Gareth, waiting beside Gawain's vacant chair, wore looks of grim concern, and even Sagramore was silent and subdued. Only Agravain, cool and impassive as ever, seemed his customary self.

"Take your seat then, Sir Mordred," cried Arthur in a high, strained voice. A feverish excitement gripped all the knights. Guenevere could see Kay's lips moving in a muttered invocation, and Sir Niamh was leaning forward, his eyes fixed with a ferocious concentration on Mordred. As she watched, a hectic flush rose up the old man's cheeks, and she felt a sudden fear—was he ill?

Flanked by Gawain and Lancelot, Mordred moved toward the chair. Arthur took hold of it to draw it back, then gave a sudden gasp. The chair would not move.

Arthur tried again, pitting his weight against the impervious wood. A sheen of distress broke over his face.

"My lord!"

In a second, Lancelot was at Arthur's side. But the chair would not be shifted from its place. Now Gawain too hastened to Lancelot's aid. At last, heaving and groaning like a living thing, the mighty siege yielded to the force of the two knights. Mordred could take his seat.

Arthur's brow cleared. Jubilantly he waved Mordred on. Mordred moved forward like a man in a trance, the pale film of sweat on his face echoing Arthur's own. Bowing to his fellow knights, he gripped the edge of the table with both hands and lowered himself to his seat.

A sigh of relief ran through the waiting crowd, followed by a swelling roar of delight.

"Sir Mordred, Sir Mordred!" they caroled with bursting glee.

Gawain and Lancelot slipped quietly to their places, to smiles all round. The knights shared a silent release of tension, then turned as one to honor the new knight.

"Sir Mordred," "Sir Mordred" echoed on all sides.

Arthur mastered himself, and raised his arms in blessing over them all. "Now God be praised, who has brought us to this hour! My son has vanquished the Siege Perilous and proved himself to be the most peerless knight!"

The cheer from the heart of the hall almost lifted the roof. As the noise grew, Guenevere felt her senses fading and her head began to swim. The air grew thin, and she was gasping for breath. As she looked round, others were struggling too. She saw Lancelot clutch at his throat, then throw her a glance: Wait there, madame, I am coming to you. He took one stride toward the dais, and was lost to sight. A blinding flash scorched her eyes; then a mantle of black night fell on the hall like a shroud.

"Goddess, Mother, save us!" Guenevere cried. Determinedly she felt her way forward through the murk, trying to find the steps down into the hall. But the crowd erupted in a babble of cries and screams and she knew it was not safe to move. Above the rising panic she could hear Arthur's deep-throated bellow, like a bull in pain, "My son—save my son!"

Then the darkness lifted as swiftly as it had come. The June sunshine poured back into the hall, and a dead silence fell as the blinking sufferers began to take stock of what had passed. On the flagstones lay the prostrate forms of Arthur's monks, weeping and gibbering and holding their crosses aloft. The Papal Legate and the Abbot were kneeling together in prayer. Every knight at the table had his sword drawn and his dagger in his hand, and Lancelot was halfway to the dais. Only Agravain and Mordred were just as they had been before, Agravain still wearing his unnatural calm, and Mordred locked in frozen-eyed disbelief.

"My son!" screamed Arthur, leaping to Mordred's side. As he moved, the air curdled and darkened again. The Siege Perilous quaked and with a violent convulsion cast Mordred out and threw him to the floor. He landed facedown with the sick thud of flesh on stone, and did not rise.

In the hall, one lady screamed, a terrible sound. But around Mordred, not a soul moved. In all the stricken crowd, the ancient Sir Niamh was the first to stir, a furious spirit straining against the confines of his failing flesh. Trembling with rage, he pointed at Mordred lying on the floor.

"Save him, you fools!" he screeched.

But Mordred was slowly beginning to lift his head. Arthur bounded toward him, weeping with relief. With a swift glance at Guenevere, Lancelot turned back to Arthur's aid. Gawain was already at Arthur's side. Together they helped Mordred to his feet.

Mordred's face was a blank, all expression razed by the unearthly power that had cast him down. But his black eyes were burning with a bright blue fire.

"I am unharmed!" he shrilled, brushing off Arthur's touch. "I am ready, sire, lead me to the throne!"

Was it then, Guenevere mourned later in her inner soul, *that our world turned and all we loved was lost?* Arthur had been moving to embrace Mordred, his arms outstretched. Now at Mordred's words he checked himself and fell back.

"Not now, son," he said, in a different voice. "Not yet."

"What do you mean?" cried Mordred, beginning to shake.

Arthur spread his hands "You have taken a fall—your head—you cannot be well." But a deeper doubt was engraved on his face.

"I am as well as I've ever been in my life!"

Arthur frowned. "The time is not yet ripe."

Mordred threw back his head like a wolf at bay. "I am your son!" he howled. "Do you deny me now?"

"Never!" growled Arthur in an answering rage. "But the Siege Perilous spoke out against us both. I wanted to place you in the seat of kings. And the hand of fate proved that we both were wrong!"

"Father—" Mordred implored. Tearing his hair, he fell weeping to his knees. "Do not shame me here before this throng! Give me my birthright. Name me as your son!"

Arthur moved forward with a bearlike tread. Firmly he raised Mordred to his feet. "You are my son," he said with infinite tenderness. "All the world knows that. We shall seek a better time to enthrone you as my heir."

"Now!" cried Mordred. "Now! It must be now!"

"No!" A thunderous cloud darkened Arthur's face. "I have spoken!" he said angrily. "Remember who is King here, sir—"

Mordred gagged with rage. "You—you—" he shouted, and could not go on. His eyes bulged, and he threw himself to the floor.

A high scream like that of a woman betrayed tore through the air. Old Sir Niamh was on his feet, his vanquished frame trembling with a force too great to resist.

"Arthur—" he screeched in a wild, accusing tone. Quivering, he pulled his dagger from his belt. A thin froth dribbled from his writhing lips, and his body jerked with a feeling he could not control. He lifted a skeletal accusing hand. "Traitor!" he screamed, and fell senseless to the floor.

Lancelot was at his side as he hit the ground. But Niamh's body was no more than a shell, a gaping hollow where his soul had been. His chest buckled, one last breath rushed howling from his body, and he gave up the ghost.

CHAPTER 13

T hrough the window, the sun was cascading down the sky. In the heavens beyond, a shooting star blazed for an instant and was gone, scattering a trail of stars. Guenevere turned away in a sorrow too deep for tears. The soul of old Niamh had taken to the astral plane, winging its way to the world of delight. But here on earth, only pain and peril loomed.

High overhead, the spirit took refuge between the rafters, huddling under the greenery to lick her wound. A livid, pulsing slit lay open in her heart, and she gazed at it in horror, weeping at the hurt. "Arthur!" she howled. "Traitor to your son!"

How weak, how vile he was proving, this man she had loved! And Sir Niamh, how frail the old fool had been too! His body had been hers to command, dagger in hand, only a pace away from Arthur, and it had failed.

"I could have cut Arthur's heart open, as he did to me!" Morgan screamed to the stars.

Raging, she sought some balm for her great wound. Mordred would still be King, she would make sure of that. And Arthur would pay for this, along with everything else.

Oh, he would pay. For eternity and longer, he would pay.

The remains of what had been Sir Niamh lay huddled on the floor. Arthur stood transfixed, staring at the mortal ruin at his feet. Kneeling beside Niamh, Lancelot felt for the pulse in the old man's shrunken neck, then looked up at Guenevere and shook his head.

Guenevere was aware of a weeping at her side.

"He was your mother's champion and chosen one before me. He was the truest of all. He worshiped her."

Guenevere looked up into Sir Lovell's watery eyes. "He will be buried next to her on the Hill of Queens," she said huskily. "My mother will have his love in the world of stars, as she treasured it in this." She turned to the nearest knights. "Sirs?"

Under Guenevere's command, the old warrior was gently lifted from the unforgiving stones, covered with his cloak, and carried from the hall. All the court stood in silence to watch him go.

She could not speak to Lancelot. Though his brown eyes were alive with their brightest flame, there was no hope of a word in the crowded court. She watched with a fresh pang as he moved across to Arthur, who was still standing over Mordred like a wounded bear.

But Arthur was rousing himself to take care of his son. "Sir Vullian! Sir Ozark!" he called thickly, casting around.

Arthur, no! Guenevere could have cried aloud. *Mordred's young cronies owe no faith to you. They will feed his resentment, and sow nothing but discord.*

She moved toward him, putting her heart in her eyes. "My lord, one moment—"

"Sire?" Two figures appeared from the crowd, pointing like dogs. "What is your wish?"

Arthur gave a hopeless wave: "The Prince."

Guenevere paused, and forced herself to sound calm. A hundred eyes and ears were hanging on her every word. "Why not ask Sir Kay, Sir Lucan, and Sir Bedivere to attend him?" she asked.

Arthur turned an empty gaze on her. "I have spoken, Guenevere."

Ozark and Vullian were already scrambling to raise the prostrate form of Mordred from the floor. His arms stretched across their shoulders, he swayed between them like Christ crucified. Then with a glance of darkness fathoms deep, he turned his back, and the three of them left the hall.

Arthur—oh Arthur—

Guenevere reached out for Arthur's cold hand and drew him away. Weeping, praying, and reaching out to touch the train of their gowns, the people parted to let them go.

Arthur was shivering like a man with an ague. He was moving badly too, she saw; his wound was clearly troubling him again.

"Why, Guenevere?" he muttered. "What did I do wrong?"

Guenevere did not want to look at his stricken face. "Mordred was not destined for the Siege Perilous," she said quietly. "We know that now."

Arthur groaned. "Dear God, forgive my folly—the sinful pride in my own flesh and blood!" He shook his great head. "And why did Niamh accuse me of treachery? I never betrayed him in my life."

Guenevere threw a glance over the troubled crowd. "Think of the people, Arthur," she said in low, urgent tones. "They are shocked and grieved. We must tell them that all will be well."

"Will it, Guenevere?" he mourned like a lost child. "Oh, if only Merlin were here!"

"Come." She drew him back onto the dais, and they took their thrones.

Already the people were beginning to settle down. The ladies were smoothing down their flowerlike silks, and the knights and lords were almost themselves again. The Father Abbot and the Papal Legate were erect and watchful, their eyes on the throne. Even the monks had regained their dignity, twitching their rumpled habits into place and loftily staring down the Druids with their unruffled brows. In a moment she would say a few peaceful words, and then she and Arthur could withdraw.

Her mind raced on. Then she could send for Lancelot to hear what had happened at Castle Corbenic. She would learn the truth about Elaine and his evil dream—she would hold him in her arms, perhaps even tonight—

"Your Majesties!"

It was the Chamberlain. "Strangers, my lady, seek admittance."

A cold wind reached Guenevere from far away. She tensed. "Who are they?"

"The leader says he brings greetings from one you know. One who walks the hillsides in the wind and rain, sleepless for Pendragon all his days."

"Merlin!" A tearful hope invaded Arthur's face. "A messenger from Merlin, it must be!" He gestured to the Chamberlain. "Admit them, man, at once! Show them your best haste!"

"Sire!"

The Chamberlain waved his staff, and the strangers were ushered in. First through the door was a crabbed, ancient king, prancing in with an unseemly haste. His eyes were alight with a fanatic's fire, and his burning pallor was accentuated by a rusty black gown. The monastic severity of his dress was strangely contrasted with the rich furs he wore and the massive gold cross around his neck. Rubies the size of damsons encrusted his crown, and his white hair streamed down his back like a fall of snow. He had aged twenty years since she saw him last. But Guenevere would have known him anywhere.

King Pelles of Terre Foraine! What——?

Her eyes were out on stalks. Behind Pelles came a woman in nunlike white, hands folded modestly in long trailing sleeves, but she moved down the hall in a sensuous rustle of silk, and men's heads throughout the hall turned to watch her pass. From her tall headdress, as white as sun-bleached ivory, a gossamer veil frothed down around her face and neck and flowed out as a train behind. Her face was as pale as a lily, and her eyes were cast down to the floor.

Goddess, Mother, this is the virgin princess—this is Elaine, the daughter of the ancient prophecy—but the youth with her—?

He was clad like a knight in palest silver mail, but his pure white cloak and tunic bore no knightly badge or crest. From his pale blond hair to the tip of his gilded sword, he gleamed with his own light. He had the look of one who neither ate nor slept, but lived in freedom from the tyranny of the flesh. His pale gold eyes were from the Otherworld, and his spirit seemed yearning to slip its earthly shell.

In his fragile beauty, he was his mother to the life, and he glanced at her often with a boy's doting love. But his ardent yet grieving air, his lithe step and springing walk, the shape of his face, even the careless swing of his thick, bright hair were not from her, *no, not from the pious Elaine—*

Who, then?

Goddess, mother, say it cannot be—

Limping down the hall behind him came an ancient, crippled dame, with a troop of men-at-arms bearing a great box. And behind her, hardly registering in Guenevere's distracted gaze—

"Merlin!" Arthur exploded, surging to his feet.

"Hold your place, lord and King!" the answering cry rang out. "Let no one stir."

Merlin came forward in a gown like storm on the mountain, moody and blue-black. His spirit crackled from him as he walked, erupting in flashes of blue and green fire. A deep band of gold bound his brows and held back his wiry crown of gray hair. Gold dragons swung from his ears, and tourmalines as blue as owl-light hung round his neck on a chain of gold.

In his hand a long carved wand of golden yew murmured and hissed to the people, *Be still.* When he raised both arms in the air, not a mouse stirred. His yellow eyes swiveled like an eagle's over the throng, and his words were loud enough to carry through the hall. But Guenevere knew that the old enchanter was addressing himself to her.

"Gods and Great Ones, hear the tale I tell," he began in a high bardic voice. "Long ago I dreamed a dream, at peace in my crystal cell. The King would set up the most noble order of knights, and each would emblazon his name upon the world. But I heard the command of the Old Ones even then: Remember to make a seat for the boy still to come. He will be the son of the most peerless knight in the world, and he is destined for the highest adventure of all. There should be one siege left unfilled for him till time brought him forth. Call it the Siege Perilous, were the words of my ecstasy then, for he will face many dangers and defy them all. He will be the best knight in all the world, and when he comes, the table will be complete."

A ringing silence fell. Guenevere was choking, half out of her body and mind.

He will be the son of the most peerless knight in the world—there's only one man alive who—

"By your leave, then, my King!" Merlin cried. He crossed to the boy and hoisted his thin right arm in the air. "I give you Sir Galahad, the peerless knight. He has come to take his place at the Table now."

The crowd round the Table melted like midsummer snow. Merlin's claw-like grip tightened on the boy, and he drew him toward the Perilous Chair. The entire court watched in a trance of dread. The old man and the boy were two steps away when Arthur spoke.

"Merlin!" he cried in a voice full of pain. "Once this seat was destined for Amir. Then it seemed that Mordred was the chosen one. Yet today we discovered that this was not so." His voice rose to an anguished roar. "Who is this boy that he should take their place?"

"Who, sir?" King Pelles's answering scream fluttered the banners in the roof. "He is a Christian knight and the grandson of a king. He is the off-spring of a pure virgin, as clean of sin as Mary, Mother of God."

"And he is the son of the most peerless knight in the world!" Elaine's low, rapturous chant was even more arresting than her father's strident tones. Her large eyes with their twilight shadows slipped slyly round the court. "His father is here today. And he is too fine to deny his son."

His father here? A hungry buzz ran round the overstrained crowd: *Who? When? And where?*

"Here now?" bellowed Arthur, his eyes bulging. "Who are you claiming, lady, fathered this knight?"

Guenevere reached out a nerveless hand. *No, Arthur, no, don't ask—*

A gleam of triumph flashed from Elaine's face. Then she cast down her eyes to the ground and only Guenevere caught her hidden smile.

"Who?" shouted Arthur, baffled by her calm. "Be warned, madam, who you accuse of this!"

"I accuse no man!" she cried in ecstasy. "The knight himself knows the truth I speak." Her pallid face took on a gleam like her son's, then she turned aside and drew something from her sleeve. Out, out it came in an endless length, white like her gown and then a blossom of red—

Goddess, mother, no—oh, my trusting heart—

Elaine held the bloodstained sheet up before all the court. "One man here knows this for my virgin pledge," she shrilled. "He took my maidenhead and fathered my son. He is the finest knight in all the world. And I was destined for him by Our Lord Himself!"

"The finest knight—and he's here—?" Arthur gasped. "Why, that's—"

All eyes turned to Lancelot. And no one needed to ask, Is this your son?

CHAPTER 14

But Merlin was blind to all save his own concerns.

"I bring you the virgin knight!" he screamed in a transport of delight. "The chosen one!" He advanced on Arthur, fixing him with one agate eye. "The Great Ones themselves watch out for the fatherless child. As you were, boy! As I was in my time."

There was a trembling pause. No one moved.

Merlin turned toward Galahad with an inhuman smile. His pointing hand snaked out. "And as he is now. Both he and I are only sons of princesses of the blood." He bared his yellow teeth. "Both our mothers were chosen for a purpose beyond their power to comprehend."

He is mad, came to Guenevere dully, like an ache. *Why should women be chosen, when they have the right to choose?* But the thought faded in the face of the anguish that beset her now.

Lancelot, my love, my lord, my life, to betray me so, for all his protestations, all his vows. Just as Arthur did with Morgan, when I still loved him with all my heart.

Lancelot lay with her—with Elaine, that pious, whey-faced nun! And she has a son, while I am barren and bereft of the son I had—

And now she comes here in triumph, just as Morgan had Arthur's son to triumph over me—

She caught Lancelot's eye and gave a mad shake of her head. *No, tell me it cannot be. Say it was not so—*

A stare of liquid fire was all she had back.

I beg you, sweetheart, she implored him with her eyes.

But the fire in his gaze had burned out, and all that was left were black hollows where his soul should be.

"Galahad chosen?" caroled King Pelles ecstatically. "You say true, Lord Merlin, our virgin knight was chosen indeed by the Lord God Himself, for a higher purpose than any here yet know." He pointed toward Arthur, but it seemed to Guenevere that the triumph in his gaze was meant for her alone. "We bear the proof! Trust the evidence of your own eyes."

He turned and waved up his men-at-arms, signaling them to lay the great chest at his feet. The old woman in black hobbled forward, and threw back the lid.

Wait—wait a moment. Who is this woman? What is she doing? Arthur, Arthur, order them to wait!

Numbly Guenevere moved her lips and found she could not speak. She looked toward Lancelot, but could not read his black and empty eyes. At her side Arthur sat massive and immobile, his great head craning forward, frozen in time like one of the Great Ones at the ending of the world.

The old woman bent over the chest and seemed to whisper to what lay within. There came a humming in the hall like the pulse of life itself, a high singing like the Fair Ones' own dawn song. Then an ethereal fragrance drifted down, the scent of all the roses breathing out their sweetness in far-away deserts many worlds ago.

At the Round Table, Lucan, Kay, and Bedivere groped madly for their swords, then lost themselves in long-forgotten memories of delight. Gaheris and Gareth heard the seagulls calling on the shores of the eternal summers of their boyhood, Tor and Sagramore the whinny of horses in an upland glade. To those in the body of the hall, it seemed they fed on milk and honey and bathed in gold.

Guenevere's ears filled with the soft plashing of the waters of Avalon and the cooing of doves in the island's leafy shades. *Green—green—* She wanted to lie down, to stretch out her body in a cool hallowed glade—

The old woman's murmuring had risen to a drone. *"Advene demogorgon, venite alla baal princips noctis, domines tenebrae sint mihi propitii…"*

Guenevere gasped for breath. Where had she heard these words of power before? *Arthur, Arthur, we have to stop her now—*

"Behold!"

Who cried out, King Pelles or the old dame? Together they stood by the finely wrought old chest, heavy with the brass shapes of crosses and fish and symbols of the East. A muttered incantation filled the air, and a golden light flooded the hall, so bright that it turned every gaze to milk. Through the white haze the chest and the Table shimmered as one, and when Guenevere looked again, the surface of the Table shone with gold.

No—no, it cannot be—

Guenevere struggled to draw together the last remaining ragged threads of thought.

Goddess, Mother, can it be? Is this Your will——?

On the Round Table, glittering in the sun, stood a great gold loving cup, large enough to feast the Great Ones in their hall. Beside it lay a massive golden platter, its outer edge embossed with raised fruit and corn. Between them, drawing light from the Round Table's moonlike glow, were a long slender lance and a sword, both of fine gold.

The Hallows of the Goddess, lost at Corbenic and now restored to us—

Guenevere could scarcely contain her joy. Awe and wonder drifted down on the crowd like a soft mist.

"Now God be praised!"

The stentorian bellow terrorized them all. The Father Abbot strode forward, the light of battle flashing from his eyes.

"The Holy Grail!" he shouted. "Give thanks to God, who has sent us back the Grail!"

What? What did he say?

King Pelles bounded toward the Table, and took up the cry. "The cup and plate of Christ Himself," he trumpeted, "from the Last Supper Our Lord shared on this earth." He jabbed at the weapons of power, the sword and the lance. "And the instruments of His Passion, as He suffered for our sins!"

Again the high keening whine sounded through the air. Throughout the hall, the golden light thickened into an amber dusk. Small pinpoints of light appeared in the quivering gloom, floating like fireflies around Galahad.

Galahad's face was transfigured, bathed in pearly light. Tongues of fire flickered round him as he moved, and the light formed a halo round his head.

"Come, boy!" breathed Merlin.

Groaning aloud, the old enchanter took the boy by the hand and led him to the Table, casting his charms and spells freely into the air. Ahead of them the Siege Perilous glowered ominously, threatening their approach. But as Merlin laid a hand on its wooden back, it yielded to him with an answering groan. Merlin drew back the chair, and Galahad took his seat.

On the Table, the Hallows glowed and throbbed and seemed to grow larger to welcome him. At the center the great loving cup filled with tongues of fire from heaven, and the rubies round its rim burned as red as blood.

"Guenevere! Guenevere! Look!"

Arthur's voice seemed to reach her at the bottom of a lake. She was drowning, she knew, unless she swam up to him.

"It's the Grail, Guenevere," came Arthur's voice again, trembling with joy.

"The blood of Our Lord Jesus Christ! We are redeemed! Christ's purpose is fulfilled. The Round Table is complete."

No, Arthur, no! she wanted to cry out. *This is the Table of the Mother, not the God from the East. The Christians cannot claim our Hallows as theirs.* But why could she not speak?

"Glory be to the Lord! Praise His name!"

With monks from all over the hall hastening to his side, the Father Abbot was thrusting toward the Table, brandishing his cross. Waving the heavy jeweled crucifix in the air, he kissed it reverently, then cast it down at the foot of the loving cup. Behind him the Papal Legate had assumed the position of power, feet wide apart, legs braced, and both arms flourished high in the air. He too was praying in a strong tenor that carried round the throng. "O God our Father, we thank Thee for Thy blessing on this house of pagans, this benighted court—"

"Amen!"

"—that now will be a Christian place indeed—"

"Amen!"

Now she could hear Galahad praying too, his ecstatic treble rising above all other sounds. "Father God, You who take away the sins of the world, may Your holy purpose be fulfilled through me. Grant me to do that for which I was born..."

From beside the Table came a low whisper, almost inaudible above the Christians' cries and groans: *"Tene, tene, dominus noctis ut crescam in totis malis, sint mecum proh superior—"*

It was the old woman in black, the servant to the princess and the king. Hunched toward the Table, she was muttering as if her life depended on the stream of words pouring from her mouth.

Guenevere felt a stirring in her depths.

The old woman—mouthing the words of power—and this vile Christian priest prays down our Great One at Her own Table—

At last a healing fury flooded her veins. Transcendent with rage, she surged to her feet and hurled herself down from the dais. Behind her she could hear Arthur's startled cry of protest, but it meant nothing now. She flew down the hall, pressing through the courtiers as if they were shadows or unreal things. Approaching the Table she saw Lancelot, but the face he turned toward her she did not know.

On the Round Table, the Hallows shrank from her like living things. As if in answer to some unheard call, a drop of blood formed on the tip of the lance. Then the sword and plate were both bedewed with blood, and the loving cup was brimming with the same ruby red, pulsing like a heart. And it seemed to Guenevere that they were evil beyond compare.

Goddess, Mother, save me from all hurt—

Around the Table, the knights were still frozen in their sieges, bewildered by what had passed. Ahead of her, Kay and Bedivere made way as she drew near. Thrusting between them, she reached onto the Table and seized the sword of power, then almost dropped it as the jeweled hilt seared the flesh of her palms. In the agony of the moment, her mother's battle cry rose unbidden to her throat. Howling for blood, she swung the shining weapon round her head. As it carved through the air, it dissolved in her hand and the air was full of drifting flakes of gold.

The anguished cry of the Abbot rang through the Hall. "Lord, save your Holy Grail from this witch!"

"Amen!" wailed the wide-eyed monks, crossing themselves. "Amen, amen!"

"Hold your peace!"

Guenevere's cry overtopped them all. "This is not your Grail!" she cried, glaring at the Abbot passionately. "You only want to destroy the Mother-right! You think yours is the only faith in the whole world. But let me tell you, monk, that the truth is greater than us all." She gestured toward the Hallows. "And these are nothing but a false fetch, a sham. Your greed to secure our treasures makes you see your wretched Grail where none exists!"

"Not so!" the Abbot blazed. "The Holy Grail is here with us today, sent by Jesus and the Blessed Mother Mary, heaven's Queen, and we shall have it—"

He reached forward, grasping with both hands.

"Keep back!" Guenevere howled.

Panting, she reached for the lance, and felt it shudder and draw away from her hand. Her fingers scorched till she smelled her own burning flesh, but she gripped it with mad fury, and the next moment it had dwindled to a long length of shining dust. She stretched out both hands to the dish, and the Abbot's cry became a scream. Above it, the old woman's drone ascended to a fever pitch.

The gold platter heaved and buckled in her grasp, and crumpled to nothingness. Left alone amidst the ruin of its mates, the great gold cup

swelled and puffed itself up in a blaze of yellow light. She heard a hiss, and
a breath of sulfur blinded her eyes. The pain in her hands was almost more
than she could bear. But half mad with grief, she threw herself forward and
seized its wide graceful handles with both hands.

Bolts of lightning coursed through her scalded palms, and a thunderclap
darkened the air. But the loving cup turned to ashes in her hands, with a
stink like the rotten heart of the earth. Then the miasma lifted, and the
stench was gone. The next moment the sun poured streaming into the hall,
like the Mother's blessing on a wasted land.

Outlined in its rays, Arthur was sitting frozen in his place and King
Pelles was a statue of despair. Beside him Elaine's gossamer white gown was
filmed with ash and dust. Guenevere looked her way, and loathing filled her
soul. She wanted to fly at Elaine, to tear the clothes off her back, shrivel her
soft smooth skin, and drive her with whips and scorpions naked from the
court. From the way Lancelot was staring at Elaine, it seemed he was feeling
the same.

But you lay with her! the thought ran screaming round her head. *You called it
a dream—was that a lie, all lies? Did you even ride back to Corbenic, as you said you did?
Or did you go only as far as your mistress, waiting outside the town, and enjoy a tryst with
her while I wept and prayed?*

Sick to vomiting, she clutched her stomach and turned away. Galahad
stumbled to his feet and stood swaying from side to side. He spread out his
arms, more than ever like a young angel of death.

"This is all God's will!" he cried, blazing with pale fire. He leaned forward and placed both his hands on the Table, palms down. "This is God's
Table, and He will make us whole!"

The silence that followed was too deep for sighs or tears. But later, some
swore that they heard a low, musical lament, like the voice of a woman dying
of grief. Others heard an angry roaring, as if the skies themselves protested
at what had been done. Then the shining surface of the Table dimmed like
stars before dawn, and there came a mighty crack. As they looked on in horror, the great disc of the Summer Country split across its heart. Guenevere
felt her own heart riving too. The Round Table had shattered. The fellowship
of Camelot was no more.

CHAPTER 15

"*G uenevere!*"

With a furious bellow, Arthur leaped from his throne and vaulted down from the dais in a single leap. He came raging toward her down the hall and thrust a distended face into hers.

"It was the Grail!" he shouted in a voice between rage and tears. "The Holy Grail, sent to bless our court. And you made it disappear!"

"Arthur, you were deceived!" she cried, fighting back furiously. "It was not the Grail! The Hallows were a fraud. It was only a filthy trick—"

He gave an angry laugh. "Who would do such a thing?"

She wanted to scream. "Morgan, of course, who else?"

"But the Grail vanished because of you!" Arthur struck his head. "And why would the Table crack, except for what you did?"

She moved forward, ready to face him down. "It cracked, yes, but Arthur, Arthur, remember what you did. You tried to claim the Hallows for your God—"

"It was the Grail! We saw the Holy Grail!"

Looming beside her was the Abbot, his monks clustering all around with the secret glee of children who see another in disgrace. His deep-set eyes flayed her with open contempt. *I have you now, madam,* his inner soul rejoiced. *And may God permit me to catch all pagan whores like this.*

"It was the Holy Grail indeed," he boomed, rising to his task. "And only witchcraft could have made it fly away."

Witchcraft—?

The pain in her hands was raging out of control. But the age-old accents of hate must not prevail. "Hear me, monk," she cried, "and obey my command! There are no witches, only maggots in men's brains! I am Queen here, and you will guard your tongue!"

His pale face flushed as if she had boxed his ears. She could see his sub-

tle brain flashing like fire. "Yet Your Majesty saw the great treasures disappear," he said with a silky effort at self-control.

Arthur clenched his jaw. "At the very least, Guenevere, admit that."

"No!" she howled. "The Hallows were never here! All we saw was a
phantom—"

"A vision from heaven." The Papal Legate cut her off, ice glinting in his
clear blue gaze. "A spiritual promise of the Grail itself."

"And now it's lost!" Arthur took a pace or two, raging in pain. "It would
have purified our court, and renewed the fellowship of knights."

Arthur, there is no fellowship, now the Table has gone—

"It would have inspired our new quest for empire, when Mordred and I
set out from these islands to take the rule of the Britons as far as Rome—"

Guenevere forced her mind away from her suffering hands. "My
lord—"

But King Pelles had rallied to join the debate. "It was pure, as Our Lord
was pure!" He directed at Guenevere a glance of open hate. "And the evil
here would have vanished as the Grail has now!"

With a face as gray as her gown, Elaine took up the lament. "And the
great chance we had has gone, never to return!"

"Yes, gone, Guenevere," snarled Arthur, gripping her wrist. "Lost and
gone, far away!"

A pale treble voice came pealing through the Hall. "Far away, yes. But
not lost forever, my lord King." Galahad was stepping toward them, his eyes
blind with desire. "We must have a quest—a quest for the Holy Grail."

He fell to his knees. "King Arthur, grant it to me to lead this sacred
quest," he cried in a trance. "The path may take us as far as the Holy Land,
the home of the Grail when it graced Our Lord's hand at the Last Supper
that He shared on this earth. Bid all your knights to take the road with me.
We shall ride high and low till we find the Grail."

"A quest for the Grail!" Arthur too was transcendent with delight. "To
purify our table—renew our vows—"

"Arthur, think!" Guenevere cried. "Would you risk the knights' lives to
follow an evil dream?"

"Not so, Guenevere! What we saw was real!" Arthur was deaf now to all
but Galahad's voice.

"And your knights will do good, sire, along the way." Galahad's eyes had turned hopefully to Elaine now. "And win the approval of those they love and admire—"

"All your knights to go forth adventuring for the risen Christ?" The Abbot's mottled flush had given way to an unearthly pallor mirroring Galahad's own. His eyes caught fire. "My lord, this is the way to serve God indeed!"

Arthur fixed his gaze on the light from above pouring into the hall. "Yes, a quest!" he cried in a high, febrile tone. "My knights will ride out, to renew and relive their vows." He swung round to address the knights as they stared wide-eyed, some out of their sieges, some transfixed where they sat. "Remember your oaths!" he called. "You swore to defend the poor, and honor all widows and orphans with your strength and might. You bound yourselves to poverty and chastity before God, and these holy truths will lead you to the Grail. You may find it in your hearts, or at the tomb of Christ where Joseph of Arimathea laid Our Lord to rest. Go even as far as Babylon, or the Holy Land itself. Follow the Quest where it leads—to the death, if God wills—only be fearless, and be true!"

There was a low muttering in the silent court. One by one the knights murmured to their neighbors and glanced around at one another, half fearfully at first, then with growing awe. Gawain was the first to take up the gauntlet Arthur had cast down. "To horse!" he cried. "The Orkneys for the Quest!"

Gaheris and Gareth were on their feet in an instant, straining to be off. Agravain was slower to rise, but not long behind his brothers, while all others gathered themselves together and prepared to leave.

"The Quest!" "The Quest!" flew through the bewildered court.

"Go with God!" bellowed the Abbot, raising his cross to the skies.

"And the blessings of the Holy Father on you all," the Papal Legate seconded him fervently.

"Amen!" cried all the Christians with one voice. King Pelles embraced Galahad, weeping on his neck, while the pale youth gazed in rapture at the sun. Elaine fell to her knees, praying and weeping with joy, and Guenevere knew that all was lost, and never would return.

"To horse!"

From cellar to battlement the castle was aflame. In the stable yard, the sudden cry sent grooms and ostlers jumping like fleas at the crack of the Horse Master's whip. The blacksmiths were already pumping up their fires, and the saddlers were furiously setting out their leather patches, needles, and catgut for the repairs that some would surely need.

"What's happening, sir?" a stableboy gasped in dismay.

"Don't ask, boy!" the Horse Master roared. "Just see to the horses—all the knights are taking to the road!"

In the knights' quarters, squires and pages were at full stretch, some packing up their masters' saddlebags, others assembling weapons and shining up the multicolored shields. Shouldering down the central corridor, Bors and Lionel were still trying to recover from their shock.

"All this time he had a son," said Bors through chattering teeth. "And we never knew."

"He didn't know himself." Lionel shook his head in bewilderment. "What's going to happen now?" he demanded numbly.

"How do I know?" Bors gave a savage laugh. "Lancelot's waiting to see the Queen, the Queen is in attendance on the King—"

"—so we wait for him, while he waits for her."

Lionel's level tone betrayed the disturbance in his soul. The thought that his gentle brother felt such pain angered Bors more than he could say.

"It was bad enough," he ground out, "when he galloped off to Corbenic, and wouldn't let us ride with him on the way. Then he didn't get back till the last minute before the knighting—"

"—and we had to dismiss his page and work like madmen to get him ready in time." Lionel gave a pale reminiscent nod.

Bors ground his teeth. "And whatever he went for, the whole thing was a wild goose chase, we could tell."

"And now this." Lionel's fair skin was unnaturally pale. "As soon as he's seen the Queen, he'll have to do something for Princess Elaine and the boy—"

Bors gave a tight nod. "A knight must acknowledge his son. The boy and his mother will have to be given their due." And what then? was the thought splitting his mind. Gods above! he cried in inward fear, what will become of us?

"Bors! And Lionel!"

Ahead of them Sagramore was plunging out of his quarters with a laden squire and page laboring behind, and a pair of bulging saddlebags over his arm. "To horse!" he cried exuberantly. "It's the Quest!" His expression changed. "You're going, aren't you?"

Bors met the boisterous greeting with a forced smile "Are we going on the Quest? That depends on Lancelot—"

"And he depends on the Queen!" chortled Sagramore. "Who'll doubtless be pleased to see the back of him, after what's happened today. Who'd have thought Lancelot had a secret son? So much for his claim that he served only the Queen!"

Bors gritted his teeth. "We don't know the full story, Sagramore—"

"We know enough!" Sagramore's eyes lit up with a lecherous gleam. "A handsome lad, and a young Lancelot to the life. And a fine piece like the mother tucked away for all these years—any man in his right mind would—"

Any minute now, Lionel knew, Bors would plant his fist in Sagramore's grinning face. "Where are you headed, Sagramore?" he said in an overly loud voice.

"Where?" The stout knight paused. "Oh yes, the Quest! Ride far and wide, the King said, wherever the road may lead. Gods above, it's a long time since we all went off adventuring, knights-errant out on deeds of derring-do!" He punched Bors' shoulder, grinning again. "Fear nothing, the King said. Risk anything, for God will protect us whatever we do—"

Bors could have screamed with rage. Sagramore was a blind fool; the King had said nothing like that! He opened his mouth to remonstrate when a commotion farther down the corridor drew all eyes that way. Outside the chambers shared by the Orkney brothers, a clutch of attendants scattered, catching cuffs and blows as Gawain strode through, bellowing like a wounded bull. "I said we go, Agravain, and that means tonight!"

Agravain came stalking behind, his calm rejoinder sounding like sweet reason itself. "I only asked where we're heading, brother. It might be better to wait till tomorrow at first light."

Gawain's voice was verging on a shriek. "Are you deaf? Gareth, get down to the stables and see the horses fettled, we ride tonight! Gaheris, order the pages, and Agravain, take charge of the squires. Get to it, all of you!"

Nodding to the knights in their way, the Orkney brothers passed through the low corridor and were gone. Bors watched them go, vexed to the

depths of his soul. In all the apartments he could see knights readying themselves for departure, or standing at a loss amidst piles of their effects, uncertain what to do.

As he looked around, Bors could hardly quell the bitterness springing in
his soul. All the knights to take to the road? What would that serve?
Through one door he could see Kay, Lucan, and Bedivere, heads together in
earnest discourse, and through another a group of the young knights who
attended on Mordred, deep in their own discussion of what they should do.
Bors gave a bitter laugh. Over there was Dinant, always ready to adventure
but unaware that he had long forgotten what adventuring was. By the light
in his eye, he would get no farther than the first inn where a greasy tavern
maid would open her scrawny thighs and offer him what he never got at
court. In the next chamber Tor, rugged and unmoved, was stolidly stowing
his few soldierly accoutrements into a battered leather bag.

Tor felt Bors' glance and looked up. "I'm going, yes—back to the Saxon
shore." He shook his grizzled head. "All this talk of the Quest, when we have
work to do there, real work, keeping the Norsemen at bay, not this idle fool-
ery of rushing off to the Holy Land." He nodded at a young knight coming in. "Some of the lads are coming along with me. They're not going to
chase after Galahad through the world."

Bors turned away. Tor was right. But wherever they went, the fellowship
of the Round Table would be scattered to the winds.

"Guenevere?"

"Yes, Arthur, I'm here."

The light was fading in the King's apartments, and Arthur sat hunched
in misery over a dying fire. The June dusk was humid but not warm, and
beneath their feet the flagstones of the floor sweated like living things. The
servants had been dismissed, and they sat alone in a silence that neither could
break. On the far horizon the sun was dying in a blaze of pewter and gold,
but here the gloaming had deepened till all she could see was the outline of
Arthur's massive form. Guenevere was craving to be alone to nurse her hurt,
and by now her rage against Arthur had passed beyond speech, but still she
could not leave him as he was.

She rose and lit a candle between their chairs. Arthur sat shivering like a
man with a fatal ague. She crossed to a table and poured him a cordial to
revive his heart. Returning to her seat, she made herself touch his hand. Yet

as she did so, her heart protested till she thought that he must hear. *He betrayed you and you must comfort him? He meant to hand over the Hallows to the Christians and you must still do your duty to him like the lowliest maid?*

"Why, Guenevere?" he muttered wanly. "Why did the Table crack?"

"Because it belonged to the Goddess." *Arthur, Arthur, do I need to tell you this?* "And Galahad tried to claim it for his Christian God."

Arthur held his head. "And Mordred was rejected too, cast to the ground." He raised his eyes hopelessly to hers. "Was it all my folly, a father's vanity, to think Mordred was destined for the Siege Perilous?"

Guenevere paused. Angry though she was, she had no wish to add to Arthur's confusion and distress. "Mordred was not peerless, we know that now."

"And Galahad is." Arthur gave an unhappy smile. "Well, Lancelot is the finest knight in the world. He's the soul of honor, he'd never do anything wrong."

"No—" *Goddess, Mother, give me strength to endure this!*

"So it's hardly surprising if his son is peerless too."

"Galahad's still a boy, he's never been tried." She tried to keep the hostility out of her voice. "We have yet to see how peerless he will prove."

"But the idea of the Quest was inspired," Arthur said fervently, "you have to grant him that." He took a long pull on the ruby liquor, and the life began to return to his ravaged face.

"Arthur—" She forced herself to stay calm. "Surely you can see that once the knights are scattered through the world, we'll never see the fellowship of the Round Table again?"

"Still doubting, Guenevere, after all we've seen today?" The strength was coming back to Arthur's voice. "Isn't it wonderful that Lancelot has a son?" A look she could hardly bear crept into his eye. "And a secret little lady love too!" He chuckled as men will over such things. "The Grail princess! He was destined for Elaine after all. D'you remember we once talked of making her his wife? You didn't like the idea then, but clearly Lancelot took things into his own hands. Well, she's a fine wench and no mistake!"

Goddess, Mother, why do you torture me?

She dug her nails into the flesh of her aching palms. "Arthur, this is nothing at all to us—"

"But it is!" He leaned forward urgently. "You have to see God's purpose in all of this. Galahad will find the Grail, we're assured of that—"

"Assured by the Christians!"

"Of course," he returned in surprise. "And the knights will all come back purified by the Quest. Then with the Table renewed—"

"But Arthur, how can it be? There is no Grail, we saw the Hallows of the Goddess if we saw anything at all—"

Arthur smiled wisely. "To each what he saw, Guenevere. You can't argue with that."

Furiously she pressed on. "And the Table can't be renewed by the Quest—"

"What d'you mean?" he interrupted sharply, lifting his head.

"Arthur, the Table is broken! It's shattered, it'll never—"

"Guenevere—" With a ponderous air of discovery, Arthur held up his hand. "Don't you remember? It cracked once before, when Agravain was made a knight."

She drew a deep breath. "Yes, it did," she said slowly. "But it only shifted on its trestles then, and took no harm. Not like today." She covered her eyes with her hand.

Why should the Table crack, he asks? Why doesn't he feel this heartache, this terrible pain? Gods above, Arthur, have the Christians stolen your brain?

"But it can be healed!" Arthur cried heartily. "We'll send for the best joiner in the islands, and have it mended in no time. Then we shall have the Grail, all our knights will be renewed, and we'll be ready for the greatest adventure of all!"

Her heart froze. "Arthur—"

He swept on, his face now alight with a vivid glow, his great fists clenched. "Remember what I was telling you about Mordred?"

"Mordred—Gods above, we've forgotten him, we should go to see how he is—"

"Not necessary." Arthur gave a confident shake of the head. "He has his knights with him, so we can let him rest—young people are always happy to be left alone. Mordred won't go on the Quest, of course—"

"Arthur, why not? Surely he'll want to go."

Arthur looked at her blankly. "He can't go, Guenevere, I need him here. And besides, I have other plans for him. No, he and I will strike out from here when the Grail Quest is done, and build an empire that any son would be proud to call his own!"

Mordred is not my son, Arthur, came as a new pain. But a conviction deeper than all overwhelmed her now. "It's the end of the Round Table, Arthur, don't you see that?"

"No, Guenevere, I don't!" he cried euphorically, throwing down the last of the blood-red drink. "In fact, you're wrong, you're completely wrong! The Table will have a new purpose, the greater glory of God. It will be restored and remade, stronger than before. No one will remember the old deeds of the knights of the Round Table, once Mordred is ruling as far as Rome and a new Camelot brings in the age of Christ!"

Arthur, Arthur—

All that was left was to weep. Guenevere got to her feet. She had done her duty, for today at least. Arthur had lost himself in a world of his own, and when she bade him farewell, he hardly saw her go.

Resolutely she moved out into the night. Time now to turn to her own concerns. *I must see Lancelot,* she thought dully. *But what can I say to him or he to me?*

After all that has happened, all that has come to light— Her flesh shrank from seeing him again. Still, it had to be done. She must get back to her apartments, he would be waiting for her there. Slowly her bruised mind turned back to Lancelot, and with every step her longing for him grew. *There must be a reason for this, there's always a purpose in what the Great Ones do. He was tricked into betraying me, he would never have chosen that terrible girl by himself. I have loved him so long, I cannot abandon him now. If he can make me love him and trust him again, Goddess, Mother, help me to forgive!*

She would not weep, not while she still had hope. Overhead Venus was rising in the west. Guenevere lifted her eyes to the love-star and doggedly pressed on through the twilit court. And all around, the demons of pain and distress reveled through the sky and danced about her head, laughing with glee at the horrors that lay ahead.

CHAPTER 16

The purple threads of dusk wove across the gold of evening as a perfect night darkened over Camelot. In the guest apartments, King Pelles rocked back on his heels and surveyed his work. Yes, Galahad would do very well indeed.

In the oriel window, Elaine was on her knees, praying for the success of the Quest. If a tear or two escaped her tightly closed eyes, King Pelles did not care. His daughter was nothing to him now. Aided by the crooked old dame Brisein, he had made his grandson a miracle to behold. Disdaining the menservants under his command, he had prepared the boy entirely by himself.

Now Galahad stood tall and erect, shining in silver mail from head to foot. A cross of silver gleamed on his white tunic, and a larger cross in gold adorned his white shield. In the crook of his left arm, he held a silver helmet with a full white plume, and his gauntleted fist clutched a slender golden sword.

"The virgin warrior to the life!" breathed Pelles, entranced. He raised his clasped fists to the sky. "He is Yours, Lord! Do with him as You will."

Galahad gave a graceful inclination of his head. But if anyone had looked into his eyes, they would have seen traces of bewilderment and fear. "God's will be done."

"Kneel," ordered the old man peremptorily.

Galahad fell to his knees. His pearl-pale mane of hair fell forward over his face, and the king laid both his hands on the boy's bent head. "Go forth in the name of the Lord," he intoned, closing his eyes. "Tread the way of truth and life even as far as the Holy Sepulchre. Find and bring back the Grail, and the purpose of your life will be fulfilled."

"Amen."

The youth took his grandfather's hand and brought it to his lips. In the window, Elaine was still busy at her prayers. Galahad moved toward her and treated her to a beseeching smile. "Give me your blessing, Mother," he breathed. He turned back to King Pelles. "I pray you, take care of her, Sire."

"I—"

Grief choked Elaine's throat. Was this it, the great moment of fulfill-ment that her father had half-promised, half-threatened for all these years? Her son leaving and going she knew not where? The son in truth she could hardly call her own, the child taken from her at birth, and trained like a sapling to her father's will?

"Elaine—" came King Pelles's threatening voice.

Her soft flesh crawled, and the harsh discipline of years came to her aid.

"I do, my son," she forced out. "My prayers will follow you everywhere, night and day."

"Farewell, madam."

"God be with you, Galahad."

She stepped forward to embrace him, but his painted linen tunic and cold mail resisted her grasp. She gave him her hand and brushed his cheek with a chilly, fleeting kiss. He stiffened, and she did not know that he was aching for her touch as a starving child craves food. Then King Pelles's clutching hand drew him firmly away, and the last of her unborn hopes died in her famished heart.

"So, so, enough!" cried King Pelles tetchily. "Time to go, boy, no more dallying now. The men will make camp for you tonight, but still you should be on your way—"

"Grandsire, by your leave—" Galahad held up his hand. "I will not endanger the men. These are men with wives and children. I do not need to make widows and orphans on my journey. Our Lord had no soldiers to accompany His steps."

"What? This is nonsense, son! The men will go with you!"

Elaine's stomach heaved. Her father was angry, and she would pay for it.

"If you will not think of them, think of the Quest," the earnest voice wound on. "To find the Grail, a man must be free from sin, nor must he be tainted by another's deeds. The guards are no more than simple sons of Eve. For my companions on the Quest, I cannot ask a purity they do not have."

"You think so? Let me tell you—"

Elaine could hear her father preparing to attack. But again the bell-like treble cut through the air. "Sire, I speak only the truth."

"Do you defy me now?" Pelles roared.

Galahad's limpid stare seemed to pass through the furious old man. "You are my grandsire and my king," he said with an untroubled brow. "If you order the men to accompany me, I must obey. But on the road, I am master of my Quest. From there, I shall order them to return." He smiled serenely. "Tell me, then, lord, what is your will?"

"Young man—"

Bullying, threatening, King Pelles escorted his grandson to the door. But shout as he might, he would not prevail over Galahad, Elaine knew. For the first time in his life, King Pelles had met his match. And he was not a man to stomach the defeat. He would forgive the Grail child, but not her. Elaine's tender inner being shrank at the thought of the night ahead. Her father's nature would be raging out of control once Galahad had gone.

A tear of utter hopelessness squeezed from her eye. She wanted to die, to be dead long ago, no more than a cage of bleached bones and a lock of silver hair. He had not come—he had not looked at her—

"You are grieving for Sir Lancelot."

It was Dame Brisein at her elbow, her old face suddenly alive and young. How was it that she came to life like that, when other times she was only a dried-up shell? Elaine shook her head, but the puzzle was too familiar for her to care. Her tears overflowed and ran like rain.

"Yes," she whispered, her soul a waterfall of grief.

Dame Brisein fixed her with a hypnotic stare. "You hoped he would see you in your white gown and gossamer veil and love you and come to you again," the old-young voice went on.

"Yes." The sound was no more than the dying of a leaf.

"And instead he ignored you, to dance attendance on the Queen."

Her heart burned. "He loves her! And she's old—she's already forty, she'll be fifty soon!"

"He chose her over you." Dame Brisein's words were like knives to her wounded heart. "He was false to you, when you have borne his child. The child of the Grail."

She could only nod.

The old woman pursed her full mulberry mouth. "But still you want to see him, and you want him to see and acknowledge his son?" The cracked voice was a mesmeric whisper now. "You want to hold your knight in your arms once again."

Elaine could hardly breathe. "If only once—"

"Once may be all that we have," the old woman hissed. "All men play false." Her eyes were pools of ink. "But leave it to me, lady dear—leave your false knight to me."

SHE WILL NOT COME.

In the hours of waiting for Guenevere, Lancelot had entertained this thought a hundred times, only to dismiss it as fainthearted, not worthy of her trust. But suddenly he knew with certainty that his hopes were in vain. She would not come.

Under Ina's direction, the servants were bringing the candles into the antechamber and preparing a fire. All at once the Queen's apartments seemed dark, cold, and mocking, instead of the warm, well-lighted place he had come to love. The maid approached him again with eyes begging him to stay and offered him refreshment, as she had done more times than they could count. With a brief word of thanks, he hurried away.

Now he was cursing every second he had spent idling in the deserted chamber, watching the dusk come down. The boy—he had to see the boy.

But first— He redoubled his strides, pressing as fast as he could down the miles of corridors, through courtyards and cloisters crowded with chattering throngs. From princes to potboys, all Camelot had turned out to marvel at the day's events. On all sides Lancelot caught sideways smiles or frank, knowing grins, and snatches of gossip that the speakers did not bother to hide.

"A son!"

"Yes, twelve or fifteen, maybe more—"

"And a love-nest, was it—?"

"A fine-looking woman tucked away in the north—"

He wanted to vomit. He wanted to kill Elaine. That he had been so entrapped— He burned with shame. The sense of intimate violation was so strong that it came to him: this is how women must suffer when they are raped.

On the next corner, a group of men-at-arms straightened up at the sight of him and came to attention respectfully enough. But the look in their eyes made him feel unclean. Would he ever escape the greasy complicity of men enjoying a furtive leer at another's expense?

The cool of the evening air was balm to his soul. All round the walls, the June roses were pouring out their hearts' sweetness in the silver twilight of a perfect day. The faint breath of wild honeysuckle drifted down from the woods, and the birds were coming home to their drowsy roosts. When night fell, the young lovers of Camelot would slip out into the welcoming darkness of the woodland to wander the green hills and hollows where the Fair Ones walked. Once again, the evil of his fate struck Lancelot to the quick. All nature's loveliness, and he the only ugly thing alive!

On the far side of the palace, the knights' quarters lay dark and deserted, and his overburdened spirit plunged again. Had he missed them? Where could they have gone? Half frantic he plunged down the central corridor to the small whitewashed chamber at the end. There, sitting in the gloom, were Bors and Lionel, each perched dejectedly on the edge of his narrow bed, Bors with his head in his hands, and Lionel staring into space. Beside them on the floor lay their saddlebags, neatly packed, and their swords and lances stood ready by the door. They looked up at him, bemused and unsmiling, and he saw the doubt and apprehension in their eyes.

Shame and fury tore his heart again. "I am glad to find you here," he managed to say.

Where else? said Bors' sad, untrusting shrug.

Lancelot found his voice. "We shall join the Quest. We ride tonight."

Bors pursed his lips. You're overridden already, he wanted to say. You must be exhausted, racing all the way to Corbenic and back. And now you're talking of setting off again tonight? But the words died in his throat.

Lionel looked at Bors, then gave Lancelot a nod. "Very well."

"You will set off first," Lancelot went on. "I still have to attend the Queen."

The Queen.

Always the Queen.

Who else?

Bors rose stiffly to his feet. "She has ordered you not to go?"

Lancelot tried to keep the bitterness out of his tone. "I waited, but I couldn't see her. She's still with the King. I came to find you because the boy will be leaving, and you must ride with him."

"With the boy?" Bors knew he was being deliberately obtuse. "With young Galahad, you mean?"

They all flinched a little as he said the name.

Lancelot held Bors' gaze. "With Galahad, yes. With my son."

There was a silence that none knew how to break. Lancelot felt his throat burning and his eyes on fire. "I swear to you I never knew he lived," he said hoarsely. "More—I never knew his mother, as men think."

Both his cousins now were watching him like hawks.

"When I told you what had happened at Corbenic—" Lancelot paused, then forced himself to go on. "I told you as it was." He swung away, and bunched his fists with rage. "I did not lie to you!"

Lionel's fair skin flushed to the roots of his hair. "We never thought you did!" he cried angrily. Bors reached out a hand and laid it on Lancelot's arm.

"But now the boy is here," Lancelot resumed with an effort, "I have to look after him—help him on his way—"

Bors could not stop himself. "And what will the Queen have to say about that? You leave her for the son of her rival, you help the Christians to attain the Grail—"

"There is no Grail!" Lancelot forced out. "Not as the Christians think. What it is lies beyond their power to comprehend. They will never find it, so I am not betraying the Queen. And I must take care of my son!"

Lionel hastened forward with a glance at Bors. "Just tell us what we can do for Galahad."

A spasm of hopeless pity twisted Lancelot's mouth. "It seems he's determined to go on this Quest. But he's not thirteen, and if he takes to the road alone—"

"With outlaws and vagabonds, rogue knights and worse—" Bors shook his head furiously.

"It's madness!" cried Lionel, coloring up again. "Gods above, what can King Pelles be thinking of?"

"We have to protect him," insisted Lancelot, half under his breath. "He's my son." A brief smile of embarrassment shadowed his face. "Your nephew. Our blood kin. Will you go with him?"

In the silence that followed, Bors felt the world he had known shifting on its axis, and heard a new call from the astral plane. He would rather have been kin to any other creature in the world. Must he take up a burden that his loyal soul would not permit him to lay down in this life, or the next? He looked at Lionel, and received a silent nod. He managed a smile. "Very well then. We shall go."

Lancelot felt his eyes pricking with tears. "Let's get down to the courtyard then, before they all set off."

Bors squared his neat shoulders. "So we ride with Galahad—"

R O S A L I N D   M I L E S

A raw fervor swept over Lancelot that he had never known before. "—and guard him with your lives!"

Lionel smiled sadly. "You know we will," he said.

"And you——?" Bors took a breath. His nerves were screaming. Will you see the boy's mother? What about his grandfather, the mad old king? How long will you wait for the Queen? Will she keep you dangling till you crawl on your knees to her? What's happening, Lancelot? he was crying out inside. But none of it could be said.

"When will you follow?" he got out at last.

Lancelot turned his head away. "I don't know. I have to see the Queen. She thinks I lied and betrayed her, and she won't forgive that."

Oh yes she will, said Bors' ugly inner voice, because she'll never find another knight like you. But he caught Lionel watching him, and knew that his younger brother could hear his thoughts. With an effort, he mastered his rage.

"She will," he said.

"No. Not after the King betrayed her with Queen Morgan, and she had a son too, while my dear lady lost her little boy—and now I have a child—"

The thought of Guenevere's pain was more than he could bear. Pain, always new pain—would it never end? He closed his eyes, and could no longer hold back his tears. "I want to speak to my son—if only for a little time."

"Come." Bors moved toward him and gently took his arm. "Let's get down to the courtyard," he said stoutly, "and meet our young kin." He nodded to Lionel with a watery smile. "And then, brother, to horse for the Quest!"

THE GUARDS OF the Queen's apartments threw wide the great doors. Guenevere flew through to her inner sanctuary and her heart died. She cast around, forcing herself to stay calm. "Oh, Ina—where is he?"

The maid came forward, deep grooves of sorrow marking her small face. "He left, lady, a few minutes ago."

"He's gone?" Guenevere brought her knuckles to her mouth, stifling a howl. *Goddess, Mother, what is my sin? Why must I suffer so?*

Ina's eyes welled with tears. "He waited here, madam, all the time you were with the King."

She felt a pain in her head and lifted off the heavy crown. "Why didn't he stay?"

"The knights are leaving, lady. He wanted to see his son."

"His son!" She echoed Ina's words like a raven of doom. "Yes, his son!" Tears sprang to her eyes. "He betrayed me, Ina—"

"No, lady, surely not—"

"Yes!" Guenevere cried. "Just as Arthur did."

"There must be a reason—"

"What reason could there be? And he lied about it all these years—"

"Lady, don't torment yourself—"

"I'm not! He's tormenting me! He told me some wretched story about having a dream. And I believed him! Was there ever such a fool?"

She roamed round the chamber, clenching and unclenching her fists. "Ina, he's worthless, he's just a breaker of hearts. I think he's the vilest man in all the world. He should go on the Quest, I'll never see him again."

Never again—

She felt her mind splitting, and clutched at the maid for support. "Ina, Ina, I have to see him, send for him again! Go and find him yourself, don't trust anyone else. But bring him back—I shall go mad if I don't see him tonight!"

CHAPTER 17

The evening deepened over Camelot into a silvery twilight midway between night and day. From the side of the stable yard, Kay, Bedivere, and Lucan watched in silence as the knights rode out. A long and tense debate in the knights' quarters had left them still unsure of what to do. But as they saw knight after knight leaving in high excitement, yet with no clear idea of where they were going or why, it seemed to them they had been wise to wait.

At least until they were able to see the King. But did Arthur himself know what he wanted to do?

Kay groaned and wrapped himself tighter inside his cloak. The evening was warmer than it had promised at first, and the stable yard was alive with bustle and noise. The blacksmiths' braziers were flaring and hissing as teams of boys vigorously plied the bellows to keep up the heat, and their flames lit up the sky. As the sweating, toiling smiths hammered and shod, the sparks from the beaten meal caught the horses' coats, and the sour tang of singeing horsehair rose above the sweet stable smell of straw and hay. Piles of steaming droppings testified to the fever in the yard as the great beasts jittered about, resisting the grooms struggling to bridle them and fasten up their girths. Kay could see Lucan's eyes shining in sympathy, and knew his fellow knight was longing to ride out. But the dew of evening was coming down, the last of the sun was gone, and a night on a hard bed of earth seemed more unwelcome than ever now. Surreptitiously massaging his crippled leg, Kay did not know whether he was suffering a malaise of body or of soul.

"Gods above," he grumbled, "I'm too old for this game."

Bedivere gave a rueful laugh. "So are we all, if the truth is told."

With an unpleasant sensation, Lucan thought of his recent discovery that strands of silver were invading his red-gold hair. "Speak for yourself," he said a shade too heartily. He gestured at the knights getting ready to ride out. "We're more than a match for any of these. We'd achieve this Quest."

"Good of you to include me in your boast," snapped Kay, his sallow face alive with anger and regret. "But if we go, who will defend the King?" He pointed a scornful finger at Sagramore, huffing and puffing as he marshaled his page and his squire to get him mounted along with all his goods. "When these imbeciles have flown out, who's left?"

"We shall be, never fear," Lucan came back. Resolutely he shut his mind to dreams of glory, and long lost days on the road. "Our place is with the King."

"We'll stay with him," Bedivere said simply.

To the death was the thought in every mind.

Lucan was the first to break the silence. "And not all the firebrands are taking to the road." He gave a meaningful nod. Across the courtyard stood a dozen or so young knights, watching with nervous attention as the others left. From their leering grins and unconvincing jocularity, he could see they were torn between mirth and envy, as one by one the knights were mounted, their shields slung on their horses, and their bright banners unfurled.

"Mordred's cronies," Lucan said with undisguised contempt. "They won't go without him—"

"—and the King will never let him go," Kay finished the thought. "Especially if everyone else rides out and the King's left alone."

"What about Lancelot?" Bedivere said. "What will he do?"

Kay turned his head. "We can probably ask him ourselves," he said sardonically, pointing across the yard. "He must be here soon to join the fond farewell."

Near the open arch leading out to the castle gate, Galahad was standing serenely while the king's men-at-arms attended him with the stolid acceptance of men who never had to decide their destination or fate. Opposite them, waiting to bless the Quest, were the black figures of the Father Abbot and the Papal Legate from Rome. Weaving to and fro among them, King Pelles buzzed with tension like an angry wasp.

Under the old man's eye, every item of the boy's knightly accoutrements had been checked and checked again. Waving aside the attentions of the grooms, the old man plucked compulsively at harness and saddlebags, packing and repacking their contents, pulling out swords and daggers for fresh scrutiny before slotting them away again. Even the great gray stallion, bearing the delay as patiently as its master, had to suffer having its nose and ears inspected and its legs palpated for the hundredth time.

At last the youth stepped forward and touched his grandfather's arm. "It is time, sire," he said quietly. "The night is coming, and I have far to go."

"What?" cried the old king. He clutched at Galahad with a desperate air. "No, you're not ready, you can't go——"

Galahad gave a gentle smile. "It is time."

"Time indeed." The Papal Legate gave a reproving nod, and fixed King Pelles with his bright blue stare. "God's will be done." He beckoned Galahad and gestured to the Father Abbot at his side. "My colleague will invoke God's blessing on the Quest."

Galahad came toward them and knelt on the cobbled yard.

Lord, Lord, prayed the Father Abbot, be Thou in my words and the truth of my heart. His lungs swelled with the sweet savor of heavenly grace, and he knew himself possessed.

"Approach, my child," he cried ecstatically. "The mantle of God's peace and protection descends on you this day. Gird yourself in the cloak of humility and the armor of righteousness, and the shield of the Lord will guard you as you go. Let your soul rejoice in the knowledge that you do God's will. Follow the Holy Grail to your journey's end!"

The Papal Legate's command fell like a voice from heaven. "And when you have the sacred vessel of Christ, *bring it to us!*"

"Amen!" cried the Abbot.

"Amen," murmured Galahad through bloodless lips.

King Pelles skipped in the air and writhed with glee. "Amen!" he caroled, waving his bony arms. "Amen! Amen! Amen!"

No, NO—MY SON should not be kneeling to Christian priests—

Entering the courtyard with Bors and Lionel, Lancelot could see Galahad on his knees surrounded by men in black. The evening starlight gilded the boy's bent head, and the waiting servants and men-at-arms behind were dimly lit up by the rising moon. From the cloisters, the group around Galahad seemed frozen in time, a vision bathed in the amber light of memory. Lancelot saw the dark-robed figures leaning over Galahad, and spurred his pace.

"You may go, sirs!" he dismissed the monks. Thrusting through the inner group, he reached down and placed his hand under Galahad's arm to raise him to his feet. Galahad lifted his bent head and opened his eyes, and for the first time Lancelot looked his son in the face.

At first the baby-blond hair, the softly translucent flesh caught Lancelot like a blow in the stomach with their violent reminder of Elaine. His gorge rose, and he wanted to turn away. But then he saw the hero worship in the eyes, eyes that he knew without a second's doubt were the echo of his own. Griefs and memories as sharp as elf arrows stung Lancelot to the quick. In the mirror of time he saw the boy's ardent, Otherworldly air, and knew that he must have looked like this himself when he was young. With just such an air of hope he must have embarked on his own quest, riding down into the Summer Country to seek out its Queen. His faith had brought him to Camelot, and to Guenevere. Loving, hoping, trusting, as Galahad did now, he had knelt at her feet. Had she caught then those lights at the corners of his mouth, lifting the long, full lips in the shadow of a smile? He smiled at himself that he should even ask. Of course she had. She had seen him as he saw Galahad now.

Except that—

When he had sought out Guenevere, he was a man full grown, young to be sure, but no babe in arms. He had known love and life and the joys the Goddess gives. But this boy—

Courteous as he was, and reared in chivalry, his son was a still a child. A child vowed to the Grail. A living sacrifice on the altar of his God.

His throat convulsed. He forced himself to speak. "This Quest—are you vowed to it? Must you go?"

"Sir, I must." The boy's face was ablaze.

Lancelot fought down his grief. So his son would leave as suddenly as he arrived, making him a father then taking it all away again? He suppressed a sardonic smile. Many a knight he knew would be only too pleased if the proof of an old indiscretion would disappear. But his mind, his soul were aching with a single thought: How would it be if I could truly father this boy?

Lancelot drew a deep breath. "Can nothing persuade you to remain in Camelot—at least for a while?"

Again the white-hot gaze. "Nothing, my lord, though it grieves me to deny you."

Lancelot wanted to tear up the earth, rip apart the sky. "I am your father," he said huskily. He waved a hand at Bors and Lionel behind. "These good knights are your near kin. Their father and mine were brothers, kings of Benoic. If you will stay—or even delay a little"—he was appalled to hear the agony leaking into his voice—"we would embrace the chance to know you, and welcome you to your blood."

"No!"

A wild cry of anguish racked the air. "Don't listen to them, son!" panted old Pelles, thrusting himself in front of Lancelot. "You are vowed to the Quest! For that alone—"

Lancelot's heart burst. "Old sire," he ground out, "I may not tell you what a vile thing you did when I was your guest, and you abused my trust. But I must and will reprehend what you do now. You may not call this youth son. He is my son, not yours, and he will answer to me!"

"Father, I will."

Galahad's pure youthful voice fell like cool water in a land of fire. The love in his eyes was almost shameful, it was so naked and unadorned. "You are my father and my lord. I shall die happy knowing that you have acknowledged me. But if I am to live up to your fame and honor, I may not break a vow that I have made. I have sworn to perform this Quest since I was born."

You did not swear! You were sworn! And a child's oath is the work of adults, not of his own soul! The vain protest ran screaming through Lancelot's head, and died. The boy has vowed, came the urgent word of his inner voice. Do not disgrace him now.

"Very well." He arranged his face in a smile. "But you will not refuse your father one request. You have dear kin here, Sir Bors and Sir Lionel. They wish to go with you on the Quest. I shall join you later on."

"No, no!" yelped King Pelles. "Remember, boy, you said you would go alone. If you need men, take mine, not his! You are the child of the Holy Grail—"

But Galahad was staring at Lancelot. A glow like fire transfigured his boyish face. "You will join me? On the Quest?"

"I will."

Galahad turned to Bors and Lionel, and humbly bowed. "My lords," he said, in a voice that betrayed his youth, "you will accompany me? I am honored—beyond words—"

Bors and Lionel exchanged the briefest glance. Then both stepped forward and warmly embraced the youth. Around them King Pelles gibbered with rage. "No—no! They are not pure! They are not of the faith—son—son!"

A furious pity stirred in Lancelot's heart. He raised his head and surveyed King Pelles's band of men. In the front, his eyes locked on Lancelot, their Captain stood poised and ready for command. Lancelot met his gaze.

"Escort King Pelles to his quarters," he said in a level tone, "and give orders that His Majesty is to have the best of care. See him well settled and content in his mind until the time comes for him to return with his party to Corbenic. In case of any trouble, come back to me." He favored the Captain with the glimmer of a smile. "But I do not expect to see you and your troop again."

"No need, my lord," said the Captain. Briskly he signaled his men. Forming a wall around the loudly bleating Pelles, they half-marched, half-shuffled the old king out of sight. Lancelot turned back to Galahad. Gods above! his soul cried. Must I lose him now?

Blindly he laid a hand on the horse's neck. "A good mount," he said, feeling the distance already creeping between him and the boy, sensing a chasm of sorrow, darkness, and fear lying ahead. "He will carry you well. And your kinsmen will be behind you and before."

There was no more to say. Wordlessly he threw his arms round Galahad's neck. In a leaden silence he took farewell of Bors and Lionel. The grooms already had their horses waiting to mount. Within moments all three were aloft, and leaving him.

"Farewell!" he called out in his strongest voice.

And "Farewell!" all three returned, the three voices he loved best in the world. With a wholly new tearing sensation in his soul, he watched them ride away.

The stable yard was almost empty now. From the corner where they had drawn themselves up, the Abbot and the Papal Legate surveyed him with eyes of stone, then stalked away. Now the last stragglers hurried through their preparations and spurred out of the gates after Galahad, Bors, and Lionel, anxious to trail the knights of the Holy Grail. The blacksmiths and their boys had faded away, and the grooms and ostlers were slinking off thankfully to their beds.

"My lord—anything I can do for you?"

The Horse Master was making his final rounds. With only a few poor old jades left behind, horses too strangled or spavined to take to the road, his last check on his charges would be brief, Lancelot knew.

He raised a smile. "Thank you, no. I shan't be riding out tonight."

"Good night then, my lord."

"Good night."

In the stable yard, night had come down at last. A ragged wind leaped up, whipping the clouds, sending them scudding across the troubled sky. One by one the stars and the moon went out. Lancelot stood in a darkness that perfectly mirrored the midnight in his soul.

How long he stood there brooding, he never knew. The three cries of farewell were still echoing through his head, the voices he loved best in all the world.

Best in all the world?

Yes, he loved Galahad, with a primal depth. As for Bors and Lionel, they were his, they were part of him, and he was theirs, from the time before thought. The best loved in the world, indeed they were.

Except one.

My lady! came to him like a sword through the heart. How could he ever convince Guenevere that he had to support Galahad on the Quest? To her this would be another great act of betrayal, like lying with Elaine, giving comfort to the Christians and furthering their desires. Their aim was nothing less than the theft of the Hallows, through which they sought to bring down the Goddess and all who followed her. And he was helping his son to be part of this?

He groaned aloud. If I could talk to her, ran frantically through his head—if she would listen to me—if I could see her—but she can't bear me now! Gods above, she'll never speak to me, never see me again—

Suddenly he was aware of a female form beside him in the dusk. Muffled though she was and hunched inside her cloak, he knew her from her very first whispered words. "Come to the Queen," she breathed. "She has sent me to bring you to her side."

Lancelot's eyes and throat burned with a rush of tears.

Goddess, Mother, thanks—that my lady can find it in her heart to forgive—

"We must go in silence and darkness, my lady says," the voice went on. "Say nothing—follow me—I will lead you there."

Dimly he could see her making off. His heart leaped. He would see Guenevere, all might yet be well.

"I am with you, Ina," he rejoiced in his lowest tones. "Lead on to my lady, I shall follow, I am yours!"

CHAPTER 18

"Follow, all of you!"

Mordred flung out of his apartments, fighting down the blind choking round his heart. Navigating the twilit corridors, he did not recognize the darkness that had invaded him. All he knew was that he had suffered slights no mortal man should endure.

"With you, my lord!"

Behind him, the ferret-faced Ozark darted nimbly along with his fellow knight Vullian and the rest of the young knights who had gathered to comfort the prince. Already the pair were composing the words and phrases to console their master for this new turn of events. But Mordred was deaf to his followers, lost in a dreadful new world of shock and shame. Ever since he knew that he was Arthur's son, he had looked on the Siege Perilous as his destiny. To be rejected by the great chair, spewed out like a thing unclean, sent sprawling facedown in front of the whole court was a humiliation that he would never forgive.

The handsome mouth worked convulsively, chewing on his anger and its bitter cud. One thing could have saved him, and that had been denied. If Arthur had taken him by the hand and led him to the throne, installed him in the place standing ready on the dais, it would have proclaimed to the world that Mordred was still his son. Still the heir, still the beloved, the chosen one. If Arthur had seized the moment, the hateful disappointment could have been passed off, and he could have taken comfort from a title and an honor that would long outlast the memories of his shame.

But Arthur had refused to save him. He had denied Mordred his natural right and due.

And I begged him on my knees? raged Mordred in his darkening soul. Never, *never* again.

He had thought then that his life was at the worst. Yet there was worse to come. As Vullian and Ozark were with him in his chamber, soothing the sense of outrage that had left him writhing on his bed, one by one had come the whispers as the other young knights slipped in. Rutger, was it, or Blithil? One of his followers had finally divulged what they knew.

"After you left, my lord," the knight muttered, avoiding Mordred's eye, "a stranger knight came in and took the Seat."

"What?" Mordred cried in horror. Another had sat in the Siege Perilous destined for him? "Who was he? A great warrior, a king from another land?"

"Alas, no—"

"Who, then?" Mordred screamed. Who had defeated him? *"Who?"*

"A boy from Corbenic. An untried knight, twelve or fourteen years of age, no more."

Mordred's fury then had known no bounds. Following him now, Ozark and Vullian exchanged a glance, silently preening themselves on a job well done. The two companion knights had labored long and hard to restore Mordred to this semblance of calm, and when Mordred came into his own, they must get their reward. And if their lord's anger with his father continued like this, that might be sooner than any man would think.

"My lord, you do well to bring your grievances to the King," Vullian ventured ingratiatingly. "The King is bound to answer your just concerns."

Mordred gave a laugh that sounded like a cry of pain. What nonsense was this? A king was never bound. A ruler was always a law unto himself, or what was kingship worth? Arthur did not have to do anything for him at all.

And what then? Mordred's heart moaned and tossed. Aloud he cried, "Follow!"

And be ready to attack! was his secret command to himself. His hand flew to the comforting hilt of his sword, nestling against the dragon-hilted daggers at his belt. Let any man laugh or smirk, and the villain would be dead. Women too, he thought vengefully, why should he spare them?

They had come to the cloister leading to the King's apartments, where Arthur would be found. The torches along the walls were guttering in the low night wind, throwing out patterns of shadow and blood. For a second he thought of Guenevere's world-without-end gaze, and the anguished pity in her eyes when the Siege Perilous had hurled him to the ground. He longed to lay his hurt in her soft lap, to crawl into her arms, feel her sweetness around him, have her salve his deadly injuries.

Guenevere? A mocking inner voice awoke inside him and laughed. She did not pity you, Mordred.

He winced at the lash of contempt on his raw wound. She did. I know she did.

The spirit of Morgan writhed contemptuously round his head. You are fooling yourself, came the cawing laugh again. Guenevere cares for no one but herself.

Mordred shook his head like a dog. She cares for Arthur.

And Arthur is your enemy. He knew the Siege Perilous was not meant for you.

No! No! It cannot be. Mad anger spiked Mordred's heart, only to yield to sudden waves of fear. Had Arthur been playing with him all along?

Oh yes. He never loved you. So you must fight on—revenge—punish him—make him pay—

No!

Yesssss—Arthur is your enemy—

No—

With his knights on his heels, Mordred paced onward down the halls of night, possessed by the fate of men, driven by the voice of his mother echoing inside his head.

PENDRAGON.

Merlin closed his eyes and let the high ethereal chant from the cradle of his dreams wind itself in and out of his Otherworldly ears. First Mauther and then Gawther, then Deither and old Gwithin, High Kings of Pendragon all the way back in time to the days of the Old Ones, when the lords of Pendragon were half men, half Gods. Nowadays the title belonged to Uther, then Arthur, then Mordred—Mordred, it had to be, there was no child else—

"Merlin!"

Arthur was leaning forward urgently in his chair. The finery he had worn for Mordred's knight-making sat sadly on him now. "Tell me what it all means."

"What it all means?"

Merlin brought the tips of his finger to his lips. Restlessly he prowled away, tugging on the ends of his long hair. His heavy, storm-colored gown swept around his feet as he paced, and his yew wand dangled from his hand with a low, unhappy whine.

It was beyond him to admit he did not know. He was a Lord of Light, a spirit of the All-Being, one who guided souls and settled destinies as easily as others read the stones by the wayside, or cast the runes. He had brought Pendragon from the mists of dawn to its present power and glory, he had made Arthur High King of this golden land. He was a Druid of the ninth circle, at one with the eagle and the sightless mole. His chest swelled. *I am alive, I once was dead, I am the rock, I am the tree,* he called into the void. *I am Merlin! Why do I not know?*

His eyelids flickered, and the flame in his eyes flared blood-red. "The Grail child was destined to come," he said brusquely. "He took the Siege Perilous, and through him the prophecy was fulfilled. We may not question that."

Arthur brought his great bulk restlessly to his feet. "And the Quest— that too was fated, no? For the glory of Christ?"

Merlin lifted one skinny shoulder in a scornful shrug. "There are many more Gods in this kingdom than the God from the East." He gave a sudden cackle. "Not forgetting the first and greatest, Magna Mater, the Mother of them all."

Arthur groaned. "For Pendragon, then? Surely the Quest will renew the Table, and do us a mighty good?"

"Arthur, you forget." Merlin's harsh laughter cracked his wizened cheeks. "The strength of Pendragon does not lie in the Round Table. In truth, the Table was never ours at all. Oh, we've given it out that it was Uther's once, but remember the Great Ones themselves gave it to the Summer Country and its Queens. The Table belongs to Camelot and Guenevere. The Grail of the Christians can neither help nor harm it at all."

Arthur thrust a hand through his fading hair. "But we saw the Grail, before it vanished away—"

Merlin gave a loud, derisive snort. "Flashing lights, tinted shadows, shapes in smoke!"

Arthur turned pale. "What do you mean?"

The old enchanter favored Arthur with his hawklike glare. "We saw nothing, boy! Think on this." He leaned forward, and his voice took on a manic note. "What did we see? Nothing that advantaged Pendragon. Nothing to benefit you or your son. And he should be our prime concern now!"

"Mordred, yes—" Tears came to Arthur's eyes. "Guenevere says I should

THE CHILD OF THE HOLY GRAIL ❖ 121

have gone to him. But I can't undo what's happened, and I won't insult him with idle words. Besides—" His great body rocked and he turned his head away.

A sharp pain awoke behind Merlin's eyes. After so many lives, his own troubles were nothing to him, but Arthur's grief was more than he could bear. "Besides?" he probed with soft intent. "You fear he is not worthy of what you planned for him? Not fit to be your heir?"

Arthur raised his head. "Merlin, I—"

From the outer chamber came a sudden scream. "Don't touch me, you filthy wretch! The King my father will hang you if you deny entrance to his son!"

"Prince Mordred—"

"Off, away!"

The door flew open and Mordred came storming in. Crowding behind him in the doorway were Ozark and Vullian and twenty or so other young knights.

"Mordred!" cried Arthur, wide-eyed. He forced a smile. "We are glad to see you. Come in." His smile faded and he withered Mordred's followers with a glance. "Perhaps your knights will be good enough to wait outside."

Beware, Mordred, beware—

Mordred caught his breath. He did not need the voice to tell him what to do. At the sight of Arthur, all the old loving-kindness had risen up to embrace him, as it always did. But now he knew that he could trust no man.

"Indeed, sire," he cried brightly, dismissing his men. "Forgive this unseemly intrusion." He bowed to Merlin and fell gracefully to one knee. "A boon, my lord," he proclaimed. "Grant me leave to go forth on this Quest."

"What?" Arthur blanched. He drew a ragged breath. "No. Do not ask—it is not possible."

"But my lord—" Fixing his eyes on Arthur, Mordred put all he had into his plea. "All the knights are riding out. If I stay behind, I shall be shamed, even more than I already have been today." To his horror he felt hot tears rising to his eyes. "You have knighted me," he said, strengthening his voice. "Let me prove my sword."

"I have said no."

But if Mordred heard the rising anger in Arthur's voice, he did not care. "Sire, I can defeat the boy Galahad and achieve the Grail!" he burst out. "And win honor for myself that I sorely need." He was weeping openly now.

"The Gods know how I need it, no man more!" He took a step toward Arthur and threw himself onto his knees. "I beg you, Father! Do not deny me now!"

Arthur stood his ground, angry and remote. "Sir, I do. Now let me hear no more!"

The voice he dreaded stirred in Mordred's head: *And you swore you would never beg—?*

Mordred leaped to his feet. "Why?" he screamed. "Why do you treat me so?"

Arthur drew himself up. "Mordred, beware!"

But Mordred was deaf. "You forbid me to go?" he howled, beside himself. "If you call yourself a man, be ready to defend your good name in the field! Or shall I tell the world that you hold me back only because you're too old, finished, and afraid to go?" The next second, his hand was on his hilt, and the shining blade halfway out of its sheath. "I challenge you—to the death!"

To the death? Death of me if Pendragon dies—

Merlin felt his heart tearing out of his breast. He lurched forward in terror and tried to throw himself between Arthur and Mordred's sword.

"Hear me, both of you!" he cried. Sweating, he knew that his effort had been in vain. His outstretched arm would not obey his will, and the rings on his fingers seemed too heavy for his papery hands.

But Arthur had bounded forward like a great bear. In one powerful move he knocked Mordred's sword from his hand, then sent the young knight flying to the floor.

Panting, he surveyed his handiwork. "If you want my forgiveness, cub, on your knees and beg for it!" he growled. "No man defies Arthur Pendragon and lives!"

Dazed and reeling, Mordred scrambled to his knees. Abjectly he knelt for forgiveness, bowing his handsome head. Muttered apologies and broken professions of remorse poured from his lips. Listening to the voice full of tears, Merlin could almost persuade himself that Mordred was making his peace. But when the young knight looked up, his eyes were pits of ink.

No, worse—pinpoints of shining black, like the moon at midnight on the tip of a murderer's blade. Merlin gasped. He knew those eyes. Where had he seen them last?

Today—

Only hours ago, here in the Great Hall—

A spasm shook Merlin's frame. As if through a veil he saw again young Galahad and King Pelles, and behind them the old woman, Dame Brisein. Her head was low, her crooked body stooped and immobile, frozen in submission to the scene. Only her eyes were alive, leaping black points of fire, wriggling like maggots as she glanced to and fro.

Black eyes—long face—and that mouth—

Howling from the depths of his gut, Merlin groped madly at the veil blinding his sight. Where the old woman's face had been a moment before, there was nothing but vacancy. The black garments were hollow, held up by nothing but air. There was a rushing wind, and for a moment, time congealed. A second later, the tall headdress, shawl, black gown, and underskirts crumpled to the floor.

The eyes—the eyes—

Mordred's or Brisein's?

The blackness in Mordred's eyes sucked the life from Merlin's heart. With a gasp of horror he felt again the stabbing in his thumbs, the old sign of evil, worse than ever now. The agony could hardly be contained. His whole hands filled and swelled with a searing pain.

"So, sir?" Arthur demanded roughly.

Mordred found some tears. "Forgive me, Father, I am yours," he wept, dropping his head.

"So!" A glimmer of warmth lit Arthur's ravaged face. "Come then, my son." He drew Mordred to his feet, then folded him in a bear hug that almost knocked the younger man off his feet again.

"Arthur—"

Merlin reached out for Arthur. As he moved, the pain in his hands shot up his arms and exploded in his brain.

"So, Mordred, no more of this, eh?" cried Arthur in a hearty voice. "And do not fear to live with shame, my son. There is a world for you larger than this single Quest. Leave that pursuit to the child who was called to the Grail. I have a path for you to tread that will eclipse all the Kings of the Britons before your time."

Mordred looked up wonderingly. "What is there but the Grail?"

Arthur let out a triumphant bray of laughter at the look on Mordred's face. "Why, a mighty empire of our own! Think upon this, my son. Rome was only a single city when her armies reached out to conquer the whole world. We are an island of many kingdoms, all united now, with warriors as good as any the Romans had. May we not retrace their retreating footsteps and build our own empire even as far as Italy and beyond?" He clapped Mordred's shoulder encouragingly. "Leave it to me, I have long had this in mind. You shall not want for honor and action, mark my words."

"Thank you, Father," said Mordred submissively.

"Arth—" Merlin tried again.

But Arthur was escorting Mordred lovingly to the door. "Go and rest, my son. Tomorrow we will hunt, and everything shall be as it was before. We shall make no mention of this to a soul, not even to the Queen. Indeed we shall feast her in the Great Hall more joyfully than before."

Fool, Arthur! Fool! And thrice fool!

Merlin's head was screaming, though his tongue was dead. He could feel the storm within him raging like mountain clouds in jagged peaks of blood-red and blue-black. His felt his mind splitting, and his coronet slipped from his head, releasing the heavy locks of close-curled hair. He clutched at the chain of tourmalines round his neck, and his long carved wand tumbled weeping to the ground.

"Arthur," he said clearly, "beware Mordred, for he is no longer your son. I can feel his black fury of betrayal, and I can feel another too inside his skin, and one I know. One we both know. Morgan has come for her son, and has made herself a lodging in his heart. He is your enemy now, because she hates you, and he is hers, body and soul. Beware, Arthur, beware."

Swaying, the old enchanter considered his words. He was pleased with the speech, except that he knew it had not escaped his mouth. A great chasm had opened between his mind and his tongue. His left arm, his whole side were silent too. Soon, soon, the silence would take over his whole body, and he would sleep forevermore.

But the eyes—he could still see the eyes—

Morgan's eyes.

He gasped with dull amusement, though he knew he made no sound. All his work to be undone by a woman's stronger power? A power darker and more ancient than he had ever known? Was this how the world ended for a Lord of Light, a slow slide into unmoving, then unknowing, and thence to unbeing itself?

"Arthur," he tried one final time. He could think of no better way to take his leave of the light than by saying the name he had loved most in the world. *ArthurArthurArthur* rolled with relish round his mind.

Perhaps Arthur heard it, for he turned back into the room. He was just in time to see Merlin mouth his name lovingly, close his tired eyes, and slump smiling to the floor.

"Merlin!"

Screaming, Arthur leaped forward to catch the old man. Caught off-balance and straining to hold him up, he took the dead weight of Merlin on one outstretched leg. At once he felt the old wound in his groin reopen and the muscles tear like tissue from the bone. Still supporting Merlin, he fell in agony to the ground. "Give me some help here!" he howled to the servants outside. "And fetch the Queen—run for the Queen!"

CHAPTER 19

*G*oddess, *Mother, bring my love to me!*

Guenevere came to herself with a shuddering start. Brooding in the window, watching the night descend and the troubled stars weep their way down the sky, she had lost track of time. How long had passed since she had sent Ina scudding out of the door with the frantic command, "Find him, Ina, bring him to me *now*"? Long enough, perhaps even too long. Lancelot could be here at any time.

She crossed stiffly to the table by the wall, where she used to watch her mother enhancing her flowerlike beauty in the days when she herself was still a little girl. The bright bottles of blown glass from the East glowed red and blue and gold, and a glimmer of their warmth crept into her heart. Hurriedly she dabbed at her wrists and temples with rose water, and bathed her swollen eyes. In a sandalwood box she found a salve for her blistered hands. She tried some color on her cheeks, then in a passion of disgust scrubbed it off again. Without Ina's skillful touch, the soft peach and carnation were too garish for her pallid skin, and only emphasized the purple shadows under her eyes. After one long last look in the mirror, she stood up and moved away. When he came, Lancelot would have to take her as she was.

If he comes, ran bitterly through her mind. She gave a sardonic laugh. *Perhaps he won't.* Ina had been gone for a long time; she should have found him by now. But a man caught out by an old flame and a long lost son had good reason to avoid a woman who had thought he was true. *Perhaps he's gone to her, and he's with her now, making love to her in her bed.* She grinned madly. Well, so be it. She knew where she stood.

And she stood in danger now; they all did. Whatever had possessed Merlin to bring Galahad to court, the damage had been done. Sorrow came down upon her like a cloud. The Round Table was shattered and all its knights dispersed. The golden dream they had shared was destroyed. And unless she could save it, Camelot itself might soon be no more.

And she would have to do it alone, with only Lancelot to help—if he was still her knight. For Arthur was not well, she saw that now. Had his old battle wound ever truly healed? Certainly it was threatening him again. *He is sick in his soul too,* came to her with equal certainty. *He has placed his life and his hopes in Mordred's hands, and the burden is too much for a young man to bear.*

Especially now that Mordred had failed to take the Siege. Now Galahad was the hero of the hour. If the boy-knight achieved the Grail as well, and came back in triumph to Arthur's court, Mordred's shame would be complete.

Yes, Mordred will have to be watched. She laughed again, a dry mirthless sound. *And the Christians too. You are a witch to them, as you always were. And you know what Christians love to do with a witch.*

She stood in the oriel window, looking down on the world below. From the Queen's tower all Camelot's courtyards and arched walkways, sturdy battlements, stables, and spires lay spread out in the shining gloom. Suddenly she spied a tall, knightly figure in the dark, slipping through a distant cloister many feet below. Like the hunched female figure who led him through the night, he was muffled from head to foot. *Lancelot!* Or was it? She could not be sure. But the thought was enough to bring tears to her eyes. *Goddess, Mother, bring my love to me!*

She hastened back to the dressing table and caught up a pot of patchouli, her long-loved perfume from the distant East. Its haunting, musky fragrance was the very scent of the love between them—surely he would remember the long woodland afternoons lying among the bluebells, and the all-too-short nights of breathless bliss? Her fingers trembled as she lightly touched the balmy paste into the hollows of her neck and arms, and between her breasts. *Do you remember, love?*

Suddenly she heard feet at the bottom of the stair.

Already? She started toward the door.

Come in, my love, she opened her mouth to say. Then a loud and fearful shouting broke though her dreams.

"Majesty, it's the King! He's lying injured in his chamber calling for you, and Lord Merlin's dead!"

"We're here."

Lancelot could scarcely hear the low voice breathing through the dark till the whisper came again: "It's the Queen's chamber, sir."

Ahead of him he could just make out the maid's huddled shape in the gloom. "Thank you, Ina," he said.

Goddess, Mother, bring me to my love—

Suppressing a groan of relief, Lancelot offered a blessing from the depths of his overcharged heart. He had hardly dared to hope they could get here unseen. The whole palace was still buzzing from cellar to battlements with the events of the day, and the chances of slipping undetected past guards and servants had seemed remote, even impossible. How Ina had done it he would never know.

And how would he leave again when the tryst was done? The maid had led him by such a roundabout route that he did not know where he was. The darkness was so deep that without a lantern, he could not see a hand in front of his face. A second later he let the fear fall from his mind. Ina would lead him back the same way they had come. The maid was of Otherworldly stock; she could see in the dark. Of course she was at home in the midnight passages of Camelot.

"This way, my lord," came the whispered voice again.

A latch clicked, and the door opened silently on a pitch-black room. The maid's shape in the doorway glimmered through the dark. "Remember my lady said no words, sir," she breathed in his ear. "The court is full, and even walls have ears."

Lancelot nodded. "If you say so." Privately he knew this could not be the last word. Sooner or later, they would have to speak. Guenevere had to believe him, and accept that he was true. But just to touch her, to be with her, his burdened soul would accept anything now. Exhausted and distracted, he had only one thought in his head: *If I can see my lady, hold her again, I can prove to her that she is my world without end.*

Guenevere—

And these young knights had raced off on the Quest? He wanted to laugh. Only a virgin youth like Galahad could prize a gold cup above a woman's love. Guenevere was his quest, as she had been from the first. Only in the circle of the Goddess could a man find himself.

Lose himself.

Find Guenevere.

He was stumbling with fatigue. But his eyes, his arms, his loins were hungry for her now.

He felt a tug on his sleeve, and a light push.

"In you go, sir."

The door closed behind him. He stood in a darkness so deep that he might have been underground. The air was thick with chamber fragrance, and for a second he could hardly breathe. A sudden sharp sense of danger came to him, and involuntarily his hand flew to his sword. Then a series of little lights danced before his eyes, and he saw flashes of fire. He pressed a trembling hand to his aching lids. Gods above, he was more tired than he thought. He could only thank the Great Ones that his desire for Guenevere was so strong.

He took a careful step forward, breathing more easily. She could well have fallen asleep, he should try to wake her in the gentlest way. But his heart was thudding so loudly she must hear it now. And with every breath he took, his senses swam.

He would know the fragrance anywhere, Guenevere's favorite, juniper and pine. But did she always perfume her chamber so heavily? For a second he thought he could smell civet, the rank, sour smell of a cat. But he knew his senses must be deceiving him.

The darkness was shimmering, and tiny flames waved before his eyes. For a second time the same cold thought descended, every man's most lonely fear. He was so exhausted, would he fail tonight, fail Guenevere and himself?

The air moved beside him, and a soft finger brushed his lips. He almost screamed with fear. "My lady?" he choked.

"Hush."

Her voice was so low that, like her presence, it hardly disturbed the blackness all around. But the throbbing in his head intensified. A great weakness came over him, and he did not know where he was. To lie down now— if only he could lie down—

As if in answer, he felt himself being led toward the bed. Something between a sob and a laugh rose in his throat: "Oh, my love—"

"No words."

A woman's fingers, soft and strong, worked on his sword belt, then turned to his clothes. He felt himself released from his tunic and shirt, and pushed down on the bed. Now he was free of his boots and breeches, stretched out naked on the welcoming sheets. There came a rustling in the darkness as a shift slipped to the floor. Years of memory threw up the image of Guenevere disrobing for love, her full body emerging from her gown as a lily flourished free of its green sheath. Groaning, he felt his flesh stirring and growing strong.

Her body was next to his, naked on the bed. He reached out for her, words of grief and regret falling from his lips. "Lady, I—"

"Hussssssssssssshhhhhhhhh—"

She pressed her body against him, and silenced him with a kiss. Her lips were hungry and yet apprehensive too, and for a second his heart quailed: what is this? Then it came to him that she too had passed a day of torment, hours of anger and fear. Yet in spite of it all she had sent for him, she loved him still. The knowledge flooded through him that she had forgiven him, that she was renewing their love and trust with this deep kiss. In that precious knowledge he would have laid down his life and welcomed death. Yet he had never felt more intensely alive. Almost maddened with joy and thankfulness, he folded her in his arms and kissed her till he was drunk on her lips, drowning in her love.

It seemed to him that the fragrance in the chamber was stronger than ever, almost suffocating now. His hand found her breast, and the nipple was waiting for him, longer and stronger than ever before, quivering for his touch. Roughly and tenderly he stroked the soft skin of her breasts, his desire for her growing and swelling with the hopeless weight of his love. His own body was lost in sensation, all trace of the outside world drifting from his mind. He coaxed and caressed her soft places till her grasp on him tightened, and her fractured breath was coming in soft hissing moans. On the brink of losing control, he took her fiercely, and abandoned himself to her. She crushed him in her arms, opened her body to him, and drew him in. Riding the waves of darkness, his senses swooned and he knew no more.

CHAPTER 20

From the castle, the road wound downhill through the town. Soon the three riders were in the forest that encircled Camelot, sheltering the ancient citadel of Queens since time was born. Overhead the huge mossy oaks and stands of primeval yew wove their branches together to form a dense canopy. Under lofty pines and straight beeches stretching their slender limbs up to the skies, they rode through a living green cathedral roofed with stars. In every thicket and clearing, the fragrant incense of the living earth wrapped them all around. The rich leaf-mold underfoot was still warm and breathing from the kiss of the sun. The soft, dry, whispering leaves beneath the trees would make a welcome bed for their weary heads later on.

Too welcoming, perhaps. Bors felt for his sword, and looked sharply all around. Over the years, the soft loam of this woodland must have been the last resting place of many a mother's son who'd had no desire to lay his head down here. Madmen, outlaws, villains, and landless men roamed these hidden places, as all men knew, and preyed on passing travelers without fear. No knight in his right mind would have taken this route after dark. But Galahad had chosen this way, and would not be denied.

And mortals were not the only dwellers in these groves. For a while now Bors had been catching slight movements out of the corner of his eye, and high, bell-like laughter far away. Will-o'-the-wisps flitted through the distant trees, glimmering lights that were here, and there, and then lost to view. Once he saw a bonfire flaring up through the dark in a blaze of red and gold, and shadowy figures dancing in a ring, but when he looked again, they were gone. Well, the woodland belonged to the Fair Ones, every man knew that. And nights like these were when the Fair Ones walked.

Look after Galahad—

Lancelot's voice came back to Bors with a start. He raised his voice. "We should think of stopping soon," he called. "It's not safe to ride all night."

Galahad favored him with a radiant smile. "God will protect us."

Bors stared. "D'you mean we should go on?"

Galahad looked back at him serenely. "To the end of the road."

"Well and good, cousin." Lionel gave an uncomfortable laugh. "But we have to rest."

"Yes, of course." Galahad was suddenly contrite. "Forgive me—I was not thinking of your needs. All my life I have thought of nothing but the Grail."

"The Grail, yes—" Bors looked at Galahad and took a breath. "Where will it be found? Where are we making for?"

"Where but the East?"

The East—

Bors could hear Lionel's thoughts turning as fast as his own. That meant sailing over the Narrow Sea to France, or else to their own kingdom of Benoic, then riding down through Gaul to Italy to take another ship across the Middle Sea. Or else there was the long route overland in the midst of savage tribes, to take ship again where the Saracen lands began. Gods above, it would take a year, two years—

"The East," repeated Galahad reverently. Again the boy's certainty shone like a beacon in the night. His fair young face was alight with hope and desire.

"The Holy Land," he breathed, his pallor ebbing to an unearthly glow. "The cradle and grave of Our Lord, where sweet Jesus died for our sins." He nodded fervently. "We were shown the Grail to inspire us to this pilgrimage. The Grail is awaiting us in its eternal home."

There was a low murmuring from the forest, then the echo of a hiss. A hostile breeze picked up and pecked at them through the trees. From high in the branches overhead, round eyes scrutinized the speaker with an unblinking glare.

A deep foreboding settled on Bors' soul. "And if we do not find it?"

Galahad's smile now outshone the stars. "Have no fear, dear cousin. We shall."

THE SERVANT COULD hardly speak for haste and fear. "My lady, come to the King! He's had a fall, he sent for you—"

Guenevere leaped to her feet. "Where is he?"

"This way, Your Majesty!"

"Hurry, lady!"

"In here, my lady—the King's here, and Lord Merlin's dead—"

Guenevere flew through the clamoring mob on wings of fear. The tight knot of servants in the center of the chamber dissolved as she approached, and there lay Arthur, stretched out on the floor. One leg was drawn up under him, the other thrown wide. His eyes were closed, and he was deathly pale.

Beside him sprawled the body of Merlin lying on its side, one withered cheek pressed against the cold flagstones, one eye closed, the other set in a round, glazed stare like the yolk of an egg. Kneeling over them both was Mordred, his hand reaching for the pulse in Arthur's throat. As she came in, there was something she did not recognize in the young man's gaze. But when she looked again, his face was the picture of sorrow and concern.

Mordred leaped to his feet. "The King—" he cried in distress, gesturing to the great unmoving figure at his feet.

"What happened?" In two steps, Guenevere was at Arthur's side.

Mordred was very pale. "I don't know. I had been with the King and Merlin, and all was well then. But as soon as I left, I heard the uproar and came rushing back."

"You've sent for the doctors?"

He shook his head, confused. "I did not know what to do."

Guenevere raised her hand. "Fetch my Druid healer to the King," she ordered in low, rapid tones. "Make Lord Merlin a bed on the sofa here, and call the King's physicians to see to him. And hurry! There's no time to waste."

They scrambled to obey. She dropped on one knee beside Arthur, took his hand, and stroked his tortured face. Her heart contracted to feel the chill of his skin.

"How are you?" she whispered in his ear.

He shook his head, in too much pain to speak.

"Is it your old wound?"

His clenched jaw and closed eyes answered yes.

"Can you bear to be moved?"

He squeezed her hand: Go ahead.

She got to her feet. Some of Arthur's most trusted servants were crowding round in silence, frantic to help. She nodded to five or six of them. "Carry the King to his chamber, and lay him on his bed."

She hurried ahead of them to the inner room. The great bed of state loomed up against the wall opposite the door, its billowing hangings and red silk canopy like a ship in full sail. After her came the menservants, handling Arthur's massive body as tenderly as a babe's. Mordred followed, aiding and supervising every careful move. But when they laid Arthur down, he was paler than ever, gray against the sheets. Beads of dew stood out on his knotted forehead, gleaming unnaturally in the candlelight.

She took his hand again and leaned over the bed. "Arthur, I'm just going to see that they're taking care of Merlin—I'll be straight back."

"He's dead, Guenevere. Merlin's dead—"

His voice was like a death rattle, thin and hoarse. From him came a faint, fine stench of decay.

"Don't try to talk, Arthur!" she cried in alarm. "We've sent for the doctor, and Mordred will stay with you till then."

Again a faint pressure on her hand was the only reply. She hastened back to the antechamber, where Merlin had been laid upon a couch. With his garments straightened and his wand restored to his hand, he looked more like the Merlin of old, the ancient man of might. But while one side of his face was fixed in the expression of angry contempt she knew so well, the other hung like a door on a broken hinge. One eye, one cheek, one side of his mouth gaped slack, as if the Gods had cut his facial strings.

A group of anxious onlookers surrounded the couch.

"He was touched!" moaned the voice of an old retainer from the back. "The Dark Lord came from the Underworld and marked him out for death!"

"He's dead, Lord Merlin's dead!" cried another.

Guenevere looked around. "No ill words here!" she cried. "Unless you have reason to be here, leave the room."

Reluctantly they complied. Guenevere turned back to Merlin with a heavy heart. No wonder Arthur's old wound had broken out, when his dearest friend had been struck down so grievously and died in his arms. Merlin had been Arthur's counselor, confidant, and guide. The old man had made Arthur King, and had been the nearest thing to a father he had ever known. Arthur would never recover from this grievous loss.

Beside the couch two or three of the attendants were on their knees, weeping and praying for Merlin's soul. Another placed a candle beside his head. The flame danced and flickered in the cavern of Merlin's one open eye till it looked as if the old man were still alive, grinning and mocking as he always did. Moved beyond words, Guenevere reached out to close the eyelid in the last office for the dead.

But the leathery skin refused to yield to her touch. Instead the cold eye-

lid jumped and twitched against her fingers like a living thing. With a thrill
of recoil, she pulled away, and stared at the stricken, split face with new eyes.
Merlin's one eye stared back, alive with the same harsh, ironical glint it always
had.

"Here!" she hailed a manservant, "loosen his collar, let me feel his neck!"
The man obeyed. The skin of Merlin's throat was as clammy as a toad's, and
his withered dewlaps hung down cold beneath his chin. But still she detected
a heartbeat—a faint pulse.

Curse you, Merlin!

She could have laughed aloud. *Alive after all? Trickster to the last! If you have
brought on Arthur's death with this charade, I'll finish you off myself!*

"Majesty?"

Behind her stood a broad-shouldered man of middle height, robed in
white, with the sacred mark shining between his brows. It was her Druid
healer, a former warrior now deeply versed in the ways of Gods and men.

Her heart heaved with relief.

"Greetings, sir," she breathed. She turned to the attendants around
Merlin. "Bathe Lord Merlin's forehead, stroke his temples, and chafe his
wrists," she directed them. "And wrap him in blankets, keep his body warm."

The Druid nodded, eyeing Merlin keenly. "That is the way to keep him
alive," he conceded. He gestured to the inner salon. "But the King—?"

"This way, sir."

Inside the chamber, Mordred was leaning over Arthur's prostrate form,
rubbing his hand and whispering in his ear. As the Druid approached,
Mordred moved back from the bed. Guenevere saw the healer touch Arthur's
wrist and then his head, and the years fell away. She had stood by this bed,
by this same sturdy man, how long ago, when Arthur first took this blow?
Mesmerized, she watched the newcomer throw back the sheets, part Arthur's
clothing, and reveal his wound.

It was worse than she had dared to think. At the top of Arthur's leg, per-
ilously near the organ of generation, black blood oozed from an empurpled
wound. A deep gash had reopened in the angle of his thigh. To one side,
Arthur's sex curled pink and defenseless, as if shrinking away from the pain.
The Druid touched the flesh around the scar, and Arthur threw his arm
across his eyes.

Part of Arthur's shirt had dried across the wound. The Druid ripped it
off. A fresh line of blood broke out along the edges of the gash.

"Gods above!" Gagging, Mordred hurried from the room.

The healer pushed Arthur's shirt back to his waist. His stubby hands dug and probed. "How long since the King suffered this wound?"

Guenevere steadied her voice. "Ten years, fifteen—?"

"A sword slash right between the legs, was it not?" His fierce blue eyes delved into her soul. "And we feared for his manhood then?"

She swallowed. "Yes."

More digging and exploring. "And we were wrong?"

"Indeed, yes." She gave a pallid smile. "Thank the Gods, the King was restored to himself again. We—we were able to resume our married life."

The Druid was suddenly still. "But latterly—?"

"Oh, sir—"

Arthur, Arthur, her wounded soul cried out, *how long since you took me in our bed? Or even held me in your arms and called me 'my love'? How long since I wanted or welcomed your loving touch? In this chamber, here in this bed, we once bestrode the summer earth and played among the stars. Here we brought to life our beloved Amir, who died. Here we were heaven and earth, you were my all in all—*

"—latterly, we were saying, my lady?"

She came to herself with a start. "Forgive me, sir." She composed herself to reply. "These days the King has kept much to himself. And I—I am not as young as I was."

He nodded his head, though his eyes quested on. "It comes to us all." Then he turned again to his work, his blunt finger jabbing at the oozing wound. "I do not like the blackness of this blood. The King has been suffering with this for many moons. We shall have hard days before he can be as he was."

Guenevere put her heart into her words. "Whatever it takes, I beg you, make the King whole."

MERLIN—

What of him now?

In the antechamber, half a dozen venerable heads were bent over Merlin's recumbent form. As Guenevere entered from the inner chamber, the earnest dispute was reaching a fever pitch. One younger man was ranged against the rest.

"Signs of life—"

"Nonsense—he has suffered the stroke of the Gods—"

"A definite pulse—"

"He's dead, I tell you. Dead!"

"The Gods decide that, not we."

The urgent voices fell silent as Guenevere came in. The gray and white heads bowed in unison. Only the younger doctor remained upright. "Your Majesty—"

"So, the Lord Merlin, sirs—?" Her voice was unnaturally calm. "What is your view?"

A flurry of aged heads came together again. Then the leader stepped forward, his hands in his sleeves. "Lord Merlin is dead. We are all agreed."

"All?"

Hot-eyed, the young doctor thrust forward a jutting chin. "I believe I detected a fleeting sign of life."

"I thank you, sirs," Guenevere said. "I know now where I must take him—where he must go."

THE HOURS CREPT BY as she took care of the two sick men. By the end, her body, her blood were as weak as the waning stars. She wanted to cry, to die, to creep into a hole. But she had done all she could. Arthur's wound had been dressed with the best of healing salves, and tomorrow it would be sutured again, to repair the damage he had done. The Druid physician was on guard beside Arthur's bed, and the patient was sleeping peacefully after the healer's draughts. Merlin too was at rest, warmly wrapped up and attended at every point. Tomorrow, when Arthur had safely undergone the ordeal of needle and knife, she would take Merlin to the place where he might be healed. The boat had been ordered, and the way prepared.

But tonight—

Tonight, or what remained of it, was hers—and Lancelot's.

Oh my love—

Exhausted to the point of collapse, she left the King's apartments with her guard and made her way back to the private quarters of the Queen. One thought obsessed her now.

Lancelot—

This time, she knew he would not fail. Earlier in the day, when he had lost faith and left, he did not know that she had been longing for him too, although her duty had forced her to be with the King. But now that Ina had reached him, he would know that she loved him still. Loved and hated, but had to see him, be with him, hold him again.

He will be there.

And there will be a fire, lighted candles, a great bed, and warm honeyed wine—

At every corner she met signs of life. Few people were sleeping in Camelot tonight. Was it wise, was it safe to see Lancelot now? She thought of the risk she was taking, and thrust it away. Somehow, she knew, Ina would have brought him to her. Greeting the guards on the door, she entered in.

Lancelot, my love—

Inside, the Queen's apartments were like a midnight graveyard, cold and bleak. There were no lights, no fire. The whole apartment breathed the dark night of the soul. In the inner chamber, Ina was sitting beside a long-dead fire. The maid raised a gray face as Guenevere hastened in. "He's not here, lady."

"Where is he?"

Ina shook her head. "I couldn't find him anywhere. I've searched the castle, and there's only one place he can be." She got stiffly to her feet. "He must be with her. The princess from Corbenic."

CHAPTER 21

Fools!

Fools!

All fools!

Locked in his half-working body, Merlin took stock of his state. Warm, safe, and alive—good, good—and wrapped in sheepskins, laid out on a sofa in the King's antechamber, attended by the most devoted care—all well enough. In the next room, he knew, Arthur slept safely in the care of his Druid, a gifted healer Merlin himself would have called to Arthur's side. Merlin pondered on. Soon he would put it into the minds of those around him to move him next door. Then he would be with his Arthur, his heart's darling boy.

At least until Guenevere came back.

Guenevere, yes.

One half of Merlin's face twitched in its sardonic grin. That he owed his salvation to Guenevere, his bitterest foe—it was enough to make a dead man laugh. Yet left to themselves, those clodpoll doctors would have had him in his grave by now. And what a fine fate that would be!

He cackled inwardly. So Guenevere had saved him from being buried alive? No matter, it was too late for him to warm to her now. After all these years of wrestling for Arthur's soul, he would not rest until Pendragon was secure.

Pendragon.

His purpose.

His quest.

One that bore no relation to the madness seizing Camelot.

Merlin laughed to himself again, but a bitter tear welled up in his one open eye. The Quest would destroy the Round Table, there was no doubt of that. When the Table itself shattered and split in two, it was only an echo of what Galahad had already done.

Galahad?

The cold hand of fear gripped Merlin's gut. Could he rightly say that

Galahad was the cause? Or had he done it himself? Had his bringing Galahad to Camelot been the fatal madness he now blamed others for? He struggled violently to make sense of what he knew.

The first sign was the pricking of his thumbs. He was warned then to beware the coming of a child. When he'd met Galahad, his thumbs had pricked again. Yet he had been so sure that he could handle the boy! He had seen no evil in the old king and his troop. On the contrary, they had played into his hand. Yet when he had come to play this hand, all had been lost.

"Why?" he tormented himself. "What did I miss?"

Once when he'd traveled in the East he had met a sage so ancient that his voice was a husk and his flesh no more than grass. His sightless eyes as milky as blown glass, the seer had favored him with one saying before lapsing into a trance.

"When the wise man points at the moon," the old man had breathed, "the fool looks at the finger." Merlin groaned. Had he watched the finger and missed the moon?

"Yes, yes!" he moaned in an ecstasy of self-disgust. As pleased with himself as any simpleton, he had quite mistaken Galahad; he had been entirely wrong.

And Mordred—his soul slipped deeper into darkness with an anguish greater than all. When Mordred rebelled against Arthur, Arthur had risen to the challenge like a father and a king. He had put Mordred firmly in his place, the two of them had been reconciled, and that should have been a cause for unbridled joy. Yet after that he had had the worst warning of them all. This time when his thumbs had exploded, his brain had too.

He could not bear to think what this might mean. Was Mordred the thing of darkness after all? Was he the child who would bring Arthur down? And had he, Merlin the Bard, striving to save Pendragon, hastened the doom of the whole house?

"Grief upon me!" he wailed in the caverns of his mind. With a savage detachment, he noted that he could not raise his fists to beat his head. Would the Gods release him from this entombment in his body over time? Or was this his long farewell, trapped in a coffin of flesh?

Either way, the Great Ones would choose.

Or—

Bolts of lightning coursed through his wounded brain. Or else this affliction was not from the Gods.

Who then? No man alive hated him enough to strike him down. All his enemies were dead, many moons ago.

No man—but a woman?

A woman, yes, he knew it, it had to be!

Yet what woman had he offended? the silent howl went on. No trusting virgin had lost her maidenhead to him. No widow cursed him for the death of her lord. He had killed no man for his own advantage—

A thunderclap invaded his being now. Not for his own advantage, but for Pendragon—

And no human woman had he offended, but one who walked both the stars and the earth.

A blinding light split him from the root to the head, and he saw what he had missed. And then he knew who had brought him to this place.

Morgan!

"Aaiii!" he screamed in the wilderness of his pain. Yet he had to make the leap. Fixing his eye on the candle beside his head, he sent his spirit spinning into the void. Like a hawk he soared up through the dancing stars till he was floating free. At last he came to rest above the astral plane, and there she was, as she had always been.

All he could see in the darkness were her blood-red eyes. She twisted her body sharply, and he was scalded by her scattered flakes of fire. Hungrily he drank in her strong savor, relishing her stench. How long had he loved her, this spirit woman of his? Loved her and hated her for all she had done?

"So, Merlin," she cried harshly, "have you taken farewell of the earth, have you slipped your mortal shell?"

And she laughed. And then he knew that she had contrived all this. It was she who had laid the chains on his earthly tongue, hung the dead weights on his chest, and cut the cords that connected his mind with his body to carry out his will. Would she release him from this thrall? Only when she wearied of the game. And that would be only when all her desires were fulfilled.

Whatever they were. Some of them he was sure he already knew. But her crucial new urges he had yet to find out. And that would mean tracking her scent like a fox.

"You," he said with soft certainty, "you were Dame Brisein."

"Yeesssssss!" Her rasping laugh echoed through the void. "Of course I used the old dullard's body, yes indeed. Half dead as she is, she never feels me come and go. And the old fool Sir Niamh at the knight-making, I used him too. I made him serve my turn."

Merlin nodded. Why was he surprised? She could always change her shape and appear as anything from a modest maiden to a horse-goddess with cartwheel eyes. But why?

"Why did you bring Galahad to Camelot? What was the trick with the Hallows? *Why?*"

"Come now, Merlin—"

With a shudder he felt her nails sink into his ear. Soon, soon she would claw him to the earth, mount him, and drive him to madness, terror, and delight. His flanks heaved, and he felt his withered loins begin to stir. Always, always she had been his pleasure and his bane.

"Why, Merlin?" Her breath scorched his neck. "Think, only think." The flash of her white teeth lit the farthest star. "Through Galahad I can strike at Guenevere, who always thought that Lancelot was true. By making the Hallows appear and disappear, I torment the Christians, a poor repayment for a childhood of suffering at their hands. But most of all, the Quest will destroy the Round Table, and break Arthur's heart. As he and his father broke mine, and my mother Igraine's." Her glee bubbled and hissed like a pot on the boil. "And you ask me why?"

"Will you ruin Arthur to bring about your revenge?"

"Yesssssssssssssssss!"

"But you love Arthur!"

"Our love will be even greater after death! Only there will we be together as I planned!"

Then he saw that she would spare nothing, not even herself. The sins of Uther were coming home at last. The golden dream of Pendragon was no more. The world was ending, and he must end so too. It was coming, he could feel it, it was here—

"Is it Mordred?" he cried in anguish as the darkness invaded his soul. "Is it all for him?"

"Mordred?" she spat. "He is nothing, nothing to me!"

"Morgan, he is your son!"

There was a scream like the sound of the living dead. "He is Arthur's too! And Arthur tried to kill him when he was born!"

Frantic, Merlin launched a final plea. "Only out of madness and fear, not from hatred of you. For ten years and more, he has loved Mordred as his own." He gathered his waning strength. "Mordred is the only Pendragon heir. He will inherit Arthur's name and throne."

"Pendragon?" Her anger flared. She fell on him, biting and tearing, slashing with talons and teeth. "Pendragon was the death of all my house! Uther Pendragon took my mother against her will. From a Pendragon rape your precious Arthur was born!"

Grief upon me, that I named the fatal thing! Merlin cried inwardly. But she heard every note.

"Yes, grief upon you, old fool!" she snarled. "Grief upon all of you! Pendragon will go down to the house of death!"

"Never!" he cried recklessly. "I can raise magic against you older than that of all Druidkind!"

"Dream weaver!" She throbbed with cruel mirth. "Soon you will be no more. The ancient race of Druids is passing away. And the power I have is the oldest on the earth."

He was lost, he knew it now. But madly he tried again. "And Mordred, your son? Would you destroy your own child to pull Arthur down?"

"*Yes!* And you too, Merlin, and you!"

She howled, she danced, she wove patterns in the air. Merlin felt his mind melting, dissolving like flakes of fire. Hold on! he shrieked to himself. But he knew she was sucking his soul out, sucking him dry.

He cracked a terrible laugh. She would not spare him this torture to the death. For he had raised the mist in which her father, Duke Gorlois, had died, he had brought Uther to her mother, Igraine. He had done these things, and here was the reckoning. Whatever she did with his body, he would not know. For she would kill him in the worst way that she knew, she would take his mind.

He could feel her talons now inside his brain. One by one her nails, dripping with his blood, picked out his thoughts and hopes and ate them alive. One by one she devoured his plans, his schemes, above all his golden dreams. Daintily she filleted the contents of his skull, till he knew he was hollow, a man without thought, a creature without meaning, purpose, or faith.

And what man would choose to live a life like that? was Merlin's last conscious thought. Already the chasm was gaping for him now. He was destined for the darkness, without hope of return. Yet still he was a Druid of the seventh seal, a Lord of Light and a Chosen Son. He had always known that this time would come. The last power was the power to embrace his fate. To go as a hero, not a coward, into the Beyond.

And he would not delay.

"Bless Arthur, all you stars!" he screeched. "And may the Great Ones guard and keep Pendragon for all time! Adieu!"

Weeping, cursing, and calling on his Gods, Merlin readied his soul, and leaped into the abyss.

CHAPTER 22

The first faint sensation of dawn fingered Lancelot's closed eyes. He felt the light at the window change from gray to pink, then gold, and a humble sense of wonder flooded his soul. How she had forgiven him, he would never know. But if Guenevere still loved him, all would yet be well.

He stretched out with a drowsy, unaccustomed luxury, relishing the aching in his weary limbs. The bed was wide, the sheets cool and lavendered, the chamber quiet, the peace of love profound. And he had passed a whole night here with Guenevere? In all the years he had loved her, how often was that?

Guenevere—

He wanted to seize her, to hug her in his arms, to shout his love aloud. But the slightest movement would break the mood of tremulous joy. Beside him he could feel her asleep lying on her back, her long legs stretching down to the end of the bed. Her full body lay at ease in blissful repose. A small smile of pain and love crossed his sleepy lips. Like all women of passion, she slumbered heavily when she had given her all, and taken her fill of bliss.

Soon he would open his eyes and embark on the day. I should leave, his soul mourned, for her safety and my own. I should have been gone by now; it is almost full dawn. But at least if she woke, they could take a true farewell. All the more, his heart plunged, now that he had to leave. If his young son led the Quest, he could not stay behind. But how could he tell her he must follow him?

The Quest—

She would loathe it, she would scream at him and shout. To her it would be the supreme betrayal, that he should choose the Christians over her. But he could not avoid it and still call his honor his own. He had to make her see that he did not seek the Grail, he did not for a moment believe the Christians' lies. But he could not abandon his son to adventure alone. He could not be shamed by the courage of a child. If Guenevere refused to accept that, then so be it. Goddess, Mother, he prayed behind closed lids, give me the strength to deal with her anger now.

He heard her breathing change, and his sad heart rejoiced. Wake up, my love. Wake up and play with me.

The gold had faded from the sky, and the day was gray. He opened his eyes and reached out and touched her hip. "My lady—oh my love—"

He turned a sleepy head to her morning gaze. But the eyes that met his were not Guenevere's. Pale and triumphing, they were chips of ice as foreign as the farthest ends of the earth. The face on the pillow was a stranger's, the tumbled hair not Guenevere's thick mane but as fine and blond as a child's—a stranger, and yet known from long ago, as the boy had been, the child of the Grail—

The next moment he leaped screaming from the bed. Scrabbling for his sword, he slashed wildly about him in terror, fighting the air. Then the demons and monsters faded and he was alone.

Alone but for the monster in the bed.

The woman who had stolen his essence once before, and had now come back to prey on him again.

Elaine of Corbenic.

The thought of Guenevere flashed through his mind like a knell, weeping and waiting for him all the night. She would never forgive him now. He had had one chance to win her forgiveness and had spent it in a new betrayal, far worse than the first.

Thanks to this—this—*thing.* He could not say her name. She sat up in the bed, clutching the sheets up to protect her breasts. Modest now, was she? After all that had happened last night? Rage flooded him. A virgin again, to be sure—until she came again in a new guise. A killing fervor possessed him from head to foot. He felt his sword cold and true in his hand, and advanced on the bed.

"No!"

As naked as a needle, she skipped out of the sheets and came toward him, her body like a corpse in the thin gray dawn. Her eyes were round with vainglory and a sense of power.

"All that I did, I did for love of you!" she shrilled, throwing herself at his feet. Her belly was soft and round, her breasts tender and full, her nipples engorged with his handling through the long night of love. He wanted to bruise her, to kick her, to beat her to death.

The next moment his heart turned to water at the sorrow of it all. Her father loved her, she had fixed her love on him, he loved Guenevere, and Guenevere loved in vain: all this love misplaced and doomed to miss its mark, an endless daisy chain of broken lives.

She saw the change in his eyes and misread the signs.

"Don't forget I am the mother of your son!" she shrilled in a fit of terror that matched his own. "If you kill me, Galahad will have revenge—"

He threw his sword to the farthest corner of the room. "I shall not kill you, madam," he said hoarsely. He could hardly speak. "But neither shall I see your face again."

"No!" Her pale eyes goggled and gaped with grief. "But my maid said— she promised me—"

He felt infinitely old. "Said what?"

She gulped like a beaten child. "Dame Brisein, my gentlewoman—she told me that if you came to me again, you would love me, and all would be well—"

"Ah, lady—"

He could almost have loved her then for her childlike trust, the abuse of her innocence betrayed. "She lied to you," he said.

"No!"

She reached up and flung her arms round his naked waist. Her touch was lizards and scorpions, and he threw her off. Wailing, she fell awkwardly to the floor. Averting his gaze, he scrambled into his clothes. By the time he had retrieved his sword, she was still weeping her heart out on the cold stone. Taking her by the arm, he led her back to the bed.

"Lie down and take comfort, madam," he said with forced calm. "Your gentlewoman will be here soon. May the Gods bring you safely back to Corbenic."

She shrugged off his hand. The weeping was louder, the abandon more pronounced. Reproach was written in every trembling line of her long back, heaving shoulders, and shuddering flanks. He nodded grimly. Grief was her destiny now.

"I will not say forgive me," he said heavily. "But take this from me, lady, as my last farewell. Whatever sorrow I have brought on you, be assured that my life lies in ruins now as well."

❖   ❖

IT WAS THE grimmest dawn of all her life. All night she had had no thought of going to bed. Side by side she and Ina had waited for the light, dozing and waking, locked in silence and dread. At last the first faint fingers of gray stroked the sky. Guenevere flexed her stiff body and sat up in her chair.

"He will be here soon," she muttered to herself. She straightened her back. She must not let him see how much she was hurt.

Ina got to her feet. "Yes indeed, madam!" she cried with false gaiety. "Let me get you ready for the day."

Ready, how? Guenevere pondered for a while. She had a gown of misty blue that he used to love. Ina read her thoughts, and produced it in a trice. *Is it too young for me?* passed between them without words. No, madam, was the promise in Ina's eyes. And she could see for herself that the soft woodland hue was a kindness to her skin, and lent some color to her empty eyes.

With it she wore a veil of gossamer like the mist weeping from the mountains when winter comes. And pearls for her neck and ears, pearl bracelets and rings, everywhere pearls. For pearls were the Mother's tears for love betrayed. She would always wear pearls now for the rest of her life.

The light was stronger now. Ina looked at her, her head on one side. "A little color, lady, for your face?"

"No."

"Madam, I beg—"

"No, Ina. Let him see me as I am."

"But you aren't yourself when you look as sad as this—"

In the end Guenevere succumbed, and allowed a trace of carnation on a face that she knew was otherwise like chalk. But anything more would be foolishness and false.

She thanked Ina, waving the maid away. "This is good enough." The savage truth crept up on her unaware. "He's only coming to say farewell, after all. No knight who has done what he has can expect anything else."

The same moment they heard the guard at the door. "Sir Lancelot for Her Majesty?"

"Admit him," Ina said.

He stood in the doorway, tall, tense, and aloof. Averting her gaze, the maid dropped a curtsy and whisked out.

Guenevere's eyes burned, seeing him as he stepped into the room. She hated him—how could he look so fine? So good and yet so bad at the same time, pale and ravaged in the dawn's watery light. He met her gaze, and for a second nothing had changed. Then she saw the traveling cloak on his arm, his leather tunic and thick boots: he was dressed for the road. So already he planned to leave her, whatever she said? A fury of grief overwhelmed her; she could hardly speak.

"You have lied and betrayed me, Lancelot," she forced out. "That woman was your lover in Corbenic, you took her to your bed."

He shook his head. His eyes were terrible. "My lady, hear me—"

But she could not stop. "That ridiculous tale about having a midnight dream—it was all true, the tryst at Corbenic, and every word you told me was false!"

He clenched his fists. "Madame, I did not—"

"Don't lie!"

"Lady, I never lied to you in my life!"

"You said nothing had happened between you and Elaine. But I've seen the proof. The living proof—your son!"

He tossed his head in pain. "Believe me, I never knew!"

She gave a cruel laugh. "Do you know who you were with last night?"

He caught his breath. "Last night I was deceived." His throat was raw with tears. "Ina came to me in the dark—"

"Not Ina!"

"—and brought me to your chamber—"

"Not mine, Lancelot!" she ground out between clenched teeth. "Gods above!" She beat her head in rage. "Last night the whole court was awake, after all that had gone on—would I choose a time like that to send for you?" She could not now admit to him that she had.

"I thought Ina knew the way to get past the guards!" he burst out. "I thought I was coming to you!"

"You thought she was me? After all these years, you couldn't tell us apart?" She was seized with a vicious mirth. "What are you saying? All cats are gray in the dark?"

He struggled to be calm. "Lady, I won't take all the blame on myself. Others are preying on us unaware. In Corbenic, the old woman drugged me with a drink. And I never consented to what took place last night."

"Oh, so? The peerless knight was a victim of an old woman's schemes?" she sneered, hating herself as much as she hated him.

He drove his fist into his palm. "I never offered her love! I never loved her. When she came to court, the princess was loathsome to me." His warm brown skin turned a dull shade of gray. "And when she brought out her proof, waving the bloody sheet before all the court—" He closed his eyes. "I beg you, madame, have pity on my shame!"

"Have pity on you?" Again she could feel the pain boiling up out of control. "You talk to me of shame, when I am the laughingstock of all the court! Haven't you heard the talk?" She let out her breath in savage mimicry. "'The Queen fancied she was Sir Lancelot's only love. And all along he had a little sweetheart tucked away, and a fine son too!'"

"Yet there's comfort in that, if you'd take it, madame," he cried furiously. "We should welcome anything that makes all men believe I'm only your knight. If it ever came out that I loved you forbiddenly—if anyone told the King—"

"Stop it!" she screamed. She could not bear to think of Arthur now.

Inexorably he pressed on with the hateful truth. "The princess Elaine is young and a beauty too. Many men would be glad to have her for their love. If I let it be known that she sent for me last night, that would protect you—"

"Don't say it!" she howled, bursting into tears. She pressed her hands over her ears. "Not another word." Suddenly she knew that she could bear no more. She could say no more, hear no more, and any moment now she felt she could live no more.

She turned her huge tragic eyes on him, and his heart failed. Never had she looked more strange and beautiful. She was a lost flower of the forest, alone in a woodland glade. He wanted to crush her to his chest and kiss her mouth till it bled. He wanted to throw her to the floor and enter her, fill her with his love, and comfort her against all the world. Time after time he had soothed her like this before. But suddenly he saw that she was a stranger to him now.

He stared at her, breathless with pain. For the rest of his life, he knew he would carry this memory of her like a wound, her misty gown and silvery floating veil, her clustering pearls, her eyes like the end of the world.

They stood for a while in silence, feeling the distance between them stretching to the breaking point. Around them lay the wasteland of their love, barren of hope.

Guenevere looked at him as if he were a ghost. "It's over, Lancelot, don't you see?" she said unsteadily. "Everything we had has been founded on a lie. We thought we were the only lovers in the world. But for years, a decade and more, you had another woman, whether you knew it or not. And more—you had a son."

He could not speak. Every word she said was true.

"And now your son needs you, whatever his mother has done. Go to him."

He bowed his head to keep the tears at bay.

Her voice flowed on. "Perhaps we could have endured through all this, who knows? You were drugged and enchanted in Corbenic, I know that. What you did there was not of your own free will."

"Thank you," he breathed out like a dying man.

She gave him a distant nod. "But that was not all. Whatever the reason, you went back to her bed. When you slept with her last night, you killed our love."

A mad flash of fury lit his dying fire. What of Arthur? he was crying out inside. I was trapped into going to another bed. Yet night after night all these years you have gone willingly to bed with the King, and I have had to stand by and smile as he led you away.

But he could not add to the torment she suffered now. Her face, her whole body was fractured with pangs of grief, her whole being breaking down under the strain.

"Go with your son," she said. "Go to the Holy Land."

"Wherever the road leads." He nodded hollowly. "I must follow him. And he must follow the Quest."

She drew herself up. "But whatever happens, Lancelot, don't come back. Go to your own kingdom, stay in Benoic. Don't think that you can ever return to me. It's all over, the dream we've had for so many years."

He was standing before her, unable to speak or move. Her sight shivered, and she saw him standing alone, the last survivor on a battlefield. Around him stretched the carnage of their years together, all their thoughts and hopes, each kiss and tender promise lying bleeding and mangled, hacked limb from limb. Nothing but blood and pain—pain and blood—

She closed her eyes and willed him away. He was fading before her sight like a dream walker, a phantom of the night. She was losing him in the gray-green morning light.

"Go." She moved to the door and passed through. "You are free. It's all gone, everything we had. Go to her if you want to, do whatever you like. We shall never see each other again."

CHAPTER 23

The tang off the sea was sharp and clean and cold. Ahead of them the little ship bobbed up and down, bright with pennants and fluttering sails, flirting like a maiden on her first May day. The midday sun bounced off the dancing waters in glittering shafts of living green and gold. Bors stood on the dock next to Lionel and Galahad and felt his spirits rise. He was no sailor, and with every buffet of the keen salt air, he prayed his Gods to be mindful of that. But the long-buried boy inside the dutiful man was rousing to this adventure with a joyful heart.

"To Benoic, then, is it, sirs?" The Captain surveyed the three knights, then turned his weather-beaten face up to the sky. Tiny white puffball clouds chased each other playfully across a wide expanse of flawless blue. "Couldn't have a better day," he pronounced in a rich southwestern burr. "Tide'll turn at noon. And we'll be away with it."

Aboard the ship the sailors were setting more sail, scrambling round the rigging as swift as monkeys with their sure, grasping hold. Overhead a flock of seagulls wheeled and cried. The piercing, two-note lament hammered through Bors' head like a sorrowful farewell. Yet what was he leaving behind that he had cause to regret?

The Captain squinted at them against the sun. "You want to sail with us?"

Lionel turned to Bors. "Lancelot isn't here. Should we wait for him?"

"We left messages all along the way." Bors paused. "I thought he'd be here by now."

The Captain shifted the weight of his wiry torso from one bowleg to the other, and turned away. "There's other ships and plenty of tides, good sirs. You may take your pick."

"Thank you, Captain." Galahad's brisk tone surprised them all. "But we sail with you. The summer days are slipping by one by one, and we may not delay. This is God's business that we go about."

The Captain nodded dubiously. "None of my business, sir, whose work you do." He nodded to the saddlebags on the dock. "Shall we board your traps?"

Galahad looked at Bors and Lionel. "Let us go, cousins," he said confidently. "Sir Lancelot will find us—if God wills. Meanwhile my heavenly Father calls me on."

"Very well." Bors nodded.

He reached for his purse, and counted out the coins for their passages into the Captain's callused hand. Then he watched the man stroll off to order the crew and get their bags aboard, marveling at himself. What had happened to him? Who would have thought that he and Lionel could tolerate this pale, thin youth and his constant Christian talk? Yet Galahad's childlike trust and burning faith had carved its way into their hearts. The lad was Lancelot's son without a doubt, honest, clear-sighted, and true to the core. Not a mile of their journey but his courtesy had shown through, with no thought for himself. In one sorry town he had given the contents of his purse to a woman half-mad with hunger, savagely gleaning the forest for acorns to feed her starving children. On the road, they had come upon an old man weeping by the wayside, too exhausted to walk to his daughter's house. Galahad had seated the ancient on his own horse and led him to the house many miles away. Yet there was always a gladness and a joy about the journey too. It reminded Bors of his lost boyhood days in Benoic, when he had ridden out for weeks on end with Lionel and Lancelot, to hunt all day in the blazing summer sun and at night camp by an open fire, cooking what they caught.

Bors smiled. "We can deny you nothing," he said. "But when we get to Benoic, you must follow our lead. We are going to the land of your forefathers, kings of Benoic from time out of mind."

Lionel put a light hand on Galahad's shoulder, nearly of a height with his. "We want to ride down through the country, to show you the kingdom that will be yours one day."

Galahad shook his fair head. "Not mine, cousin," he said with shining certainty. "I shall not rule in Benoic. Nor in Terre Foraine, though my grandfather King Pelles would have it so." He paused, then gave a smile of radiant happiness. "I do not think to fill a place on this earth. I know my fate. Mine is the kingdom of God."

PERHAPS THEY SHOULD have followed Galahad after all.

Sagramore fixed his eyes on the woodland path ahead and tried not to let the thought prey on his mind. Behind him he could hear the familiar murmuring of his squire and page, and knew that they had been muttering this too. Yet what did Galahad know, after all? For all his airs, no more than the rest of them. Whereas he, Sagramore, the stout knight they all laughed at, he knew his idea was better than them all.

Even now, lost in the forest with the afternoon well advanced, rain in the air, and nowhere to sleep tonight, the memory of it made Sagramore's weary heart pick up. Galahad was going to seek the Grail in the East, they all knew. That would mean first riding south, ever south, then taking a ship to avoid the last unnavigable overland terrain. But surely, any man who sought the East would find it down the path of the setting sun. Riding due east from where it vanished would surely locate the Grail. Where else would it be but along that golden road?

Sagramore nodded owlishly. When they had set out, it had seemed a wonderful idea, the journey of a lifetime, to be taken slowly and savored at every step. But after all these weeks, it had begun to droop and fade. They had traveled for miles, riding hard and living by the wayside, the clean life of pilgrims or soldiers of Christ. They had succored the weak and given generously to the poor, so much so that Sagramore was uneasily counting his purse. Now in his wakeful night hours, lying on ground increasingly growing cold, Sagramore was contemplating the prospect of having to crawl back penniless to court. Returning without the Grail, and with his tail between his legs—Sagramore knew he would never live it down.

A thin mist wreathed the mountains up ahead and made the afternoon air dank and chill. A cold accompanying drizzle began in Sagramore's soul. Where were the thankful maidens and grateful old grandsires, the worthy opponents and vanquished ne'er-do-wells he had pictured to himself when the Quest began? He had foreseen great adventures and rich rewards, hard jousting by day and soft feather beds at night, himself the honored guest of some hardy rural knight, or the favored friend of a lady of fine estate. How tedious it had been, how awkward and painfully sore to ride in full armor all day, preparing for the challenge that never came. They had met no one worthy of his sword. Instead they had trailed through village after petty village, greeted by surly, starving, dark-faced brats and chased out by a pack of flea-bitten mongrels when they left.

And never a sign of the Grail.

Perhaps they should have followed Galahad after all—

Or perhaps the whole thing was a wild-goose chase, a trick—

It had begun to rain. A thin trickle of water made its way down Sagramore's neck. He shifted stiffly in the saddle and raised his eyes to the sky, suppressing an angry curse. No more than an hour left of daylight, and then another wet night in this Mother-forsaken forest, with not a bite to eat—

He lapsed into a dismal reverie.

"Sir!" shrilled the terrified voice of his page.

Sagramore looked up. Ahead was a sight that made his blood congeal. Some fifty yards up the track, standing foursquare and blocking the woodland path, was a knight in black armor on a dark bay horse. The black plumes of the stranger's helmet nodded fearsomely, and his massive mount snorted and pawed at the earth. The knight's long black lance lay idly in its rest. Whatever hurt the charger did not accomplish, the weapon would.

The strange knight lowered his visor with a clang. "A challenge, sir," came the hollow cry from within, "or you go no farther today. This is the land of the mighty Sir Brunor de Gretise. All who venture here must joust for the right to proceed. The best of three falls, to be fought out on the ground."

Sagramore bowed his head. He could think of no honorable reason to refuse. A sharp smile of self-knowledge came sadly to his lips. Why had he seen himself jousting only with hopeful young knights, green beginners, wet behind the ears, who would be easily bested, and thankful afterward? How had he never thought he might meet a hardened warrior, one who would fight for his lord to the death? It came to Sagramore that he could die here now. He laughed. What kind of fate was that? One that the Gods had long ago written for him. And sealed in the stars, when the moon itself was still liquid fire, before the Mother divided the sea from the sky and danced upon the waves to make the earth.

So be it.

Strangely calm, Sagramore turned to his white-faced squire behind.

"My shield and lance, if you please," he said.

Legs buckling, the young man slid from his horse to the earth, and fumbled to pass up the knightly accoutrements. Sagramore lowered his helmet into place and roughly laced up the thongs. He did not need to lash it firmly into place. He knew he would not survive three passes with this knight. One charge would be all that he and his armor had to stand.

Gauntlets on, lance in its rest, he raised his hand to the knight. "Have at you, sir," he called.

The black knight nodded. "Come on!"

Sagramore eased his horse into a trot. But the trained charger facing him had already leaped into a canter that sent the dead leaves flying from the forest floor. His opponent was thundering toward him down the path. Sagramore felt the earth shake and heard the birds rise shrieking from the trees. He saw the black eyes of the horse burning with blood and fire. Level with its head and steady in the black knight's iron hand, the oncoming tip of the lance called out for him with a hungry gleam. Silently, soberly, Sagramore offered up a blessing for the love of his parents, long gone, and gave up his soul to his Gods.

Nevertheless, as the strange knight approached Sagramore strove valiantly to place his lance in the center of the black breast. But his enemy's shield deflected the point with almost contemptuous ease. The black lance struck Sagramore amidships with a killing force. Gasping, Sagramore felt something rupture within. A moment later he was flying backward out of the saddle, tossed through the air. As he crashed to the ground, he heard his poor bones crack.

He lay on the ground, and knew he could not move. The heavy armor bit into his flesh and crushed his joints. All round him the cold loamy smell of the earth mingled with the fresh sour smell of his blood. The pain in his head was intense, and the whole of his body was shot through with different agonies, some greater, some less. But one by one they were joining together now.

"Arise, sir." He heard a distant roar. His squire was trying to lift him, and his page was weeping brokenheartedly at his side. But Sagramore knew he would never rise again. Heavy footsteps approached, and he felt the helmet being roughly torn from his head.

The black knight stood over him, sword in hand.

Sagramore tried to smile. "Pray you, sir, be good to my lads," he began. Take care of my squire and my page, he wanted to say. But he could not speak. Without warning he coughed up a lungful of blood, and slipped away without another word.

CHAPTER 24

"How goes the Quest for the Grail?"

There was a sudden stillness in the corridors of the Vatican. The Cardinal gave a practiced laugh, but in truth he was surprised to know that the word had made its way so speedily around Rome. "Well enough, Giorgio," he said guardedly. He took a step back and looked at the rotund monk down his thin nose. "How did you hear of it?"

The faraway chant of monks hung in the air, and all around them the corridors teemed with life. The speaker waved a hand at the busy clerics plying to and fro and gave a laugh of genuine merriment. "Boniface, you know Rome's a village, full of old gossips and craning ears."

And you know you can't mystify me, my old friend, he wanted to say, but he had more tenderness for the Cardinal's stiff self-pride. He would never forget the years he and Boniface had spent as young monks on Avalon, struggling to bring the Goddess island under heel. For himself, he had never been happier than when he was called back to Rome, the mother of all cities, the center of the earth. But Boniface, he knew, had found his heart's home on that pagan isle. His old friend had done well, and this lean, scarlet-clad apparition standing tensely before him was now secretary to the Pope, one of the Supreme Pontiff's inner cabinet and a prince of the Church. By contrast, Giorgio had risen no higher than to be music master of the Vatican here, in charge of the choir and the sacred chants. But they both knew who was the happier man.

Sensing this, Boniface felt his anger rise. Jesu Maria, look at Giorgio now! Fat and foolish and decaying too, the product of too many good dinners and beautiful boys. Yet he still had his first love, Tomaso, near him among the throng, a lovely lad no longer, but as plump as Giorgio was. And they all seemed to find a joy that evaded him.

Boniface stiffened his back. His joy had to be in the service of God, and he could not waste God's good time gossiping here. Bidding Giorgio a brisk farewell, he hurried off down the corridors of power, drinking in the sooth-

ing scent of incense as he went. Passing out of the main highways, he came
at last to a small hidden door and entered without knocking, as he always
did. But once inside he fell reverently to his knees. "Your Holiness!" he said,
bowing his head.

He was in a small chamber as red as his cardinal's robes, the walls and
ceiling lined with ruby silk. Thick drapes the color of blood shut out the
daylight, and the candlelight danced off a great gold crucifix bearing a marble Christ. Opposite stood an outside throne with a mighty canopy bearing
a massive figure also swathed in red. Above the robe and cope a large white
face seemed to float like a sleeping moon. But Boniface knew that beneath
the slumbrous weight of flesh lay a reptilian brain, constantly flickering, like
an envenomed tongue.

"Arise, my son." The Pope extended a fat, ring-laden hand. "What news
of the Quest?"

Boniface frowned. "Not good."

The Pope raised his eyebrows. "How so?"

"They have not found the Grail."

The Pope smiled urbanely. "Was it our expectation that they would?"

Boniface's thin face took on a pale flush. "Why not?"

The Pope spread his hands. "Surely better by far that they should continue to search—that our followers should always be seeking what may not
be found—?"

An unpleasant thrill ran through Boniface's veins. "But no man should
labor in vain! It is the true vessel of Christ, and it should be found!"

"To be sure, yes indeed," said the Pope soothingly. "But in the meantime"—something flickered in his small black eyes and was gone—"this
gives us a reason now to send in more monks. This is the island where the
Grail came to light. Now that Our Lord's last vessel has been revealed to us,
it is only right that we should protect our own."

"More monks—" Boniface echoed, his swift mind instantly at work. It
was one of the young Cardinal's strengths, the Pope mused benignly, that he
could pick up a suggestion and act on it at once. He fondled the arms of his
throne. That gift of Boniface's would take him far, perhaps even to this very
chair, the papal seat. But for now—

"More men," he said softly. "Especially those who joined our ranks
when their fighting days were done, monks who will do for us what they did
in the Holy Land, battle the infidels and tear their temples down."

Boniface's eyes fired up. "Yes, sir!" he cried passionately. "We must throw all we have into the island war. The tide is turning, but the land is not yet ours."

"Not as long as one pagan soul worships beside a lake, or hangs offerings on a tree," the Pope agreed. A shadow passed over the moon face. "Or while pagan queens like Guenevere uphold the Mother-right."

Boniface tensed. "Arthur has done much, but he fails to see that we must work by force." His color changed. "We must kill the Goddess who still lingers there!"

The Goddess—memory broke through him with a sudden stab, and he felt again the youthful agony of leaving the island he held dearer than his life. Deep in the stifling chamber like a womb he heard again the waterfowl's mournful cry and knew he too was weeping for Avalon. Above the sound of the birds came a voice finer than any organ and sweeter than a mother with her child: "Religion should be kindness. Faith should be love..."

Oh, Lady, Lady, you gave us peace on Avalon—

Yet why was he thinking of that pagan whore? Changing color again, a furious Boniface caught himself up. The Pope was watching him impassively, waiting for his next word. "Fighting monks, yes!" Boniface cried more shrilly than he'd meant to.

"And builders and workers to make churches everywhere," the Pope put in. "We do not win hearts only with the sword. Send warriors and worker bees to swarm over all the isles."

"Holy Father, your word is law." Boniface knelt again to kiss the large, still hand. War on the pagans! A pale fire warmed his veins. "Trust me, Holiness, it will be done!"

CHAPTER 25

"We should have followed Galahad."

Gawain looked at the speaker and felt a cold core of iron hardening in his heart. It was true that they were deep in a tangled woodland, but they were not lost. Why did they need Galahad to show them the way? Whatever airs the boy had given himself, he knew no more than any other knight.

Yet ever since they had left Camelot, Agravain had been jabbing away with remarks like this. They always came out with the same bland smile or innocent air, but more and more Gawain could see that they were unsettling Gaheris and Gareth and disturbing the natural order of things.

"I've told you, Agravain," he began dangerously, "I'm the leader here. You follow me and keep your thoughts to yourself, or else get on your horse and be ready to take a fall."

Agravain uncoiled his sinewy length and looked around. The broad forest clearing where the brothers had dismounted lay smooth and open to the late summer sun. A wide track led into it and straight out again, perfect for a charge. They were miles from anywhere, deep enough in the woodland for all manner of things to happen, and no man would ever know.

The midday sun was strong and warm on his back. Agravain felt his Gods smiling on him, and smiled to himself. He turned to Gawain.

"You're offering me a challenge, brother?" he said casually. "Why not now?"

Gawain gave a deeply startled laugh. "You'll get a thrashing, Agravain, I promise you."

"Perhaps not." Agravain thought of all he had learned in his years in the East, and smiled again.

In all his life, Gawain had never feared a fight. But now a sickness gripped his stomach, and his bowels heaved. He had jousted with all his brothers ever since they were old enough to ride, and he had often taken Agravain to the tilting yard before, trouncing him till he was bloody for some offense. But this was different, they all knew that. Agravain was jousting for the leadership of the clan. He was out for Gawain's blood.

Gawain gazed off at the serene horizon with the sudden desperate awareness that the world he knew was shifting beneath his feet. What he did now would shape all their lives to come. Sweat glistened on his forehead, and he gave a warning cough. "Agravain—" he began stoutly, as man to man.

Agravain's smile spread like oil across his face. "Best of three falls, brother?" he inquired easily. "And to be determined on the ground?"

The words were out, and could not be withdrawn. With a curt nod, Gawain turned on his heel and strode off toward his horse. A leaden-hearted Gaheris followed him down the woodland track, and assisted his brother to arm. Wordlessly he buckled on the big knight's armor, then laced on the heavy helmet as firmly as he could. Gaheris needed no urging to fasten each piece on its tightest hold: both men knew that the fight would be the worst of Gawain's life. In the same grim silence, he assisted Gawain to mount, passed up his gauntlets and sword, and watched as Gawain settled his lance in its rest.

On the opposite side of the clearing, Gareth was pacing out the charge, furiously wishing he did not have to be Agravain's squire. The baby giant of the clan, known for his gentle heart, he dreaded nothing as he did what lay ahead. At best, the battle between his brothers would be bloody and prolonged. Gawain was a fearsome fighter, gifted by the Gods with massive weight and skill. Of all the Round Table knights only Lancelot could bring him down. But Agravain, though leaner and less strong, would give no quarter, and expect none. He would fight like an Orkneyan, to the death.

And at worst—if Agravain won—then Gareth's plunging heart knew with black certainty that Agravain would kill Gawain. So Gaheris would be forced to take on Agravain, and if Gaheris failed, Gareth would stand alone. Before nightfall, the floor of the clearing would be soaked with blood, and the rooks and crows would be feasting for weeks to come.

A fatal calm hung over the forest as the two knights prepared. In the wide clearing, the sun turned every blade of grass to gold, and made a pool of slumbrous heat in the leafy glade. Under the trees, small drowsy insects droned in the summer afternoon, careless of what might come.

Armed and mounted, Gawain and Agravain saluted each other, then turned away. Slowly their horses paced up the opposing tracks, then turned for the charge. Standing in the clearing, Gaheris raised his arm. The world trembled on its axis; then the arm fell.

"Set on!" Gaheris bellowed at the top of his lungs.

The cry echoed through the forest. Slowly at first, and then with increasing force, the two chargers hurtled forward down the track.

Why was this happening? Gawain shook his head. Despite the urgent drumming of his horse's hooves, he still could not believe that it was real. Think! he told himself furiously, *think!* Before, he had always beaten Agravain in the tiltyard or at the joust. This time he knew his brother would not submit. A fear like the wind off a grave sneaked round his mind, and a ghostly thought took shape: I'll have to kill him now.

Through the grille of his visor he could see a dark form thundering forward against the sun, and in front of it a wavering pinpoint of black light. Mesmerized, Gawain watched the bright tip of Agravain's spear floating up and down. So much for the vaunted new prowess, the tricks he had learned in the East. Agravain could not even keep his lance steady as he came on, but was handling it like a novice, or a feeble old man. You'll have to do better than that, brother, Gawain thought with amusement as he hefted his lance and took aim. A moment later he felt a shattering blow to his chest, and felt himself crashing to the ground.

As he fell, he knew he had broken a rib. Blood oozed from beneath his breastplate and down his side, and remounting cost him more strength than he would have wished. Already Agravain had taken up his stand at the far end of the track, waiting to charge again.

"Come on!" Gaheris called.

This time Gawain knew he would not underestimate Agravain's trickery, nor his skill. His horse went forward eagerly, aroused by the smell of blood, and he felt the sweet assurance of power at his control. Sitting back in the saddle, he made a cool appraisal of the point in the center of the oncoming breastplate where he intended to give Agravain the fall of his life. Then throwing himself forward, he took full advantage of his longer reach and, as Agravain approached, struck the first blow. But Agravain had mastered the art of making himself, not his weapon, the moving target now. Feinting to the left and right, he lithely evaded the impact, while Gawain's ferocious lunge almost unseated him. Gawain ground his teeth. So much effort for so little gain. As both riders thundered past without a fall, he smelled fresh blood, and felt it running down his side.

"Come on!" came the final call.

Gawain gritted his teeth. His effort to unseat Agravain had opened the wound in his side, and every jolt of his horse's hooves made the pain worse. But he did not care. He focused his eyes, his whole being on the black figure hurtling toward him over the grass, and prepared his lance. Third time pays for all, brother, he swore in his soul. Agravain was only yards away now. Giving his horse its head, Gawain sank his spurs deep into the animal's side. Screaming, the beast leaped forward with a massive bound, and Gawain knocked Agravain out of his saddle and back over his horse's tail.

But Agravain's luck had not deserted him. He landed as lightly as a cat and was instantly on his feet, sword in hand. Dismounting, Gawain could feel his blood congealing round his waist. Inside the heavy armor, he was sweating like a pig. He had to finish the fight quickly, while he still could.

His first blow dispelled any hope of that. It landed on Agravain's shoulder with the force of a rock fall, and would have driven any other knight to his knees. But Agravain simply slithered away from the blow. How did he do that? Gawain shook his head. It was like fighting a snake. Seen through the black bars of his visor, dodging and weaving, Agravain shimmered before him in the sun, a mirage, not a man.

The next moment he was reeling from a low stroke that Agravain had unleashed from nowhere, it seemed. For the first time, Gawain felt panic rising in his throat. Gripping his broadsword in both hands, he went forward swinging and slashing in a frenzy of fear and pain, and knocked Agravain to the ground. But as Agravain surged back up, he contrived another treacherous stroke, a cruel slash to the inner thigh. Grimly, Gawain knew that Agravain had drawn blood again.

Then he knew too that the fight would take all he had. They battled on all through the heat of the day. Overhead the relentless sun stood still in the sky, bathing them both in streams of molten gold. The smallest creatures of the forest fell silent with dread, and the very trees seemed to hold their breath. Gaheris and Gareth looked on in growing despair as the two brothers fought and feinted and came again, churning the ground in their fury like wild boars. The grass beneath their feet was dark with their blood, and high overhead a lone crow watched and waited with the light of death in its eye.

What, Agravain—? How—? Panting, Gawain gasped with disbelief. Time and again Agravain was shrugging off his blows. His ten years in the East had taught him a sweet treachery such as no knight in Britain knew.

Gawain gave a groan of fury and despair. How could he fight an enemy who melted away from his sword?

His blood was running down in many places now. How many ribs he had broken, Gawain could not count. His sword grip was no more than a frantic spasm, and when he unlocked his hand, the weapon would fall. All he had was his power to endure, and he had to trust to that. Sooner or later Agravain had to fail.

Yet Gawain was failing faster, as both men knew. He had paid a heavy price for the early fall. Stumbling now, and weak from loss of blood, he felt Agravain's sword find a gap in his armor and slice his skin again. It was one barb too many for Gawain's tormented flesh. With a howl, he hurled himself forward onto the sword, driving it deeper into his shoulder and turning the impact back on Agravain. Recoiling from the force of his brother's weight, Agravain lost his grip on his sword, caught his spur in a tussock of grass, and fell backward to the ground.

In an instant Gawain was upon him, pinning him down. Agravain felt Gawain's sword point piercing his skin, and did not move. Kneeling across his brother's recumbent form, Gawain looked at the blind helmeted head, and lifted the visor with a trembling hand. Agravain's face stared up impassively, black-eyed and streaked with blood.

"Yield!" Gawain croaked.

A flicker of—what?—some emotion Gawain did not know crossed the blank features in the iron casque. "I yield."

"What?" Gawain was dumbfounded. "And swear to obey—?"

Agravain looked up. There was an unearthly glitter in his eyes. "I swear."

There was a baffled pause.

"He's lying," came a furious voice from behind.

Gawain turned. Gaheris was leaning over them, his milky skin and pale eyes alight with rage. "Kill him, Gawain."

"What?"

Gawain looked at Gareth. There were tears in the eyes of the youngest of the clan, and his mouth was twisted with grief. But he did not evade the question in Gawain's gaze. After a second's hesitation he nodded and turned away.

Gaheris stood looming at Gawain's side. "This is just another of his filthy tricks," he said hoarsely, as if Agravain were not there. "He agreed too readily, don't you see? He's lying to save his hide." He gripped Gawain's shoulder in the nearest thing to brotherly love that he had ever shown. "He would have taken you from us if he could. He meant to destroy our clan. Who knows what else he'll do if you let him live?"

Kill Agravain? Gawain heard the voice of darkness in his heart. This moment had been coming all their lives, ever since Agravain knew he was the second son. Agravain had made love to this death, Gawain knew. If his brother could simply disappear—go away—

Heavily Gawain dropped the point of his sword. "I cannot kill a fallen enemy."

Gaheris stared at him madly. "Gawain—!"

Gawain got to his feet. His wounds had hardened, and every move was a separate agony. "He yielded to my hand. I can't take his life. It's all against the laws of chivalry."

Gaheris's eyes bulged with disbelief. "He'll only give more grief. He always has—"

Gawain tried to shrug, but his shoulders would not move. "On my head be it."

"He deserves to die." Gareth began to weep. "He killed our mother, she died of grief when he killed her love—"

Gawain's voice was a dried husk. "Then let her spirit be his executioner." He turned back to the motionless figure on the ground. Agravain lay on his back, watching the proceedings as calmly as though he were in bed. If I lay there and he stood over me, Gawain thought, he would have stabbed me through the neck by now. But he knew that I would never take his life.

Nausea shook him, and the fear of vomiting. He forced himself to be calm. "Hear me, Agravain." He looked into the empty black eyes and put the last of his strength into the fateful words. "You are banished from the Quest. Go back to court, to the Orkneys, wherever you will. But never call me brother anymore."

He threw down his bloodstained sword and moved slowly away. Gaheris hurried after him, tense with concern, and Gareth followed anxiously behind. Together they shouldered the weight of the wavering bulk, and when they reached the shelter of the wood, they laid Gawain carefully down.

Cautiously Agravain hauled himself to his feet. One by one he tested out his wounds, and knew that he was well enough to ride. Gawain, however, would remain there for many days. Gaheris and Gareth would be kept busy for a good while, making up a bed of bracken for the injured man, erecting a tent to keep him from the rain, binding up his wounds and dressing them every day, and letting nature take its course till the great body was whole again.

If it ever was. Agravain felt a comforting warmth around his heart. God knows where in a forest they would find the necessaries to heal fighting wounds: spiders' webs, cow dung, and thick red wine. Gawain's wounds would fester; he could be scarred or crippled for life. He could die.

How wonderful life was. The possibilities were infinite, and the game had only just begun. Agravain's smile spread across his face. As it did so, a cut of his own broke out on his head, and a fresh red spurt of blood streaked his brow like the mark of Cain. "Well, brother," he said softly, trying the word out. "Not this time, it seems. But soon, dear brother— *sssooooooooooooonnn!*"

CHAPTER 26

*A*valon, *Avalon, mystic island, home...*

The oars beat on the water like the wings of wounded birds. Guenevere stood in the prow of the boat watching the island loom up out of the water, green above the still and silvery glass. Behind her in the well of the shallow barge, Merlin lay at peace, his long body robed in the royal red of Pendragon, his wand in his hand. His iron-gray locks, sweetly perfumed and curled, were held in place by a golden coronet, and thick chains of gold adorned his neck and waist. His hands, clasped on his breast, were burdened with great rings, each stone as big as a thrush's egg. The agates he wore were as yellow and strange as his eyes. But no one had encountered his gaze since the day he fell.

Guenevere sighed. She had known from the first that she had to bring Merlin here. Once, long before, he had been grievously sick and they had brought him to Avalon to be made whole. Oh, he had his own underground home, everyone knew that—his cave in the Welshlands where he could sleep his fill. But here he could rest in the island's crystal cave, the best healing for a broken mind.

"Lady, see there!" One of the boatmen pointed toward the shore, addressing her in the odd, coughing sound of the Old Tongue. Through the twilight haze, a light flickered in and out on the hillside like a magic thing. She looked at the Lake dweller, and saw his bright black eyes burning behind the thick thatch of wet hair. Who would take care of these people when the Lady was gone? Who would even understand them when they spoke?

Together they watched the lantern coming down the Tor. The Lake dweller's eyes turned uneasily to the still form of Merlin lying at his feet. All men feared the enchanter, Guenevere knew. "Have no fear, sir." She addressed him gently in his own rough tongue. "They are coming to greet the Lord Merlin and bring him home."

Around them the air was soft and comforting. The parting waters purled away beneath their bow. The sweet living smell of the Lake rose like a blessing on Merlin, on her, on all who suffered pain. At the watery edge all the unseen creatures of the Lake, otters, coots, and voles, hooted and snuffled off to their tranquil beds. On the island itself, she knew, thousands of white wings were settling into their roosts. A sharp shaft of envy pierced her to the quick: *Oh, to be a wood pigeon, and sing all day in the trees—*

She bit her lip, nipping it between her teeth till she felt the blood run. She was blessed among women; she had no reason to mourn. Blessed in always calling Avalon her home.

Avalon, Avalon, mystic island, home—

The light ahead continued to call them on. But where was Avalon now, all its great green bulk? It seemed to be fading before them as they drew near. And where was the scent of apple blossom that had always heralded the approach to the island before? Guenevere stared through the silver-gray gloaming till her eyes were on stalks. And there it was, no more than a dark shape in the last of the light. Not until day would she see the long-loved places of her heart again, the drifting apple orchards, pink and white, and the green flanks of the Mother at rest rising up above the waters as still as glass.

Now the dancing lantern flame had come to rest at the foot of the Tor, on the small stone jetty where the boats put in. Behind it Guenevere saw a familiar form, and knew the Lady had sent her chief Maiden to welcome them. As they drew near, Nemue's low voice, as rough and sweet as an otter's, reached them through the dark. "We are glad to see you—welcome to you all."

Moments later, she had Guenevere in her arms.

"Gods above," Guenevere whispered tremulously, "what a blessing to be here!"

Nemue nodded. "Bring Lord Merlin in."

The men raised Merlin's litter from the well of the boat. More eager hands on the jetty lifted him to the shore. More candles joined the small procession as it set off up the hill. Guenevere felt a glimmer of comfort warming her heart. With fire and starlight they were bringing Merlin home.

Nemue plodded beside her through the velvet dusk. "How did Lord Merlin die?"

Guenevere shook her head. "He is not dead," she said doggedly.

A small smile lit Nemue's dusky face. "We thought as much."

Guenevere sighed. "All men think I am mad for thinking so. But—"

She hardly knew where to begin. A man like Merlin did not die as others did. Yet there was no man like Merlin on the earth. Did that mean that for him there could be no death?

"You are confused." Nemue looked at her shrewdly. "Indeed, you have had much to bear. Your Arthur has had a cruel blow, we hear—his old wound broken out, and infected within?"

"My Druid healer managed to close it up," she returned in the same dry, drained tones. "With time and care, he will be himself again."

Nemue looked at her. "But the King will heal quicker if his old friend gets well. Is this why you cling to the hope that Merlin lives when others swear that every breath of his life has fled?"

"No," she said abruptly, stubborn again. She took a breath. "In truth, I do not know what to think. The first time he fell, we took it for a stroke of the Gods. Even then one of our Druids saw signs of life. While they were attending him, he cried out and convulsed, and they said he had been struck again. Since then he has not moved or drawn a breath."

"Is his flesh warm?"

"No."

"And he has rigor in his limbs?"

"Yes." Guenevere paused. "But he shows no signs of decay. The Druid mark still pulses on his brow. His body breathes out a rich incense like fire. When I sat with him in the night, he cried to himself, like a child. But then it passed, and a sweetness came into his face." She clenched her fists. "He lives!"

Nemue touched her hand. "You have done right to bring Lord Merlin here," she said in her strange rusty voice. "No man should be hurried to the grave before his time. And of all men on earth, he is most likely to be still alive."

Guenevere stared. "How so?"

"He is a Lord of Light," Nemue said simply. "They can send their souls out of themselves, and slumber many ages before they return." She glimmered at Guenevere like a water vole. "A true Lord of Light can never die."

"But why would he choose to go when Arthur needs him so?"

Nemue's dusky face closed up like a flower. "Perhaps to avoid a greater grief to them both."

The path wound upward round the side of the Tor. Their unseeing feet traced out the ancient paths, the serpentine tracks carved out by those who had danced to the glory of the Goddess before time began. They came to a halt beside a hawthorn tree. Behind it on the hillside stood a great white disc of stone.

Almost above their hearing, a fragment of high, sweet humming sounded through the air. Nemue smiled. "Lord Merlin is singing. Our old friend is rejoicing to come back to his crystal cave."

She gave a signal to the men. Two of the strongest stepped forward and rolled back the stone. Inside the hollow hill lay a cool, quiet space cut out of the living rock. A flight of gentle steps led down into it, and inside, all the walls, the floor, and the dome of the roof glittered with diamondlike shards of crystal quartz. Each dazzling white facet threw off a separate gleam, and the cell itself was a haven of shining peace. It was the healing chamber of Avalon, a cavern of new reflections for a broken mind.

Beside the opening rested a doe hare, quite unafraid. Her large brown liquid eyes watched over them with a mother's loving care. The sound of Merlin's strange melody filled the air. Guenevere caught the hare's gaze, and a sudden conviction came into her mind.

"His singing robes," Guenevere said suddenly. "Merlin must have all his glory when he goes to his rest."

Nemue raised her cool gaze. "Be it so."

Guenevere turned to those standing behind. All Merlin's possessions had come with him to Avalon: chests of his books of magic, his jewels and pomades, the candles he lit to burn in a ring around his head. When the menservants opened the first chest, Merlin's sweet song increased. It sounded like the music of the spheres. With reverent hands, Merlin was robed in a long cloak of black and white feathers, raven and swan adorned with flashing discs of gold. Each tiny moon caught the last of the dying light and seemed to echo the strains of Merlin's song, throbbing and humming with the old man's every note.

Now the inside of the cave was vibrating with the thin, beelike drone, a high, ethereal song of love and loss. It told of the beauty of the midnight moon, and the strength of the warrior's arm in the heat of the day. It sang of the warmth of the love in a true lover's eye, and the fire in the hall with snow and ice outside. Then it came to the death of hope and the heart's long decay, when the body fails and all must go down to the dark. Yet all souls, living and dead, the song wound on, may know the glory in the eyes of a child, the sweetness of the sun in the sky, the white blossom on the bough, and the home that awaits us in the arms of the one we love.

Guenevere stood entranced. She did not know she was weeping till she felt her face wet with tears.

"He is ready." Nemue's husky voice sounded in her ear. "The old man is ready to go to his last home."

Guenevere could not speak. Nemue gave a sign. Reverently the Lake dwellers took up the pallet and carried Merlin within. His books were laid ready to his sleeping hand, and a circle of candles like stars bloomed round his head.

One by one they withdrew, and stood on the hillside above. Merlin lay in sleeping majesty in the shining space.

"Farewell!" cried Nemue.

"Farewell," echoed the Lake dwellers with one voice.

Two of them rolled the great stone across the door. As it closed, the mother hare slipped smiling through the crack. Guenevere gave a watery smile in return. Merlin would not be alone.

Nemue read her thought. "We will take care of him," she said. "The old lord will have whatever he needs. Above all, we shall help him to find himself again."

Guenevere forced a smile. "All of us do that on Avalon."

"Alas, no." Nemue's smile faded. "Not as it was before. But the Lady will tell you all. She will see you now."

A WEEPING MOON was climbing up the sky. Together they trod upward through the groves of apple blossom and the stand of ancient pines looming above. The night was chill, and it came to Guenevere with a creeping shock, *I have never been cold on Avalon before.* Approaching the Lady's house, she was lost again: *Surely it was here, right where we are standing—where has it gone?*

The path ahead of them wound onward into the trees, skirting the steep mountainside. Nemue closed her eyes and held out her hands, palms outward toward the rocky face, muttering to herself under her breath. Beads of sweat dewed her forehead, and Guenevere could feel the words of power. The air shivered and changed shape, and the frontage of the Lady's house came into view, the white stone gleaming in the moonlight like a living thing.

"Hurry!" Nemue urged her toward the door. "The Christians are ever lying in wait to discover the House, so we always conceal it now. Go in. I shall be waiting for you when you come out."

Already the door was gaping to beckon her in. Guenevere went forward without fear. In the House of Maidens when she was a girl, it was whispered that the Lady's House was not a house at all, but her enchanted way down to the Lake below. Yet the low, domed chamber within was always warm, with no more than a faint echo of water farther down. She had first been admitted with Arthur when he courted her, and she had come back since at times of sorrow and loss. Never had she failed to find comfort and succor here. But this time she knew that her grief was beyond repair.

Yet in spite of herself the wide, welcoming space touched something in her heart. The rough loamy walls still glowed like ripe honey, and the dragon lamps crouching in every niche cast the same pools of gold over bright mats woven in all the colors of the East. Against the farthest wall, a tall throne stood on a dais, its long legs and highly wrought back strangely alive. A pack of sleek water hounds lolled around its foot, their collars as heavy and golden as their eyes. On it sat a muffled figure, leaning her head on her hand.

Guenevere started. "Lady!"

The figure on the dais rose to her feet. She was veiled from head to foot in soft gauze, her floating draperies echoing her every move. Above the misty veil covering her face she wore the diadem of the Goddess, a perfect moon of pale gold set with pearls. The Goddess ring gleamed on the second finger of her right hand, while the other hand cradled an orb of shining rock crystal bound in gold. Erect and shapely, she waited in silence for Guenevere to approach, then resumed her seat, gently motioning Guenevere to a stool in front of the throne.

"Welcome, dear Guenevere," came a low, ringing voice. "You are always welcome back to your long-ago home. But I grieve for the sorrows that have brought you here."

It was a voice of power, low and musical, imbued with all the sadness of the world. In its sweet tones Guenevere could hear the white mist mourning on the mountain, the cry of the mother for a baby lost, the low, lingering lament of the lover for hope betrayed. Grief ambushed her, and the tears flowed like rain. "Oh, Lady," she gasped, stuttering with pain. "I— Lancelot—"

The tall shape leaned forward and reached out a hand. "I know, I have read it in the stars."

"How could he—?"

There was a rhythmic sigh. "Do not ask. Fate spins where it will, and dark hands have been turning the wheel."

Morgan! Guenevere caught her breath. *I knew as much.*

The Lady gave a slow answering nod. "You have lost your true love, and your husband is suffering too. And more lies ahead before your way is clear."

A bleak acceptance swept through Guenevere. "Oh, Lady, the way ahead is clear to me. I must care for my husband and say good-bye to my love." She paused and checked herself. "And Merlin too—I have to care for him." She gave a small, sad smile. "We were never friends, because of Arthur—how could we be? But I won't abandon him now." She looked up. "He lives, I swear it. And I want to keep him alive—for Arthur's sake."

The Lady waved a hand, and her filmy draperies fluttered and danced through the air. "Lord Merlin will live forever in the hearts and minds of all the world. You need have no fear for him."

No fear for him—

The Lady spoke in riddles, Guenevere knew. "But for someone else?" she demanded. "Who?"

"For all of us." The Lady sighed heavily. "Dark and deadly happenings are afoot. The wheel of Fate has begun to roll downhill. Many will die before it runs its course."

Guenevere felt a wind from the Otherworld. She could not speak.

"The world as we know it is coming to an end," the Lady's musical tones wound sadly on. "The blossom is fading on Avalon. Soon it will be no more."

Guenevere started as if she had been stung. "What?" she cried. "Oh, I noticed I couldn't smell the blossom when I arrived, but I thought—"

"The apple trees are dying." The Lady's voice was stark with pain. "Like the island itself."

Guenevere was seized with a terror she could not name. "What?"

"The Lake waters are receding. Soon the Lake will be no more."

Guenevere gasped. "No—!" She ran a hand wildly over her forehead. "But the Lake dwellers—?"

"—must learn to live on land, without the fish and fowl that feed them now."

Guenevere gasped. "They'll die!"

"We must all go down to the darkness in the end. Some will live."

"But you and the Maidens—the Goddess people here—"

"The same is true for every one of us."

Guenevere felt a pain stabbing her heart. "Why, Lady, why?"

"The Christians are turning the waters into a new course. To rescue the drowned land, they say, for the use of men. They claim that the Island will be the same as before. But without the streams that feed the marshes, the Lake will die." She sighed like the wind off the mountains. "In time it will be only a hill rising from the plain. The world will forget it was once the Isle of Glass."

Guenevere's eyes were huge and terrible. "Avalon no more?" she whispered in dread.

"Ah, that is something else."

Guenevere looked up. A new note had come into the Lady's voice. The tall figure surged to her feet. "Follow me!"

Behind the throne, a low arch gave onto a wide stone stairway leading down into the dark. Mesmerized, Guenevere followed the rustling draperies down the steps. Around them the air was alive with unseen wings. Soundless calls and small scurryings betrayed the presence of many other dwellers in this land of night. Carefully Guenevere felt her way over the slippery stones, going down, ever down, till at last her feet touched sand. Now she could smell the water she knew was here.

There was a movement ahead, and lights blazed up all around. A thousand dragon lamps played on soaring walls and arched roofs formed out of the living rock. Sparkling crystals of red and white gleamed from the walls, glinting in and out of the folds in the natural stone. A vast cavern floored with white sand ran away before Guenevere's gaze.

She knew it as the sanctuary of the Goddess, and Her ancient treasure chamber of the offerings made to Her from the world above. She knew too from her girlhood days on Avalon which of the Maidens were trained to swim up to rescue the gifts cast into the Lake and bring them down to the rocky caves below. But still she was startled by the wealth of silver and gold. Since the last time she was here the heaps of drinking cups and bowls and great platters of shining metal seemed more numerous than before. There were cauldrons, too, and swords of bronze and copper, pewter vessels and precious stones, all objects of beauty treasured for a lifetime or more. Guenevere's eyes roved over swords and daggers with jeweled hilts, ropes of coral and amber, and turquoises as round as owlets' eyes.

And the treasures seemed housed more spaciously than before. Guenevere looked around in wonderment—surely the cavern was bigger than when she last came? In the center of the great stone chamber the Lady stood on a platform of rock between twin basins containing the waters of two springs, one red, one white. As Guenevere watched, the veiled figure opened her arms, and whirled in a circle through the pulsing void.

"The body of the Mother!" she cried, embracing the wide space. She gestured to the red spring at her feet. "The blood of the Mother, which was given for you." Another fluttering wave encompassed the white. "The milk of the Mother, which feeds all who come. The love of the Mother who made us all!"

"So be it ..."

"So be it, so be it, so be it ..."

Guenevere had not seen the Maidens at the back of the cave. Now they came forward singing, their eyes on fire. All robed in white and crowned with a moon of gold, each of them had a wide-eyed child by the hand. These were the Star Children of the Goddess, vowed by their parents to Her service from their earliest days, just as the Maidens studied to be priestesses when their time came. Guenevere felt the familiar tug at her heart. *Amir was like these sturdy little ones. But the Goddess called him to serve Her in the Otherworld.*

Still singing, they crossed the treasure chamber and disappeared. Guenevere was stunned. "Why are the Maidens down here? And where did they go?"

The veiled figure saw her confusion and stretched out a hand. "Here, Guenevere—come here."

Beckoning, she led Guenevere to the back of the cavern and through a series of passageways and arches to another world. They passed through a grove of silver blossom and golden apples to a garden where the Maidens and children were at play. The air was alive with birdsong and happy cries. Beyond lay a smiling landscape of upland meadows and gently wooded hills. Sheep grazed in the pastures, and the hedgerows were heavy with honeysuckle and wild rose. The scent of blossoms was everywhere, and a basking summer sun beamed down on all.

Guenevere wanted to laugh, to weep, to pinch herself and cry. How could this be, a land of eternal summer in the heart of the Tor? In the cavern she could feel the weighty mass of the hillside looming above. Yet here they were in a rare kingdom, a country under land.

"The blessed land."

A sudden radiance filled all the place with light. Guenevere turned. The Lady had unveiled her face. Youthful and yet ageless, it was alight with a wisdom as old as the hills, and the sweetness of a child. It was all that was ever feared and desired. The Lady was shining forth as she truly was. At first Guenevere had to turn away and close her eyes. But when she looked again she saw her mother's face, lit with her loving, joyful, undying smile.

"So now you see."

She could feel the Lady's hand warm on her arm. She nodded, unable to speak.

"Avalon lives!" came the rich throbbing voice in her ear. "The people of the Goddess are leaving the earth for a better place. From now on we shall walk the world between the worlds. Nemue and a handful of others will remain over ground for a while. When their work is done, they will come to join us here."

"Here?"

"There is room here for all who choose to come. It is only required that they love the Mother in their souls. All who believe will always find us here. Avalon will endure away from the eyes of men."

Guenevere felt tears of joy flooding her soul. "Blessed by the Great One, thanks and joy to Her name!"

"And the Hallows too will one day be ours again." The Lady smiled at the mingled doubt and hope on Guenevere's face. "No, little one, they are not lost, as you feared. What you saw at Mordred's knight-making was a trick of Morgan's, no more. She produced a mirage to convince the Christians of the Grail. To destroy the Round Table and scatter all the knights."

Guenevere nodded numbly. "I feared the Hallows were gone for ever-more—"

The Lady placed her hand along her heart. "Like Avalon, they live. I know it. They call to me."

Guenevere could feel the tears beginning again. "When will we get them back, Lady, when?"

"Ah, Guenevere." The lovely face clouded. "My sight is failing, I cannot see so far." She straightened her back. "But the way ahead is plain. I will stay here, keeping Avalon safe. And you will go back to Camelot, and wait."

CHAPTER 27

The highway lay open ahead, and a wintry sun shone down. The days were shortening now as the old year died, but there were still hours of good riding to be had. Sir Dinant picked up his horse's head and urged the beast on. He should reach the nearest town before nightfall if his luck held.

And that would not be so long away now. Dinant bared his teeth in a humorless grin and looked up at the sky. Two hours, maybe three if the weather held clear till dark. Otherwise—

He would not think about otherwise. *I was never a thinking man*, he thought to himself with the strong sense of a simple nature pushed beyond its bounds. *Before all this, we never had to think.* His mind turned to the ease of the olden days, when such things never troubled a single soul—when he and Sagramore had held court in the knights' hall, eating and drinking and gorging to the full on jokes and rough humor and dishonoring their fellows in play at every turn.

Well, all that was over now.

And Sagramore—

Well, he would not think about Sagramore.

Dinant tensed, and a bleakness bit into his soul. And all for this damn fool Quest. What a fool he had been to follow them all riding out. How much cleverer it would have been to smile nobly, vow to stay and comfort the King, and sit tight.

Furious, he resisted the urge to dig his spurs into his horse. Spurring on the mare would only finish her off. Overridden now, the poor beast might go lame or worse. She could founder in this wild and distant spot, and then how would he get out?

His money, too, was running short after so long on the road. He had had to get rid of his squire and send the lad back to Camelot. Whatever was left, it was not enough to buy a horse. So he'd best look after the sorry jade that he had.

Far on the horizon, the little town sat smiling in the sun. Dinant cocked his head to get a better view. Tonight, he swore, he would lie in a feather bed. An inn in a byway like this could not cost too dear.

But before that, there were miles of virgin forest to cross. Dinant looked at the native woodland, and his heart twitched. Since losing his squire, he had had to travel alone. And who knew who held the castle in the wood?

For there must be a castle in a wood as deep as this, doubtless in the keeping of a savage lord with knights to defend it against all who came. Dinant felt for his sword, and knew that his lance was at hand. Unreadiness would never bring him down. But others had fallen that way, too many to count. What was it that Helin had told him when they'd chanced to meet? Sitting in that stinking alehouse where their roads had crossed?

Of all the Round Table, Helin had never been a friend. But it was strange how glad he had been to meet a fellow knight now. And Helin had been only too eager to talk. Wild-eyed and unkempt, the knight had had a tale to tell.

"No, none of us has yet won the Grail," Helin had said hoarsely, nursing a pint of rough ale. "Nor got anywhere near it, if the truth is told. Last I heard, Galahad had reached the Holy Land. And he's the only one who knows what all this is about."

"Galahad's got that far? But surely not by himself?" Tough as he was, Dinant did not care to think of a twelve-year-old fighting the hazards of the road.

Helin shook his head. "No, he's with Bors and Lionel." He paused for another heartening swig of his ale. "But not Lancelot," he said curiously. "I'd like to know what's become of him."

Yet Lancelot was the only blank Helin had to concede. Sticking to the high roads and stopping at every alehouse along the way had allowed Helin to find out more than Dinant wished to know. Names and fates of other knights poured from his lips. And every one of the knights had suffered some misfortune, it seemed.

"Poor Erec was waylaid by outlaws and stabbed. He'll live, but he'll never ride a horse again. Balin and his brother Balan were both traveling with borrowed shields. When they met and challenged each other on the way, they fought to the death before they found out."

Helin paused and gazed into his drink, then looked around. Dinant saw his eyes wander over the bosomy, compliant inn maid and gave him a frown. Helin should know that Dinant had earmarked her for his bed tonight. The silver to pay for a night of harmless joy was already with the landlord, and the deal was done. Useless for Helin to think of muscling in now. But a second glance showed him that Helin's thoughts were not tending that way at all.

Dinant's face grew grimmer as Helin's tale wore on. Too many had died on the road for the true figure to be known. Accidents, misjudgments, and disease had claimed many lives. Rough jousting had been the end of many more. And malice and cruelty stalked them everywhere. Sir Griflet had been lost in the East. Sir Almain had been made amply welcome by the lady of a castle, then had been surprised by the lady's husband in her bed, and had had his manhood removed and his throat cut for his pains. Sir Ladinas had been seized and held for ransom by a renegade band. When no ransom was forthcoming, they had starved him to death.

Dinant looked at Sir Helin and drained the last drop of his ale before ordering two more goblets of the dark, frothy brew. No wonder Helin looked haunted, with all he had heard. Misery hung on him like a cloak as he told his tale.

"And all for what?" he ended with a nervous laugh. "There was never a sign of the Grail." He rolled his eyes. "The Grail. Whatever it is."

And Dinant knew then that Helin had lost his faith. He no longer believed in the Grail, if he ever had. Now he was treading water, simply casting around. When they parted the next day, each taking to his own route, Helin bade him farewell heartily but would not meet his eye. Melancholy settled on Dinant as he rode away. The Quest is over for Helin, he thought, it's finished now. He'll find a safe place to hole up through the winter, then when spring comes, he'll slink back to court. It won't be too much of a defeat, he'll live it down. No one expected him to win the Grail anyway.

Now a wintry wind stirred the dry leaves underfoot. And it came to Dinant that he did not want his Quest to end like this. He'd never thought that he would win the Grail. But to crawl back to court with nothing to show for his jaunt was an ignominious outcome he had not foreseen. Only, how to keep on with the Quest when he had no money, no destination, and no hope?

There was a sudden movement in the forest ahead, and a loud cry rang out.

"Halt! Hold there, or accept my challenge for your life."

A hundred yards down the path sat a knight in red armor on a red horse. The glory of the joust flooded Dinant's brain.

"Have at you!" he roared. Slamming down his visor, he hefted his lance in his fist, gathered up his reins, and put his horse to the charge. Moments later he saw his opponent turn tail and flee. Gleefully chanting his battle cry, Dinant gave chase.

The red knight left the pathway and vanished down a side track into the wood. You can't hide there! Dinant thought in high delight. Already he was counting out the spoils. When he caught up with the cowardly fugitive, he'd strip him of his arms, his armor, and his horse as well. Red was not a color he would choose. But a whole set of knightly accoutrements would fetch good money in any hue.

Dinant could have rubbed his hands and laughed aloud. With one of his problems solved so expediently, the others would surely go the same way. Doggedly he pursued the red knight on a headlong passage through the trees. "Stand or yield, recreant!" he cried again and again.

At last the red knight seemed to hear, and turned to stand his ground. Sir Dinant rode forward along the narrow track. As he did so, a dozen men-at-arms came softly out of the thick undergrowth. Dinant wheeled round to flee, and saw another dozen coming up behind.

A ring of shining spears was pointed at his heart. Cursing, he knew he had fallen into a trap.

"Out of my way, you clowns!" he called in lofty tones. "You can't hold me. I'm a knight of King Arthur, following the Quest."

"Not anymore," came the voice of the red knight. "No more Quest for you." He pushed up the visor of his helmet to reveal a lupine grin.

Dinant's blood ran cold. "Sir—" he began, but the red knight simply laughed.

"It's over for you," he said, as if talking to an imbecile. He paused and gave another nasty shake of his head. "This side of the grave, at least. Come on then, sir. This way, if you please." Without waiting for an answer, he pulled round his horse's head and set off into the wood.

CHAPTER 28

The horse limped onward through the frozen grass. As white as the frost descending through the trees, the great stallion caught the last of the daylight and even seemed to shed a little luster of his own. Leading him tenderly along the edge of the stony road, Lancelot scented the air with a sinking heart. A lame horse, a lonely highway, and an icy night ahead—it could hardly be worse.

Already he could feel the cold biting his face. His shoulder, too, was aching from the fall he took when his horse stumbled and threw him, then went lame. He was dearly hoping that the dim light on the road ahead would prove to be an inn, or else he was destined for a bitter night outdoors. Truly the Mother was punishing him for his sins.

Enough! He shook his head and tried to clear his mind. Useless to add to his miseries with such thoughts. Things might still turn out better than they seemed. As soon as he caught up with the others—whenever he did—

Gods above! he groaned. Where were Bors, Galahad, and Lionel? Surely he ought to have overtaken them by now? He had followed them mile by mile and never once lost the trail, they had taken such care to leave word at every stage. But as he had trailed after them, he had been dogged by misfortune every step of the way. From a broken bridle to a fever that had laid him low, every incident had conspired to hold him back.

Yet still he knew he was on the right track. At every alehouse, every petty village, every wayside cell, his loyal cousins had left word for him. He could hear Bors' very tone of voice in the careful directions passed on to him, and knew that the little knight must have laid out his money with a lavish hand to ensure such faithful transmission of his words. Bors and Lionel too—and now Galahad: the very thought of them made his eyes sting. Well, he had to catch up with them soon.

But not tonight.

Tonight he would have to try to take shelter at the alehouse here: alehouse and pig-house too, to judge by the smell and the squealing coming from the rear. Dubiously he eyed the low dwelling looming up out of the dusk. Hardly more than a hovel, it offered a cold comfort to the weary wayfarer. A single lantern glimmered through the small, unglazed window on the front, and only the rough clump of bush suspended over the door gave any sign that this was a public house. Tethering his horse, Lancelot approached the threshold and went in.

The stink within met him as he opened the door, a foul mingling of human and animal, bad ale, and rancid tallow smoking in the lamp. Inside, turning toward him, huddled round a table by the light of one candle, were a set of faces as bad as any he had ever seen. The low foreheads of the half dozen inhabitants, their suspicious, piglike eyes, sickly complexions, and undershot chins were all alike, each uglier than the last. The worst of them all was the oldest and a woman to boot, the matriarch, he now saw, of the whole ill-favored clan.

The alewife lifted her head like a sow about to charge, then stiffened, staring at him as if she knew who he was. The same understanding passed between the men in the sweaty room. Objects on the table melted swiftly from hand to hand and out of sight. Moments later the old woman was bustling to his side.

"Good evening, sir!" she hailed him, her misshapen, leathery face wreathed in smiles. "You're out late for a winter night like this. We didn't expect any travelers at this hour."

Close up, she was even uglier than he'd thought. One small eye had to do the work of two, the other being sunk into itself, and only one tooth remained in the mouth below. Coarse black and gray hairs sprouted on her lower face, and her jaw was lost in a welter of withered chins. Beneath her splayed bosom and greasy apron a mighty stomach thrust out, and her mountainous frame ran with grease despite the cold. Though she seemed more pig than woman, the demeanor of the others in the room indicated that she was nevertheless the owner of the place.

Lancelot's spirits shrank. Where was the cheerful landlord of his wishful hopes, with his merry band of cronies and his wholesome wife? A bright fire should be burning on the hearth, with the rich scent of broth or hot brawn in the air. But here the only warmth came from a few bricks of peat smoldering on the hearth. Standing by a cauldron slung over the low fire, a sour-eyed slattern was resentfully stirring the pot. She was as thin as her mother was fat, but from the cast of her features, the two were flesh and blood. Lancelot watched as her dirty fingers fished into the stew and brought a dripping lump of fat to her lips. His stomach heaved. If it meant a hard fast, he would not eat here tonight.

The alewife leered at Lancelot. "My daughter," she said. Another one-toothed grin took in the four or six outsize figures he had seen before, lounging round the table in the gloom. "And my sons."

Lancelot nodded bleakly to himself. However unsavory the place, it would have been preferable to a night in the cold. But with so many in the family, there would not even be a length of floor by the fire. So be it. A sharp night outdoors would make him more thankful for a warm bed when it came. No man in his senses would regret leaving here: the place was no better than a nest of thieves.

Out then into the night with me, Lancelot resolved, before an iron midnight locks all the land in ice. Aloud he had one request: "The knights who came through here before me—did they leave any word of the way I was to go?"

The alewife fixed her one good eye on Lancelot, and an evil as old as the hills swept her meager soul. This was the fine knight, for sure, the one who the other three had told her would follow them. The gold they had left her had gone to save her eldest son, who had had the bad luck to beat a man to death. The blood-gelt settled, she had dreamed of more to come. And here he was, as handsome as the day in his fine armor and shining silver mail, his sword alone worth God knows how many crowns, and doubtless an equally fine horse waiting outside. All this for the taking, and no one to know where he went. She'd be a fool to let this golden goose fly away.

"The way you're to go, good sir?" She grinned, and her one tooth gleamed like a tombstone in her ruined mouth. "The three lords left word for you, indeed they did. They're taking the great road south, they told me to say, making for the port. They went through the forest to the highway over the hill."

A soft snicker came from the watchers around the fire. The largest and ugliest of them drew his knife from his belt and began to pick his teeth. The old woman took no notice, and pressed on. "From here you take the track hard by the house, up to the left beyond the stricken pine."

"I thank you, madam," said Lancelot courteously. He bowed and left the house.

The lone candle in the hovel shimmered and spun. Watching it dance in the draught of Lancelot's passing, not a soul moved. Then the old witch's index finger began to itch. Rubbing it against her thumb in the age-old gesture of counting coins, she stared out greedily beyond the smoke-stained walls of her hovel to a better place.

"Sword, daggers, armor, silver chain mail, and a fine horse for sure," she snuffled in glee. "And who knows what he'll have in his saddlebags? Come spring, we'll have a new byre for the pigs and a new roof for ourselves too if our luck holds."

She gazed lovingly at her cluster of hideous sons. Still picking his teeth, the eldest treated her to a vicious grin. "He's yours, Ma," he said, his mind already running ahead. Horse, saddle, armor, and all of the best, he calculated—never had such a prize fallen into their hands. Can't sell that stuff round here though; we'll have to go to the city or farther still—

Another large, greasy head shook doubtfully in the gloom. "He won't be easy pickings," its owner complained. "He looks like a fighter, and he's well armed."

The eldest laughed in rank derision. "You 'fraid?" he sneered. "When there's five of us against a long, drink of water like him? We'll cut him to pieces and bring his kidneys home for the pot."

A strange sensation stabbed the alewife to the quick. Pig-woman and thief-mother as she was, the sad knight had reached into a long-forgotten chamber of her heart where she had once been female, and young and loving too. She surprised herself and her offspring with what came next.

"No blood!" she commanded. "And no violence. Let him live."

"Let him live?" The eldest son gaped, baffled. "Why, Ma? Dead men tell no tales."

"And neither will he," said the alewife confidently. "He'll never make trouble for us. He won't come back here—he's too keen to catch up with the knights who've gone ahead."

Her son stared her out. "You don't know that."

"True." The old witch was starting to think again. "Well, do what you like. He's sure to fetch up at the old Lady Chapel to rest, you can take him there in his sleep." She paused, and laughed heartily at her own foolishness. "But whatever you do, my boys—don't spoil his pretty face!"

LANCELOT STEPPED OUT in the dark, happy to breathe again the pure night air. Untying his horse, he led the beast back on the road, his eyes searching the frozen route ahead. Soon he came upon a cloven tree shadowing a path leading into the wood, and without hesitation turned his horse that way. With memories of the hard glint in the alewife's eye, he had no faith at all in the woman's words, for all her ratlike grinning smiles. But he knew that the highway must run beyond the hill, and this track would be the shortest way to it.

The air was a little warmer under the trees, and the wind had dropped. Overhead the stars winked and called him on, glimmering through the leafless roof above. Watching the singing, dancing points of light, he could hear the eternal star-song, high and clear, and his soul mourned with every plangent note. Oh, I have lost my love, my life, my soul, Guenevere my dear one, Guenevere the Queen.

On they went, and on. But every step he took was slower now, and it came to him that he would not catch up with his cousins before the Holy Land. Bors, Lionel, and Galahad would continue the Quest alone. He trudged on in a trancelike state of misery, his only thought to keep walking if he could into the red, freezing dawn.

Now visions came to him as he went along. He saw three figures on horseback riding away out of sight, then a sun-baked landscape and a shimmering sea of sand. He saw a shining city on a hill, and within it a golden palace with silver doors and windows and towers of bronze. But imprinted on his eyelids was one sight above all, a white cross rising from a hill of green. Standing alone in its eminence the cross bore a name he could not read, the letters vanishing as he strained his eyes to see.

But one of them would die in the Holy Land, that much was plain. Was it Bors, Galahad, Lionel, or himself? A sorrow greater than any he had ever known invaded his soul. Now pain and fatigue wracked his every joint. He was too tired to walk, to think, even to breathe. But he made himself join the star-chorus to keep his spirits up. "Guenevere," he sang, "Guenevere the Queen..."

The dead leaves, crisped by the frost, crackled softly underfoot. The horse was still limping, but moving more easily now. Lovingly Lancelot caressed the warm, smooth nose. "Soon, soon, old friend, we'll find a place to rest," he promised. But the faithful beast knew that he was too tired to stop.

He did not know how long they plodded on before he saw a faint glow through the trees. Leading the horse behind him on a single rein, he left the path and shouldered through the dense scrub and undergrowth. In a small clearing stood a low stone building roofed with flint and moss. The light he had seen came from inside, warm golden beams pouring out on the frosty night.

Lancelot stood outside and drank the whole scene in. Despite the cold, a slow warmth gently suffused his limbs, and his deep fatigue and hunger ebbed away. Half ardently, half in fear he hastened to unsaddle the horse and turn it loose to graze. Carefully he laid the horse harness and all his gear in the shelter of the wall, and approached the open door.

He saw a simple stone cell, deserted except for a plain altar of black basalt in the center of the floor. A fine cloth of silk and gold adorned the primeval stone, and countless candles blazed around the walls. In the world outside, frost and ice were weaving their crystalline magic to cover every twig, every blade of grass, in shades of glittering white. But here in the rosy glow of the candlelight, the old chapel was as warm and welcoming as a loving kiss. A sweet savor breathed from every ancient stone, and the rugs and cushions on the floor begged him to lie down.

Lancelot felt a sweet liquor rise within him, unlocking his eyes and his throat. Joy and sorrow combined in his heart, and his tears overflowed. Weeping gently, in a grief as soft as summer rain, he unbuckled his sword and took his armor off. Piece by piece he laid his weapons of war by the door. They did not seem to belong in this house of love.

Unarmed, peace flooded him like a blessing, and he turned to the altar once more. Black stone, he thought, like the altars of the Goddess: where am I? Pondering, he gazed around, and saw that the four angles of the walls, the threshold where he came in, and the lintel over the door were ancient bluestones, the standing stones men had raised to the Mother since time began.

Then he knew that he had come to a sacred place. From the flint infilling of the walls and the roof covering of moss, he saw that some hermit had taken the framework of the standing stones and made them into his home. But wherever he slept, moldering in the green earth nearby, he was long gone. And now the Great One had reclaimed the place as Her own.

He stood still for a moment, rejoicing in where he was. Then he moved reverently to the altar and fell to his knees. Clasping his hands, he brought them to his lips. That made him dream of kissing Guenevere, and his soul took flight.

Guenevere—

How long he remained there praying, he never knew. The rich sweetness in the air fed the hunger of his body and lifted his soul. Transported with tiredness and hunger, his body slipped its earthly shell and winged its way up to the astral plane. And there, amidst the stars blazing with cold fire, she came to him.

"My love——" he thought she said, and he cried back to her, "Lady, speak to me—let me hear your voice——"

Gleaming like the moon, she spread her long white hands. "Take care of my treasures," she whispered in a pale, astral voice. He looked, and saw she had the Hallows spread at her feet.

Murmuring, she set them on the altar one by one. "The cup of love," she crooned, stroking the gold as if it were a child, "and the plate of the Mother that feeds all who come." Her arms in their golden sleeves shimmered as she touched the sword and the lance. "The weapons of truth, which comes only through love."

Before him the Hallows glowed and flashed like stars on fire. His whole being pulsed in unison with them, the very force of nature unconfined. He heard the eternal harmony of the singing spheres, and the voice of his mother from his cradleside.

"Love," breathed the music.

"Love," echoed his mother's undying voice.

And "Love," cried the owl on the frozen branch and the glowworm in the grass.

Then his sight darkened, and the black figure of the Father Abbot strode into the cell. With him came an odor of righteousness, sickening in this clean and holy place.

The Prelate took up his stance before the altar and seized the loving cup in both hands, hoisting it high above his shaven pate. His pale eyes flashed and passion dripped from his contorted frame, suffusing his every word.

"Only a Christian will achieve the Grail," the black vision intoned. "You are not he, Sir Lancelot, sinful man! You are fated to fail this test of holiness. Avaunt then, sir, be gone and quit this place!"

But Lancelot could only smile and laugh quietly to himself. Above and beyond the shriveled figure of the priest he could see Guenevere in the world between the worlds. Clad in starlight and crowned with the tears of the moon, she leaned down from heaven and brushed him with a kiss. A joy sweeter than he ever knew ran through every vein. He was drunk with delight, alive with living bliss.

"Hear me, monk," he cried ecstatically, "I have won the Grail! Every man seeks the woman of the dream, and he who enters the circle of the Goddess finds all he desires. Guenevere is the dream of all the world! She is my grail, there is no other in all the world. And I will proclaim her love through all the world, though I never see her on this earth again." He laughed again, too happy to contain his joy. "Away with you, then, sir priest, for I would be with my love."

The black vision screamed and threw his arms about. But to Lancelot he grew smaller with every cry. Slowly he watched the priest shrivel away. Then he reached out his arms and thought that Guenevere came to him. In a dream of bliss, he lost hold of himself and swooned away.

He dreamed long and hard, stretched out on the frozen stone, lying in a dead sleep as only those do who are taking flight from consciousness, broken in heart and hope. In the barren cell, not a mouse stirred. Lancelot slept as sweetly as he ever had in his life. Meanwhile, at the edge of the forest round the clearing, the two-legged wolves were gathering to tear out his heart.

CHAPTER 29

"The Grail! The Grail! The Grail!"

Bors was instantly awake. Beside him in the gloom he could hear Lionel stirring too.

"Brother?" came Lionel's soft query through the dark.

"Yes?" he responded at once, though both knew there was nothing to say.

For their quest had changed in a way that neither of them understood. From the moment they had first sighted the Holy Land from the deck of the ship, Galahad was transformed from the ardent youth they had both come to love. Refusing to eat or sleep, he had remained rigid in the prow, his eyes fixed on the far horizon, with its squat, white flat-roofed houses and shimmering sand.

Before this, he had won all hearts onboard with his kindness. The lone sailor at the helm on a starless night, the hapless seasick traveler, all were grateful for his quiet company. He had willingly given his own heavy cloak of Welsh wool to a shivering cabin boy who could not stop coughing in the cold sea air. "Where I am going," he merrily proclaimed, "there is no need of wool." Of course, he caught cold himself and now coughed too, but he laughed it off, despite his cousins' concern.

Belowdecks, heaving his heart out, Bors had known little of this, and cared less till at last they put into port. But as soon as his feet were on the blessed earth once more, he could not fail to notice the change in the young knight. Always pale, Galahad was waxing more translucent every day. He simply forgot the normal demands of the flesh, and his body ceased to interest him at all. He seemed to feed on some savor in his soul, and never looked hungry or starved. But in truth he grew thinner every day.

And the calling, the cries, the talking in his sleep—that was enough to drive a man raving mad. Bors shifted uneasily on his pallet and tried to think. If only it weren't for this infernal heat, perhaps Galahad's transports might be less. Lord, Lord, he gibed to himself, is this Your Holy Land, or are we in hell?

For the heat—it was like nothing Bors had ever encountered before. By day they had to hide from the blistering sun. Even now, at dead of night when the undead walked, the heat lay on their limbs like molten copper, too heavy to shift. Bors moved his sticky arms away from his body and thought hopelessly of cool, leafy forests and sheltered glades. Both he and Lionel had felt the strokes of the sun in scorched skin, violent headaches, even lights before their eyes. Only Galahad stayed pale and cool and sweet, as white as a lily in a world aflame.

For his young heart, his mind were on other things. No sooner had they disembarked than he was asking, "How far to the Sepulchre of Our Lord?" When Lionel, loving Lionel, had resisted him, citing Bors' weeks of seasickness as a reason to delay, Galahad had shown that rest and recovery were nowhere on his mind.

"Well, cousins, I shall see you at the Sepulchre of Christ," he had said, and they had had no choice but to accompany him.

For however he had grown and flourished in their long months on the road, he was still a boy. Not yet fourteen, Bors groaned to himself, hardly more than a child. If only I'd had a child of my own, he thought, I'd know what to do. Then he caught himself up: This is the first time in my life I ever had such a thought. And where's Lancelot? He above all ought to be here with his son. But as it is, we must do the best we can.

So he and Lionel had brought the cherished boy south, then east, ever east toward the sacred land. Mile by mile Galahad's joy had grown greater, and his body's health worse. He was so pale, so weak, he could hardly sit his horse. He was coughing now too on almost every breath he took. And with the ragged, rasping remains of his breath, he was denying that he ever coughed at all.

From the air above Bors' rough pallet there came a low drone. Bors pulled up the sheet and wrapped it tightly round his head, enduring the heat, sweating in despair. The creatures that stung in the night were a torture to him. Like the sun in these parts, their bite was too much for his tender skin.

Wretchedly he forced his mind back to something worse. Galahad was sick, there was no doubt of that. Those whose flesh melted away from their limbs were destined for the world between the worlds. And they saw and heard things too that others did not. As the boy did now, dreaming of the Grail.

And if Galahad was failing, where was Lancelot? Why on earth had he not caught up with them by now? Only one thing would have kept Lancelot from joining them. And what that was, Bors would not, dared not think.

"All well, brother?" came Lionel's voice through the dark.

"As well as can be," Bors' answering grunt conveyed. "Go back to sleep."

"The Grail! The Grail! The Grail! Let me see the Grail!" sounded above the feverish tossing from Galahad's bed.

Huddling under his sheet, sweltering in his misery, Bors raised a frantic prayer: *Goddess, Mother, save this child of the Grail! Or else may his God from the East grant his dying prayer.*

"DINANT? GODS ABOVE, Dinant, is that you?"

Stumbling forward in the subterranean gloom, Dinant raised his head. He never thought to find another living soul in this noisome cell. But he knew the voice calling him as well as his own.

"Ladinas?" He burst out into a cackle of disbelief. "Helin told me you had starved to death."

"The Gods know how I didn't," came the low rumbling voice in the dark. He gave a sepulchral laugh. "And let me tell you, now you're here, we may yet."

"What?" Dinant cried, loosing a volley of oaths. The fury he felt with himself was with him still, and would not soon subside. To fall for that trick in the woods with the strange knight, and ride straight into an ambush—he spat in disgust. If ever a knight deserved his fate, he knew he did.

Yet still it was shaming to be dragged to this castle on foot, a prisoner walking at his horse's tail. When his captors thrust him into the hold at the base of the keep, into the darkest dungeon without food or water or regard for nature's needs, he was only glad that his plight was no worse. They had taken his armor to be sure, and relieved him of his weapons and every trace of knighthood he carried with him. But they had not stripped him and beaten his body with thorns. They had not turned the dogs on him for sport, or strung him up by his thumbs. They had not— Enough! he chided himself. All this they still could do. Or starve him to death, as Ladinas said.

"Why are they keeping us here?" Dinant found his teeth chattering, though he could not have said whether through cold or fear. Let it not be gaol fever, Gods, he prayed. Even the strongest did not survive that. "What do they want us for?"

"For ransom," Ladinas laughed hollowly, "from the King."

Dinant's spirits revived. "Then we'll be saved! After all, we know the King will do anything for his knights. And Guenevere will—"

"If the King knows. Or the Queen. If they've sent word to them."

The first tendrils of real fear wrapped themselves round Dinant's heart. "What?"

He felt a rustling in the straw, and a few feet away from him a pair of maddened eyes shone in the midnight blackness of the cell.

"How long d'you think I've been here?" the raw voice demanded hoarsely. "Gods above, man, I've lost count of time. All these months, it must be a year, two years—"

"No, surely not?" Dinant protested, but without conviction. His voice faded away.

The hollow voice rasped on. "I fell into their hands within a week or two of beginning the Quest. Some will have been to the Holy Land and back by now. They talked of ransom as soon as I was seized. And all these moons later, I languish here still."

The stink of Ladinas was terrible. Dinant could feel the fetid breath on his face. He forced himself to stay calm. "But why would they keep you here?"

A madman's cackle rang round the dripping walls. "The Gods alone know that."

Goddess, Mother, save us, save us now— "Who are they, Ladinas, do you know that?"

"No. But what's a castle without prisoners?" The wild eyes flared again in the bitter gloom. "What's a dungeon without captives rotting in their chains?"

WE SHOULD HAVE followed Galahad.

Gawain rolled his aching shoulders and shook his head, gazing round the barren landscape in despair. The Quest was leading them nowhere, he knew that now. Agravain's taunting refrain had come back to haunt him with every pointless step, just as misty sunsets like this awoke every one of the wounds he had taken at his brother's hands. They had been slow to heal, till Gawain was forced to admit in the silence of his heart that he was too old—the fight in him was waning. His next hard battle would likely be his last. And then? He thrust the thought away.

He wanted to weep. They should have followed Galahad as Agravain said, he knew that now. But that he should ever agree with Agravain—the thought was bitter to him, like chewing sloes in winter for want of better food.

Agravain—

A savage sadness gripped him, and the ache in his heart made him forget the pain in his limbs. Where was he? What was he doing now?

The next moment a bitter laugh rocked Gawain's frame. That he would find himself missing that dark, still presence, sorrowing for his hateful brother like a lost limb—

He threw a glance behind, where Gaheris and Gareth sat their weary horses just as he did, staring out into the setting sun. At least they, thank the Gods, were as true as the sun rising in the morning and sinking in flames every night. They had stayed by his side as he set their course steadily east. On the way they had done all that could be expected, and striven to fulfill every demand of the Quest. They had succored the weak, put down the strong, and defended women and children everywhere.

And then they had come to the edge of the land, and there was no more. Only the salt sea's savage spray on their faces and the crying of the birds. A poor cluster of half a dozen hovels was all that passed for human life. But there, too, they had comported themselves like knights of the Grail.

Three women whose men had been swallowed up by the sea had madly craved their love. "But for you, strangers," they wailed, "there'll be no bairns in this place, and our village will die!"

But Gareth, bowing to the leader as if she were a queen, had said sweetly, "Madam, we may not avail ourselves of your love. Our Quest is pure, and our hearts must be so too."

Curse him for a great looby, mused Gawain fondly, easing himself in the saddle and feeling his manhood stir. The leader had had a marvelous pair of breasts, and even the short one, a weedy, mouse-colored thing, had had a look in her eye that any man would know. They could have rested there, and done fine deeds by all three of the women, for as long as they cared to stay. But his virtuous brothers had decreed otherwise.

So what now? Where now? Gawain gnawed furiously on the end of his thumb. There was nothing here in the east but acres of drowned land, half sea, half marsh. His great idea for the site of the Grail had proved false, and the Quest itself was hollow after so long on the road. Months and months, far too many to count, had flown by them as apple blossom falls from the springtime bough. And as fast and as cruelly, their cash had ebbed away too. Soon, soon, they would have to turn back to the court.

But for tonight—Gawain's spirits revived. Tonight they would be housed as befitted knights of their order and kin of the King.

"At the fork in the road, take the left," the old publican of the last hostelry had confided in his cups. "'Tis a meager bypath, and most pass it by. But the right-hand track is guarded by a troop of knights. Take the left, winding up to the castle, and the lord will welcome you in. 'Tis his humor to put strangers to the challenge in this way. But he's no fighter himself, and when you and your brothers get to his gate, he's knightly enough to take you in and do you all the honor that's due."

Never one to miss a good fight, Gawain had hesitated at the fork in the road. But an unaccustomed prudence had turned him left. They were due for a rest in soft beds, all three of them, not to mention a hot trencher and a goblet brimming with spiced wine. Now they were fast approaching the castle the old man had described: a massive curtain wall around a mighty keep, with towers at each corner of the battlements, and twin towers guarding the gates and portcullis in front. The guards at the gatehouse had seen them coming, they knew. Moments later the challenge rang out through the dusk.

"Hold there! What's your business here?"

"Knights of King Arthur!" bellowed Gawain across the moat. "We bring greetings to your lord and seek shelter for the night."

A light, reedy voice joined in the colloquy. "Welcome, knights, to the castle of Sir Brunor de Gretise."

From the archway across the drawbridge, the lord himself leaped forth. A small, smiling figure, he could have been any age. He was clad in the finest armor, with a great sword at his side and a set of silver daggers through his belt, but every piece was as pristine as the day it was made. For no knight would offer combat to this odd little man. With his diminutive limbs and strange movements, it was clear that the Old Ones had sent him into the world imperfect and unfinished, though his fate had made him the last heir to a noble house. His scrubby, colorless hair stood up all over his head, and his wide-spaced eyes were as guileless as a child's.

"Come in! Come in!"

He beckoned them forward eagerly across the moat, reaching up to take their hands before they could dismount. "I thank you, sirs, for gracing my poor house," he caroled enthusiastically, prancing around. "I keep knightly traditions here, and the fellowship of the Round Table is an honor beyond words." A flourish of capering movements concluded his words. "Come in, come in!"

All well enough till then, as Gawain later told all who would listen back at Arthur's court: a knightly welcome from a lord who would never be a knight but who strove to maintain the traditions nonetheless. A manly welcome too from the knights who did their lord's work of challenging strangers on the road through his land for the right to pass: they were happy to see strange faces in the knights' hall and hear word of the Quest, who lived and who had died. An unobtrusive welcome from the servants, pages, and squires, all unnoticed as they sat down to dine, until one young face and then another caught Gawain's eye.

Gareth too had noticed the sad-eyed boys who served at the high table with so little joy. "Tell me, sir, about that squire and page—?"

"Those lads at the end?" Sir Brunor responded to Gareth's question, squinting at them through the flickering candlelight on the board. "Oh yes, I had to take them in last year. They lost their lord, an errant knight who came this way. He was from Arthur's court, just as you are. He made a doughty challenge to my knight, but he was no match for him at the joust, and took a bad fall." He laughed unconcernedly, nodding like a child. "A big, hearty fellow he was, on a fine roan. But too fat, too fat—when he fell, he broke his back."

Gareth caught his breath. Already his soft heart was pregnant with foreboding, and Gaheris's color too had turned milk-pale. But it was left to Gawain to put their fear into words. "This knight, sir—was he called Sagramore?"

It was after midnight by the time they had heard the story in full, and questioned the page and squire to learn all they knew. Afterward they had lingered long in the castle chapel, weeping and praying beside the handsome tombstone hung with Sagramore's banner and shield. Then they had been escorted to the finest chambers, each equipped with a handsome feather bed. But none of the brothers slept well that night. And Gawain as the leader slept worst of all.

One by one they passed through his mind, all the sad ghosts of those who were no more. He saw Sagramore again in the knights' hall, fat and expansive, roistering with his peers, and wondered what prize was worth that joyful life. Then Lamorak came to him from the astral plane, a face from the Orkneys of so long ago.

"Remember your mother, Gawain," said the shining shade. "I was her champion, and I died for her."

Last of all he saw Morgause, his mother herself, her womanly form just as it had been in life, her rich red hair tumbling down over her ample breasts. She wore the royal robe and crown of the Orkneys and the look of a woman in love.

"Lamorak and I are together now for all time," she told him with starlight in her eyes. "But why do all these others have to die? For the Grail? What is it to you, Gawain?"

And now he saw that in truth he did not know. All he had seen was the dull gleam of gold, the lightning flash, the piles of smoldering dust. All he had felt was the call of the road, the urge to adventure, the thrill of the Quest. Then he saw how he had led himself astray and taken his brothers on the same lost errand too, and he suffered as he had never suffered in his life.

By daylight he had come to a plan. As gray as the dawn and suddenly looking old, Gawain called his brothers to him, and began to speak.

"We won't find the Grail." Gawain stared out on a vision of a lesser world. "It's over." Never had two words been harder for him to say. He felt sick and spent. "There is no Grail. We're going back to court."

SO ENDED THE QUEST.

One by one the knights returned, or came trailing back in hollow-eyed twos and threes. And then it was seen that the Quest had begun the breaking of the Round Table, when the knights rode away. They were scattered far and wide in pursuit of the Holy Grail, for none knew where it lay. Some traveled to the holy places in the heart of the islands, where the Old Ones had left sacred signs upon the land. Some scoured the hills and hollows where the Fair Ones loved to hide, disturbing the ancient dwellers in those parts, the land kin, the dark, shy folk born of the union between the Old Ones and the first creatures of the lakes and caves and woods.

Others crossed overseas and followed the pilgrim path to seek the God from the East, the sacred way leading to the Holy Land. Still others voyaged on to the ends of the earth, where humankind ended and the halflings began, savages who went naked but for barbarous garments of scrawny fur, who gobbled at each other in outlandish tongues and, as rumor had it, ate their own young. There they saw wonders no man could believe, massive beasts as big as houses with curved horns of ivory growing out of their mouths, and great birds that snatched sheep from the hillsides and tore full-grown infants from their mothers' arms.

Long years afterward they were still returning home, wild-eyed ancients with tales no man would believe. But many never came back to Camelot at all. Some were set upon far away from home, and robbed of horse and armor and all their goods. Stripped of their knighthoods, stranded in foreign climes, they had no choice but to labor for their bread, and watch their past receding year by year till Camelot was no more than a gilded dream. Others saved themselves from such enemies, but lost their faith after years of questing for the Grail in vain. Some lost their reason and ran mad from loneliness and despair, till they found peace at last in some quiet hermitage far from town and court.

Many perished, gloriously or hopelessly, without a trace. Some rode into dark forests and were lost. Others fell among thieves and had their throats cut before they could cry out, or were taken by pirates and sold as slaves. Not a few were held for ransom, and then held for malice after the ransom came. The fever claimed many, and the flux many more.

None was more mourned than Galahad, who was never seen again. Many rumors attended his passing, for his holiness had been a cause for wonder everywhere he went. It was said that he became king of a holy city before he died, revered by the inhabitants as their gateway to God. After a year he was taken up to the Father by bands of singing angels, cradling him softly in their mighty wings. Other knights heard another tale: that he had drawn his last breath quite alone but for the kind attentions of a passing pilgrim, in whose fatherly arms he fell asleep. But one thing was certain: that he had joined the ranks of those lost on the Quest.

And those who survived limped back to Camelot.

CHAPTER 30

long the riverbank, all the green rushes had withered into brown, and the willow trees had lost their silvery leaves. An endless autumn was dwindling into winter, and already it was too cold to linger here. Guenevere stood at the water's edge and looked out across the level plain beyond. How long had she lived without Lancelot—without love?

The great river rolled indifferently along, winding its way round Camelot, meandering through plains and water meadows down to Avalon.

Avalon.

Guenevere nodded somberly to herself. All waters led to Avalon in the end. The thought was a dull comfort and something more, a promise of escape. *How blessed it would be to step into the river, become one with the rolling waters, and drift down to the Sacred Lake—to cease forever on the setting sun, and float into infinity with no pain—*

Brooding among things dead and dying, Guenevere saw bleakness everywhere. Arthur had recovered in body but not in spirit, and she feared he would never again be wholly well. The Round Table still lay in two broken shards, and no joiner in the land had been able to mend it again. Nothing disturbed the dull rhythms of her days. Yet still she stubbornly allowed herself to dream. *One day I shall be free of this sad burden, my unending life. Till then, I have to wait—wait and endure.*

But Goddess, Mother, tell me, tell me, how long?

That was the question that dogged her night and day. How long must she go on living in grief like this? The love between her and Lancelot was over, dead and gone—why must she go on suffering for him? Panic seized her, and she threw off her thick cloak, careless of the cold. Already she had borne more than she could stand. And the seasons had come and gone without relief.

For time had rolled by like the river and left no trace. Every day she hoped for something new, and hoped in vain. *When you left, you took my life along with you,* she said to Lancelot, but without reproach. She often spoke to him alone like this, though it was still hard for her to understand that he could not hear, and never would reply.

Or was it *could not* reply? Had he left the land of love and laughter and gone down to the world beneath? Shivering with dread, she felt for her cloak and pulled it close around her again. Absently she took note of her hands as they drew up the cords, blue and shriveled in the raw, damp chill. *Old woman's hands,* she thought. *Well, I'm an old woman now.*

Maiden, mother, and then crone—this is the way of the Goddess since time began. Ah, Lancelot. Our love was like a sweet apple ripening in the sun. Now summer's gone, and we are for the dark.

She wanted to weep, but she had no more tears. All she had was a raw inner dryness where the wellsprings of nature should be. She wrapped her arms tightly around her cold breasts. *I am old and alone, without a lover, without a child. My life is as empty and bare as these leafless trees.*

Without Lancelot—

Before, when he went away, he would always return, she always knew that she would see him again. Every dusk when the love-star bloomed in the evening sky, she would light a candle in her window to shine for him. And every dawn, she had only to close her eyes to see him at his morning ritual, kneeling to face the rising sun to renew his vows to her. The fierce purity of their devotion, the unwavering concentration that each had had upon the other, had made their love burn as ardently then whether they were together or apart.

But now—

"Goddess, Mother," she moaned, "let me be free!"

Freefreefree... the evening breeze whispered mockingly among the reeds.

Then a cry from behind broke in on her reverie. "Lady?" came the voice of Ina waiting in the rear. "Lady, see—"

She turned. Two men were coming down the path from Camelot, the taller of the two giving his arm to help the older one across the water meadow in between. The idle thought floated into her mind, *That old man looks like Bors.* The next moment a thrill of horror passed through her frame. *It is Bors, it's Bors himself!*

Even from a distance, he could read her face. She saw him draw himself up as he approached, and shake off Lionel's supporting arm. "Your Majesty," he said stiffly.

"I am glad to see you, Sir Bors," she said tremulously. She bowed to Lionel. "You and your brother too." She tried not to look at Bors' drawn and wrinkled face, his stooped shoulders, the unhealthy pallor beneath the sunburned sheen. "I am sorry to see you looking so—" Her voice trailed off. "Have you been unwell?"

Bors shook his head. "A wretched ague I took in the East, madam, nothing more." He forced a smile. "I'll soon be my old self." He threw a glance at Lionel, and a look of inexpressible suffering clouded his gaze. "As much as we'll ever be the same again."

Lancelot is dead, came to Guenevere. *Of all men, they would know.* She could not breathe. A strange sound came out of her mouth.

Lionel stared at her. "Majesty?" he said anxiously.

Somehow she opened her mouth and moved her lips. "Sir—whatever it is—tell me—" She could not say any more.

"Alas—" Bors aged again before her frightened eyes. "I can't deny it, madam, I wish I could." His shoulders moved in a defeated shrug. "We've given him up for dead."

My love dead? Yes, I knew it. Well, soon I will be too.

"Dead?" Ina flew at Bors with a wild scream. "How did he die? Who'd kill Sir Lancelot?"

Ina, Ina, don't ask—death comes when it will—

"Lancelot?"

It was Lionel, his worn face alive with surprise. "No, not Lancelot," he said hollowly. "Galahad."

The voices reached Guenevere like sounds underwater. Was she already in the river, floating away? *Oh,* her heart cried, *ohhh—*

"Lancelot? No." Shaking his head, Bors hastened to second Lionel. "We haven't seen him since the start of the Quest, but we've got no reason to think he's dead."

A somber Lionel took up the tale. "No, it's Galahad we're concerned about. We had to leave him in the Holy Land. He—"

Lionel's voice wound on. Guenevere stood as motionless as a stone. *Galahad? What do I care about that fanatical boy? Especially when they say that Lancelot lives!*

She wanted to leap in the air, to dance and cry out. Instead she must try to cheer the brothers' pain. For they loved Galahad, there could be no doubt about that.

She drew a breath, and made her voice very calm. "You had to leave Galahad? Tell me," she said.

Bors stared out across the river with unseeing eyes. How could he tell the truth about the Quest, the miracle, the terror, the pity of it all?

"We were almost in sight of the Grail," he began hoarsely. "We were in the East, and the heat was terrible—" Then he felt the weight of Lionel's gaze, looked up, and caught his brother's eye. And suddenly, inexplicably he was there again.

THE WAY HAD been weary and long, and the going hard. Once over the Narrow Sea, they passed down through France into stranger and stranger lands.

The farther south they went, the more often they had to change their mounts in the heat. Even so, they found themselves making slower and slower progress, condemned to ride fly-blown, broken-down, and pitiful nags. "These people don't care for their horses the way we do," Lionel had observed with dismay.

But Galahad grew more joyful every day. For now they had reached the Holy Land, and every night he had visions of the Grail.

"We'll come to a hill outside a city wall," he said huskily. "And on the top we'll see a castle of gold with a tower of silver and gates of pearl. The Grail is there, in the keeping of an ancient king. Inside the Grail Castle, all who truly believe in Our Saviour may taste the blood of Christ. And I shall be among them, if God wills!"

Such dreams fed his soul and kept his frail form alive.

Yet every day his body grew weaker as his spirit blazed and grew strong. His flesh was translucent now, the bones in his hands visible through their paper-thin covering of skin. Eating was something he had forgotten how to do. He had bursts of strange energy when a hectic flush in his cheeks would make him look healthy again. But then he began to cough and his fever came and went, leaving him bright-eyed and restless, wakeful and tossing all night.

At the last inn, the owner complained that Galahad was ruining his trade when he kept everyone else awake. He brought in an ancient crone from the desert outside the town, to silence the boy, he said, or else he would throw them out. She was old and poorly dressed, swathed and veiled in the dark blue robes of her tribe, and her sunburned face and hands were deeply wrinkled and work-worn. But her large, liquid eyes were fathomless pools of love, and their hooded gaze held all the wisdom of the East. In spite of himself, Bors' heart revived. All might yet be well.

She entered the wretched room where Galahad lay, and the comforting smell of sweet herbs came in with her. Fresh bunches of all-heal dangled from her belt, and a glowing phial of cordial hung round her neck. Approaching the tumbled bed with its sweated sheets, she favored the boy with a glance as old as time. She took up a pinch of skin on the back of Galahad's hand, and pulled down his lower eyelid to look inside. Then she turned away and spoke directly to Bors.

"His blood has turned to white," she said impassively. "And you hear him cough. The fever has rotted his lungs. He will not live."

"For Gods' sake!" Bors cried in anguish, glancing at the wasted form on the bed. Not in front of the boy, he besought her without words.

But Galahad only laughed.

"You are wrong, good mother," he said cheerfully. "I shall live forever in the love of Jesus Christ." His eyes were glowing. "I shall sit at the feet of His throne among the cherubim and seraphim, and all the angels and archangels shall fly about my head." He laughed again, a simple, joyous sound. "My mother told me so when I was young."

"He will die crying for his mother," observed the old woman dispassionately. "All men do. But the Great Mother called for this child long ago. There is nothing to be done."

They hardly saw her go. A sadness beyond speech gripped the room. Bors' heart was bursting, and he knew that Lionel too was aching to discharge his grief in tears. But neither wanted to be the first to speak.

"We must part." Galahad's voice when it came made them both start. "Now you see why I must go on alone."

"What?" yelped Bors. "Alone?" A moment before he could not have imagined a crueler truth than what they had just heard. Yet suddenly, here it was.

"Tomorrow I shall see the Holy Grail," Galahad said serenely. "And I must see it alone." He turned to Lionel and took his hand. "We must part."

"And leave you?" Lionel was aghast. "Never!"

"You must," Galahad persisted gently. "Both of you." The effort of speech had filmed his forehead with sweat.

"Why?" Bors demanded thickly. He wanted to scream.

"Because you doubt." Galahad's voice was suddenly strong and clear. "And the Grail Castle is only for those who believe. None who doubt the truth of Christ revealed may enter there."

Bors could feel his mind splitting in two. Suddenly he felt worthless, less than dust. "It's true that I doubt," he cried, frantic with pain. "But Lionel can surely go with you! He loves and trusts. His nature is not like mine."

"No," Galahad conceded with a loving smile. "But you two must not be parted for my sake." The pale smile faded, and Galahad closed his eyes. Suddenly he was remote and terrible. "Accept the truth, Bors. I shall leave tonight."

A howl rose from the depths of Bors' gut. *What shall we tell Lancelot?*

The semblance of a smile returned to Galahad's cold lips. "The truth," he coughed. "What else?"

"And so we left him."

Bors' broken voice tailed off. The air shivered and the shadow of a hot and fetid room rose before Guenevere's eyes. For a moment she saw the pale, tortured body on the bed, the eyes raised to seek a heaven beyond. Then the sight was gone, and with it the smell of sickness and decay. In the fresh, cool air off the river, she tried to understand. A foreign land, a dying boy, a parting beyond pain—no wonder then that Bors had aged twenty years, or that Lionel was weeping in the way grown men rarely wept, hopelessly, like a child.

These two good men suffering a cruel grief like this—and still their Quest was not over, would never end till Galahad was at peace. The familiar fury pounded through Guenevere's veins. A thousand curses on this evil Quest! The knights who pursued it were all destroyed by it, whether they lived or died. And it would also destroy the finest fellowship that the world had ever known.

She could not find her voice. A few odd crying sounds fell out of her mouth before she was able to speak. "And Lancelot? You said he didn't join you—*where is he?*"

A swift bolt of understanding passed between the two men. They did not need to speak.

Guenevere clutched her head. "You think he's dead?" she gasped, almost blind with grief. "You do!"

A thin cry, far away, cut through the air. "My lady—"

They turned. A manservant was running across the darkening plain, waving his arms. "Sir Gawain and his brothers have returned! The King is calling you all into the Great Hall."

CHAPTER 31

"**S**ir Gawain and his brothers!"

The excited servants ran shouting to and fro. "Sir Gawain—!"

Gawain, Gawain—

Agravain hastened through the failing light, making for the Prince's apartments with an eager step. Welcome back, Gawain, brother of mine, he mused sardonically, I have been waiting for you a long time now. He lengthened his stride across the lower court. Now, Gods, give me good fortune. Let me be first to bring Mordred the news.

At the door of Mordred's quarters the guard's spear was at Agravain's throat before he knew. "Who goes there?"

Contemptuously he brushed the deadly point aside. "A messenger from the King."

"Admit him," rang out a command from within.

Agravain stepped into the long chamber, suppressing a smile. Already Mordred knew how to live like a King. Twice as many torches flared against the walls as Arthur ever commanded to light a room, and every corner of the whitewashed space boasted a polished bench, a padded footstool, or a thick rug. Around the blazing hearth a handful of young women reclined on sheepskin couches or sprawled across plump cushions on the floor, ready to make music when their lord desired. Their books and instruments lay at their feet, and one plucked away disconsolately at her harp. Attired in springtime silks of lily and rose, they bloomed expectantly as Agravain came in. Then a damp disappointment made them droop again: this man would not distract the Prince from his warlike concerns and bring him to the fireside for songs and airs.

At the far end of the chamber Mordred sat enthroned on a low dais with Ozark and Vullian on either side, and the rest of his knights clustered tightly at his back. Twenty pairs of curious, hostile eyes watched Agravain intently as he approached.

"Sir Agravain!" Mordred greeted him heartily. "What brings you here?"

Agravain made a sketchy bow. "News, lord." Casually he flicked his eyes to the left and the right, taking in the knights hanging round the throne. *Let us be private, Prince,* his manner said.

Mordred smiled at his knights and waved a dismissive hand. "Go and amuse the ladies, will you, sirs? Vullian and Ozark, remain here with me."

Concealing their resentment, the rest of the knights trooped down from the dais and joined the flowerlike girls round the hearth. Mordred listened for a moment as one struck up a soft, plaintive air, then leaned forward, smoothing down his velvet gown. His face was alight with its Otherworldly glint. A circle of gold held back his thick black hair, the gold torque of knighthood gleamed round his neck, and his eyes were very bright. He gazed at Agravain almost mockingly, inviting him to speak. "Well, sir?"

"Gawain has returned. He and my brothers are back."

"So?" Mordred raised his elegant eyebrows in a cool stare. "Where's the news in that? A dozen servants will bring me word of this." He laughed. "Unless they have found the Grail. And I fancy we would have heard if they had."

"We would indeed," Agravain agreed. "But win or lose, the King will make much of them for going on the Quest. They ventured forth, and doubtless did great deeds." *As you did not, Prince,* his bland stare conveyed. "As heroes, they will win acclaim on all sides."

Mordred's face tightened. "So they are heroes now. What's that to me?"

"They'll be men of fame, and also the King's nearest kin." Agravain paused, then gently stabbed again. "Nearer and dearer to him for all this time away."

Nearer than I am? Dearer to Arthur's heart? The painful thought was plain on Mordred's face.

Yes, Mordred, yes, sang the voice inside his head.

From either side of the throne, his two attendant knights shot angry glances at Agravain. Vullian's face darkened as he leaned down to speak. "The King will never forget his own son, my lord."

"Never," seconded Ozark doggedly, his eyes hard.

"Ah, but—" Agravain held the pause, and nerved himself for the leap. "In the old world, lords, a sister's son was held to be a man's closest kin, closer indeed than the child of his own loins. Where the Mother-right prevails, the son of a king's sister has a stronger claim to inherit his father's throne. Our mother was Arthur's elder sister, and a great queen besides. To many here, Gawain is the King's rightful heir."

Mordred's mouth opened in a silent cry: *Not so! Your mother married King Lot and had Gawain. But her younger sister Morgan lay with the King and gave birth to me! I have the right twice over on my side. My claim derives from my mother and my father too!*

Agravain read his thought and had to suppress a laugh.

You make your claim through incest then, my lord?

He knew that was the question Mordred dared not raise. In the thirty years that had passed since the Prince was born, many had forgotten how he came into the world. Many others, born later, had never known. All those who knew the truth had long ago agreed to let it lie. Raising the specter of the offense that had given him life could only hurt Mordred now. No, the young Prince was trapped by the ghosts of his past. He had no choice but to stand as Arthur's son.

Which left Gawain the heir of the Mother-right.

Agravain watched the dark struggles on Mordred's handsome face without pity or remorse. Smoothly he pressed his advantage home. "And Gawain has yet another hold on the King," he observed in tones of sorrowful regret. "He was there, remember, when Arthur pulled the sword from the stone. He saw the King acclaimed, and declared for him then. He and Arthur have a lifetime between them now." Carefully he eliminated any sneering tones from his voice. "He always says he was the King's first companion, and he'll be the last."

"There at the last, you mean?" Vullian put in sharply. He looked at Ozark, and saw his concern mirrored in Ozark's troubled gaze. *If Gawain is there when Arthur breathes his last, will he snatch the crown from under our Prince's nose?*

Mordred too was sharing the same thought, it was plain. Agravain watched the fear blossom in three darkening minds, and inwardly rejoiced. He made his voice sound very reasonable and quiet. "So you see, my Prince, why you need to take care of your interests now that Gawain is back."

Mordred stared at him. The lustrous purple and blue had left his eyes, and his gaze was black. "I do."

Agravain bowed. "Then forgive me, lord, if I raise something else?"

Mordred's head went back, and his eyes flared. "What now?"

Agravain looked down and sighed, collecting his forces for the final leap.

Now, Gods, he prayed, be with me as I make my cast. "Your Highness must already have thought of this," he said easily. "But when you are King, sir, and come into your own, what of"—he gave a delicate cough—"Queen Guenevere?"

"Guenevere?" Mordred gave him a stare as black as ink. "What to do with her, you mean?" He let out a humorless laugh. "We'll have to see. Keep an eye on her, will you, Agravain, and let me know what you think?"

HER HEART POUNDING, Guenevere reentered Camelot on flying feet. In the King's apartments she found Arthur hastily robing for the Great Hall. His face was glowing, and the ardent hope in his eyes almost stopped her heart. *Oh, Arthur, Arthur, your hopes will betray you, I know.*

"Guenevere, you've heard that Gawain's back?" he cried joyfully as she hastened in. "D'you think he has found the Grail?"

She wanted to weep. *There is no Grail, Arthur. Everyone knows that now, except you.*

"We'll soon find out," she said huskily.

Waving the attendants away, she took his cloak from the nearest hands, then reached up to fasten it in place. The red of the silk warmed his skin, but his face when she touched it was cold. She watched in pain as he settled the crown on his head. His hands were trembling with elation, and he was on fire to be gone.

"Hurry, Guenevere," he cried urgently as the chamber women fluttered round her to brush down her cloak and gown and smooth her hair. She thanked them all, and sent them on their way. There was little they could do in any case to put a bloom on her pale skin, or a smile like Arthur's on her wasted face. *What does it matter now?* drifted through her mind. *All that remains is to take whatever comes.*

But like a Queen—always like a Queen.

She lifted her head. "I'm ready, Arthur," she said.

AS THEY ENTERED the Great Hall, she could see Kay, Bedivere, and Lucan all embracing Gawain, and the gentle Bedivere weeping on his old friend's neck. Standing quietly to the side were Bors and Lionel, their eyes full of feeling they did not try to hide.

"Damn you, Gawain," Lucan fretted, half laughing, half in tears. "We'd all but given your wretched hide up for lost—"

"—but we knew they'd never have you in the Otherworld," Kay bantered sardonically to cover his joy.

Beside them Gaheris and Gareth were surrounded by an excited group of the younger knights. Only Agravain stood apart from them in the rear, his long, scorched face impassive as he waited for the welcome to die down. The greeting he had had from Gawain moments ago had been barely civil, and it rankled still.

"So, Agravain?" Gawain had said coldly, then had turned away, snubbing him openly before the full court. Not so full these days, to be sure, with none but old men and boys left once the Quest knights were gone. But still, a public insult from his own blood was not something any knight should endure. *Sssssssssooooooooooon, brother, sssoooooon,* came into Agravain's seething mind, *ssssooon—*

Stepping in at Arthur's side, Guenevere saw Agravain's tall black shadow amidst the bright silks and felt his dark glare turn from Gawain to her. His eyes never left her as she pressed on through the throng, and a new and unpleasant sensation crept over her: *Agravain is watching me.* A cold inner laugh shook her silently. *You may watch till your eyes burn out, Agravain. My love has gone. There's nothing to see anymore.*

"Your Majesties—"

She had not seen him come. Surging through the crowd to thrust himself in their path, the black figure of the Father Abbot cast a dark shadow just as Agravain had. With his angular face and lean, attacking form, he stalked like a heron bearing down on its prey. Behind him were twenty other black-habited monks, all sporting the same shaven heads, rough rope girdles, and cracked, raw, sandaled feet. The very sight of them hurt Guenevere's eyes. *Goddess, Great Ones, you give so much beauty to the world. Why do they make themselves so ugly and all alike, a set of hideous dolls proclaiming their faith to their God?*

"Sire—" The Abbot blocked Arthur's path, reaching for his hand and bringing it to his lips.

Ever courteous, Arthur turned a bewildered face to him. "Yes, Father?"

The Abbot gestured to his monks. "We have heard the Grail has been found," he said urgently. "If this is true, and God in His Mercy has delivered us the vessel of Christ's Passion, then Your Majesty must—"

"By your leave, sir—" With a fixed smile, Guenevere pointed to Gawain and his brothers standing by. "His Majesty desires to greet his kin." She waved the Abbot away. "He will speak to you as soon as he can."

Her reward was a look of hate from the angry monk. She schooled her-self not to flinch from his livid face. *Well, sir, may your God be with you. Mine is a faith of love.*

She looked up to see Arthur and Gawain falling into a joyful embrace, the two massive forms locked in a mighty hug, weeping as one. Looking on in wonder, the busy crowd was still.

Guenevere waited, beyond fear, beyond hope. *So the monks have heard that the Grail has been found? By Galahad? A crazed child an inch away from death? Glory be to your God if this is true.*

In the hushed court, not a soul moved. Gawain was the first to break through his tears. "Arthur, my lord, forgive us—we rode the length and breadth of the land, but we did not find the Grail."

Arthur hugged him to his chest. "God will have mercy, Gawain," he cried fervently. He turned a tear-stained face toward Gaheris and Gareth, both weeping openly at Gawain's side, and thrust out a battle-scarred fist. "God bless you, sirs," he cried huskily, wringing first one mighty hand, then another, in a passion of joy. "I have prayed night and day to have you all safe home."

Gawain broke away. "But sire—"

Arthur laughed fiercely through his flooding tears. "No buts, Gawain! You and your brothers are home—and no men in the world are dearer to my heart than you!"

Pacing into the hall behind the King, keeping an appropriate distance in the rear, smiling joyfully and maintaining an attentive stance, Mordred fas-tened on the words, and his heart froze.

No man dearer in the world—?

The sounds and their meaning went echoing round his head. And again the mocking, cawing voice that lived in him now took up the theme. *No man dearer—you are not the man—no man dearer than Gawain—Gawain is the man—*

Behind him he knew that his henchmen and all his knights had heard the words too. No one in the court could mistake what Arthur meant. Mordred's soul shriveled with the sense of public shame. *The King is mak-ing his choice, and I am lost. Gawain is preferred as his heir, and I am cast away.*

"Hear me, sire!" Gawain ran a trembling hand through his unkempt hair. "The Mother Herself knows how glad we are to be back. But many of our fellows set out on the Quest too. Sire—" Tears filled his large blue eyes. "I fear you don't know how many knights you have lost."

Arthur's eyes widened. He nodded grimly. "Tell me." He was very pale.

Gawain swallowed. "Sagramore is dead."

Arthur closed his eyes. "How did he die? In combat? Like a knight?"

"Indeed, sire. They all did."

Arthur gasped and turned a ghastly hue. *"All?"*

Gawain threw an anguished glance at Arthur, shaking his head. "And I wish I could spare you the worst of it."

"The worst?" cried Arthur hoarsely. "What do you mean?"

Gawain raised an arm. Two of his squires struggled forward, carrying a deep wooden box three or four feet long. Groaning, Gawain signaled them to throw back the lid.

Guenevere could not move. Inside the box, carefully bedded in straw, lay a white and gold breastplate, and a golden sword. From beneath them protruded the crest of a golden helmet with a white plume, and below that she could see the outline of a long heart-shaped shield. She would have known them at the ending of the world. And there could be only one reason why they were here now.

White and gold, Lancelot—the colors of our love.

How did you lose your arms, sweetheart?

How did you die?

"Lancelot!"

Arthur leaped forward, bellowing with grief. "It's Lancelot's armor! No one would get it from him while he was alive. If he's lost it like this, he must be dead! How, Gawain—? Where—?"

"Soon told, my lord." Gawain's great beefy face was pale, and his voice bespoke a thousand years of grief. "We saw it for sale in a faraway marketplace. It was easy to track down the villains who had brought it there. A nest of villains, indeed, and the worst was their dam."

He paused, wiping tears from his eyes. "They were thieves and murderers, every one of them. We hanged them all, but we got their story first. A generation of vipers, they kept a mean tavern to prey on travelers in the woods round their house. They sent them to a hermitage in the depths of the wood where they could take them as they slept. Lancelot was only one of many good knights they killed."

"Killed?"

Guenevere did not know the sound of her own voice. All she knew was that the cry must be hers.

Gawain looked at her, and broke down before her gaze.

"Killed, lady," he forced out. "They admitted it. They knew him well enough: 'The knight in white and gold.' That's what they called him. The leader told me all."

Gawain paused. He knew he would never reveal the boastful glory in the great brute's eyes, as the outlaw defiantly faced death.

"Split his skull like a rotten apple, with the first blow!" the man had boasted jeeringly. "I did it myself, and then the others had their fun." He laughed, a hideous sound, and threw a contemptuous glance at his mother, standing aside cursing venomously among her sons. "The old woman told us to spare his handsome face." He spat at her feet and laughed horribly again. "Disgusting, at her age. So we made sure he had no face left by the time we were done."

Moments later, the filthy wretch was dead. And his story, Gawain vowed, would die with him. No one who loved Lancelot should hear of his cruel death. Neither the Queen nor the King would ever know.

"They killed him as he slept." Gawain braced himself. "His body they buried in a woodland grave. His armor is the only thing we have."

Guenevere could not move. A world-without-end lament was rolling through her head. *Dead, my love? I knew it. And now am I dead too.*

"Lancelot dead and all my knights lost too?"

Arthur threw back his head and screamed till the Great Hall rang. Then he clutched at his head and fell howling to the ground. "They're all dead, Guenevere," he cried hoarsely, reaching for her hand. "And it's all my fault! Why should I live, now that they have gone? Take me to Caerleon, and let me die!"

CHAPTER 32

A t first she thought that his great wound had opened up again. But when they had carried him to his chamber, the wisest of the Druid healers shook his head. "The King is sound enough now in his body. The injury he feels is in his mind."

"Get him to Caerleon" was the advice she had on all sides. "There, if anywhere, he will be restored."

Some voices in Camelot were heard to mutter that Arthur did not deserve to be himself again. This was his reward, the people said, for believing the Christians when all the world knew the Hallows of the Goddess were no Holy Grail. The Queen had been proved right all along, and the King should have listened to her. But Guenevere took no comfort in being right. The task ahead was enough for her now.

It was the worst time of the year for a journey, they all knew that. The dying winter ways were muddy and slow, and every dawn was late, stillborn and dull, as if the sun begrudged shining on the earth below. Another month, and the snow would lock up hill and vale. Progress was slower, too, because Arthur could not ride. While others on horseback endured the biting air, Arthur lay in a litter and wept the days away.

"I have lost the most peerless knight in all the world," he was heard to lament hour by hour, "And the fellowship of the Round Table is no more. Oh, Lancelot! Griflet, Helin, Sagramore! What you meant to me!"

Riding at his side, Guenevere heard every groan, but her ears were dead; the sounds meant nothing to her. Another voice was sounding inside her head, and sweeter scenes by far filled her wounded mind. She saw again a full midsummer moon shining down on a woodland by night. The silver branches of the golden trees leaned tenderly down to kiss the sweet green grass, and a light mist lay like wisps of enchantment on the woodland glade. There in a circle of ancient mossy oaks stood a dark stranger, tall and unsmiling in the glimmering light. He looked at her with eyes from the Otherworld, and knelt to kiss her hand.

"You are the woman of the dream," he had told her in the musical accents of his home across the sea. "I am Lancelot. My sword is yours, my life is yours to command."

Or did he say that later, as their love ebbed and flowed through all the years to come? *Eighteen years, Lancelot, eighteen sweet springs and eighteen wild Decembers have come and gone and still I called you mine. Now you are twice lost, gone from my arms and my heart.*

She thought of his grave in the woods, his long body's length of shallow, sandy earth mantled only with dead leaves and rotten loam. *You must be cold out there, my darling, let me make you warm. I'll come to you, sweetheart, I won't be long. Wait for me there in the world between the worlds. Let me do my duty here a for a little while. Then we shall be together—and with Amir.*

Amir.

Her breath left her lungs in the shadow of a sigh.

Amir, yes. I shall see my child again. You remember him, love? I lost him long ago. His grave is cold too, he lies on the edge of the sea.

Cold, cold...

But you've always been warm in my heart, haven't you, little one? Do you hear me, Amir? Soon I shall be with you—

"Madam?"

She heard Ina's voice behind her, frozen and low.

"Yes, Ina?"

"You were talking, madam. I thought you were calling me."

She laughed, though she did not know why. "Talking? No, not at all. What have I to say?"

Was that a sigh from Ina, or a hidden gust of tears? "I don't know, lady," came the maid's faint response. "Forgive me, I must have made a mistake."

Later she saw little lights flickering far away, shimmering through the trees in the dead, dank winter air, and heard distant laughter as soft and sweet as bells. She thought she saw slender forms flashing through the night, dancing and feasting and reveling without care. *Lancelot? Can you hear me, love? If we could get to that place, I could meet you there. Then we'd go hand in hand barefoot through the flowers, and lie together, and whisper and kiss in peace.*

She heard herself laughing again, a foolish sound. Why had she cared about the Grail princess Elaine? Why had she sent Lancelot away for that? What was one night, even two in another woman's bed, when he was only there by trickery, blandished and enchanted against his will? She had had his love, his body, his heart and soul for eighteen years. Did she care that a young witch had preyed on him for a few hours, and stolen his mind away?

No-no-no-no—

She shook her head mournfully from side to side, and found she could not stop. *No-no-no-no-no-no—*

I thought you betrayed my love, Lancelot.

But I betrayed you.

I had no faith, no trust.

No-no-no-no-no-no-no-no-no-no—

"Lady?"

It was Ina again, her voice more urgent this time. "Lady, you must rest. You are not well."

"Rest?" Again the strange, high laugh. "I'll rest soon enough, you'll see."

GODS ABOVE, what had come over the Queen?

Riding immediately behind the King's litter, his eyes fixed on Guenevere, Mordred watched intently the distracted form swaying on the horse ahead. Of course she'd be sick with worry about the King, that was only natural. This grief over Lancelot had overwhelmed Arthur's mind, and no one knew when he would be himself again. And Gods above, this mad move to Caerleon, and having to ride out at this time of the year! Mordred flexed his frozen feet inside his boots, muttered a curse, and watched the white plume of his breath cloud the icy air.

But perhaps there was something too in what Agravain said. Whoever they were, women always thought of themselves. Women— Mordred's mind played over his most recent diversion with a fond mixture of lust and contempt. They were all the same, the greatest necessary evil in the world, obsessed with their own petty plots and plans at every turn. And a queen like Guenevere would be concerned with her country, her power, the continuation of her rule. She'd be in mortal dread of what would happen when Arthur was no more.

Mordred felt his mouth curl in a smile. Well, Agravain had had some interesting thoughts on that.

Agravain—

Mordred smiled again. It was good to know where his new follower was, even if it meant Agravain's eyes forever boring into his back. The Orkney prince was riding directly behind, he and his brothers abreast at the head of the knights, in pride of place as Arthur's favored kin. The knights they were leading were poor and few these days, and as soon as they got to Caerleon the task could begin of renewing the Round Table again. Before all this happened, the King would always ride out with a forest of glittering lances ahead and behind, and a bevy of bright banners all around. Now Arthur was followed by old men and cripples and those who had failed the Quest. All the heroes like Lancelot were dead, never to return.

"No matter!" Mordred cleared the bile from his throat and spat on the ground. All the better, in fact, that most of the Quest knights had died. They knew nothing but Arthur and the older ways. Yet change had to come, and the wiser sort knew that.

Change—

Things are changing, my son. Are you ready? What will you do?

Mordred's inner eye blazed with blue-black fire. The King can deny me nothing, came the voice in his head. I am more to him than Gawain, I can defeat the great Orkneyan for his love. And now that he is ill, he must yield up his power to me. I can enroll the new knights in his stead; they will kneel and swear their oath of allegiance to me—

"King Mordred! Mordred for King!"

From out of the air of the world yet to come, Mordred heard the wild cries of acclaim, and his head swam. Under him, the new order of knighthood would be greater than it had ever been. The deeds they would do would be known throughout the world. Arthur would be forgotten, and men would talk of King Mordred and the Round Table for a thousand years…

First catch your bear and then skin it—eh, boy, eh?

Without warning, Merlin's cackling laugh burst through his mind. Mordred snarled, caught between fear and surprise. What, old man, not dead? Is your spirit prowling still? he challenged the empty air. But in all the frozen forest, nothing stirred. Only the soft clopping of the horses' hooves and the light jingle of their harness answered him. With a violent spasm Mordred shook off the shadow of foreboding and calmed himself. None of this mattered. The wise man learned to turn such things to his own use.

Which was why, when the column pulled up to rest, he sent Vullian and Ozark to encounter Agravain and draw him aside. While the grooms watered the horses, the knights and their squires waited quietly in companionable groups or strolled off to answer the needs of nature under the trees. As his two followers stood in talk with Agravain, it was easy enough for Mordred to cross the glade, dismiss Vullian and Ozark with a nod, and engage Agravain in casual chat.

Within moments Mordred learned that the watchful Orkneyan had seen all that he had, and more.

"The Queen's not herself," Agravain told him dismissively, staring out at the gathering dusk. "But why?"

In a few cryptic sentences, he gave Mordred all he knew. Knew, but did not fully understand. As the column was mounting up at the start of the ride, he had seen Guenevere twisting and kissing a ring on her finger in such distraction that at last her maid Ina, with tears standing in her eyes, had taken her mistress's hand and drawn the ring off.

What ring?

Agravain did not know. But the Queen had worn it now for ten or twenty years.

What became of it?

The maid had slipped it onto a chain around her mistress's neck; then they had both wept.

Why would the Queen play with it like that?

Again, who could say?

But it bore watching, did it not?

Indeed it did. And it would be watched.

Good.

Satisfied, Mordred strolled on, and Agravain melted away into the darkness of the wood.

From his vantage point in a clearing beyond the trees, hugging his frozen body and blowing on his hands, Gaheris watched them go. Beside him a shivering Gareth was stamping up and down, and Gawain was resting on a fallen log, his elbows on his knees, his great head buried miserably in his hands.

Lancelot—

It was all Gawain could do not to howl aloud with distress and smash his head into the nearest tree. Perhaps that would bring relief from this torrent of griefs and the remorseful thoughts that tormented him by night and by day. If you'd come with us, old friend, you'd still be alive. If I'd waited for you instead of pushing on—if I hadn't neglected our brotherhood of knights—

Behind Gawain's shoulder, Gaheris gave him a nudge. "See there, brother?" He pointed across the clearing. "Our Agravain, in colloquy with the Prince?"

Gareth stared too. "You're right." His fair skin colored up, and he gave a startled laugh. "Yes, there he goes. What d'you think it means?"

Gaheris's milk-blue eyes were as cold as ice. He prodded his older brother once again. "Trouble, wouldn't you say?"

And Galahad too. Reluctantly Gawain nodded his heavy head. *If I'd thought to take care of the boy, he'd be with us still. If we had to lose Lancelot, at least we'd have his child—*

He felt a thump on his back, and an insistent voice. "Gawain—"

Gawain moved his shaggy head like a bear in pain. "What did you say?" he cried irritably, peering through the dusk. The black-garbed Agravain had vanished between the trees. "Agravain talking to Mordred?" He shook his head. "So what? The Prince is polite and civil to everyone." A grim smile twisted Gawain's mouth. "He wouldn't have time for our dear Agravain. Take no notice, brother. I can tell you it's nothing at all."

CHAPTER 33

All that dread time, Caerleon slumbered on its citadel of rock. Behind it the primeval forest huddled close, sheltering it from the worst of the winter storms. The rough stones of the old castle, already ancient when the first Pendragon seized it for his own, had withstood wind and weather for a thousand years. Yet still the night-riding demons howled round its high towers, tore its banners from the battlements, and battered its courtyards and cloisters with snow and hail. And all winter long Guenevere cared for Arthur as he slowly recovered his strength, and not a moment passed in all that dead waste of time that she did not wish her life over, and feel herself dying too.

At last the earth stirred again and slowly awoke. A late spring came trembling down from the mountains, and a primrose-colored sun ventured into the sky. It melted the snow that locked up all the roads, and the rivers ran freely again, released from their chains of ice. Among the new season's travelers, one knight limped back to Camelot with another on his heels, then both struggled on to Caerleon to catch up with the King.

"Griflet!" wept Arthur, crushing the knight to his breast. "And Ladinas!" His long arm extended in another bear hug. "God be praised!"

Ladinas wept on Arthur's shoulder. "Dinant is lost."

Arthur stiffened. "How?"

"We were imprisoned together by a cruel lord. He caught gaol fever in the foulness of our cell."

"How did you both survive?"

Griflet's jaundiced complexion and the yellow in the whites of his eyes betokened the disease from the East that would never leave him now. But his wry smile held all the old Griflet, and more. "Barely, my lord," he replied. "But you shall hear—"

Ladinas nodded fervently, trembling all through his thin frame. "There is much to tell."

Their stories held the court enthralled all through the winter's end, night after night when the candles danced in the draughts of the Great Hall, the fires roared up the hearths, the hot mulled wine went round, and the sleet fell like elf arrows through the blackness outside. Both the survivors brought a warmth to Arthur's face and a spring to his step, and when the hard weather broke he was hunting again.

But the full tally of losses had yet to be told. Gawain, Kay, Lucan, and Bedivere were given the task of gathering the names of the dead.

"Erec—Yvain—Helin—"

One by one they went through the names and their fates. "—perished in an ambush—hung on a tree till he starved—taken by the Saracens, blinded and made a slave—"

"Alas, no—!" Arthur wept piteously again. "So many lost? Lancelot gone, and all my good knights dead?"

But his spirit gained no relief from his scalding tears. Though he rode out every day, and doggedly tried to sustain his recovery, the loss of his knights was a wound that would not heal.

"WHICH MAKES IT a sign from God that this is our time," observed the Father Abbot somberly, looking round the group of monks. The circle of intent faces told him that his listeners were absorbing his every word. On another occasion he would have taken pride in the fine new chapter house where they sat, a lofty whitewashed space the King had built for them when he turned Caerleon's small ancient chapel into a splendid church. But there would be another time for that. "So, brother?" he said brusquely. "Say on."

Before them stood the young monk under orders to watch Arthur in his privy chamber, under cover of praying for the King's recovery on each of the holy hours.

"The Queen has been tireless in attending on her lord," the eager youth announced impressively. "And the King has had her with him day and night to ease his grief. But tonight she was fainting from weariness and strain. So the King sent her to rest, at least till the dinnertime." His round eyes in an even rounder face were alive with the thrill of it all. "At last, Father, he's alone."

The Abbot made a steeple of his hands. "So," he said softly. "Then Arthur may be ours."

Silently he repeated his prayer of the last twenty years: Lord God, give me the King's soul. He scanned the keen eyes and monkish faces all around, and knew he was fighting with the best he had. Every one of them knew what was riding on this throw. His eye fell on the monk opposite, a stone-eyed man approaching middle age. "Brother Sylvester, time to tell the King the news from Rome?"

Sylvester nodded. Whatever he thought, his smooth, composed expression and taut body gave nothing away. He gestured to the monk seated at his side, a squat, ugly creature with a brutal grin who looked as if he would be more at home on a battlefield than in a church. "We are ready, Iachimo and I."

Iachimo gave a slow, broken-toothed smile and an answering nod. Acquiescing, the Abbot suppressed an inward sigh. God's will be done. Sylvester and Iachimo had done good work together, and would do more. The bright force of Sylvester's will and his shrewd skills in the battle for hearts and minds depended on his coarse companion in ways none could know. Did it matter then that Iachimo bore all the signs of his unsavory past? That he grunted rather than spoke, and smelled like a dog? Lord, open Thou my heart, the Abbot prayed. Spare me from pride, let me not disdain. We need such warriors for Your holy word. Grant me to use this blunt tool in Thy eternal name.

He leaned forward, hungering to strike. "One thrust," he said intently, "one final thrust now, and the King is ours. He is weakened by the loss of so many knights, and his heart is craving a poultice for his hurts. The Queen will not oppose us as she always did, for she too is not herself anymore."

Sylvester glanced at Iachimo, and they shared a cruel smile. "Her wits are unraveling. She knows not what she does."

"It is the vice of women," came a harsh voice at the Abbot's side. "It comes from their grandmother Eve, she who first led Adam into sin—"

"Quite so," said the Abbot tersely, with a frown. Brother Anselmo was a spiritual force to be sure, and his knowledge of the Scriptures cut like a falling blade. But he was as unnaturally given to his texts as Iachimo was dull and devoid of any spark. Lord God, send me some well-tempered men!

"Their weak wits, yes, but also their wandering wombs," put in Anselmo's pupil Roddri, the novice monk who tended his master's books and shared his cell. "The pagan philosopher warns us about that—"

Anselmo's beetling brows shot up. "The Athenian, you mean?" he quizzed sharply.

"Aristotle, sir, indeed," the novice confirmed. He looked round the table, warming to his theme. "The old sage says that women's inner parts are not secure. When they have hysterics, their wombs swell up and choke them in their throats." His small, pebbly eyes began to burn. "They are governed by the parts below the waist, while we men are ruled by our Godlike intellects. That is why they are all hot and lustful, full of sin and loose in the loins—"

"Women are whores indeed," snapped the Abbot, raging with cold fire. God, Lord God, help me to curb the lascivious thoughts of these men! "But we need no pagan Greek to tell us that. The question is, What do we do here? From Queen Guenevere herself down to the lowliest maid, these women believe that their Goddess grants them free will, and gives them the right to dispose of their bodies themselves."

He paused and saw to his satisfaction that he had the full attention of every monk. "And while they think that, they will never be subject to men. Weaker vessels as they are, they will continue to resist God's decree." He lifted up his eyes, and his face lit with incandescent glow. "That is why we must destroy the Great Whore in her sacred place. We must root out Goddess worship from Avalon."

There was a general murmur of fervid assent.

"And we shall triumph, brothers!" the Abbot breathed. "Already the Great Mother has been driven before our sword from the white wastes of the north to the edge of the Inland Sea. In all these islands now, only this kingdom holds out."

Sylvester gave a hard and mirthless smile. "And only because it's the home of Avalon." He coughed, feigning modesty. "But you know, Father, what progress we've made there. The Lake is almost gone and the river too, and only one last channel feeds the so-called isle. The Lake dwellers have departed, and the old witch of the place, who called herself the Lady, is nowhere to be seen."

"Good, good," said the Abbot tensely. His eyes bulged with desire. "We shall secure Arthur, and then we may move against his rebellious Queen."

"Not Queen, Father," Anselmo interjected, brimming with righteous zeal. "Not in herself, for a woman may never hold power over men. Our Lord God has expressly forbidden it. And she cannot be Queen through being King Arthur's wife, for they were not married by the rites of the Holy Church. She is a whore, then, and lives in sin—"

"Thank you, brother!" Crisply the Abbot cut Anselmo off. Time enough for theology when the war was won. He rose to his feet abruptly, gathering up his gown. "Come then, all of you," he ordered, striding from the cell. "Queen or concubine, Guenevere has left Arthur's side. We burn time as we speak. Now is the moment to strike!"

THEY FOUND ARTHUR on his knees in his private chapel, hands clasped and eyes uplifted to an ivory carving of a tortured Christ. Beneath the crucifix stood a fine altar covered in purple and gold. A gold cross with a cabochon ruby at its heart glowed on the altar like an evil eye. A lone monk chanted mournfully in the rear, and the sick scent of incense lay in the air.

In the outer chamber a bevy of monks were praying inside the door while the guards stood watchful but bemused outside. The Father Abbot brushed unseeingly past them all.

"My son—"

"Father—?"

Rising from his knees, Arthur received the delegation warmly and without surprise. "You come to call me to my devotions?" He smiled wanly and waved a hand around. "You see I am already at my prayers."

The Abbot shook his head. "Son, no," he said with a sorrow he could not explain. "I have never had cause to question the depth of your faith. I know too that it has been sorely tried, and never more so than now."

"Now?" Arthur turned color. "Yes indeed. All my good knights are dead. You heard that, Father?" He grimaced. "And the way they died?"

"I did," the Abbot said. He raised his voice, and beckoned his monks to draw near. "The wages of sin, I fear, is always death."

Arthur bowed his big body like a bear in pain. "Was it sin, then, that kept them from the Grail? That caused so many of them to lose their lives?"

"Sin, for a certainty," the Abbot intoned. "Or else the Grail would be ours."

Sylvester leaned forward hungrily. "Sin inescapable, sire."

"As black as Satan's hoof!" Anselmo cried.

A spasm of terror ran through Arthur's frame. "The sin that leads to the eternal fire?" His eyes widened as a new thought took root. "My sin?" he said with a terrible laugh. "Would God take the lives of my knights for that?"

There was no reply. Arthur felt like a rat in a trap. All around him burned a circle of accusing eyes. He struck his head. "God knows I sinned," he cried hoarsely. His vacant eyes showed a mind burrowing into the past. "I broke my vow to Guenevere—lay with my sister—killed my son—"

The Abbot joined his hands as if in prayer. "These are sins enough for any man."

"But have I not atoned?" Arthur cried out in anguish. "You know how many times I have confessed. I have done penance, suffered for my sins." He began to weep wildly, blindly, like a child. "Did I fail to atone in the eyes of God? Are my sins still heavy on my head? Did the best knights in the world die because of me?"

The Abbot's pale eyes flared. "Sire, who can say? You have sinned greatly, that much is true. But think, sire, where the Quest began. The Grail appeared before us in Camelot, then vanished again. And why?"

Arthur looked up, bewildered. "Why? I don't know."

The Abbot leaned forward. "Because it could not abide there. The stronghold of the Goddess is a sinful place."

Arthur groaned. "What shall I do?"

The Abbot spread his long, lean-fingered hands. "There may yet be a way to reconcile your sin and the sin of Camelot with God's purpose here on earth." He gestured to the monks standing at his side. "You remember our brothers Sylvester and Iachimo? These two have been furthering Christ's purpose on the Sacred Isle. For many years now they have kept a house of God on Avalon, joining their Christian prayers to the worship there, while I have led the Christians in these parts. But now the Lord has a new purpose for us all."

He stepped forward and knelt before Arthur, bowing his head. A heightened color had come into his hollow cheeks. "Give me your blessing, sire, for I must leave this place. I have received a commandment from the Pope. I am called to Canterbury, to be Archbishop there."

"Now God go with you, Father," said Arthur fervently. Raising the Abbot to his feet, he kissed both his hands, then glanced at his companions with a bow. "And Brother Sylvester, I guess, will take your place?"

"With your permission, sire, he will indeed," the Abbot replied. "And I crave a boon from you to bless his work."

He paused. No one moved. All around him he felt the force of the brothers' will, and his own passion flowed through his veins like fire. Now Lord God be my speed, he prayed, and committed himself to the boldest throw of his life.

"A boon for the church of God," he said with all the power at his command. "And this will save you too, sire, as you struggle to free yourself from the mire of sin." Greatly daring, he made the final leap. "And your Queen, sire, Queen Guenevere—we have been most concerned—"

"Save me?" Arthur started. "How?"

The Abbot took a breath. *Lord, give wings to the words of my mouth.* "'We must do good,' you have always said. Hear me out, Majesty, as I tell you how—"

CHAPTER 34

Guenevere awoke from a sick drowse with a sudden start. At first she did not recognize her own chamber, or the hangings on her bed. *I should not have gone to sleep* was her first thought. *I only meant to close my eyes before dinner, and now it's almost dark.*

She sat up, struggling to collect herself. The window stood open on the raw spring air.

How?

Ina must have been in to open it.

But why?

She felt chilled to the bone, and the evening mist was clammy on her skin. The next second a strange thought came to her like a blow. *You left Arthur undefended, and yourself too. He cannot protect you if he cannot save himself.*

On the open windowsill sat a white dove. She fluttered her wings in distress and fixed Guenevere with her large, mournful eyes. Again the message dropped into Guenevere's mind. *Why have you left Arthur? Go to him, go to him now—*

"Tell me, Mother, why?" Guenevere cried in anguish. "Save him from what?"

But the dove only spread her white tail and flew off.

Guenevere grabbed for the overgown lying at the end of the bed. "Ina, help me!" she called madly. "Where are you?"

"Lady, I'm here!" Eyes wide, the startled maid flew into the room.

"Hurry, hurry," Guenevere panted. "Help me with my gown, I beg you, settle my hair, I must go to the King."

But even as Ina did so, the thought came, *It may be too late—*

TOO LATE, too late—

She covered the ground to the King's apartments in frantic strides. Arthur knelt before the altar in his chapel, his eyes closed, and his face wet with tears.

Too late?

"Praying, Arthur?" She could hear the sound of fear in her own voice.

"Guenevere, welcome," he returned. He got to his feet, assuming a cheerfulness that pained her heart. "I was praying for the success of God's purpose here on earth."

Your God or mine, Arthur? But she could not say it now.

"My dear——" He came toward her and tenderly took her hands. "You should rest more, you know. You don't look well."

How can I be well now that Lancelot's dead? I shall never be well now until I am dead too.

She freed herself from his grasp and pulled away. She was suddenly suspicious, though she did not know why. "What did you mean, God's purpose here on earth?"

She saw at once that he would not meet her eye. "You're not well, Guenevere," he persisted, moving away. "Others have noticed it too. The Father Abbot came to express his concern. The Christian brothers have seen you walking and talking to yourself."

"I've been——very sad." She drew a labored breath. "This is a terrible time. You have been grieving too." She fought down a spurt of rage. *Trust the Christians to take advantage of Lancelot's death. But I must beware, if the Christians have been here. Arthur listens to them, and they have no love for me.*

Arthur nodded heavily. "But we shall make amends," he said in manful tones. "There's no sin so great that we may not seek God's love, and win His forgiveness with good deeds here on earth."

"Sin——? Heavenly forgiveness?" Again her suspicions leaped up. "What are you talking about?"

She knew she sounded sharper than she meant. But Arthur was looking at her with an unfathomable distance in his eyes. "Sin, Guenevere," he repeated bleakly. "Sin and death. My sin." He drew a ragged breath. "And the death——" He faltered and broke down.

A rush of pity seized her. *He means Amir.* She could hardly speak. *Oh, Arthur, Arthur, why didn't you turn to me? Or did I fail you when you needed me?*

"I should have realized," she managed at last, "that losing Lancelot would make you think of Amir."

He gave a despairing nod. "I have to atone, you must see that, Guenevere. For Lancelot and Amir."

"Lancelot?" she repeated, baffled. "Arthur, how were you responsible for Lancelot's death?"

"His and all my knights'," Arthur groaned. "The Abbot has been with me to explain it all."

"*Goddess, Mother——!*" she cried.

"Don't take it so hard, Guenevere!" Arthur cried. "He has shown me the way that we can make amends——"

She was tearing her hair. "We? *We?* What have I got to do with this?"

He seized her hands. "Everything!" he cried. "The Father Abbot has shown me the way——" He broke off with a self-conscious laugh. "I'll have to remember not to call him that—he's Archbishop of Canterbury now."

"Oh, so? A great leader then? Must we kneel to him?"

If he heard the sarcasm in her tone, he gave no sign. "Yes, he tells me he's been summoned by the Pope. His Holiness himself wrote in his own hand——"

"Arthur——" Her voice cut mercilessly through his words. "All this is nothing to me. What is the good thing that will make amends?"

"Great news, Guenevere." He gave a smile of joy. "The Archbishop came to ask permission to build a great new church."

"Not another——! Haven't they built enough throughout the land?"

"Wait, Guenevere, hear me out. It will be finer than any church so far, the finest in these islands, perhaps in all Christendom."

She could hardly contain herself. "So the Christians want to display their wealth and power?" She laughed harshly. "What's that to us?"

"Wait, dear, I said." He gave a forgiving smile. "Will I ever convince you that these are good men? This new church—Guenevere, you won't believe——" His eyes welled with tears, and his smile was mystical now. "The Archbishop has begged for permission to dedicate it to Amir." He paused in triumph. "To Amir—to our son, Guenevere. What d'you think of that?"

To Amir?

She could not speak. *My son to be in the mouths of those Christian toads, his memory gnawed at by those weevils, crawled over by those worms—Amir—Amir, my son—*

She was blind and gasping with pain. Clutching her stomach, she tried in vain to speak. At last a few husks of protest fell out of her mouth. "Arthur—it's nonsense—there could never be a Christian church of Saint Amir——"

He gave an unconvincing laugh. "Of course not, Guenevere. We all know that. But remember that Amir's name means 'beloved.'"

"What?" Her mind was cracking. She could not take it in.

" 'Beloved,' Guenevere." His eyes widened again in that look of delight and triumph she had come to dread. "And who was God's beloved? Why, Saint Michael, the brightest of the angels, and dearest to God's heart! It is to be the Holy Church of Saint Michael, not Saint Amir."

"*Where?*" But she knew already from the way he spoke.

He did not seem to hear. "So when they begged my permission, I gave it at once——"

Pieces of her heart, her brain, were breaking off. She reached out her hand and frenziedly clutched at his arm. "Where, Arthur? *Where will they build this church?*"

He met her eye with another joyful smile. "Why, on Avalon, my dear, in the country's most sacred place. As a shrine to our beloved Amir, where else?"

Oh, Arthur, Arthur——

Her mind exploded in a burst of grief. The still-living memory of all their golden days and tender whispering nights came to her in spurts of fresh agony as she remembered the time when they were young. For one eternal moment she felt all the love between them as it once was. And as she stood not daring to move or breathe, she felt it floating away.

Now all the bonds between them, all the golden ties that had held them together for so many years frayed to a thin filament like a spider's web. For an endless moment the slender thread hung in time and space; then, one by one, its tiny, hairlike tendrils frayed and snapped.

Amir——

A Christian church to Amir on Avalon——?

Arthur had betrayed her in her deepest place. Nothing now tied her, held her to this man. For all the years together, there was nothing between them but dust and ashes, dry bones and abandoned earth. She tried to speak, but her mouth was choked with disgust. She was lost in the place beyond Eden, the eternal wasteland of trust broken and hopes betrayed.

Oh, Arthur——

Amir——

And Avalon, Avalon, sacred island, home——

There came a sigh from Avalon like the world's last breath. Already she could hear the thud of the Christians' axes and their shouts of triumph as the apple trees came crashing to the ground. She could see the doves rising in terror from their roosts, and the silver blossoms trampled under monkish feet. No more would the faithful follow their hearts up the Tor, honoring the slumbering Mother with their songs, tracing her serpentine flanks with dancing feet. No more would the spring breezes blow Her fragrance across the Lake—there would be no more Lake—

No more, Arthur.

Nevermore.

Aloud she said with a fatal calm, "Do you think you should have discussed this with me?"

"Of course." Arthur stared at her earnestly. "We're discussing it now."

"Arthur, there's no discussion when you've already agreed. You've told them to go ahead without my consent."

"Your consent?" A sudden anger crept into his voice. "Haven't you been listening to a word I said? I have to redeem my sin, and this is the way. My sin, Guenevere," he repeated with rising force. "My chance to save my soul." His voice was raw. "Do you begrudge me that? When my son is lost, and all my knights are gone, and now Lancelot's dead too?"

He could not go on. She watched his great shoulders heaving and turned away. *I would not begrudge you if I believed the Christians' lies. But you do, alas, and I never can.*

She drew herself up. "Avalon is mine, Arthur," she said coldly in clear, bell-like tones. "It is the heart of my kingdom, and was never yours to give away. You have broken the vow you made when you swore to be mine. You promised then to defend the Mother and Her worship, and now you join with the Christians to root it out. You have betrayed me, you have condemned the Lady and her Maidens to the hands of men who hate, and worst of all you have dishonored our son."

"Dishonored? When we'll build the grandest, greatest church—"

She shook her head. "Religion should be kindness, Arthur, you know that. Faith is love."

"God is love! And Jesus Christ His Son!"

Guenevere turned her head. For a moment she heard the marching feet from the East, an army of fanatics on the move. In her mind's eye, swarm after swarm of mad-eyed muscular monks struck out from Rome and colonized the earth. Intolerance was their creed, and their weapon was death. Only those who believed could be saved. The rest were damned.

"No." She felt her love, her will, her life draining away.

Arthur drove his palm into his fist. "Guenevere, listen to me!"

She turned her gaze on him. His angry, staring eyes and open mouth would have been comic if she had any feeling left. But she was empty and echoing like a shell. She looked through him and moved toward the door. "Farewell."

He stared at her furiously. "Where are you going?"

She did not turn back. "To Avalon—where else?"

CHAPTER 35

valon, Avalon, sacred island, home—
Must get to Avalon—
Go—go—!
Guenevere flew out of Arthur's chamber, on fire to avoid him
before he spoke again. In the antechamber Mordred was waiting
to go in, surrounded by his knights. His handsome face changed
at the sight of her, and for an instant she saw herself through his
eyes, bursting through the door in wild disorder, tears down her face, hair
streaming about her madly as she ran. What would he make of it? She did
not care.

"Come in, Mordred, come in!" she heard Arthur booming hollowly as
she fled.

Mordred murmured a sharp query, and then Arthur's bluff jovial tones
rang out. "The Queen? Oh, she's a little indisposed indeed, but she'll be with
us for dinner, she'll be herself by then—"

No, Arthur, no—
Never again.

She rushed through the antechamber talking to herself, and let all the
round-eyed stares roll off her back.

Avalon, Avalon, that's where I have to go—

Yes, it was all clear now, the way ahead. She and Ina would take horse
straightaway. Her guard was standing by; they were prepared. It would mean
a ride through the night, but they had all done that a thousand times and
more—

Must get there—
Hurry, hurry, get away—

She lengthened her stride across the courtyard with no thought but
to reach her apartments, do what had to be done, and be gone. Outside the
night air was fresh and keen, and a million stars were glittering overhead, dancing through the cavern of the void. On she went, and on. *Hurry,
hurry, go—*

And suddenly the voice of her long-dead mother came purling down toward her through the dark: *You may not go.*

"What?" she cried out.

Little one, hear me: You may not go.

"Not go?"

Not to Avalon. You must stay here.

"Mother, mother, how can I stay?"

You are the Queen. A queen may not depart.

"But a woman can't stay with a man who betrays!"

You may leave a man. You may not leave your people. You are wedded to the land.

Guenevere tore at her hair. "Mother!" she screamed. "Hear me, let me go!"

But still the echo came: *You may not go.*

Somewhere, she knew, her mother was with her, walking through the mansions of the dark, calling her through the halls of space and time. A spirit like hers would light the lamps of heaven and roam the astral plane scattering bliss. In life she had been one of earth's shining souls, blessed with the gift of quicksilver delight and a smile to melt the world. She had always loved her people more than she had loved herself. And if she had come down from the world between the worlds—

"Mother, no!" Guenevere cried. "I cannot, I cannot stay!"

Casting aside her veil, Guenevere roamed on frantically through the gathering dark.

And coming toward her through the cloisters like a phantom in the night, Agravain watched her go and shook his head. Any woman talking to herself, addressing unseen spirits and calling on the Mother like this, was in no state to be Queen, let alone the consort to a King like Arthur, so much in need of advice and guidance. And her men-at-arms too, trotting after her as trustingly as fools or children, not like trained soldiers, ready to give their lives!

Well, he would take Mordred news of this, and soon.

Soon, soon, another hand would rule in this place.

With a new King, this place would run as it should.

"INA, INA, we must—"

Guenevere burst through the door of the Queen's apartments and cried out in frustration at the busy scene within. Three or four women were feed-

ing the braziers in each corner of the room with fresh herbs, sweetening the
air with rosemary and rue. Two more were straightening the great bed,
punching the plump pillows into shape and turning back the covers for the
night. Another was tidying up the dressing table, arranging the fragrant
pastes and potions, and setting out the colors in their bright glass pots.

"Be off with you all!" Impatiently Guenevere scattered them aside. "Ina,
where are you?"

The door to the bedchamber flew open and there stood the maid, her
eyes in the candlelight alive with their catlike gleam. She brought her finger
to her lips and drew Guenevere urgently into the room. As the heavy oak
swung behind them, she pressed a scrap of paper into Guenevere's hands.

"Madam, see!"

The black runes ran together before Guenevere's eyes. She struggled to
make out the straggling script:

> *Bring your mistress from the castle after owl-light, when no one sees you come.
> This messenger will help you find the way. Let her come with no other, for the sake
> of her dearest friend.*

Guenevere stared, bewildered. "Ina, what is this? When did it come?"

"Just now, lady. I was coming up from the courtyard when he gave it
to me."

"Who?"

"A man—not from the court—short and dark, shy like a wild
thing—"

"One of the land kin?"

"Or like—" Ina hesitated.

"Go on."

She shivered. "One of the Lake villagers from Avalon."

"What?" Guenevere gripped the message in a shaking hand. "Did he
speak to you? Did you recognize the tongue?"

"Not a word." Now Ina was trembling too. "He just slipped the message
into my hand and disappeared."

"So after dark he will lead us to this place—"

Ina nodded. "—for the sake of your dearest friend."

*I have no friend, not since my marriage died. I had a lover, but I sent him away. Now
he's dead too, I have no other friend.*

Anxiously Ina read her face. "You will not go?"

Ina, Ina, wait—I do not know—

MOONLIGHT HAD FADED to starshine when they left the old castle brooding on its rock. The owls had come and gone from the high tower, and all
the world slept. Together they drifted down through the shadows like shadows themselves, veiled from head to foot in draperies that blended with the
night, and no one saw them go.

Silently they wound down the hill from the castle and passed over the
causeway into the little town. The closely packed buildings nestled together
like dogs in a basket, all slumbering as one. They plunged into the warren of
narrow streets where the houses hugged the base of the castle rock, and soon
another shadow melted into theirs. The air stirred as a short, dark form fell
in behind them, keeping pace with them on silent feet.

Swiftly they passed down through the sleeping town, the lanes and
streets getting narrower as they went. At last they came to an alley so dark
that they could not see their way. Like a breeze off the Sacred Lake, their
shadow follower slipped past them, beckoning them on. They came to a low
doorway so old and gnarled that it looked like part of the wall, and he
knocked softly, lifted the latch, and went in.

Guenevere hesitated at the open door as her eyes adapted to the dim
light of the dragon lamp within. Ahead of them a short flight of steps led
down to an earthen floor. A fire crackled merrily on the hearth opposite, and
a faint scent of applewood hung in the air. The warm darkness, the low ceiling, and the rich loamy smell of the earth underfoot welcomed them like a
burrow, but the human inhabitants had left their traces too. A wooden table
and chairs stood against the wall, and a rough hanging curtained off the rear
of the hovel, where the sleeping quarters must be.

Seated at the table was an old crone in a ragged cloak. Her back was
hunched with age, and the gnarled hands in her fingerless gloves were
crooked in every joint. She wore a shapeless black hat with a deep brim, and
a wild fringe of gray hair sheltered her face. Somewhere within lurked a pair
of piercing eyes, and Guenevere felt a feral but friendly stare. *Come in,* she
seemed to hear, *you are welcome, Guenevere.*

Squatting beside the old woman was the messenger who had brought
them here, a short sturdy man with thick black hair in a damp tangle over his
eyes. He was clad in pelts of otter and waterfowl, and the tang of the Lake

seeped from him as he moved. He was one of the Lake villagers without doubt, but she could never remember one so watchful and fearful before. His left hand played with the dagger at his belt, while his right gripped a stout stave lying on the floor. *What, fellow, are you afraid of me?* was Guenevere's angry thought. *You should know a queen attacks no one. Do you fear two women alone and unarmed?*

She moved forward, gesturing Ina to stay by the door. She could see the old woman's eyes through the veil of tangled hair, and the feeling they gave her was sad and tender now. A strange thought came suddenly into her head. "Mother?" she whispered.

In a voice like the wind in the trees, the old woman began. "You are alone?"

"Except for my maid."

"No one saw you come?"

"No."

"Or knew where you were going?"

"No."

"Not King Arthur your husband?"

Guenevere gave a mirthless smile. "Least of all him."

The ragged head nodded slowly. "He is much with the Christians now."

Guenevere set her jaw. "I know that."

"They do not catch your soul?"

"The Christians?" Guenevere had to laugh. "When I have felt the love of the Goddess, seen Her power in the wind on the mountain, heard Her in the wave of the sea and every newborn cry? When the Mother gave me my own mother, and the love of my dearest lord?"

Her voice broke as she thought of Lancelot's hand on her shoulder, his touch on her cheek. But she clutched at the cruel memory with all her heart. Every trace of Lancelot was welcome to her now. "Would I betray this for a faith that worships torture and death?" she demanded fervently. "A faith that forbids women the enjoyment of their bodies and makes men mortify their sex?"

The old woman nodded her head. "It is well." She waved toward Ina. "Will you ask your maiden to wait outside? I have things to say for your ears alone."

Already the Lake villager was on his feet. Mutely Ina followed him out of the house. The door closed behind them, making the flame in the dragon lamp dance. The air shivered, and the old woman straightened her back. As she rose to her feet, she seemed to grow taller before Guenevere's eyes. "So you do not forget your days on Avalon——?"

Avalon, Avalon, Mother, Goddess, home——

"Never."

"You remember the Sacred Isle and its holy treasures of love and faith?"

Guenevere felt her grief rising like a flood. "As long as I live."

The old woman's rags were fading into a mist. Now the old cracked voice had become a lyrical chant. "And your good friends there—one above all, who loved you like a mother——?"

Guenevere heard, and her senses were singing too. *Goddess, Mother, come to me, help me——*

The tall figure seemed to light the room. Her gauzy draperies gleamed with stardust, and the radiance of the moon shone round her head. She held out her hand in blessing and the scent of apple blossom filled the air. Then she spoke in the voice Guenevere remembered from her dreams.

"Ah, little one—do you not know me, Guenevere?"

CHAPTER 36

"**L**ady!"

Guenevere fell to her knees, half mad with fear and joy. "Oh Lady, Lady," she babbled deliriously, "forgive me that I did not know you before."

"Little one, there is nothing to forgive."

Slowly the Lady let down her gossamer veil. The long, pale, powerful face still had the strange beauty of all eternity and the grace of a new dawn, but now a raw sadness carved every feature and haunted the brilliant eyes. She looked at Guenevere and waved her to a chair. "Sit down, my dear, for there is much to tell. I bring a messenger from an unknown land. The word he speaks will be hard for you to hear."

Guenevere shook her head. "What messenger?" she said stupidly. "What word?"

"All in good time. First we must share bad tidings of our own."

There was no mistaking the sorrow in her voice. Guenevere flinched. "Is it Merlin?"

The Lady raised her hand. "Merlin's mind still sleeps, but he is well. He rests peacefully among us, awaiting his return. Nemue and the Maidens thrive too." She gave a terrible sigh. "But alas—"

"What?" Guenevere cried.

"We have a greater grief than any earthly thing. The Christians have cut down the last of the apple trees. Avalon is no more. All the blossom is gone."

Glimmering through the darkness Guenevere could still see Avalon and its sweet apple orchards, white above the lake of shining glass. Her heart froze. "All the orchards gone?" She laughed savagely. "I never thought they'd dare."

"Oh, they dare. These men dare anything. They have the future on their side."

"But you made them welcome on the Island when they came. How can they repay your trust like this?"

"Where we see faith and love, they see one God. In their own Scriptures he calls himself a jealous God, and boasts they shall have no other Gods before him. In their Holy Book he teaches them to rage and destroy."

"So will they overthrow all we hold dear?"

A thousand years of sorrow bloomed in the Lady's eyes. "Alas, we have no defense. Looking out from Avalon, we have seen the writing in the stars. They will seize all our sacred places and build their churches there. They will take our special feasts, and use them to honor Christian gods."

"*Goddess, Mother, yes!*" The last scene with Arthur flooded Guenevere's mind. "Lady, Arthur says they will build a church on the Tor. We have to stop them before they can begin—"

"Guenevere—" Great tears stood in the Lady's eyes. "The church is already begun."

"*What?*"

"The foundations were laid before they asked Arthur for his consent. They know their leader has your husband in his pocket, heart and soul, to do with as he wills."

Guenevere nodded bleakly. "Arthur wants to be magnanimous to all. He does not see the harm that goodness can do."

The Lady's voice took on a harder edge. "No man should place Christian goodness above his wife." Her every word tolled like a judgment bell. "Still less a Queen—still less the Mother-right."

Guenevere drew a breath. "Lady, I can't live with Arthur after this. I shall go to Camelot and keep my own kingdom there." She forced a watery smile. "I'll stay on good terms with him, but we'll grow old apart. He has Mordred and his knights in Caerleon, everything he wants. I'm sure he'll live to a ripe old age."

There was a chilling pause. "Alas, Guenevere, that cannot be."

Guenevere felt a cold breeze from Avalon. Her soul shrank. She wanted to ward off what was coming, and did not know how.

The Lady fixed her with her piercing gaze. "You remember when Arthur wanted to marry you? When he loved you so much that he begged you for your hand?"

Guenevere bowed her head. "We came to Avalon to betroth ourselves before you."

"And he promised to love and honor you all your days." She paused. "Then he swore to defend the Goddess against all men."

Guenevere nodded, sick with dread. "Yes—"

The Lady's voice rang out like thunder at the ending of the world. "He swore by his honor, by his sword, and even by his soul to uphold that oath. If he broke his word, he said, may he lose life and honor too."

Guenevere could not move. High overhead she felt the heavens groan and the firmament crack.

The Lady's voice rolled on. "Arthur swore you a mighty threefold oath. He spoke his own doom if he broke his word. Now he has broken his oath. He has brought that doom down on his head."

Panic gripped her. "Lady, no!"

"Ah, Guenevere, fate spins as it will. Not even the Mother can turn back the wheel. You and he were only keepers of the golden dream. Without your consent, he has opted for the dark."

"Lady, help us! Surely I can still—"

"It is not possible." The Lady was growing taller as she spoke. "Neither you nor I can choose his fate for him. Arthur himself has numbered his own days. Now they are running down like the sands of time. Let go your hold, or you will go down too."

"But he is still my husband! My duty demands—"

"You have no duty to him now." The Lady's voice grew darker with every word. "Only to the land. You are no longer married to this man. By choosing the Christians, he has severed his bond to you."

"So I must let him die?"

The Lady laughed like leaves in the winter wind. "We must all die. You may not stop his death. The dance of life is the rhythm of rise and fall. Arthur, your husband, has flourished in his time. Now he has taken the path that has brought you both here."

"Where?"

"To the time of trial."

Her heart lurched. "Lady, what can I do?"

"Only hold fast to the faith."

"The faith?" It seemed the bitterest word in the world. "Oh Lady, whatever can I believe in now?"

"Believe in yourself. Torments you do not dream of lie ahead. But we shall be with you in your trial, your mother, myself, and the Great One we serve. Be strong in us, and we will fight for you." The Lady's voice was growing fainter with every word. "Remember, those who believe can always enter the dream. Hold fast, and you will become the dream you seek."

"Lady," she cried, "tell me, what must I do?" But there was no answer except the wind keening over the ruins of Avalon.

The tall figure was fading, blending into the shadows and the smoke from the fire. The distant voice rolled on. "One more task lies ahead of you now. I spoke of a messenger from a distant land. He brings word from one who has passed beyond the grave. Hear him, and you will know what you must do." She was dissolving softly into the shimmering air. "Never fear, Guenevere. Stand firm on what you know. In the meantime—"

The earth stood still. The voice grew heavier with every word.

"The last battle is coming for King Arthur and his knights. Soon the trysting horn will call every man to war, and trumpets and drums will darken the field of death. Many thousands will go down to the Otherworld, and all they have known will be drowned in their own blood." She paused. "One thing alone for Arthur will remain. At the last crossing of the water, I shall see him there."

CHAPTER 37

he air in the room convulsed, and the Lady was gone. A sound
like *Farewell* was drifting round the room. A mighty emptiness
drained Guenevere's soul.

Farewell, Lady.
Goddess, Mother, farewell.
And what must I do now?

She stood in a dream of grief, lost and alone. Then before
she knew where she was, a strange man was shouldering through the hangings at the far end of the room. She had no strength even to feel afraid. It
came to her in the Lady's voice, *I bring a messenger from an unknown land. The word*
he speaks will be hard for you to hear.

She wanted to laugh. *What can he say worse than I have heard?*

Tall, gaunt, and stooping, robed from head to foot, the stranger emerged
from the shadows into the gloom within. Head bowed, he kept a distance
from her, the hood of his cloak pulled down over his face. Even in the dark
she could see he was poorly dressed, a peasant or a pilgrim by his rough garb.
Something about him ravaged her numb heart. "You are the messenger, sir?"

"Yes." The strained whisper was at odds with his once-fine frame, and
she heard him cough and turn away his head. *He's ill, maybe dying, that's why he*
seems so sad. She wanted to weep. Even in her misery she had had more joy, it
seemed, than this wretched man.

"Well, sir?" she tried again. "You have a message for me?"

The hooded head went slowly up and down. A weight of unspeakable
suffering hung on him. "I lost my living, lady, and took to the roads. Then
I met a traveler in a distant land—a knight who had lost all that I had and
more—"

A message from beyond the grave, the Lady said.

Oh my love, my love—

"Do you bring me word of—?"

She could not say his name. In a moment of pure madness it came to
her that she could sense him near her again, smell his beloved body, reach out

her hand again for his loving touch. Then her loss swept over her like a monstrous thing. Ambushed by memory as sharp as a torturer's knife, she could not speak, only fight for breath.

At last she found the words. "A knight, you say?"

He nodded. "Of King Arthur's court."

"I had a knight," she said simply, "the finest in all the world. And true to me—how true I did not know." Tears leaped to her eyes. "He went away—"

There was a sound like a savage cough. "You sent him away."

She leaped as if she had been stung. "You must have known him then," she cried, "if he told you that. Tell me where!"

"In the Holy Land."

"But he was killed here! Ambushed in our kingdom before he reached the shore—"

"Not true. He died in my arms." The pilgrim turned away. "He sent you this."

He stepped forward and dropped something on the table with a light thud. Even before her pouncing fingers caught it up, she knew what it was. A man's gold ring, its deep band set with rubies for eternal love. She had had it made for him, chosen every glowing cabochon herself and the color of the gold. She could remember the moment she slipped it on Lancelot's hand.

She could not speak for pain. The pilgrim paced away across the floor. When he spoke, his voice was muffled by his hood.

"We met on a highway in the Holy Land. That night we put up at the same inn and shared our histories, as travelers do. He told me he came from King Arthur's court. He served Queen Guenevere, the best lady in the world, but she banished him and he had to obey. He knew he would never see his land again." Unexpectedly he swung round. "Why did you send him away?"

"I—" She shook her head. Who was this man? She would never answer to him. "I beg you, pilgrim, tell me how he died."

The hoarse whisper resumed. "We rode together for the next few days. Wherever we went, he spoke only of you. Every sunset, you were his evening star. He would kneel to pray and renew his vows to you."

Her tears were falling harshly, like winter rain. The pilgrim's voice wound on.

"One night he had a fever, and took to his bed. The next day he was coughing blood, and had little breath. By the evening we knew he was not long for this world. I knelt by his bed, and he put this ring in my hand. He made me promise I would say these words to you. 'Tell my lady the Queen that I loved her all my life. I never was false, except by trickery. The Princess of Corbenic was never my paramour. The son that she had from me was against my will.' "

Was she dreaming, or did it sound like Lancelot's voice? The man had caught the very echo of Lancelot's speech as he told his tale. His bearing too, his body stiff and aloof, was so like Lancelot's in the hard times they shared. Her mind was slipping, she knew, sliding away from his terrible words. She could hardly bear to hear him, and yet she must.

"He died that night as the love-star rose in the sky. He said your name and then his lips were still. He was blessing you, lady, with his last breath. But he will not walk the Otherworld in peace."

How dare he say that? She cried aloud, "Why not?"

The pilgrim seemed taller now in the tiny room. "Because you hated him, and would not forgive."

Rage and grief racked her from head to foot. "Pilgrim, know this! I would not forgive, that's true." She wrung her hands savagely, careless of the pain. "And I know my jealousy sent him to his death." She threw back her head. She wanted to scream and shout and tear the air. "But you say I hated him? Sir, he was the great love of my life!"

"Still, you would not forgive."

He sounded so much like Lancelot that she knew she was losing her mind. A great weariness swept her, body and soul. "If I treated him cruelly, I have paid for it. If he were here, I would kneel to him and beg his forgiveness now." She shook her head. "But soon I shall tell him all this to his face. In the world between the worlds, I shall see him there."

The pilgrim tensed. "How do you know?"

She lifted her face, blinded by unshed tears. "He told me once that he and I were one. We were fated to love in this world, in the world that was, and the world yet to be. If I died, he would scour the three worlds to come to me."

"So you do not wish him dead?"

"Dead?" She closed her eyes. "Sir, I would die to bring him back to life. Now my only hope is to follow where he is."

"What will you do?"

She gave a tired smile. "Oh, there are potions in plenty—hemlock, wolfsbane—and plenty of desperate wretches who have it for sale."

He raised a hand to the face buried in the hood, and she caught the gleam of an old sword scar on his wrist. *He was a fighting man once, like Lancelot,* she noted idly. *Lancelot used to have a scar like that.*

The hoarse voice was breaking. "You would die for him?"

She gave a luminous smile. "Oh, gladly, sir. After all, he died for me. And it's only a little step into the dark. Then I shall be with him till the end of the world."

Till the end of the world...

In the wall of the hovel a small casement stood open to the night. A lone star hung in the branches of a tree outside. *Venus, the love-star, is blooming in the west.* She pondered it, dreaming of Lancelot. *When I have the death-potion to drink, will this be the last sight I see? Well, let it be. I am not afraid to die. I am ready now. Goddess, Mother, bring me to my love.*

She smiled in peace, knowing that the time had come. In this rough end of town, she would surely find a poor apothecary desperate enough to sell her what she sought. With a new resolution, she turned to take her leave.

"Farewell, sir. We may meet again in a better world than this." She bowed to the pilgrim and turned toward the door. Then came a sound behind that she never thought to hear: "Madame?"

CHAPTER 38

*G*oddess, Mother, spare me—

She stopped in her tracks, staring blindly ahead. How many times had she heard his beloved voice, in the wind, in the rain, in every seabird's cry? How many nights had dwindled to an aching dawn as she lay dry-eyed in her bed and dreamed fierce dreams that he held her close and called her name?

Madame—

He always called me that, even when we were alone. And now this man has come to taunt me with the word—

"Madame!" she heard again, more urgently now.

The pilgrim stepped before her, thrusting back his hood. She saw again the eyes that had haunted her empty nights, the strong cheekbones and jaw she had stroked a thousand times, the wondrous mouth she had known better than her own. With a dull shock she picked up the lines of pain aging the long, sun-browned face, and the gray at his temples that was never there before. He wore his sorrow like a pilgrim's cloak, and his gaunt features and wasted frame spoke of a grief too deep for tears. But the burning brown gaze fixed intently on her face, the ravaged beauty, the tall, lean frame had not changed. It was—

Her mind was cracking. "Ohhhh—"

He took her hand and cradled it against his face. The rough stubble stung the back of her fingers like fire.

"Forgive me, lady, for coming to you like this," came a broken voice. "But I had to know if you still wished me dead."

She could not speak. *LancelotLancelotLancelot* was roaming round her mind. *Have you come to take me to the Otherworld? Or is this a fetch, a walking spirit sent to punish me and drag me down?* She gasped for breath with little whimpering sounds. *Wished you dead, my love, when I can't believe that you're alive?*

He ground her hand between his and crushed it to his lips. "I shall never leave you now, my only love," he said in his strange, raw voice. "Not even at the ending of the world."

His hands were warm and brown, as they always were. He drew her into the shelter of his arms, and she felt again the hardness of his chest. The rough wool of his tunic was pricking against her face, and she breathed in his unmistakable scent. Numbly she dared to bring her hands to his waist. The leather sword belt, the lean flanks, all were real. He was alive, he was here, he was—

Lancelot—

The tears came then in a healing flood. A fragile ecstasy stirred in her deadened heart, and fine shoots of rapture spread through every vein. Only her tongue lay dumb and still in her mouth. There were no words for what she wanted to say.

He looked at her half laughing, half in pain. "Speak to me!" he cried.

Lightness flooded her soul. High overhead she heard the harmony of the stars. She stared at him, owl-eyed. "I thought you were dead," she forced out, the tears starting afresh. "Gawain found the men who killed you—"

"Not me, alas." Lancelot's face darkened. "Some other poor wanderer who died in my place."

She could not take her eyes off his face. "But how—?"

"I hardly know," he admitted wonderingly. "I was traveling alone through a wood, and took shelter in a hermit's cell. I had my armor by my side and my shield under my head when I fell asleep. But then suddenly I was wide awake. I thought I heard someone calling me out of doors."

Someone? Goddess, Mother, praise and thanks to you—

"I thought at first my horse was crying for me. The poor beast was lame when I turned him loose to graze, so I wanted to go and see how he was. But I could hardly move. Lying on the bare stone floor of the empty cell, I'd almost frozen to death."

Praise and thanks again, Great One, for saving my love!

"When I got to the horse, he was lying peacefully on the ground. I stretched out against him, leaning on his flank. I stayed there all night, and his warmth kept me alive."

He sighed. "But when I got back to the cell, all my things were gone, and the stranger was lying there murdered on the floor. So I knew that someone had come to rob me, and killed this poor soul instead."

"Did you know who he was?"

"A knight or a lord by his dress. But at the end, no more than a man lost in a wood."

Guenevere shuddered. "May the Mother be with him, wherever his spirit walks."

"I would have gone after the wretches who murdered him, but they'd taken my saddle so I couldn't ride. All the saddlebags and my armor had gone too. I only had the things I stood up in."

And in that cruel cold too, my sweet love—

Her heart quailed. "What did you do?"

"I still had all my money in a pouch next to my heart. I made my girdle into a head collar and led the horse on foot to the nearest town. I knew I could reequip myself there and carry on. Since then I've managed to replace everything as I went along." He paused, remembering dark things. "But I couldn't leave the poor wretch in the cell to rot. Before I left, I took him into the forest and laid him there to rest. The ground was frozen so I could not dig a grave, but I put him in a hollow and covered him with dead leaves. I gave him to the Mother as I hoped a passing knight would do for me. Then I went onward with all the speed I could. I was afraid that I'd lose Galahad."

The way he said the name hurt her heart. She could only imagine the pain it was costing him. Again she saw him turn aside to cough. "You're not well—"

He brushed her concern aside. "Every one of us caught something in the East. I got off lightly. Soon this will be gone."

But not before it has creased your forehead and hollowed out your cheeks. Not before it has streaked your dear hair with gray, and bruised the papery skin beneath your eyes.

She reached out to touch his face. "Oh my love—"

With one finger she smoothed his troubled forehead and ran her fingers down his sun-scorched cheek. He trembled at her touch and then slowly, slowly, moved toward her again. She stretched up and took him in her arms, drawing his head down to hers for their first kiss. Their lips met like strangers, tender and unsure. Then her body surged with joy at the sweet remembered taste of his love, and she put her heart and soul into the embrace.

They clung to each other like children, lost and reunited in a dark wood. Then far away a dog began to bark, and one by one all the mongrels of the town took it up. Moments later came the crowing of a cock.

Lancelot lifted his head. "Dawn already?" he said wonderingly.

A raw pang of separation shot through Guenevere. "I must go." She made herself leave the shelter of his arms. Then suddenly the tears began again. "But I can't bear to leave you—how can I go?"

"Madame—" Tears of hopeless exhaustion stood in his eyes.

Seeing them she grew strong. She gripped his hand. "Come to court this morning, as soon as you can. All Caerleon will rejoice to know that you're alive." Her spirits rose when she thought of the delight his reappearance would bring. "And as soon as you're alone—oh my love, come to me tonight!"

CHAPTER 39

"**S**ir! Sir! Come and look over there, it's Sir Lancelot!"

"You're raving, lad, he's dead."

"No, sir, he's riding in—"

The Captain of the Watch eased his back against the hard stones of his seat in the guardhouse and raised his head. Before him stood one of the newest intake of recruits, a red-faced, goggle-eyed lad jigging madly from foot to foot. God help them all if the battlements were manned by fools like this. He scowled. "You're no use as a lookout, son, if you can't tell shadows from men and your long-lost heroes from a break in the clouds. Get back to your post."

He eyed the young guard with sour disfavor. "Gods above us, back in the old days—"

Unexpectedly his mind slipped back thirty years. He'd been like this himself once, long ago, a young lad on the watch when something strange appeared. Too young to drink, he'd been the only one still conscious on the battlements when the silver hour before dawn had melted into the shapes of fighting men.

But that had been Arthur Pendragon and his knights, not a wild dream like this. First over the causeway had been Arthur himself, sword aloft, and the rest of them had followed in his train. Gawain, Kay, Bedivere, and a handful more—yet they'd still taken Caerleon with hardly a drop of blood, and Arthur had spared and feasted all the fighting men. And the boys too had felt the warmth of the King's favor, he'd noticed them all—he could still remember Arthur's great hand ruffling his hair.

Pendragon—Pendragon *à moi!*

A smile of reminiscence curved his lips. Yes, those were the days—when Arthur was a king—

He paused. Not like today. Now the King was hag-ridden by his priests, and Christians were everywhere around the throne. Worse, they were all saying the Queen was going to Avalon, that he'd driven her away. And the Gods only knew when they'd have another tournament, with all the knights of the Round Table lost on the Quest—

His thoughts began to take an ugly turn—if only they could have a real King again—

"Sir!"

The young recruit was still dancing about before his eyes.

The Captain rose menacingly to his feet. "I've warned you, soldier—"

The youth was trembling. "Sir! If only you'd see—"

See the figure on the horizon, he wanted to say, the silver armor, the white horse, the trappings of gold. And above all, the simple pennant flying in the breeze. Every man knew the arms of Lancelot du Lac.

The boy waved a hand, unable to contain his tears. "Just look at him, sir, that's all—"

AFTERWARD NO ONE knew who had seen him first, the young lad in the guard tower on his first watch or the midsummer fieldworkers out in the pearly dawn. The laundry maidens washing at the ford had greeted him by name and let him pass, knowing he was not destined for them. As he rode through the town, the word ran before him, and women hastened out of their houses to hold their babies up for his blessing, kiss his stirrup, and throw roses in his way. Bors and Lionel came galloping down to meet him, their faces drawn with a terrible hope and fear. The three of them wept a long while when they met, speaking haltingly in voices raw with pain, and rested where they met for an hour and more. By the time they rode into the castle, all the court knew that Lancelot was back.

"*Lancelot!*"

Waiting for him were Gawain, Kay, Lucan, and Bedivere, their faces a rare study in disbelief and joy. The big knight leaped forward to embrace him and almost dragged him from his horse, while Bedivere wept openly and Kay and Lucan struggled for control.

"What d'you mean, making us suffer like this?" bellowed Gawain, crushing Lancelot to his chest, then thrusting him away. "We thought you were dead, you villain, and I told the King so! I ought to take you to the tiltyard for making me look a fool!"

"Gawain, the Gods did that already, never fear," Kay cut in furiously, his sallow face glistening with strong emotions he did not wish to feel. "You can't blame Lancelot." He reached out a hand. "The King has missed you, friend."

"We all have," Bedivere said tenderly. "Welcome back."

"My dear friends—" Lancelot turned to Lucan.

With an echo of his old panache, Lucan thrust back his hair. "You were detained with a lady, weren't you, you old wretch?" he quipped, holding back his tears. "Well, we're happy to wait for you, but the King and Queen certainly won't. They're ready for you now in the Great Hall."

FROM THE DAIS, the chamber ahead was a sea of red and gold. Every lady in the court had put on her brightest attire, every knight and lord his most colorful array. Only the monks were black clouds upon the scene. In their midst Father Sylvester stood squarely among the faithful with the ever present Iachimo in tow. One or two courtiers noticed the dark clusters of unsmiling brethren with concern: surely there are more monks here now than before? But the joy of the moment soon swept such thoughts away.

High above them all, Guenevere fought to keep down the sickness of her soul. A new awareness was invading her very core.

Yes, I can get through this—a ceremony of greeting where Arthur's attention is anywhere but on me. When Lancelot comes I can still do my duty, I won't be in danger of reaching out to touch his beloved hand or gazing too long and deeply into his eyes.

But when it's over? How can we ever live again as we did before?

At her side Arthur shifted furiously in his seat as he stared down the aisle, his eyes never leaving the great arched door.

"Where is he, Guenevere?" he muttered.

"I don't know, Arthur." She suppressed a raw sigh. Sitting beside him robed and enthroned as of old, she marveled at the way he could pass over whatever had happened between them and carry on exactly as before. Not for the first time, he had risen to a crisis by treating it as if it had never occurred. When they had met that morning to process into court, no one would have believed that she had parted from him only the night before intending to go to Avalon and promising herself that she would never return. But that was Arthur. Why was she thinking he would be different now?

For herself, she had only just slipped back into Caerleon before dawn. Since then she had spent the hours laughing and weeping in her inner chamber, passing from ecstasies of joy to a wild despair. One moment she could hardly draw a breath for bliss: *He's alive, Ina! Lancelot didn't die!* Then she would face again the unspeakable truth: *And I can never be with him or love him as I should.*

And there was a sadness deeper than all this. *My marriage is over, I can never love Arthur again. Before, I had some feeling for him, some respect. Now I am tied forever to a hollow man, while the man of my heart has to stand by and wait. And I may not do right by either of them, torn between both. Goddess, Mother, this is the worst of all.*

"There—there—it's Sir Lancelot!"

A wild hum of joy broke out among the crowd. Arthur surged to his feet and bounded from the dais. Moments later he had Lancelot in his arms. Lancelot stood with his head bowed while Arthur embraced him again and again and wept on his neck. Behind them Bors and Lionel, Gawain, Kay, and Bedivere smiled and wept by turns.

From his close vantage point among the knights, Agravain echoed the joyful smiles while a cool scorn for them all possessed his soul. It was all he could do not to laugh at Gaheris and Gareth grinning like simpletons, or Ladinas hiding his face in his sleeve, and Griflet unashamedly wiping his eye. He stared at Lancelot, observing his air of constraint, his lack of joy. So, so? his subtle mind was probing. Why so? And what follows now? You always were the King's favorite, Lancelot, the knight he adored. Now that you are back from the grave, will you displace his own son in his esteem?

His cold gaze flickered over Mordred on the dais. Yes, the Prince was smiling convincingly enough, and had even raised an authentic-looking tear of joy. But Agravain would have wagered one of his eyes that Mordred was cursing Lancelot and the day he was born. For the Prince was once again out in the cold, just as he had been when Gawain came back. And now here was Lancelot, another hero returned, while he, Prince or no, was forced to appear a man of no achievement, the stay-at-home son.

Even Mordred's hard work in pretending to be pleased was a wasted effort, in Agravain's view. For Arthur had eyes only for the returning knight, and could not rest till he heard how Lancelot had escaped.

"Thank God!" he wept, embracing him again. "And Galahad?" He waved a hand toward Bors and Lionel. "We heard from your cousins that you planned to follow him. Did you succeed?"

Lancelot caught his breath and tried not to cough. "Succeed, my lord? Even now I hardly know."

Arthur waved the court to silence. "How so?"

Guenevere watched the darkness come down in Lancelot's eyes. He

THE CHILD OF THE HOLY GRAIL

caught her gaze for a second of impenetrable pain. Then he looked away, gathering his forces to speak.

"I found him, yes, that's true—"

BUT HOW COULD he ever tell it as it was? All the scenes he had endured crowded his mind, and the weight of them stopped his mouth. He did not know how to begin.

When he lost his armor in the dead of winter, it had been hard to survive. But all that was nothing to the trials in the Holy Land. Endless white days under the pitiless sun, yet at night a biting cold that cleaved to the very bone. Traveling among a proud people invaded by the worshipers of another God, and always ready to attack in return. Passing through a poor country with little food to spare, even for pilgrims' gold. Day after day pressing onward without hope, only the knowledge that Galahad was ahead.

He caught up with him on one of the holy hills, riding unprotected through the hottest part of the day. The figure clad in white, unexpectedly taller and more adult now in his ways, was swaying on his horse and talking to himself. But the pale youth, though badly wasted, knew Lancelot at once, and wept with joy in his arms. After that, they were never apart again.

Soon he knew that the boy was sick beyond human help, and his hopes for his son died a terrible death. The birth of this child had cost him both Guenevere and his place at court, his true love and the life he had loved gone in one swoop. Now Galahad was to be lost to him too. It was a bitter draught, and he had to drink it to the dregs.

But Galahad himself saw nothing but visions of joy. He talked continually of finding the Holy Grail. He was born to it; his mother had told him so. All his life he had known that he had to do this one thing above all for her. Only so would he please her, for this was the only way that she would please the old king. For his grandfather, old King Pelles, stood in the eighth degree from the Christ Himself, and Galahad was the ninth. All this was set down in the Holy Book, which only the faithful could read. Galahad was destined to recover the Holy Grail, and lay it before Jesus Christ at the foot of his throne.

"And see, Father, see!" Galahad cried. "God's other tokens of goodness to your son!"

For Lionel and Bors and he had been shown the Grail already, Galahad boasted through white and wasted lips. He could not tell what they saw, but he had seen it all: a great hill rising out of the water on a turning island, rich with temples of silver and gold, a light shining from a great vessel on an altar, and a long procession with an ailing king—

The cracked voice of the boy went on, worn by fate and sickness to an old man's husk. "And there were three moons in the sky and seven suns, and guardians tending the king with six pairs of wings—no, don't weep, Father, it's true, it's all in the Good Book." He nodded, suddenly round-eyed and childlike again. "Christ's book of heaven and hell." He was silent for a while, then with a merry laugh, he renewed his tale.

And then there was—

And then—

And then—

Lancelot watched his son's flaring eyes, felt his burning forehead, heard his voice fading, and could only endure.

On they rode and on, from one vile inn to another, following, always following the Holy Grail. Then came the night when Lancelot lay listening to the coughing in the next bed. His sense of the suffering boy was so acute that he had forgotten his own miseries, the stifling air, the stinking room, the fleas.

Then a sudden shrill cry came from Galahad and a mighty cracking and roaring filled the room. Lancelot leaped to his feet, sword and dagger in hand.

"Father, look there!" Galahad cried out.

There was nothing to be seen. Darkness hung in the air like a shroud. Lancelot fell to his knees, groping in his saddlebag for a flint. "What do you see?" he rasped. "Tell me."

"A star! A star!" the ecstatic voice went on. "And within it a table of silver with a cloth of gold. And on the table a great chalice of crystal and pearl, set about with rubies and banded all in gold—don't you see it too?" The shrill voice soared. "It is the Grail, Father, the Holy Grail! With the winged attendants and the Fisher King!"

"Yes—?"

After frantic fumbling, Lancelot raised a light. As the tiny spark bloomed in the night he saw Galahad swaying beside his bed, his mouth wide with joy, his eyes filling his head. "The Father has come to take his children home," he gasped. "We shall play and sing under the Tree of Heaven, born again in the love of Jesus Christ."

THE CHILD OF THE HOLY GRAIL

"Galahad, lie down—"

"The sun and moon are dancing round the earth. On the earth is a hill, on the hill is a castle, in the castle is an altar, and on the altar stands the Grail." He reached out with both arms. "Crystal, pearl, gold," he crowed, "bathed in heavenly light. I have it, Father! I am bringing it to Christ's throne."

Now Galahad could barely stand upright. Lancelot moved to support him, but the boy shook him off.

"Leave me!" he shrilled imperiously, "I am King here, do you not see?" He waved his arms wildly around. "This is Mount Salvation, where every man kneels to me. See, here are Bors and Lionel, and—and—all the knights of Arthur's court—and one of them has a sister, a very holy maid—she will be my bride in heaven when our two souls join as one—" Tears filled his eyes. "And my mother will be there—and she will be well pleased—"

The sound of flowing water poured through the room. Suddenly the rank hovel was fresh and sweet and clean. Through the dead midnight poured a ray of sun, and a thousand white doves fluttered down the pathway of light.

Galahad fell to his knees and cast up his eyes, raising his clasped hands before him in the air. "Father, receive my soul!" he cried in a terrible voice. "I have done my duty. I have brought you the Grail."

Sweet savors and rich scents drifted through the air: incense or roses, white blossom or the dark odors of the Christian church? His mind splitting, Lancelot could not tell. All he knew was that Galahad was leaving him.

A roaring filled his ears. But Galahad, he knew, was hearing angel choirs and the chanting of all the legions of the blessed as heaven's gates rolled back to welcome him. The boy pressed his hand. "Farewell," he said merrily. "I shall sing for you in heaven."

Lancelot groaned as if his heart would crack.

"Oh sir, don't grieve," Galahad murmured. He smiled with all the sweetness of his soul. "Don't you see the gold letters on my forehead where Jesus has set his seal? It is only the death of my body that hurts us now. Then I shall find the life of my eternal soul."

Lancelot leaped forward and caught the frail body in his arms.

"My son, my son," he said frenziedly. "Before your Father God, there was the Mother, and She remains. She is with us in the dawn, in the sunset, in the owlet's cry. She strengthens virgins as they go to the bridal bed, She attends every mother in childbirth, She comforts us in the hour of death. A man enters the circle of the Mother when he is born, and She takes him to Her again when he dies. Call on the Mother, she is waiting for you."

He clutched the swooning boy in agony, knowing his words were falling on deaf ears.

"Goddess, Mother!" he cried with all the force of his lungs. "Take this child, let him walk among Your stars. Let not the darkness of his faith block the way to Your light and joy—"

He broke off, weeping helplessly. Galahad lay like a dead weight in his arms. He kissed his eyes, and eased the beloved burden to the ground. Then he saw the pale lips moving as if to speak. Frantically he raised Galahad's head again. The flaring eyes snapped open, and a piteous smile of hope filled the young face.

"Mother?" he whispered. "Mother? Will you love me now?"

THAT AT LEAST Lancelot knew he would never repeat, except to Guenevere when they were alone. But he got through the rest of the story with the semblance of control. Returning from the East, he had gone straight to Corbenic, to break the news to King Pelles and Elaine. There he found that Galahad's mother had indeed gone ahead of him to the world between the worlds. Coming back from Arthur's court, she had refused all food and pined away, locked in her lonely tower. Alone, King Pelles had run mad, and he lived now raving and seeing visions, in the strict care of his monks. The neighboring king had a weather eye on the lands, and when Pelles died, he would add them to his own. The Christians had been promised they could continue their worship there to ensure a smooth transition when it came.

A grief-stricken silence gripped all the court.

"All lost then? All gone?" Arthur questioned sorrowfully. "And your son died in your arms? Oh, sir, there are no words for such a loss."

He turned and held up his hands. "Enough for now, good people. You have heard that Sir Lancelot has suffered a great grief. So we shall not revel tonight in the Great Hall. In the days ahead we shall honor his return."

"But Sire—the Grail!"

The sudden, snakelike hiss brought them all up short. Father Sylvester paced forward like an avenging angel, his body erect, his hands gripped together inside his sleeves. He made a bow to Arthur so brief it was almost an insult. "My lord," he said intently, but his eyes were on Lancelot. "We have heard that Sir Galahad found the Grail. Where is it? *What became of it?*"

Lancelot stepped forward to meet him, eye to eye. "There is no Grail, monk," he hissed back. "Once there were the Hallows of the Goddess, there is no doubt of that. Another time your Jesus feasted his men, and doubtless the cup of his Last Supper was real too. But the Grail my son saw was a vision, nothing more." He laughed in rage and despair. "He died for a dream. A dream not even his own."

Sylvester's eyes quivered and his nostrils flared. "Sir Lancelot—" Behind him Iachimo eased forward like a dog on the attack. Arthur raised one hand.

"Enough! Tomorrow, Father, we shall make time for this."

Still frozen on the dais, Guenevere saw Arthur dismiss the monk and lead Lancelot from the hall. They would feast together in the King's apartments, she knew, till Arthur dispatched Lancelot to his bed.

Except that the bed he goes to will not be his.

She rose to her feet, attended by the guard, and processed after Arthur and Lancelot out of the hall. Though she and Lancelot had exchanged scarcely a glance, she knew he would not break the word that they had shared.

And the word was, *Come to me tonight.*

OUTSIDE THE GREAT HALL the babbling crowd was not ready to disperse.

So wonderful, more than wonderful, that Sir Lancelot was back! But so sad about his son!

Yet how happy the King was to see him again!

And how unhappy the Queen looked that Galahad had died!

Yet where one fine son had come, another could follow. Sir Lancelot should marry, not mourn for the Princess of Corbenic.

There were many young ladies who could give him sons aplenty.

But none like Galahad.

And yet—

On the fringe of the crowd Agravain stood apart, marshaling his thoughts. Why did the Queen look so unhappy? He'd have sworn it was not for the death of Galahad. The troubled gaze she had turned from Arthur to Lancelot and back again had other origins, Agravain dared swear.

The Queen will bear watching, Mordred had agreed.

Mordred, too, had more to lose than ever, and Mordred was where his future allegiance lay.

Well, then, the way was clear.

Agravain's mind snapped shut as all his perverted allegiances came together at a stroke. He would watch Guenevere for Mordred, and work one against the other to bring the change he sought. He would create the great wave on which he would ride to achieve his desire.

He smiled, luxuriating in the moment, feeding on the future he foresaw. For all the strange pleasures he had taken in the East, nothing compared to this. He could still see Guenevere with her guard, moving away, a woman in a dream. And in the same dream, he smirked, he would track her down.

CHAPTER 40

H e came at owl-light, when she had almost despaired. Prowling the chamber, she was prey to panic and disordered thoughts. *He's dead, he must be, I have dreamed all this, Goddess, Mother, I beg you, don't bring him back to snatch him away again—*

Then she heard the cry of the guard at the outer door and the quick stir of welcome in the antechamber as he arrived with Bors and Lionel. She stood rigid with longing as Ina received the knights and heard her attending to the two cousins as they settled down to wait. Then at last the door opened, and he was there.

Now she felt as if she were seeing him for the first time. Clad in a tunic of white wool and a glittering cloak of gold, he had never looked so fine. The gold torque of knighthood gleamed at his neck, deep bands of gold encircled both his wrists, and a fillet of gold held back his thick hair. Her eyes dazzled, and the strangeness of it all made her afraid: *He's wearing my colors, the Queen's colors of white and gold, but I don't know him anymore.* A leather belt embossed with studs of gold hung loose around his waist, and his sword tapped impatiently against his spurs. From his soft leather boots to his urgent bright brown eyes, he flamed with inner light. He was so beautiful that she wanted to turn her face away and hide. *I look so old*, went coursing through her mind. *And he is still marvelous as he always was.*

"Madame!"

She flinched. He was coming toward her with darkness in his eyes, and she knew that he too was seeing her afresh. Never had she prepared with more frantic care than in the hours before he came. But now the blue gown she had thought would enhance her eyes, the long white cloak embroidered with gold runes of love, the crystals on her fingers, at her neck, and round her waist all seemed both too much and not enough. *He must hate the look of me now*, came to her in the accents of utter despair. *He would have remembered me so much better than this.*

And the chamber too—

She glanced around, losing heart even more. That morning she had sent to the wildwood for armfuls of young boughs, and her maidens had decked out the chamber like a woodland bower. Then she and Ina had filled it with flowers, wild roses and sweet forest lilies scenting the air. Between the branches of misty viridian, she had lovingly plaited long tendrils of honeysuckle, white and creamy pink, and dark strands of ivy for constancy. Before he came she had viewed it with tender pride as a place where the Queen of the Fair Ones might have welcomed her love. But now—

Now he stood before her and reached out for her hand. "Lady," he said in a voice of wonderment, "how is it you are still so lovely—?" He shook his head sadly, with a throwaway gesture of despair. "Whereas I—"

Tears stood in the corners of his blazing brown eyes. Her heart cracked. She reached up to brush his tears away. Then without a word she led him to the bed.

THEY LAY FOR a long while in each other's arms, softly whispering and weeping as the moon rose. Then they came at last to a place beyond tears. Safe in the shelter of his embrace, her head cushioned against his chest, she drank in the miracle: he was alive, he was with her, he was *here*. She could feel his familiar body, and knew again the hardness of his flanks, his thighs, his jutting hip. The never-to-be-forgotten curve of his lean side was thinner now, and his sword hand bore scars she had not seen before. But still her blood danced and sang the length of her veins, *He is Lancelot, my love, and he is here*—

Over their heads the nodding branches wove a canopy of tender green. Hungrily, she breathed in the fresh tang of the woodland and wished they were there or anywhere miles away from here. One by one they shared small pieces of news and fitfully unraveled the larger tale too. In a voice still raw with his sickness he took her with him step by step on his pilgrimage to the Holy Land; then through every husky, grief-stricken word she traveled with him every mile of the way back.

They rested a long while in the Holy Land, as he relived with her every moment of Galahad's death. She knew now that Lancelot's son would be with them all their lives, and she bowed her head and plodded through that with him too.

"He was a holy child," she murmured to Lancelot, "and his life was perfect, although it was so short. Not many of us will be able to say the same."

And he kissed her fervently, and wept into her hair.

Afterward they kissed again, and once more she knew the raw rapture of rediscovering him, mingled with the deep comfort of what was already known. At first they were tender and tentative, like beginners again, and they laughed a little to find themselves so unsure. But then his hand moved down her body with hungrier strokes and she quickened instantly at his rough caress. She felt herself arching, growing beneath his hands. With mounting elation he delved into her gown, pushing the filmy silk aside to expose her breasts.

"Oh my love!" he muttered hoarsely in his throat as he kissed her aching nipples again and again.

She lay back, abandoning herself to him. Her hips moved luxuriously to and fro, all her longing for him swelling to a head. She struggled to undo the stiff buckle on his leather belt, then she reared up and pulled his tunic over his head. In his fine breeches and shirt of spotless white lawn, the wonder of him caught her breath again. In an answering silence he leaped to his feet and shrugged off his clothes. Then with a strange reverence he laid her down on the bed and drew off her gown.

Her arms flew to cover herself: how long since she had been naked with him? Too long, far too long. *He remembers my body as it was,* she panicked, *and now he's slept with Elaine again and she was so young—*

The thought seared her mind, but she could not stop. *She was thirty to my fifty, she must have been smooth and firm. The last flesh he handled was hers, while mine has grown old and dried up with missing him. Mother, Great One, let him love me the way he did. Goddess, Mother, be with me, smile on us tonight!*

And afterward she knew that the Mother had answered her call. For Lancelot came to her with the eyes of the shining stranger that her maidens dreamed of and prayed for in their dreams. Like the King of the Fair Ones he took her to himself, with a thousand murmured words of love and praise.

"*Ma reine—mon coeur,*" he whispered into her ear, "*ma belle—belle comme le ciel—la reine du ciel—*" Then she knew she was his queen of heaven indeed, his beauty, his love, his love at the heart of love.

And she entered his arms like a queen and woman at once, and he took her hard and long, as her heart desired. His lean brown body covered her like a banner of love and she had never felt happier and safer in all her life. Together they rode the great wave when two become one, and came to themselves gasping on the furthermost shore. Then they clung together like survivors of a mighty storm, and he kissed her eyes, her mouth, her breasts, and her eyes again.

"I shall never leave you now, my only love," he dropped into her ear with a hundred little kisses and sweet sounds. And rosy with contentment, she fell asleep.

CHAPTER 41

Mordred strode through the cloisters, surveying the clouds with a troubled eye. Dawn was long gone, and the sun was bounding up the sky. Get a move on, man! he chided himself furiously. You're late! Arthur had commanded all the knights to attend him for the hunt. And no one should keep the King waiting, least of all his son.

Hurry, hurry!

No—

Mordred composed himself, settling into an easy, regular stride. He knew better than to hasten furtively along: nothing gave a man a more guilty look. He had to suggest that he was out on a healthy early-morning jaunt rather than sneaking away from a forbidden bed.

Well, not so forbidden. The woman was a widow, after all, and he too had no marriage ties to break. But his partner in last night's pleasures was supposed to be grieving for her newly lost lord, while he himself was known to be the son of the King. In truth her husband had been the least worthy of Caerleon's knights, a vain, shallow youth who had received the kiss of Excalibur only because his father had been one of Arthur's loyal old knights. And the girl Mordred had just left drowsing in her tangled sheets had married the ninny only because her father had forced her to. When the young husband had died falling drunk off his horse, the plump-breasted, pouting young widow had lost no time in catching Mordred's eye and opening her legs for him. So he could not be accused of taking advantage of her grief. All the same, it would not do well if this episode came to light. All the more reason then to end it now, before it had truly begun.

She would howl and scream, of course. His lip curled in a contemptuous grin. How foolish women were, how fond! And how little they knew that men loved to see them squeal. His smile hardened into a determined nod. Yes, the lady was already a thing of the past. As they all were in time—until the next time.

His smile faded. Why was he doing this, when he knew what it would mean for him if it came to light? If Arthur, the soul of chivalry, ever learned that his son was a whoremonger now, or worse? That the heir to Caerleon and Camelot was a man who would break fellowship with the knights of the Round Table by lying with their wives, and deflower the virgins he had sworn to protect?

A telltale flicker of nausea seared his soul: Why, Mordred, why?

Then a self-protective frenzy came to his aid. Why not? his soul snarled. Why not, since he had nothing else to do? Since the King kept him like a prisoner, tied hand and foot?

Gods above, he swore silently, shouldering through the King's cloisters to the sound of chanting monks, another man would do more than he did, much more! And he was careful, always careful, as a matter of course. Idly his mind flickered back to the lean young wanton who had first made him a man. A hot-eyed, horny-handed serving maid at the castle where he was a young squire, she had taken him by surprise with the heat of her lust, and divested him of his breeches and his virginity in one skillful assault. Later, dazzled with mad hopes of becoming Queen, she had tried to force his hand, threatening to betray him to the lord of the castle if he did not marry her. Meeting force with force, stifling her threats with black threats of his own, then wooing the silly slut back into a semblance of good humor again had been his first test of managing the hearts and minds of those who were born to serve him.

And he had learned from it, he reminded himself. That kind of mistake was made by every young knight and had probably happened to Arthur in his turn. After that he had trodden with care, and never allowed himself to be compromised again. For years he had kept himself chaste and pursued the ideals of knighthood with devoted care. He would honor all women till he met the lady he could love and serve and make his future Queen. Fool that he was, he scorned himself savagely now. He must have passed up a thousand good offers by trying to be true to his vows. And all to become a knight *fainéant*, a worthless do-nothing held back by his father's will!

So why not a moment of pleasure taken here and there, as long as silence and discretion could be enforced? If last night's amusement with the widow gave him away, he reminded himself, striding grimly on, the fault would be his, not hers, for leaving too late. All his other recent playthings would keep their mouths shut, he knew. The young maiden on the verge of marriage whose virginity would never be missed by her love-sotted groom, the lusty wife whose husband was away, the court lady seeking advancement for her husband when Mordred became King—they were always women with powerful reasons of their own to keep the silence he craved. And to give him their deference and service, for he craved that too. His duty to Arthur was all very well, but at night he needed to call his soul his own. A soul that demanded the eternal novelty of crushing female flesh, the cruel luxury of new bodies beneath his, new creatures subject to his intimate command.

Yet where was the woman he could truly call his own—the woman worthy of his dominance, the woman of the dream? Surely his destiny would reveal her to him one day, a woman of blood and fire, made of passion and tears, a woman true and valiant to the bone?

A woman like Guenevere, crashed through his mind.

Guenevere?

What—?

He started in fear, and caught himself looking round. *His father's wife?*

A moment later he was hurriedly mending his pace. You're mad, man, if you're starting to think like that! he directed himself furiously. Gods above, the hunt will be gathered already in the stable yard, all the knights will be ready and waiting except you, and you're brooding on this! Just forget all about it and *get yourself to the King!*

"The Queen looks well. And it's a perfect day for a ride."

Standing in the little knot of knights, Lucan nudged Bedivere and directed his attention approvingly toward Guenevere. Across the stable yard stood a dainty dapple-gray mare in a saddle and bridle of royal red, prancing with excitement and frisking up and down. Guenevere was reaching up for the reins, stroking the silky neck to quiet the horse, then hooking up the skirts of her riding gown ready to mount. Her face was flushed and her eyes were very bright as she laughed up at Lancelot standing by her side. Farther off, Bors and Lionel waited with Lancelot's horse and their own, both staring out blankly, lost in their own thoughts.

Watching them, Kay turned a yellower shade of bile. Gods above, what had come over the Queen? And why were Bors and Lionel looking like that? Immediately he did not want to know, and fury made him push the thought away.

"The Queen's well enough, Lucan, without your say-so," he snarled. "Can't you think of anything but a woman's looks?"

"This isn't any woman, my old friend," Lucan put in with more good humor than he felt. "She is the Queen, the sovereignty of the land. Her health is our health too."

Towering over Kay, Gawain gave a red-blooded guffaw. "Lucan, that's your old Goddess faith talking, it's not what people think." He threw Guenevere a careless glance. "God knows we all wish the Queen good health. And in Camelot they still think she's the Queen of Queens. But here in Caerleon she's no more than a woman and the King's wife." He gestured toward Arthur across the stable yard. "And as long as the King is happy, we all are, aren't we, Kay?"

Kay did not reply. Across the yard he could see Lancelot dropping to one knee, cupping his hands to Guenevere's foot to help her to mount. From the other side, Arthur was approaching in a flapping cloud of monks, their wretched leader Father Sylvester holding forth in urgent flow, making Arthur hostage to his demands. Happy? Kay questioned querulously. How could the King be happy when his wife publicly enjoyed the attention of another man, and he himself was hog-tied and hag-ridden by priests?

A dark shadow stained the cobbles and Agravain came up. "Ready for the hunt, brother?" he addressed Gawain with a courteous smile, and all the knights watched as Gawain answered back.

"As ready as I'll ever be," Gawain said with an effort, but pleasantly enough. "And now that the King's here, as soon as Mordred arrives, we can be off."

Agravain nodded. "And the Queen?" he asked casually, his understanding with Mordred ever present in his mind. "She's riding out, did you say?"

Lucan laughed with delight. "Yes, she and her maid are taking to the woods alone. It's a long time since she's done that, and it'll do her good."

Guenevere clattered out through the gate with Ina in the rear, turning to wave to Lancelot as she went. Her eyes were dancing and her mouth rosily curved as if holding back a sudden secret glee. Lancelot gave a stiff bow and turned back to Bors and Lionel, meeting a fierce glare from the former, which caused him to look away. He moved off to take his horse from Lionel, and busied himself adjusting the stirrups and girth. Not now, Bors, his back said as plainly as any speech. Whatever you have to say, say it later, not here.

What was all that about? Uncoiling like a snake, Agravain's interest stirred. With his beloved kinsman Lancelot back from the dead, Bors ought to be the happiest of men. But instead—

Agravain turned to Bedivere, who stood on the edge of the group enjoying the scene. "So we're all off on the hunt then," he said cordially, "as soon as Mordred comes?"

Bedivere smiled and nodded. "And here he is."

Both men turned to watch the tall, striding figure hastening out of the castle and down through the busy courtyard into the sun.

"Mordred!"

There was no mistaking the joy in Arthur's face. "Where've you been, you rogue?" he bellowed, his voice ringing round the yard. "Overslept, did you, and kept us all waiting here? At your age I never wanted to stay in bed. The lure of the hunt was the only call for me!"

"As you say, sire," Mordred proffered with a self-deprecating smile. "Forgive me—I'm a filthy slugabed."

Arthur roared with laughter. "There's nothing to forgive! But hurry up now, or we'll lose the day." He turned back to Father Sylvester with a bow. "Thank you for your report on Avalon. I am glad to hear that your monks are making such good progress with the church on the Tor." He paused. "The Church of Saint Michael the Beloved. It will make a fitting memorial for—" Suddenly his eyes filled with tears.

There was an awkard pause. Embarrassed, the knights stood unhappily around, not knowing what to say.

Mordred stepped forward. "Father, with God's grace you will build a hundred of them," he proclaimed ringingly. "But now the hunt's calling, and I've delayed you long enough." Mordred turned to the waiting knights, and raised his arm. "Mount up, sirs," he called.

Arthur's face changed in an instant. "Why, there's a son!" He caught Mordred to him and hugged him round the neck. "Come on, then!"

From the corner of his eye Agravain saw Lancelot, Bors, and Lionel already mounted and waiting by the gate. Again he felt the dark worm inside him stir. He caught Bedivere by the sleeve and casually indicated the three knights. "Aren't they coming with us?"

Bedivere smiled and shook his head. "No, Lancelot begged the King's leave to ride out alone. They still feel the loss of Galahad and they're better just going to the woods alone, Lancelot says."

"Yes, indeed." With a show of indifference, Agravain turned away. But in the pit of his mind, the slimy things were now wide awake and strenuously at work.

Lancelot going to the woods alone—
The Queen going to the woods alone—
Next time you are all alone, my dears, I shall know!

CHAPTER 42

Gods above, how he loved her!

Lancelot stood in the woodland, his heart pounding while his soul, his guts ached for Guenevere. The dry loam beneath his feet was inviting him to lie down and soon, soon, he would take to it with his love. Around him the sun poured down from the melting sky and the dancing motes and little gilded flies frolicked in bliss through the glittering air. Under the trees, it was dim, cool, and sweet. All the forest lay drowsing in the noonday heat, breathing out the musky tang of elder and the sweetness of woodbine.

He was so still that he might have been part of the forest. His body had forgotten where it was. How long had he waited for Guenevere? He did not care, for the waiting was part of her and his love for her now. His spirit soared and a thousand small ecstasies came thronging through his mind: Guenevere my lady, Guenevere the Queen. If I die now, he thought hazily, I am happier than I have ever been. For my lady is coming, she loves me, she will soon be here.

The forest slept on. The only sound was the low jagged buzz of the insects and the faint jingle of the horses as they moved. At one with the earth, the three beasts grazed in contentment, sighing over every pull of the lush summer grass. Beside them in the clearing, Bors paced to and fro, and wished with every step that he were dead.

"Brother—"

Seated with his back against a tree, Lionel looked at Bors' rigid carriage, his tight face, and the yellowish sheen on his skin, and wished he had not decided to speak. In truth, there was nothing at all that he wanted to say. And nothing he could say that would change anything at all.

But Bors whirled round and desperately pounced. "Yes?"

"Oh—nothing."

Bors' face hardened. "I thought you'd seen the Queen?"

"No."

"Well, what do we expect?" Bors slapped his riding whip furiously against his boot. "Why should Her sweet Majesty deign to come on time, when she knows that Lancelot would wait for her till we die!"

He gave a savage laugh. Lionel's gentle soul shrank from his brother's wrath. "She has to be careful," he put in awkwardly. "When they're meeting like this, she has to go round and about."

"Careful?" Bors gasped with rage and fought to collect himself. "Gods' blood and bones, man, she's giving the whole thing away every day!"

"Brother—"

"Brother, brother, you know that I'm telling the truth! She goes through the court beaming and smiling at all, trailing her happiness like a milkmaid in love."

Lionel shook his head. "That's not giving it away," he said hollowly, hoping it was true. "People think she's happy because the King has recovered his health."

"The King?" Bors yelped. "He's a blind worm, a mole, a fool! He's burrowing ever deeper into the dark to please his priests, and meanwhile he's lost his wife and he doesn't even see." His short limbs jerked wildly as he stalked to and fro. "But it's Lancelot I don't understand. Why isn't he more aware of what's going on?"

Lionel nodded wretchedly. He too had watched with alarm all the little smiles, the tender secret looks, the times the Queen leaned on Lancelot's shoulder or touched his arm. "I know what you mean."

Bors agonized on, biting his lower lip. "Oh, we know the Queen's deaf and dumb to anything but her own desires, but he ought to see there are eyes everywhere."

A saturnine visage flew into Lionel's mind. "Especially Agravain," he said fearfully.

Bors suspended his restless pacing instantly. "Gods, save us from the Orkneys!" he swore. "They're bad blood, and feuding is in their bones. Agravain would love to do Lancelot a bad turn, and he loathes Gawain. Gawain prides himself on being the King's dearest kin, but Mordred's the heir—"

He broke off as a new concern darkened his mind. "Mordred—there's another with his ear close to the ground." He groaned. "We need to be wary of him too." He gave a desperate laugh. "If either of them ever got to know that the Queen took Lancelot to her bed—"

Lionel stared at the ground and wished he could lie. But for the life of him he could not say, "They won't."

LANCELOT, MY TRUE LOVE, come to me tonight—

How often did these words come to her lips and how often did he frown, pull back, and refuse?

"Madame, we must have a care—"

That last summer was golden, enchanted, steeped in love but also laced with pain.

"You don't love me!"

"More than my life. But I have to care for your reputation too."

And Arthur's peace of mind, he did not say. But she knew that his love for Arthur stained their golden hours. These days he no longer tormented them both with the code of chivalry he had cast aside. He never lamented that he killed his lord by lying with his wife, or that loving her meant betraying his fellow knights too. But in the silence of the afternoon as he cradled her in her arms, in the depths of the woodland as his kisses sucked out her soul, she could hear his deep thoughts and knew it had not gone away.

Yet the blossoming love between them drove it aside, at least when they were alone. Strange to relate, and more wonderful than strange: after all the years together they were like newborn lovers again with a love so fierce and tremulous that it could not be denied.

So she begged him often, Come to me tonight!

And in spite of his fears, he went to her more often than he should have, with less care than he might.

Neither of them saw the dark figure in the doorway, the hidden watcher in the cloisters, the ever-present shadow in the night. For they were in love and could not be denied. And they knew in their hearts that the bright day was waning and after came the dark.

So they played and laughed and trod their long-destined path as the days passed by like pearls on a chain, pink and gold dawns blossoming into indigo starlit nights, days like rose petals, twilights like violets. Every kiss was the flight of a swallow, every lovemaking a feast of summer fruit.

Even then they were counting the days, feeling the looming shadow as it drew near. But while the sun shone, they danced like the mayflies who live out their one sunlit day. And so it continued all that sweet summer long.

❖　　❖

"So?"

Mordred shouldered his way sullenly into the small room and waved a peevish hand at Agravain, entering behind. "You wanted to see me alone? What's so urgent, then?" With a resentment he could not explain, he glanced around. "It had better be worth coming to this wretched place."

In the dismal little chamber, the air was sour and chill. A hidden corner of the Prince's quarters, it had been built for private consultations of high state, the kind of meeting, Mordred reflected bitterly, that he never had. But looking at the unused council table and its solid chairs and the rich but untended carpet on the dusty boards, Mordred's spirits stirred. At least the walls were sound. The last time he had been in this room he had taken a squealing virgin on this very floor, and however she'd screamed and moaned not a soul had heard.

Remembering it, he could not hold back a sharp stab of mirth. What was her name? Something Christian, Mary or Anne, that he knew. The wench had been due to enter a convent the very next day, packed off by her father to keep his cherished daughter chaste. If she was found with child, her father would kill her, she knew. But she was not to know that Mordred did not care.

"Tell them it's holy conception just as Mary had," he had told the girl as she wept out her fear. "You're a bride of Christ, God came to you in the night." In fact the girl had escaped the fate of all women that time, and remained a virgin in the eyes of all. But it was still one of his better quips, he thought. He laughed again.

Agravain's head tightened: he's laughing at me! Smiling blackly, he made sure the door was closed and turned back with an ingratiating bow. "Sir, the news I bring is hard to tell and to hear. I knew you would want to speak of it alone."

"So?"

Agravain paused. He had rehearsed this moment a thousand times. "The Queen has taken Sir Lancelot to her bed."

"*What?*"

Mordred's eyes bulged. A wave of black fury engulfed him, and he started to shake. But at the same time he was crying inside: Mordred, Mordred, you fool, why are you surprised?

Agravain saw it all and pressed smoothly on. "You told me to watch the Queen, lord, and I have done so. Sir Lancelot lies by her day and night. By day his visits are covered by Bors and Lionel. By night he slips into the Queen's garden and enters her chamber from there."

Why was all this like a blow in the chest? Mordred fought for breath. "You're sure?"

A smile of great coldness visited Agravain's lips. "Sir, I could give you times and dates at court. They meet in the forest too, but I could not follow them there. The Queen zigzags like a lapwing to cover her tracks, and Lancelot is guarded by Bors and Lionel." He let out his breath in a hiss. "But they are lovers, I'll stake my life on it."

"Your life, Agravain? Let us hope it won't come to that." Mordred was slowly coming to himself again. What did he care who lay with the Queen? How to use this against her was the only thing. "You saw all this alone?"

"Yes."

"So there are no other witnesses? No proof?" Mordred laughed in scorn.

Agravain's soul contracted. He had killed the last man who'd laughed at him. He could not do that now. With an effort he mastered himself and shook his head. "Not yet, my lord."

Mordred turned away and dropped into the nearest chair, crossing his booted feet with a furious air. "Strange," he said in an unpleasant tone, "I thought you had them in the palm of your hand." He raised his head and gave Agravain a taunting stare. "But in fact—"

"They are careful, my lord, and clever. It's been hard to pin down."

"If it exists," Mordred sneered. "So Lancelot goes to Guenevere, what does that prove? She's the Queen, he's her knight, it's the way of the court. The King's caught up with his monks, and they want him to build a hundred churches to Amir. The court's grown stale, not a tournament in sight. The Queen wants company, and Lancelot has to obey."

Agravain's eyes were pinpoints of black fire. "I can prove it, sir—with your help."

Mordred stiffened. "How?"

"Invite the King on a hunt that will take him a good way away. Lancelot will plead some excuse to remain behind. Give me a dozen good men, and I'll waylay them in her chamber after you've gone. They'll be caught in the act. I'll deliver them into your hands."

Yes! soared and burned its way through Mordred's mind. With Lancelot disgraced and Guenevere destroyed, Arthur would be his and his alone. Once

Arthur was his, then the kingdom would be his. King Mordred would become a clear reality, not a distant hope—

King Mordred—

God save the King—

Mordred's head was ringing and his eyes were blind with desire. Agravain's voice came from very far away. "Will you do it, my lord?"

"Will I do it?" Molelike, Mordred fixed his eyes on the darkness ahead and made his choice. "I'll do it." He smiled. "Oh, I will."

CHAPTER 43

"A hunt in the Wounded Forest?" Arthur's eyes narrowed with a rare excitement, and he glanced keenly round his band of knights. "Well, don't look so startled, you heard what Prince Mordred said." He laughed with delight. "Why, I haven't been there in twenty—no, thirty years—"

"And for good reason, sire," put in Kay overhastily. "It's a long ride, too far to come and go in a day—"

"What, do you think we're too old to stay out overnight?" Arthur objected with an ominous gleam.

"Never, sire!" Hooting, Gawain gave Kay's shoulder a companionable clout. "Kay's only afraid that his bad leg won't hold out. That's the only reason he complains about how far it is."

One look at Kay's face showed Arthur that this was true. "We'll go easily, Kay," he said, moved by the sight of Kay's sallow face, the features pinched with pain. "But the Wounded Forest—bless us, what a hunt that would be!"

COME TO ME TONIGHT—

Already he had had the sweet summons from the Queen. Frowning, Lancelot swung away from the window and dropped onto his haunches on the narrow bed. Beside him Bors sat nursing his head on his hands. From the rough pallet opposite, Lionel stared at them with troubled eyes. In the cramped knights' quarters, the air was thick with distress. Lancelot shook his head. "You must go, you and Lionel."

Bors did not move. "Our place is with you," he muttered doggedly.

Lancelot smiled. "But I shall be with the Queen." He paused. "And you and Lionel have wasted too much of your time waiting on me." He raised his head to the open window, where the tang of autumn was drifting in from the woods. "Summer's almost gone, and winter will soon be here. You'll enjoy the hunt, and the King will expect you there."

"What about you?"

"I shall tell him the truth—that I have no stomach for the hunt."

Bors clenched his fists and tried not to look at Lancelot. "Cousin, I beg you—this time, don't go to the Queen—"

"Not go to the Queen?"

Bors kept his gaze fixed on the ground. How could he convince Lancelot of something he hardly knew for sure himself, the faint shadow vanishing in the half-light, the sense of a watching presence when no one was there? Don't you see how lucky you have been all these years? he wanted to shout. But things are different now, the world is changing and our days are done. Sooner or later it will all come to light, it's only a matter of time—

A voice of raw disbelief assailed his ears. "Not see my lady Guenevere?"

In spite of himself Bors looked up. The expression on Lancelot's face hurt his eyes, and Bors knew what he would say.

"I must, Bors—I must."

Ssssooo—

Sssssooooo—

Good hunting, Arthur, you'll catch nothing but grief today—

High overhead the spirit wheeled and soared, laughing to herself at what she saw. Far below, the jingling column was moving into the wood. At its head rode Arthur, with Mordred on one side and Gawain on the other, and a line of high-spirited knights following behind.

Arthur surveyed the scene in deep content. Life was good. The sun sailed the sky between bobbing white clouds, and all the world lay smiling to Arthur's view. He did not see the hovering carrion crow, the great black raven watching from high above. He saw only the black hills ahead dreaming in the distant sun, and the promise of the sweet green miles in between. At the end of the ride lay the cunning quarry and the joy of the pelting chase, the fine boar cornered at last, mad eyes and savage tusks raging in the hidden thicket, and then the evening round the fire as dusk drew in. With so many knights on the ride, they should take two boars if not three, with ample helpings of the tough gamy roast pork scenting the night air. With those he loved around him, and not a care in the world, it seemed to Arthur that he had never been happier in his life.

The raven that had followed them from Caerleon wheeled low overhead. As they left the open track and entered the welcome shelter of the trees, its shadow fell on Arthur unaware, and he felt strangely sad. "Lancelot should be here!" he sighed fretfully.

Mordred nodded in pious agreement. "He should indeed." He paused, picking his words with care. "I fear that Sir Lancelot is not the man he was. His heart is not with Your Majesty anymore."

Arthur stared. "What?"

Mordred arranged his face into an expression of concern. "Never before was Sir Lancelot ill-disposed to hunt." He shook his head sorrowfully. "And unless he is ill, his duty demands attendance on his King."

"Sire, by your leave—"

Gawain urged his horse forward to join in. "Lancelot is the most loyal soul alive," he said explosively. He turned to Mordred. "Think of it, Prince: a man gets a son he never knew he had, then has to watch the boy die in his arms." He gave his boisterous laugh. "The sons of the Orkneys are not tenderhearts. But few of us would relish life after that."

The sons of the Orkneys—

Riding behind Gawain, Bors caught the passing phrase, and a violent jolting thought ran through his mind. Gawain is there with the King, and Gaheris and Gareth are here somewhere, riding behind. But on the day when Lancelot is going to the Queen, *where's Agravain?*

Ahead of him Gawain was still speaking, making no attempt to hide his glee. "Bad stomach, Agravain says," he guffawed, in answer to a question from the King. "Sent me word this morning to make his excuses to Your Majesty. But you know Agravain—he's always full of bile!"

Bors' gut convulsed with fear. He did not dare catch Lionel's eye. But he could hear his brother's thought as clearly as his own.

You know Agravain—

A wave of foreboding hit Bors and he gasped in pain.

Know Agravain?

Goddess, Mother, be with us—if only we did!

WHAT TIME WAS IT?

Guenevere awoke in a warm pool of gold. Normally she was up with the dawn or before. But now the sun was above the horizon, pouring blessings through the window without a care. Why had Ina allowed her to sleep on like this?

Already the sweet answer was forming through the mists of sleep. *Ina knows that Lancelot will be here tonight. We have had so few times in all these years when my love could hold me all night in his arms. She knew I would want to be well rested and joyful when he comes. And if he came this minute, it would not be too soon.*

She yawned luxuriously and stretched herself like a cat. Her body, her breasts, felt ready and firm and good. Her arms were already reaching out for him, and her fingertips were dreaming of his skin, his face, his hair. Now, how to get through the day before he came?

She rolled over, her mind moving sweetly this way and that. "Ina?" she called.

Time passed that day in a hundred pleasant ways. With Ina she reviewed her wardrobe gown by gown, laughing at herself for bothering at all—would he leave her because he disliked what she wore? At last she settled on the dress she had chosen at first, a fine chamber gown of great simplicity, all its beauty in the rich viridian shade of its silk, a true woodland green. Her jewels she kept simple too, beguiling herself with the thought *Just so would I dress for Lancelot at Joyous Garde.*

For the faint wisp of hope never left her heart that someday she might live with Lancelot as his wife. They would share his castle, she would be his lady there, they would be good to the people for miles around. This fragile dream she kept locked up in her mind, never telling it to Ina, still less to Lancelot. Yet at the same time she knew it could never be.

She heard the Lady's voice from far away, repeating her warning from an earlier time. *Ah, Guenevere, you are not like other women. Ahead of you there lies a great and mighty love, a love you do not think of—dare not dream—*

She nodded to herself. She had had the great love, and she had it still, indeed stronger than ever since Lancelot had returned. Why then should she expect the humbler comforts of hearth and home to be hers as well?

Still, we shall have tonight.

Tonight he will be mine.

She brought the ring she wore for Lancelot to her lips and kissed the cool moonstone with a grateful heart. Tonight was a gift they had not hoped for, a rare moment they had not thought might come. Tonight would be for them both an unforgettable memory.

So she had Ina perfume the chamber with the fragrance of the Queens of the Summer Country since time began. Now the throaty scent of patchouli drifted from the hangings, the rugs, and the draperies of the bed and, as she moved, from her wrists, her temples, and the hollows of her neck. Her skin shone, and every strand of her hair gleamed fresh and fair. Maid and mistress laughed together quietly over this. Did they really need the costly saffron from the East when Lancelot never seemed to see the threads of silver making their way in among the gold?

When he came she was ready and waiting, gown, hair, jewels as fine as they could be, her heart dancing like a maid in June. He had made his way in by a roundabout route, slipping through side passages unguarded whenever the King was away, and moments after she caught the first sound of his soft step he was in her arms.

"Oh, my love!"

She showered him with kisses, then hugged him to her heart. He was clad simply in a plain wool tunic and cloak, and every fiber bore his beloved scent. With Ina on guard in the antechamber and her men-at-arms away at the outer door, they were truly alone. She lifted up her face for his kiss, marveling at the wonder that he was there. He was there, he was hers, and nothing but joy lay ahead. Afterward she knew she had never been happier in her life.

He held her fiercely and crushed her in his arms, kissing her till she lost her breath. When at last he released his hold, she was laughing and gasping at the same time. "Lancelot—"

Then she saw his face. "What—?" she cried.

Before she could say any more, he stopped her mouth with a desperate kiss, then held her to him, raining kisses on the top of her head. His chest was heaving, and she knew he was trying to speak. As she raised her head, tears started to his eyes.

"Madame—" he began so thickly that she wanted to scream.

"Whatever it is," she begged, "don't say it, not yet—"

"Lady, I have to—I must go."

She cried out in grief and pushed him wildly away. "You said you'd never leave me—"

"And I never shall, in my heart at least. But lady, this love of ours is endangering you. We have been too happy."

Her hand flew to her mouth. "What do you mean?"

He looked away. He hardly knew where to begin.

Because my cousin begged me not to come tonight, shaming himself and me—

Because Bors would never have spoken unless he was in fear, not for himself but for us—

Because his warning made me see a hundred things I had been blind to, or had blinded myself to, which is worse: the shadow in the dark archway, the muffled figure in the midnight cloister, the castle dogs barking at some unseen stalker in the night—

Once he had begun, Lancelot could not stem the torrent of memories, each one chiming like a knell of doom. With every nerve and sinew of his fighting frame he could smell *enemy*, and knew he had been watched. And any watcher would have seen him going to the Queen. Fool, Lancelot! Blind fool! he wept to himself in useless rage. He had betrayed their love and given the Queen away. He had brought into danger the only thing he loved.

And what could he tell her now? "My cousin Bors says that we should part"? Guenevere's love was at least half jealousy. Aroused, she was a Goddess in her wrath. Already she had little love for Bors. What would it be to bring down her rage on Bors' head?

Even in the greatest love, some things must be veiled. Sorrowing at his own weakness and hers, Lancelot took her hands. "I have seen the danger, lady—that is all."

The danger—disaster—the end of our world—

Guenevere's head spun. Her sight dimmed, and the smell of water told her that she was back on Avalon again. But now she saw that the Lake was a brackish lagoon, and in the pale moonlight, the river that fed it no more than a dull channel. On its black surface floated a blacker barge, with a figure lying in it clothed in sable drapes. Four queenly women guarded the sleeping form, and the darkness was shot through with myriad glints of gold. Gold coronets encircled the veils of each of the four queens, and their fingers, wrists, and waists were adorned with gold. In the barge, the shrouded sleeper wore a great crown of gold, surmounted by a dragon of rubies with emerald eyes—

She tried to speak, but her lips could only moan. The crown with its dragon crest—she knew it—it was—

And the queens—she knew them all—and one above all—

Then the scene shivered and melted into fire. Great flames licked at the Lake, at the barge, and all her vision dissolved in a sheet of flame. Now the blaze was approaching her, licking at her feet. The heat flashed up her body, and her hair caught fire. Her face was scorching, and her skin was beginning to crack. Then she knew that she was tied hand and foot and burning alive. Her eyes exploded and only her voice remained. She threw back her head and howled.

Save me—

Save me—

"Lady, lady—"

Goddess, Mother, thanks—

She was in his arms, lying on her bed. Her face was burning and her forehead was drenched in sweat. Lancelot was kissing her eyes and stroking her trembling limbs. He soothed her with a thousand soft words and sounds till the horror was gone.

Then they lay together without speaking, for he knew better than to ask her what the seeing was. Still less did he want to know what she thought it might mean. In a while she revived and took a goblet of red cordial to strengthen her poor heart. He held her close, and in low whispers they agreed that he had to leave. He would go back to his kingdom with Bors and Lionel and stay there till suspicion had faded away and died. She knew that this meant a very long time indeed. But she knew he was right in what he wanted to do.

Tomorrow he would leave. So this night was to be their last for a lifetime apart—unforgettable indeed, though not as she had meant it to be.

"Love me now," she begged him, and slipped her hand into his shirt. Instantly he responded to her caress. But after the first hot flurry, they had no desire for haste. He took her more slowly and tenderly than ever before, every kiss like a tear, every touch a long farewell. He brought her to ecstasy again and again, till she wept in his arms and he lay silent in hers.

In the deep sense of peace they had then, she almost forgot her dark seeing, the sense of impending danger and the ordeal of water and fire she had undergone. Together they fell asleep, and she dreamed they passed hand in hand sweetly to Joyous Garde with a hundred fond hopes and thoughts of how that would be.

She slept so deeply that she almost lost herself.

But when the horror came, she knew it was real.

CHAPTER 44

B ang, bang, bang—

"Traitors in there, wake up!"

She could smell in the morning air the approach of dawn. But inside the chamber it was still pitch-dark. The room was bursting with the thunderous pounding on the door.

Bang, bang, bang!

"Traitor knight, Sir Lancelot, give yourself up!"

In an instant they were out of the bed and throwing on their clothes. "What is it?" she chattered numbly. She could hardly speak.

"No matter," he said hoarsely. "They are here."

"But where's Ina?" As she spoke, she knew the answer: *overpowered, or dead—*

"Get out that way—" Shaking, she pointed to the window, but he was already halfway there.

A moment later he turned back, his face like stone. "No way out. There are four of them below."

"Who?"

"Mordred's men."

"Mordred?" she gasped. "But why—? He's with the King—?"

He shook his head. "Who knows?"

"Open the door!" The clamor of mailed fists was louder now. A dozen pounding sword hilts took up the refrain.

Lancelot cast round the chamber in something like despair. "They're all armed, and I've only got my sword." He gave a wild, cracked laugh. "And there's no armor in a lady's chamber at a time like this."

"Oh Lancelot—" She could not hold back her tears. "There's a whole troop out there, and you're all alone." The memory of last night's seeing scorched her mind, and suddenly she understood what it meant. "They'll kill you, and I'll be burned." Her fists flew to her mouth to muffle a cry. *Goddess, Mother, take my life and let my dear one live!*

"Lady, lady—" He bounded toward her and took her in his arms. "If

I'm killed, flee to France with Bors and Lionel. They'll serve you all their days. In Little Britain, you can live on my lands like a queen." He kissed her long and hard. "Just remember me there, and pray to the Mother for my soul."

"If you die, do you think I'll want to live—?" Gasping, she thrust him away, then clutched him to her again. "Wait for me, love, in the Otherworld."

"Lady, I will." He gave her a crooked grin. "And now let me sell my life as dearly as I can. I mean to take some of them with me if I go." He reached for his sword and twisted his cloak round his arm. "When I open the door, get ready to slam it again."

She nodded at him, owl-eyed, and slid behind the door.

The battering on the door was deafening now, and the ancient oak panels were beginning to crack. Lancelot stood ready, his hand on the key. For a moment he listened to the cries and threats from outside. Then he raised his voice and shouted, "I hear you! Now listen to me."

Silence fell like a stone as the unseen leader signaled to his men. Then came a voice they both knew as well as their own.

"Sir Lancelot, there's nothing you can say. You're caught with the Queen, you have to let us in. Open the door, and I'll speak for you to the King. I'll persuade him to show you mercy and spare your wretched life."

Guenevere clutched her head.

Oh, my prophetic soul, Agravain!

How long had she had bad dreams of this very man? "Don't believe him!" she mouthed to Lancelot frantically.

He shook his head and laughed. "Never," he mouthed back derisively, then turned again to the door. "Hear me, sir, and call your mastiffs off. I'm taking your offer of mercy and coming out."

"Unarmed?" came the hollow query through the door.

"Unarmed," confirmed Lancelot. "I ask for your chivalry."

"You shall have it," came Agravain's harsh voice, "on my oath as a knight."

"Very well."

With a tense nod to Guenevere, Lancelot unlocked the door. As he threw it open, he ducked and feinted to one side. Hissing softly, a shining blade cut through the air where his head had been. Sword in hand, Agravain lunged through the door intent on the kill.

"You promised me mercy!" Lancelot panted, coming up under Agravain's guard. "That was your last lie, Agravain!"

Springing up, he caught Agravain by the neck and with a violent tug pulled him into the room. Behind him stood a tightly knit group of armed knights, momentarily nonplussed by their leader's fate. Before they could move, Guenevere slammed the door behind Agravain and turned the key. Thrown off balance, Agravain crashed forward onto his face. As he hit the ground, he was already scrabbling to get back on his feet. But Lancelot planted a foot in the small of his enemy's back and drove his sword cleanly down through the bones of his neck.

"Ha—?"

A small, indistinct sound issued from Agravain's mouth, followed by a violent spurt of blood. Then the long torso heaved and twitched, and Agravain was dead. Guenevere looked at the white hair tumbled in the gleaming red on the flagstones, and a moment of overwhelming sorrow possessed her heart. *What a death, Agravain, weltering in treachery and deceit!* Suddenly she thought of Morgause, the lost mother of the Orkneys, and her grief redoubled. *What a son you were to her, Agravain! And facedown on the cold stone—for any mother's son, what a way to die!*

"Hurry, lady!"

Already Lancelot was on his knees, heaving Agravain's body onto its back. His strong fingers went to work on the straps and buckles of the dead man's armor, feverishly tearing it off. Hastily he pointed Guenevere to the shield on his arm. "Hurry, madame—as fast as you can!"

The dead silence outside had given way to howling rage. "We've got to get in! He's got Agravain!"

"Let's break the door down! What have we got?"

The pounding on the door renewed with a flurry of cries. Then they heard a harsher, heavier sound.

Boom! Boom! Boom!

A bench from the chamber outside had been pressed into service as a battering ram. A loud crack told them that the door was giving way.

"Hurry!" Lancelot panted. "Help me!"

Together they wrestled the dead man's armor onto Lancelot's arms and legs, fitting casket and breastplate and shoulder guards, piece by piece. For the rest of her life she would remember the ecstasy of fumbling with the stubborn leather fastenings, the sound of the battering ram almost splitting her head.

"So?" At last Lancelot was armed and moving to the door.

Nodding, she made a grab for Agravain's sword and took up a position behind Lancelot to defend his flank. "Ready."

At his signal she threw open the door. Waiting on the threshold, sword and dagger in hand, was one of Mordred's chief cronies, the ferret-faced Ozark. Leaping forward, Lancelot brought his upraised sword down with such force that the blade split Ozark's helmet and cleft his head. With a graveyard grin, the knight fell dead in the dust. In the same swing Lancelot parried the attack of the knight fighting at Ozark's side, and with two ferocious blows struck him dying to the ground. Screaming, the knights who remained scrambled madly to throw aside their battering ram and arm themselves against the terror in their midst. But Lancelot slashed and thrust and whirled and struck again till they all lay dead and mangled at his feet.

Guenevere threw down her sword, feeling the terror drain from her, and in its place a sick numbness she had never known before. Yet when Lancelot spoke, it seemed that she had heard the words a thousand lives ago. "It is over for us, madame, all our long, true love."

It is over—

—all over for us—

—all our love—

She fixed her eyes on him. Blood covered his breastplate and his helmet and dripped from his sword. Against the bright gleaming gore, his face was as pale as the dead lying round his feet. He sheathed his sword and cast aside his gloves and came back toward her in the chamber, walking like a wounded man.

"The King will always be my enemy now," he said hoarsely. "And his anger will surely pursue you, lady, too. Come away with me to my kingdom. I can protect you there."

Oh, Lancelot—

It was impossible. She shook her head.

He seized her hands. "You're in danger now. The Christians—"

"What can they do to me? I am Queen here still." She turned her head with an unconscious lift. "A queen may not leave her land."

Fatigue and frustration got the better of him. "Gods above, madame, you're not in Camelot!"

"I shall be tonight." A sadness like death swept her from head to foot. "I must leave Arthur and take my own throne again. We shall each keep to our kingdoms and live apart, Arthur in Caerleon and I in Camelot. And you—" Suddenly she saw his gray face and trembling limbs and was flooded with fear. "Oh my love, you must go—get away before Arthur comes back."

He gave an incredulous laugh. "Get away? They'd only take that as a proof of guilt. No, madame, I have to stay to defend you."

"Lancelot, think!" she said desperately. She pointed to the body on the floor. "Arthur could have you killed for killing his kin. If he doesn't, when the Orkneys know you've killed Agravain, they'll take a blood oath to avenge his death."

He smiled grimly. "I can beat Gawain. I'd even take on all three of them together. I have to be here for you."

"A blood feud isn't chivalry! They'll lie in wait and ambush you with a hundred men. You wouldn't have a chance. You have to go if you want to save your life."

Implacably he shook his head. "Madame, no."

She threw back her head and cried out. "I won't let you die! For my sake if not your own, you cannot choose. Lancelot, I order you, leave here at once."

He tried to take her hand, but she pulled away, becoming cold and remote before his eyes. "I am your Queen, not your lover now. Leave me. Go."

"Gods above, lady," he groaned, "you say Gawain will kill me. But you kill me by sending me away."

She shook her head. "Enough!"

"We part?"

She did not trust herself to speak.

"So, madame." He drew her into his arms. "Hear my oath. Wherever you are in the world, I will think of you. Every dawn that I live I will pray for you. And every evening I shall turn to the love-star and honor you. My prayer will be that one day you will be mine. Until then I shall never cease to live for you."

He kissed her as they had never kissed before. "Farewell."

Blinded by tears, she did not see him go, only a tall striding shape of

shining armor and blood. Subsiding to the floor, she leaned against the wall
and felt that her back, her head, her heart must surely break. Imperceptibly
time shifted itself into a new domain. Dry-eyed, she drifted off into vast
regions of unknown pain, life without Arthur, life without Lancelot—

Must get to Camelot—

Ah, little one, you will not get to Camelot tonight.

Then to Avalon, Mother——?

Avalon is no more.

Where shall I be, then?

You will know soon enough. The wheel is spinning, Guenevere, and your fate is here.

How long she sat on the flagstones surrounded by dead men and listening to this refrain inside her head, she could not tell. But at last the sound
of feet came to her ears and her clouded gaze lifted itself from the floor.

"Your Majesty."

Mordred was standing over her with a troop of armed men. A sorrowful smile curved his mouth, but his eyes were alight with a satisfaction that
seared her soul. His face wore its Otherworldly leer, and he looked like
Morgan as he stared at her.

"Lady Guenevere, Queen of the Summer Country," he said loudly, "on
His Majesty's orders I arrest you for treason to the King. You are to be conveyed to the King's Tower."

CHAPTER 45

"**S**peak, fellow." A white-faced Gawain glared at the man in front of him. "Tell the King again."

Before him stood a trembling, bloodied wreck, a huge gash splitting his head and his sword arm dangling uselessly at his side. He gave a foolish laugh. "I'll tell it till Doomsday, if anyone wants to hear." His eyes flickered nervously toward the throne, where Arthur sat blank and staring among his knights. "As long as the King—"

"He won't blame you, man," Kay put in furiously. He glanced at the loyal group huddled round Arthur in the King's Privy Chamber and wished in desperation that they could be the only ones to hear. But when this fellow had staggered into the courtyard to greet the returning hunt, half the castle had been there. The story would be all round Caerleon by now.

And Gods above, what a tale it was—

Kay's mind reeled. He fixed his eyes on the wounded knight, and dared not look at Arthur. "Speak to the King."

"A dozen of us were told to follow Sir Agravain to catch a traitor who'd got in to the Queen." The knight coughed thickly, spitting up blood. "I was one of the four set to guard the window in case he came out that way. We heard the shouts and fighting in the chamber, then it was all over and everything went quiet. We thought our men had won, so we went in. The next thing we knew was Sir Lancelot raging toward us covered in blood. He laid me out, killed two of the others outright, and the third's not likely to live. When I came round, I heard the hunt coming back and came to tell you what I knew."

When he'd first told his tale, a great silence had fallen on the group. Arthur sat on his horse like a man in an evil dream, and no one had dared to ask what it all meant. It was at this point that Mordred had keenly inquired, "And the Queen? What about the Queen?"

The wounded knight shook his head. "Sir Agravain and the others are all dead. But she's still in her chamber, sir, for all I know."

Mordred had turned to Arthur. "Sire, if this story of treachery is true, we should secure the Queen. Her life may be in danger if she's alone." He leaned forward and gripped his father's arm. "Let me take a troop of men and see to this."

Lost to the world, staring into his own inner darkness, Arthur did not seem to hear. Waiting barely a second, Mordred cried, "Thank you, sire!" and wheeled away in triumph to take charge.

Well, so be it, thought Gawain numbly, it had to be done. Whatever happened, it was something no other knight would want to do. Least of all himself, Gaheris, or Gareth—Gods above, they could hardly save themselves! With Agravain dead, all the Orkneys were badly wounded too.

Agravain dead—he knew it had to be true. But he still had not truly taken it in.

Gawain thumped his great dazed head: Think, man, think! The wounded knight had known only part of the tale. There was more, much more to come out, he was sure of that. What in the name of the Gods had Agravain done?

Agravain.

Always darkness, always grief.

Had he shamed the Orkneys forever in the eyes of the King?

Gawain felt fear and bile curdling his gut. But already he knew all that he wanted to know. Agravain had been involved in some plot against the Queen, and he'd paid for it with his life.

And Lancelot.

Don't forget that he'd tried to kill Lancelot.

Gawain gave a harsh intake of breath. Only Agravain could have turned on a knight of Lancelot's goodness and true chivalry. What maggot, what poison had eaten Agravain's soul? He deserved to die, he'd made love to it, in fact. There would be no blood-feud to avenge his death.

He must tell Gaheris so, and Gareth. Setting his face, Gawain looked for his brothers in the group round the King. In Gaheris's numb, dead look he could see the mirror of his own, and only Gareth, the tenderhearted baby of the brood, was weeping for Agravain. Around him, Kay, Bedivere, Lucan, and the rest were white with shock. Sir Lancelot a traitor? Sir Lancelot secretly by night with the Queen? It could not be true.

Lancelot a traitor?

Lancelot with Guenevere?

Bleak as a mountaintop whipped with winter snow, Arthur sat on his throne and tried to understand. But even hearing the words now for a second time, they made no sense. A treason against the King's life, the wounded knight had said—Sir Lancelot trapped in the Queen's chamber, with the Queen—they'd been watching the doors and windows, he'd been there all night—?

As uncomprehending as a bear at the stake, Arthur moved his head slowly from side to side. Agravain must have known something; he had laid the trap. But he was dead now, so who could tell what he knew? Random thoughts agonized his mind like dogs at his flesh. Traitors, Lancelot and Guenevere? Together at night, untrue to him, both of them?

Lancelot and Guenevere?

Could they—?

When—?

How long—?

Oh, God, no—

He covered his eyes with his hand.

Thank God for Mordred to handle this terror for him.

Mordred, yes. He should know by now what was going on.

There was a knock from the outer chamber and a muted murmur at the door. Lucan returned and bowed before the throne.

"Father Sylvester is here, sire, with his monks," he announced, struggling to mask his contempt. "He begs leave for an audience to consider the fate of the Queen."

Guenevere.

And Lancelot.

Arthur drew in a great gulp of the stale, crowded air. "Where's Mordred?" he demanded huskily. "I want him here. Send for him at once!"

ON THE TREES by the wayside, the leaves were turning brown. In the coppice where they had sheltered from the wind, the rotting scent of autumn was in the air, and soon all the world would go down to darkness and decay. Bors squatted next to Lionel by the fire and tried to keep the horror of it all from overwhelming his mind.

How long had he foreseen this very thing? How often had he uselessly implored Lancelot to leave the Queen and make his way back to Little

Britain with some of his pride and dignity still intact? And now they were running for their lives like outlaw knights—

Sharp tears of frustration pricked at Bors' closed eyes. Now it had happened—and worse than he could have feared—

Around him he could hear the low noises of the camp, the squires and pages making ready for the night, the quiet voices of the knights who had followed them as soon as Lancelot rode away. Some comfort there, the thought stole into Bors' bruised heart. They were the best of the Round Table, all of them, men who knew Lancelot was no traitor and would stake their lives on joining their fate with his.

A dozen campfires crackled through the dusk. The sour, crisp tang of wood smoke stung Bors' nose and plunged him back into boyhood memories. Oh, Lancelot, that was a better world than this. But this too is over for us now.

He opened his eyes. Opposite him Lionel sat cross-legged and grim-faced, while across the clearing Lancelot leaned broodingly against a tree. Bors knew that he was not the most intuitive of men. But he also knew that Lancelot was thinking of Guenevere.

For now he could not think of anything else. From the moment he had burst in on them in the knights' quarters madly muttering, "Cousins, make haste! We leave at once!" she was his sole concern. They should have ridden immediately for the coast, taken ship for France and left all this behind. Instead they were lurking in this wind-torn wood outside Caerleon while Lancelot made up his mind what they should do. He did not care that all their lives were now in danger from the King. As they rode away, Guenevere, Guenevere, was his one refrain. Her enemies were all around her, he should protect her, she was in danger, she, she, she—

He'll go back to her—he has to, Lionel had said. He won't leave her to her fate.

And what was she, after all, the object of all this? Bors turned his head and mouthed down his disgust. A faded beauty who could neither love Lancelot fully nor bear to let him go. A jealous lover who had made sure that her beloved had never a wife, nor children, nor the comfort of a home. A fatal lover and a devourer of his life.

And a destroyer of good knights. Because of her a dozen men lay dead whose only crime had been to obey their lord. And how many more would follow? Bors groaned aloud. For a black second, his mind opened on scenes he dared not contemplate. In the dark chasm that gaped before his eyes he saw the Round Table divided on itself, knights lying dead, the golden fellowship broken, their own life's adventure done…

"Cousin?"

Lancelot was at his side, his hand on his shoulder, a troubled love and care burning in his eyes. Instantly Bors felt better, though nothing had changed. He shook his head and forced a pallid grin. "I'm all right."

"Dear Bors—" Lancelot gave a short laugh full of regret. "If only that were true." He swung down to sit between them, holding out his hands to the fire. "You're too good to say, If only I'd listened to you. Then we'd all be far away from here and safe."

Especially the Queen, he wanted to add, but did not. He knew that Bors' fear and mistrust of Guenevere had reached loathing now. But how to convey to a man who had never loved the deep ache, the dread, no, the knowledge he suffered with now? The woman he cared about most in the world was alone and defenseless and surrounded by enemies. She had put his safety above her own and ordered him to go. She had honored her duty to Arthur more than she had valued her life. And by sending him away, she had refused his protection and made it impossible for him to save her from what might befall.

Impossible—

She had always been impossible, from the first.

An iron fist of pain crushed his heart. Well, now they were at the last.

It was the last of England, for they had to go.

And the last of Guenevere he did not dare to say. But in the hollow of his heart he knew it was true. And she was in desperate peril, peril of her life. She was lost to him, and she was going to die.

He gasped with pain, and found himself leaping to his feet. "I must go and see the horses bedded down for the night. And I should speak to the knights who were good enough to follow me—" He turned away. "You were right, Bors: we should have left long ago."

"It's not too late." Greatly daring, Bors lifted his head and looked Lancelot in the eye. "We must go. If we ride at dawn, we'll get to the coast in time to catch the tide." He held his breath. Goddess, Mother, he prayed, speed my words—

"It's true." Lancelot paused. He stared remotely ahead. Guenevere's last words were echoing in his ears.

Go, Lancelot, go—

He threw back his head. "So, cousins—to Little Britain then, tomorrow at first light? I'll tell the men."

He moved away. Bors shared one heartfelt glance with Lionel, then lowered his head, unable to contain his tears. He clasped his hands and brought them to his lips, weeping with joy.

Little Britain—

Home—and peace, away from all this—

Goddess, Mother, thanks!

CHAPTER 46

he crypt was not a place for every man. Most wouldn't like the blood-warm darkness that had never seen the living day, nor the cells and passages wandering underground, the grinning skulls piled up against the walls, and, over it all, the smell. But Iachimo liked the sweet, homely stench of decay. Down here, no one could ever say he stank. Besides, he was old friends with the dead. So he sat snug and still in the candlelit vault, with no sense of trouble on his mind.

No, they were well enough here, the little group huddled round the table, him and Sylvester and the old madman Anselmo and his plump-faced boy. Roddri, they called him, the old man's pupil monk, who had come from the Welshlands to take care of Anselmo's books and share his cell. A secret snigger shook Iachimo's stocky frame. Well, all the monks knew what Anselmo's pupils really learned. The sins of the flesh meant only women as far as the old brother was concerned.

Iachimo eased his heavy thighs and imperceptibly adjusted his weight on the wooden bench. Frequent tiny movements were the secret of endurance, he had found, in a lifetime that had included far worse watches than this. That, and having some question to play with in his mind. Such as, How could Anselmo be the great mind they all said he was, admired by the Pope as the theologian who would cast all the pagans of these islands into hellfire and yet, and yet, be so desperate to bend over for a boy or make the boy crack open his bones for him?

Iachimo pondered it in the muddy shallows of his mind. Why didn't Anselmo's supposedly mighty intellect see that a boy-bender was the lowest thing alive? Even simpletons knew, and Sylvester had told him often enough, that God had ordained women to be receivers of men's waste, which is why they were lower creatures in His scheme. Men should know better than to pervert God's order, Sylvester said. So when he and Sylvester relieved each other's needs, it was only because there were no women around. This was no sin, because that which was sin for the many was no sin for God's own. And an enforced sin, such as turning to a brother in Christ when the ordained vessel of seed was not to be found, was no sin at all. So Sylvester said, and Iachimo for one believed his every word.

Sylvester said—

Complacently Iachimo fixed his dull eyes on his master and saw him speaking volubly, arguing the case with his usual command. But the old man was not following as he should. Iachimo's brows darkened. What was all this?

"But is it true?" Anselmo was insisting. "Is the Queen known to be guilty, as they say? We must be assured of that." His hand flew to his pile of texts, and fondled the Bible lying on the top. "God's lowliest creatures are protected from false accusation by the light of His truth."

"Father, may I speak?" put in Roddri, at his side. Pink and tense, the young novice was agog at being one of the inner conclave deciding the fate of the Queen. He knew he was there only as his master's book carrier, and a strong shoulder for the old man to get about. But still he was determined to make his mark.

Father, yes, Sylvester thought, nodding to himself. He still had not got used to his change of name. He stared at Roddri. "Speak."

"Sir, regardless of this new charge, the Queen's a woman and a daughter of Eve," Roddri said.

Sylvester laughed coldly. "Well observed."

Roddri flushed scarlet at the open sneer. "Therefore born to sin," he pushed on hotly, "and hence guilty already against God and man."

Sylvester's eyes widened. "Is it so?" he said slowly.

"Set down in Holy Writ," the novice insisted, warming to his theme. "A witch and a whore, condemned out of God's own mouth."

"In Genesis?" queried the old man sharply.

Roddri bowed. "In Leviticus too, master, and *passim* in the Scriptures, everywhere."

"And Saint Paul." Anselmo's eyes glittered. "Yes indeed." He patted Roddri approvingly. "The woman's guilty, then, with or without this deed. We have God's word to—"

"To do what we have to do," Sylvester cut in. God Almighty, grant him patience to deal with these men! When the Archbishop had left for Canterbury, the last thing they'd expected was something like this. But it had happened, they had to deal with it, and he was the man.

He clenched and unclenched his fists. Who cared if the tale of adultery was true? It was the chance they had been waiting for, the pagan Queen given into their hand. Should Anselmo's scruples be allowed to divert them now?

Sylvester bared his teeth in a mirthless grin. Left to himself, he would have moved against the Queen long ago, without compunction or a second thought. Where he and Iachimo came from, a troublesome opponent would simply have disappeared, many years before. But Mother Church was fastidious; he had learned that early on. Her enemies had to be named and held up to scorn, plainly convicted, and brought to a public death, in the name of God. Good reason and sound Scripture had to underlie and proclaim Christ's purpose here on earth.

Hence the presence of Anselmo at this hasty, covert meeting in the crypt. Sylvester knew he had to destroy Guenevere. And he knew Anselmo— or Roddri—had to make it right.

So be it.

Sylvester drew a breath. "This is what is known. Sir Lancelot was seen to go in secretly to the Queen and remain with her in her chamber all through the night. That was a shameless betrayal of her person, and an undoubted treachery to her lord and King. The rogue himself has fled, tracked as far as the road to the coast, proof positive of his guilt—why would an innocent man not stay to clear himself?"

Anselmo nodded. "True."

"So she's a whore," Sylvester said flatly. For himself, he did not care what she was. In their earlier days he and Iachimo had seen and had them all: old, young, tall, short, women frantic with starvation whose bones stood out of their flesh, and others so fat they could hardly roll over on demand to offer their behinds. Even with his eyes open, they were all the same. But this one was the Queen. She had the power that they had to wrest from her, or watch their work shrivel and perish in this land.

"We know she was whore-mothered and whore-bred," he went on. "Born to a Queen who believed that women had the right of thigh-freedom with all men. Brought up on Avalon by the Old Whore herself. She's a whore and a witch, and we must bring her to the fire."

"How, Father?" demanded Roddri, his eyes bright.

"We need Scripture and verse," said Sylvester, nodding at them both. "So I ask you, brothers both, get to your texts. We must bring home to Arthur what the Queen is, and what he has to do."

"Not so fast," croaked Anselmo unexpectedly. He gave a warning cough. "We are only three brethren here, or perhaps four. A King is God's ordained. If we are to move against a royal whore, especially one who has called herself Arthur's Queen, we need higher sanction. We must send to the Archbishop." His eyes bulged with a new idea, and his grating voice dropped to a reverent hush. "We must notify the Pope."

Send to Saint Michael if you like, or Old Nick himself, thought Sylvester in a fury. But Jesu Maria, didn't the old fool see that there was *no time?*

"All true, brother." Sylvester composed his voice. "But above all, we need to hurry the Queen to the stake. We shall only do it while the King is still lost to himself."

Roddri narrowed his eyes. "Sir, another thought—" He bowed to Sylvester. "You have spoken to Prince Mordred?"

The ghost of a smile warmed Sylvester's face. What a clever boy. This young monk would go far.

"The Prince and I have spoken," Sylvester agreed. He extended the ghostly smile to include them all. "He and I are one. On his encouragement, I have ordered the fagots and stake."

He rose to his feet. The glow of the charnel house possessed him now. "The witch burns. The only question is, When?"

THREE PACES—TURN— *two more—turn again—three paces—turn—two more— turn again—*

Guenevere laughed. A Queen, and in prison? She was going mad.

And locked up in one of the worst chambers in Caerleon, she was sure of that. The very walls were marked with the blood of others, damp with their tears, weeping for lives foreshortened and hope betrayed. The traitors' hole—the last cell before death. How long had Mordred been planning this revenge? Why had he turned against her and Lancelot?

She clenched her fists and pounded at her head. Why had she gone so trustingly with Mordred when he came? *Trust me,* he had murmured in her ear, and she had thought she was mistaken in the first glad glint of joy that had lit his eye. Her shock, her sorrow then, had been mother to a hundred wishful thoughts: Mordred had come to her aid, he would find Ina and bring her back, they would take farewell of Arthur and leave for Camelot as she should have done long ago.

But her long imprisonment had given her time to think. *Fool! Fool, Guenevere—why would you ever trust the son of Morgan Le Fay?*

Bitterness flooded her soul. *If only* tore at her mind like thorns.

If only she had called out to her own guard as Mordred and his men led her away—

If only she had demanded to see Ina then, instead of accepting Mordred's assurance that her maid was still recovering from being bound and gagged and half-suffocated in a chest—

If only she had demanded to see Arthur, wife to husband, Queen to King, who could have said nay to her?

If only she had drawn herself up like a Queen, and refused to go with the men who had brought her here!

But she had done none of these things.

Not one, Guenevere.

And that is why you are locked up in this pen like a lost heifer in the village pound.

Fool! Fool, triple fool!

She beat at her stupid head till it ached. After that there came a certain calm.

Soon, soon, Mordred or Arthur must release her from this place.

Or—

A new shoot of fear cracked her fragile mind.

Or the Christians—Goddess, Mother, spare me from them!

CHAPTER 47

They came for her when she had slept at last, exhausted by end-less pacing and drained of life by the hours, no, days spent alone. From her wretched cell, she could not see the sun. How long had she been there?

Long enough, she knew, to look like a guilty thing. Untended, unkempt, denied her women or a change of gown, she knew she must seem soiled and suspicious in the eyes of men. Still, she held her head high and smoothed down the silk of her robe as she heard the boots and spurs that must bring her to her trial.

The cry went before her every step of the way.

"The Queen!"

"Let us see the Queen!"

Outside the palace, the people were clamoring through the chilly air, but inside the Audience Chamber the quiet was profound. Guenevere looked at Arthur seated on his throne, and saw at once that hers had been removed. *Am I guilty, then, before I have come to trial? Oh, Arthur, is this your will or Mordred's? Do you think you can strike me from your life and from your mind?*

On one side of Arthur stood his knights in a solid block, Gawain and his two brothers, Lucan, Kay, and Bedivere, all looking at her with sor-row in their eyes. But on the other—*Goddess, Mother!* Her heart shriveled and almost failed—row upon row of black monks with that toad Iachimo planted squarely in their midst and their leader, Father Sylvester, at their head.

Already she could feel her stomach turning to water, and her head swam. *They brought me little to eat, Arthur, these last few days. How can I stand up for myself against this?*

"My lord King, barons and knights, and lords spiritual of this realm!"

Sylvester twitched his black robe, and his voice filled the room. "At the King's will and pleasure," he intoned, "we are here to charge Queen Guenevere with adultery and treason to the King—"

Gawain stepped forward, his lower lip trembling, his big jaw jutting dangerously. "If a Queen sends for her knight, monk, is that treason in your book? Sir Lancelot could have been with her for no bad reason at all."

Standing before the throne, Guenevere could hardly suppress a cry. *Gawain, I thought you would be my enemy! Goddess, Mother, thanks!*

Sylvester held his place and stared Gawain down. "Let me finish the indictment, sir, by the King's will. There will be time for all who wish to speak."

By the King's will? Guenevere pondered to herself. *Oh, Arthur, do you have any will now?*

For Arthur was sitting on his throne like a great child. His hands were gripping the arms, and he was nodding and staring as if he had lost his mind. Leaning on the back of the great carved bronze-clad chair, Mordred was alternately looking at her and dropping words into Arthur's ear. Arthur himself was listening keenly to Mordred while urgently following Sylvester's peroration too. In one bleak moment, Guenevere saw it all. Arthur was not his own man. Her life lay at the level of other men's cruelty. And neither of these two had any reason to hold back.

Her mind lurched. Suddenly she could smell the flames, feel her skin cracking, hear her hair on fire. Sylvester's voice wound on.

"—caught in her chamber with a knight not her husband, rupturing her vow of marriage, disposing of her body that was given to the King—adultery a double breaking of sacrament, an offense against her husband and God Himself—"

"Hold there, monk!" she challenged thickly, almost too full to speak. "Whatever I am charged with, let the people know. What I am or do, it should be in their sight. This is an ancient right of royal Queens. And the people too have the right to judge me, if they please."

"Well said, lady!" came a growl from the ranks of the knights. Immediately Guenevere knew Lucan's voice. He was Arthur's knight now, and would be Arthur's to the death. But long ago he had been her mother's knight, and it warmed Guenevere fleetingly that he kept the faith he had sworn.

But she knew too that he might have saved his breath. Sylvester was a fighter for all seasons, high and low. She watched his shoulders drop and his fists clench for action as he leaned forward to attack: "But madam, you are not among your own people now!"

On it went, and on. "We shall show," Sylvester proclaimed, "that the

Queen has developed a traitorous hatred of the King. I have monks here who will testify to that." He waved his hand at the serried black ranks and gave a fleeting smile to the novice Roddri in their midst. "Monks from Avalon, from the King's great new church, a church he has built to honor his dead son, and which the Queen plans to destroy, to restore the old pagan rule."

"Gods above, you lie!" Guenevere choked. "If this is a court of law, bring proof of this. It's vicious, arrant nonsense, every word."

"Alas, lady." Sylvester's eyes raked her with open contempt. "It is not for me to prove anything. It is for you to clear yourself of the foul and capital charge that has brought you here." He gave a scornful laugh and moved forward to harangue the whole court. "I freely concede that this lady cares nothing for the old Druid ways. It matters nothing to her that the Queens of older times would change their consorts when they desired and give the youth they discarded to the Gods. In those days Druids would hang the Summer King upon a tree and take his manhood with their golden knives till his seed and his blood made a paste to enrich the earth so the next spring's crops would flourish in the land."

He paused dramatically and an accusing finger snaked out. "You, madam, have no need to care for this. For you changed your consort as and when you willed, and you had no care if you killed your husband thereby!"

"I have not killed him!" Guenevere countered passionately. "See, there he sits!"

"You and your lover both!" came the answering cry. "You killed your husband's honor when you lay with his knight, and he killed his lord when he lay with you!"

"Honor is a contract between men!" Guenevere cried out at the top of her voice. "Women know for themselves where their honor lies!" She could have torn her hair. "And the Mother alone knows why I wrangle here with you!" She stepped forward, thrusting aside the pikes of the guards who tried to bar her way.

"Arthur, I am falsely accused!" she urged. "Dismiss these people and discharge this court. There is no treason here. We would never plot against you, Lancelot or I."

A sudden silence fell on all the court. Sylvester gathered himself to renew the attack, then his keen instinct told him to hold fire. Let the whore speak. She will hang herself out of her own mouth; they always do.

The great figure on the throne shifted and stirred. Arthur fixed hollow eyes on Guenevere. "Lancelot was in your chamber, they all said that."

Gawain saw his chance. "Sire, a knight may be in a lady's chamber with no ill intent," he urged, leaning toward the throne. He gestured to his fellow knights and essayed a blustering laugh. "Why, like yourself, sire, I and all of us here, Lucan, Bedivere, and Kay have been in the Queen's apartments in our time!"

Arthur's face lightened a shade. "It's true."

"Many times, sire," Kay put in.

Lucan stepped forward, his hand on his sword. "And Lancelot is the Queen's champion, her knight sworn to the death. She has every right to receive him when she wants."

"Do you think so?" Arthur's tortured expression was lifting with every word. For the first time he glanced at Guenevere.

Mordred watched in growing fury and despair. And you thought that the knights would champion Arthur and turn against Guenevere? Gods above, they'll save her yet! Hurry, hurry, make them all see that Lancelot was admitted where the King was refused—wake up Arthur's jealousy—play on his lower nature, every man has one—

"Sire—" Mordred leaned forward, a look of honest puzzlement on his face. "It's true that the Queen may send for her knight anytime. But alone at dead of night?" He paused. "Forgive me, sire—how long is it since you were in the Queen's apartments at night and alone?"

Guenevere gasped. *Cruel, Mordred, oh, how clever and cruel! You know that Arthur no longer comes to my bed. You know the great wound he took between the legs depleted his manhood and left him scarred for life. And now, to defeat the knights and ensure my death, you goad him with that in the open court—*

"—as Sir Lancelot was?" Mordred finished innocently.

Arthur's skin mottled and he fought for breath. The eyes he turned on Guenevere were like those of a wounded bull. "Why, Guenevere, why? Why did you betray me with Lancelot?"

"We didn't betray you, Arthur!" she cried, fighting down the taste of brackish tears. "We tried to defend your honor, protect your name. We never intended to hurt or dishonor you."

"No, madam?" demanded Sylvester, pouncing like a rat. "Then why has your good knight fled?"

"Because I ordered him!" Guenevere fought back. "And rightly, it seems. I had good reason to fear the malice of such as you!"

"And where is he now?" hissed the monk, not at all deterred.

"Who knows?"

The stentorian bellow took them all by surprise. Arthur leaped to his feet. "Either way," he cried in anguish, "Lancelot's lost to me. If he is a traitor, he has fled to save his life. And if he's not, all this is false, and as a man of honor he must hate me till he dies!" He turned away, covering his eyes with his hand. Tears poured down his face. "I see the end—the end of the Round Table now!"

"Not so!" Guenevere held out her hands. "Arthur, I beg you, hear me—"

But Mordred was already at Arthur's ear. You are winning, you are winning, exulted the voice in his head. You need have no fear of Gawain after this. If the big knight had been after Arthur's throne, he too would have wanted to get rid of Guenevere. Instead the great looby spoke up on her behalf, too loyal to Arthur to bear the idea of her death. Mordred wanted to laugh aloud. Gawain would not seek advantage for himself. And Arthur now was clay in his loving son's hands.

"Alas, it's true, Father," he said mournfully. "Half the knights have already fled with him."

"What?" Arthur turned pale with shock. He gripped Gawain's arm. "Gawain," he cried, his voice trembling, "is this true?"

Gawain could not meet his eye. "I can't say, sire," he mumbled, staring at the ground.

"Kay?" Arthur appealed.

Kay exchanged a desperate glance with Lucan and Bedivere. Then he limped forward as reluctantly as he'd ever moved in all his life. "It's true."

Lucan came to his aid. "Forty or more."

"Then God help us all!"

Arthur turned red-rimmed eyes on Guenevere, shaking with rage. "Oh, woman," he howled, "what have you done? You have scattered the knights of the Table far and wide! You have destroyed the work of my entire life."

"Your work? Your life?" She could not contain her distress. "Arthur, we did it together all these years. The Table was mine when I married you."

He waved her words away as if swatting a fly. "I made it what it was. And you've broken it, split it in two."

She could not let this pass. "Arthur, the Table split when Galahad came to us! Ever since, it lies in two gaping halves. You broke the fellowship when you sent the knights out on the Quest. That was when you lost half your knights and more. Don't blame me for the results of what you did!"

"Enough! That concludes the Queen's speech in her own defense."

The moment had come; Sylvester felt it in every nerve. "To your judgment, then, sire!" he cried. He pressed importantly up to the throne. "The Queen's offense is plain. All that's required is that you pass sentence now."

Guenevere reached for her last strength. "Arthur, *no!*"

"Yes!" Arthur cried.

A buzz of excitement rose from the black-clad ranks.

"Sire!" Gawain made a frantic attempt to turn the tide. "The monk says Lancelot was in the Queen's chamber till dawn. But Lancelot's a man of honor above all. I beg you, trust to that!"

"Well said, brother." Standing beside Gawain, Gaheris slapped him on the back, and Gareth grunted approvingly, flushed to the roots of his hair. Murmurs of support rose from all the rest of the knights.

"You're right, Gawain, of course." Mordred nodded feelingly. He leaned toward the big knight, making sure that Arthur could hear. "But it's the honor of the King that matters, don't you see that?"

Sylvester's voice was pitched to all the court. "And the honor of the King can only be avenged by death!"

"Watch your mouth, monk!" Lucan blanched with horror and his hand flew to his sword. "You can't kill a Queen!"

The glow of a funeral pyre spread over Sylvester's face. "True, a Queen's person is sacred," he agreed smoothly and too swiftly, Lucan knew. "The Queen's blood would not be shed." He paused. "No, her body would be burned."

The words seemed to come from another world. Guenevere turned her head. *Burned——? He can't do that——*

"Goddess, Mother——" Lucan turned away and gagged. All around him the knights were too shocked even to speak.

"——for the treason she has shown, and Sir Lancelot."

Lancelot——

Guenevere came to herself. Hopelessness put words into her mouth. "Arthur, Arthur," she shouted, "there's a treason far nearer to you than Lancelot, who always loved you faithfully with all his heart!" She threw up a quivering hand. "Look to your son, smiling there like a snake. Mordred is your dearest enemy, no one else!" She paused and put all her heart into her cry. "Think, Arthur, think! You know whose son he is. Ask yourself, *has Morgan's malice against us ever slept?*"

She could see from Mordred's face that she had hit home. But her shaft had wounded Arthur to the quick. He leaped to his feet and bellowed like a dying bear. "Morgan! I have not thought of her for twenty years!"

She knew it was not true. But she knew too that the name had sealed her fate.

"Morgan, yes," Arthur howled, shaking with rage. "I see the whole thing now! They're in it together, the two of them, plotting against me."

Over his shoulder she could see Mordred's smile. All the rest was a forest of staring eyes.

"She's a traitor, they both are!" Arthur screamed. "Take her to the fire!"

"My lord—"

Lucan was kneeling before Arthur, head bowed but sword in hand. "Sire, name your proxy. I will fight any man—" He lifted his head and a sick horror crossed his face "Even one of my fellows, Kay, Gawain, Bedivere, to defend the Queen's life."

"Sir Lucan, you forget." Mordred was trying not to enjoy himself now. "No man may challenge the King. His word is law."

"That's right!" Arthur shrilled. "And I have spoken. Give her to the law!"

Already the monks were winding down the hall, a long, black deadly serpent making for Guenevere.

Kay stiffened. Gods above, he had no time for the Queen! But this? Painfully he bent his crooked knee and bowed. "Sire, in the name of God, spare the Queen's life."

Weeping, Bedivere threw himself at Arthur's feet. "Sire, we all beg you, do not do this evil thing!"

"Hold your tongues, all of you!" Braying, Arthur threw back his head and stood arms akimbo in the middle of the floor. His face was black with rage. "You dare to challenge my decree?" The column of monks had swallowed up Guenevere now, and Sylvester was leading the way out of the door.

"You!" Arthur pointed to the knights nearest the throne. "Gawain, you and your brothers, and you, Lucan, Kay, and Bedivere—I order you to take charge of the execution of the Queen. Attend the reverend brothers to the chosen place. Get her to the fire, and see that she burns!"

CHAPTER 48

She knew she should pray, but she could not find the words. Briskly Father Sylvester appeared at her side. "Madam, come!"

Around her the monks were swooping like flapping crows, driving her forward and on to her doom. She could see their eyes hot with lust for her death, and knew that nothing else would satisfy them now.

Outside the Audience Chamber stood a troop of men clad in execution drab, waiting to escort her with their pikes reversed. All the trappings of a traitor's death already in place. Guenevere gasped. Had Mordred been so confident all along?

"Forward with the Queen, all of you," came Mordred's commanding voice. "I shall stay with the King."

"As you wish, my lord." Sylvester raised his arm. "Follow me."

Surrounded by the guard, she was jostled forward and out through the main doors, a train of monks and knights following behind. In the courtyard they were greeted by an excited throng. Her appearance was the cue for wild remorse.

"It's the Queen!"

"Look what they've done to her!"

"They're taking her to be burned!"

A few of the spectators, men and women too, tried to break through the guards and were violently repelled. Crying and mourning, the crowd followed her out of the castle and down the wide paved road.

"Oh, my lady! Who will care for us now?"

"Goddess, Mother, hear us, save the Queen!"

Now all the townsfolk were out too, weeping and calling to her, casting faded leaves and rushes under her feet. A little girl, almost too short to be seen, dodged swiftly in and out between the marching men and thrust something into her hand. Guenevere brought the velvet petals to her lips—*the last rose*—

On the level jousting plain outside the town, a stake rose tall and black against the sky. Dark bundles of fagots lay heaped around the base. Nearby two brawny monks were busy preparing torches from a tub of pitch. Already she could see them blooming into flame.

Above a band of clouds, a raw red sun hung low and bleeding in the sky. The river at the edge of the plain, the far horizon, and the distant woods lay bathed in gold. She felt the beauty of life as never before, and the terror of death broke over her, drowning her mind. Her limbs shook till she could hardly walk, and her heart clenched like a rocky fist. *If I lay down here, now, in the road, they would have to carry me screaming to the stake.*

No, I cannot—

The only thing left is to die like a Queen—

She hardly felt the grass beneath her feet. She was rudely conducted across the plain, and then they were there at the stake. She saw a platform built up against it, to raise her high above the bundles of corded wood. As the guards formed a circle all around and the monks and knights poured into the inner ring, she could see why. The people had to be able to see her over their heads.

See me dying—

See the death of the Mother-right and the coming of the new God—

The guards crossed their pikes and linked arms around the base of the stake, straining to hold back the angry crowd. But the screams from the townsfolk were deafening as the monks thrust her stumbling up the steps. At the top she saw Father Sylvester waiting with Iachimo, collected, triumphant, a man fulfilled. He watched her tied to the stake and she read his thought: *Another hour, probably less, and the job is done.*

The rough cords bit into her wrists, her ankles, her neck. But the cruel pinching of her skin was meaningless to her now. From her perch the world was reduced to a sea of shaven pates. More monks had flocked out of Caerleon to swell the crowd around the stake, and Arthur's knights were all but lost in the throng. Penned in by the guards struggling against the crowds, she caught sight of Kay fighting to keep his feet. She thought she saw Bedivere with Kay, and next to them a flash of Lucan's bright hair, but the only faces she knew were the two youngest of the Orkneys, Gaheris and Gareth. They stood huddled together on the outer edge of the throng, Gareth weeping bitterly and Gaheris bending toward his brother to comfort him.

Now the air was chill in the fading sun, and an evil wind was plucking at her gown. It would feed the fire, making the kindling crackle and the flames roar. She shivered, and caught a brutish snicker passing over Iachimo's lips. Cold, lady? Soon, soon, you'll be warm enough...

"Dame Guenevere, queen no longer—"

It was Sylvester, exultant, bullying, standing too near, and she could not get away. Tied hand and foot, she could not move at all. Iachimo passed Sylvester a great Bible, and she saw that it was open at the black-lettered service for the dead.

"Woman, I am here to shrive you of your sin," he intoned, "and bring you to the love of Jesus Christ—"

She gathered all her strength and looked him in the eye. "I spit on you, monk!" she cried in a ringing voice. "Be gone and let me die in my own faith! Tonight I shall walk the world beyond the stars. I do not need your wretched shriving to save my soul!"

Sylvester laughed sardonically. "As you wish."

Turning, he swung away down the steep steps, with the grinning Iachimo scuttling in his rear. Already the two brawny monks at the foot of the stake, the sleeves of their habits rolled up, were dipping torches in pitch and setting them alight. Seconds later she felt the hot upsurge of air and the torches caught and the fagots leaped into flame.

The howling of the crowd took on a higher note, the people keening now like a great wind off the plain. The fagots crackled and the fire leaped from clump to clump, each releasing blinding gusts of gray-green smoke. The wild laughter of death rose in her throat. *The Christians have used green wood to set this fire. They want me to die slowly, feeling every flame. Goddess, Mother, help me cheat them of that. Give me the strength to run into Your arms.*

The howling and screaming was all about her now. Sparks flew from the fire below and thick stinging fumes swallowed her up, cutting off her view. The smoke stung her eyes, her nose, the back of her throat. She was choking, she was dying, *Soon, Mother, soooooooon—*

She was in a mist now, lost to the world around. With great deliberation she set herself to breathe in, to hasten her dying and bring her to the end. Now at last she was free to think of Lancelot, free to be with him, *Soon, sweetheart, soooooooon—*

Breathe in—breathe in—don't fail—

The Dark Lord, they said, came for his Chosen Ones. Penn Annywn, they called him, on his great galloping black horse, carrying white souls away to the Otherworld. Already she could hear the thudding of horses' hooves. *I am ready, Lord of Darkness, come for me, Penn Annywn!*

Sharp shrieks and the clashing of steel reached her through the mist. But the acrid fumes were deep inside her now. Her lungs were boiling and her veins ran with fire. She was blinded with smoke and her breath was almost done. *Soon, sweetheart, soon—*

For the Dark Lord was coming, he was here. The drumming hooves swept up to the side of the stake, and she felt a new presence on the platform, disturbing the air. A dark shape was approaching through the swirling fumes. He held a knife in his hand and she knew he would cut her throat, for her life was the sacrifice he came to claim. She closed her eyes and tipped back her head. *Strike, Lord! I am ready, I am going to my love.*

She felt the cold blade at her neck and waited for the fatal stroke. Instead she felt a rough kiss, and heard one broken word. *"Madame—?"*

Goddess, Mother, thanks—

She knew then that her prayers had been answered, that her soul had slipped its earthly shell and she was wandering in the Otherworld.

But how was Lancelot here? She thought she would have to wait for him in the Otherworld, walking the astral plane till he came. Had he died then, that he was here before her—?

"Lady, lady, wake up!"

She felt the cord parting that had held her neck. A hand was roughly shaking her shoulder, while at her back she could feel the sawing of a knife. "Lady, hold your hands in—the blade's sharp—"

Lancelot?

She opened her eyes. Black-faced with smoke, his helmet splashed with blood, Lancelot was beside her in the swirling fumes. "Hurry, hurry!" he gasped, slashing at her bonds. "Pull yourself away, get free as soon as you can."

Goddess, Mother, thanks—

A mighty surge of power coursed through her veins. Bunching her fists, she burst the last threads restraining her hands. Already Lancelot was on his knees, hacking at the knots round her feet. Seconds later she was kicking free and breaking away.

"Here!"

He seized her wrist and drew her to the edge of the platform in an iron grip. In the seething mass below, mounted knights struggled with monks and knights on the ground. Through the smoke and flame, as near to the fire as he dared, Bors waited on horseback holding Lancelot's great gray. Beside him Lionel fought valiantly, fending off attack.

"Jump!" Lancelot shouted. "I'll be with you. Jump!"

She did not hesitate. Tearing off her headdress, she gathered up her skirts and leaped through the air. Passing through the flames she felt her skin crackle and her hair catch fire, but a second later she lay winded on the ground. She had cleared the burning wood, she was out, safe and alive.

But now she was in another kind of hell. The clash of arms, howls of anger, and screams of pain filled the air, as Lancelot's knights fought to clear a way through the press. The guards were offering little resistance to them and many were openly rejoicing at her escape. But unarmed though they were, the monks were fighting like madmen, pulling lighted timbers from the fire to attack horses and men, dragging knights from the saddle and beating them savagely to the ground.

"Come, lady, come!"

Lancelot's gauntleted hand closed on her wrist, dragging her to her feet, while the other beat clumsily at her smoldering hair. He pushed and pulled her, staggering across the grass to the waiting horse.

"Lancelot!"

She saw the tears start to Bors' eyes as he saw them appearing through the smoke. But he gave all his attention to steadying the jittering beast as Lancelot vaulted into the saddle and heaved her up behind.

"Go!" Lancelot roared.

Pulling round his horse's head, he set off with Bors and Lionel on either side, all three swinging their swords wildly as they fought their way out of the press. *"À moi, Benoic!"* he cried again and again, rallying his knights as they left the field.

Clinging round his waist, ducking down behind the cold comfort of his armored back, she could see nothing of the fighting but the carnage on the ground. Monks, knights, and guards lay in a nightmare tangle of split heads, broken bodies, and bleeding wounds. Riderless horses leaped frantically to and fro, heedless of those groaning underfoot.

At last they gained the edge of the melee round the stake. With a cry of triumph, Lancelot broke through the last of the guard and, hallooing wildly, spurred his horse onto the open plain. Ahead lay the forest and beyond it the open road, flight and freedom, all she could have desired. Coughing, Guenevere held on to Lancelot for her life as the ragged convoy galloped full pelt into the dusk.

"Where are we going?" she shouted above the throbbing rhythm of the hooves.

"To Joyous Garde!" he cried. His voice was incandescent with joy. "Tonight, my love, you'll sleep safe in my arms!"

THEY SPED ONWARD into the darkness, weeping with relief, laughing with delight. Late at night they reached Lancelot's castle and, for the first time in all their long love, went openly to bed. In truth she did not sleep safely, for they hardly slept at all. Seared by the fire and by the terror of death, she coughed and clung to him shaking in every limb, and wanted soothing, like a child.

So he told her the story of how he had come to her aid, unable to leave as he had promised both her and Bors. How Lionel had insisted that they must turn back, and all his knights had sworn the same. So they had sent a page on a fast horse to bring word from the castle as soon as her fate was known.

Even then, she was so swiftly hustled to the stake that he had hardly managed to snatch her from the flames. And lying in wait at the edge of the distant wood, they dared not break cover and attack too soon.

"My heart kills me for the fear you suffered," he said sadly, for he knew that she would never be free of it now. But she stroked his arm and kissed his beloved face and told him to put such thoughts from his mind. They were together, and alive, and that was good enough. Then she laughed from her heart despite the pain in her smoke-blackened throat, and gently tasted the wonder of his lips.

Toward dawn they made slow and tender love, free at last, true lovers, husband and wife. They knew that the days to come would bring a hard reckoning, too much of it bad and sad. But for now they shared a joy too deep for words, too exalted for anything but the gentlest show of feeling, the most delicate caress. At last they slept a little in each other's arms, never more thankfully in all their lives.

BUT SOME WERE FATED not to sleep that night. Away to the west, out on the plain of death, Gawain knelt weeping and vowing vengeance for the last of the Orkneys, killed unwittingly in the battle round the stake. The two lovers were not to know that Gawain's brothers, Gaheris and Gareth, lay just as they did in each other's arms, but locked in the sleep from which they would never awake; nor that Arthur had sounded the trysting horn for war, vowing a slaughter that would leave none alive.

CHAPTER 49

Mother of cities, queen of the earth, beloved Rome! The Archbishop snatched deep breaths of the warm, dry air and rejoiced in the play of light from the cloudless sky. Was there a better time to tread the sun-soaked streets and shady colonnades than in these winter months when the islands he had left shivered in their damp and cold?

An old hand in the business of warding off sin, the Archbishop paused routinely to search his conscience for any trace of sensuous concupiscence or fleshly lust. But no, he decided, feeling the sun on the back of his neck, reveling in sandaled feet not cracked and bleeding from frost and snow, and drawing in the rich scent of food and life itself from every open door; this was not sin, he knew, but only honoring the goodness that God gave.

And how good You have been to me, Lord God, he mused thankfully, as he wound his way up through the teeming alleys and shadowed lanes toward the mighty Vatican, slumbering in the sun. First You brought me to the islands of the pagans, and granted me to lead the battle against their Goddess, their Mother of Darkness, the Great Whore, a battle You have ordained for us to win. Next You translated me from my lowly place to the great See of Canterbury, cradle of the True Faith, from there to rule over all the pagan isles.

And now—

He caught his breath. Now, Lord, to be called back to Rome by the Holy Father himself! Since he had left the beloved city as a boy, exiled as a young monk to serve in the benighted isles, he had never allowed himself to dream he might return. Arriving late last night, he had hardly had time to accept that he was here. But soon he would be on the rock of Saint Peter himself, and in audience with the Pope, kneeling to God's deputy on earth, kissing the Holy Ring!

Beware, beware—seek always duty, not delight—

Ever watchful, he checked himself for the sin of pride, and turned his mind to the task for which he had come. He would make a good report of his stewardship so far, he was sure of that. The Holy Father would rejoice to hear that the kingdom of the Britons was in safe hands. Sylvester would deal with Arthur and hold down Avalon without strain. And soon, soon, they would have swept away the last traces of Goddess worship in the misty lands.

"His Grace of Canterbury—"

"—Cantuariensis in regium Anglorum Archipiscopus—"

"This way, sir."

Reverently the Vatican opened its gates for him. As he stepped over the threshold, the vast echoing space resounded with the busy thrum of prayer and the dying fall of monkish voices chanting out the hours. The air was rich with the scents of Araby, frankincense and myrrh, and from the book-lined reading rooms they passed came the waft of vellum and leather moldering quietly away. It was the very odor of sanctity, the breath of God. Trembling with anticipation, the Archbishop drank it in.

Now the traffic in the wide corridor was increasing as messengers sped by on busy feet. Scarlet as poppies in the shadowy gloom, a pair of approaching cardinals turned incurious eyes on him and passed by in unbroken talk. And suddenly he was outside a set of lofty carved and gilded double doors, which must give on to the quarters of the Pope himself.

As he tried to collect his thoughts, the doors opened and another cardinal stood in the space beyond. "Archbishop?"

He bowed. "Your Excellency."

He knew him at once, of course. But respect decreed that he could not hail a cardinal by his boyhood name, though traces of the ardent, gifted young monk were still plain in the fine-featured ascetic who stood before him now. The raw lad had done well for himself, it seemed, since his time as a novice, what, twenty, no, thirty years ago? The Archbishop's mind spun back. Yes, Boniface had done good work then too, he had fought the good fight. This boy had been the first Christian on Avalon, chosen to take the battle into the enemy camp before he had been replaced and summoned to Rome. And Cardinal now, no less—a fine ascent.

Or perhaps not.

As the Cardinal bowed and gestured him within, the Archbishop thought again. From the unhappy mouth and the tightness round the eyes, it seemed Boniface had not done well enough to silence his own demons, whatever they were.

"His Holiness will see you straightaway."

Briskly the Cardinal led him through the inner hall. Do not speak of the old days in the isles, his forbidding back said. There may be time for that later on. Or there may not.

They came to another door, set low in the wall. Half-hidden by a looped hanging, it normally passed unnoticed in these echoing halls.

The Cardinal saw his surprise and gave him a curious look. "His Holiness is in camera," he said softly. "A message has come from the islands—a matter which requires your immediate concern—"

He knocked sharply, opened the door, and stepped within. Crossing the threshold behind him, the Archbishop found himself in a small chamber where the figure he was following was momentarily lost to view. Walls, carpet, ceiling were all as red as the Cardinal's robes. The windows were heavily muffled against the daylight, and the room was lit with a hundred candles banked on every side. Their flames flickered over a huge crucifix on the wall, a jeweled statue of the Virgin Mary, and countless gilded paintings of holy scenes. With a catch of his breath the Archbishop knew that he was in the heart of the Vatican indeed.

Before him stood a great dais, with a huge red canopy above. Despite the smallness of the room, a mighty throne squatted beneath it, dominating the scene. On the throne sat a man-mountain clad like his chamber all in red. A red miter crowned his great head, a red cope surrounded his shoulders, and an embroidered apron of red covered his red gown. Only his large pale face struck a different hue. Fat white hands weighed down with jewels lay lifeless on the arms of his chair. But the gleaming, coal-black eyes were very much alive.

"Holy Father," the Archbishop muttered, overawed, falling to his knees.

The sonorous, liquid tones of Italian washed over him. "Arise, my son, and give ear, for all is not well in the land you have left."

In deep alarm, the Archbishop leaped to his feet. "Holy Father, I left the best man I had—"

The Pope held up his hand. "And he has sent his best man after you."

At his signal another door opened on the far side of the room. A squat figure limped forward out of the shadows till the light from the candelabra fell on his face. From the bruises on his face to the injured leg, the newcomer had obviously ridden far and fast, taking many falls.

The Archbishop blanched. "Iachimo!"

The Pope moved his large face up and down. "Iachimo," he agreed impassively. "Ridden here helter-skelter, with a rare tale to tell. King Arthur has found his dear queen is unchaste. He condemned her to the fire, but she escaped. With her paramour, no less, who plucked her from the flames. And now they hide out in his castle while the King sounds the trysting horn far and wide, raising an army to sweep them from the earth."

"What?" cried the Archbishop, aghast. "Holy Father, I left all in peace. We were winning the battle, we had Arthur's soul! The kingdom was ours to do with as we wished."

"So your deputy Sylvester seemed to think," Cardinal Boniface put in unpleasantly. "He prevailed upon Arthur to hurry her to the stake." He jerked a contemptuous thumb at Iachimo. "Or so this creature says, who knows his master's mind."

"God forgive us!" the Archbishop groaned. He wanted to bite off his thumbs, dash his head against the floor. Sylvester had seemed like a solid, a worthy choice. What madness had possessed him? What mindless folly, to make a martyr of the concubine! To stir up the people, antagonize Lancelot, split the country, multiply the hate—God Almighty, they would never see the end—

He could see two pairs of eyes following his every move and tracking, he felt sure, his every frantic thought.

The Pope fixed his gaze somewhere overhead. "There is more."

The Archbishop flinched. "My Lord?"

"Sir Gawain also seeks Sir Lancelot's death. Lancelot killed his brothers when he rescued the Queen. He will drive the King to hound Lancelot to his grave. There must be war." The bright black eyes swiveled the Archbishop's way. "And what then?"

The Archbishop shook his head. "Lancelot is a better fighter than them all. He'll defeat Gawain and very likely Arthur too."

Boniface laughed angrily. "Then he and Queen Guenevere will rule over the whole land! She'll restore the Old Faith, and all our work will be lost."

"And the Great Whore will ride rampaging far and wide," the Pope mused, his fleshy fingers playing with his rings. "But we trust you to stop this, Father, as you must."

Boniface laughed sarcastically again. "If it is not too late!"

The Pope's gaze was opaque, his fleshy smile even benign. But the open scorn in Cardinal Boniface's face spurred the Archbishop to salvage some remnant of his pride.

"It must and shall be done." He bowed to the Pope. "By your leave, Holy Father, I shall return at once. There is still time to save these wretches from themselves."

"Save them, is it now?" A sharp flicker of amusement lit the Cardinal's hard eyes. "Time was when you too, sir, sought the concubine's death."

"That was before we were sure of Arthur's soul. Now that we have him, the need to break Guenevere's hold on him is past. She is nothing to him now, and we lose men, monks, monasteries, if they make war." He pressed a hand to his head. "Burning Guenevere, hounding Lancelot—God help us, it threatens all that we have won!"

The coal-bright eyes briefly turned his way, and he knew that the Pope had seen all this and more. The great red figure nodded his heavy head, and his moon-faced smile shone out briefly for one last time. "We shall call you back. But go with our blessing now."

The large hand flapped, Cardinal Boniface bowed, and the Archbishop found himself ushered through the door and out. Passed from monk to monk, escorted back to the gates and shown into the street, he clung desperately to the Pope's parting words.

We shall call you back, the Holy Father had said.

The Archbishop clasped his hands. There's some comfort there.

But then it came to him with a shaft of agony, I did not kiss his ring! He did not offer me the stone of Saint Peter, no matter what bland words fell from his lips. I was judged and found wanting. I have failed in my task. And the Infallible Pontiff of God does not forgive.

In the pitiless light of the glittering winter sun, suddenly the Archbishop knew that he would never see Rome again. He would never tread her streets in the chill of his old age, when her sun would be the only cheer for his ancient bones. He would never worship again with Saint Peter on his rock, or honor God's creation in the pulsing, dancing streets. His last breath would be in the damp, lifeless isles, where sun-starved faces would be the last sight he saw and pale, cold hands would seal his dying eyes.

The islands, God help me!

He heard again the hungry seas' eternal roar and the mournful crying of the seagulls overhead. His soul answered with a desolate, wandering cry, and in that instant he saw into the heart of Boniface's fate and his own, both cast out forever from the place of their soul, doomed to eternal exile from the state of grace and condemned to mourn for it till the day they died.

CHAPTER 50

he muffled figure approached on silent feet, but the guard was instantly alert. "Who's there?"

"Good man."

Mordred briefly put back the cloak covering his head and showed his face. "How goes the night?"

The guard gave a broken-toothed grin. "Like every night, sir." He lifted his eyes to the castle above the plain, its mighty towers punching upward like great fists. "They don't bother us, and we don't bother them."

Mordred followed his gaze. It was true that the dark castle seemed asleep. No lights showed in the black mass of its silent bulk, and no sounds of life reached them through the midnight air. As winter darkened down, all the world seemed locked in the same peaceful sleep. But they were there; every man in the kingdom knew that. Why, every soul in the world had to know by now that Sir Lancelot had the Queen in Joyous Garde.

The soldier shifted his pike to his other hand. Might as well ask—he'd never get another chance like this. "Sir," he said boldly, "when do we go in? The lads are fed up with waiting, they say we'll never win like this."

And they'd be right, thought Mordred bitterly. Perhaps he should get the lads to speak to the King. They might have more success than he and Gawain had had during the long, weary weeks of this siege.

"What with having their own spring up there inside the keep, and all that time to provision before we came, they can sit it out all winter, as long as they want," the guard went on. "And while we were gathering our men, knights and lords were flocking to Sir Lancelot." He laughed. "He's got his own private army in there now."

The next thing he knew was a stinging blow across the face.

"Hold your tongue, soldier, or I'll cut it out," said Mordred pleasantly. "Don't meddle with things your betters will decide. When the King attacks, you'll be the last to know. Just keep a good watch and be ready when it comes."

Turning, he strode unhappily away. The fool was right, and every word he said had been put before Arthur time and time again. But the old bear had moved at his own pace throughout. Still, the time would come.

Mordred paced onward through the sleeping camp. Most of the watch fires were dying, little more than scattered embers fading in the dark. But every army has its men who cannot sleep. Here and there a fire blazed cheerfully, and a tight group squatted round it, talking in low tones. Gods, to be beside a glowing fire now! Mordred shivered, in spite of his wool tunic, gauntlets, and thick cloak. The earth had run down to the very dead of the year, and they must attack soon, or risk being snowed in here, sitting targets for attack from above.

A few days, a week at most, that was all they had. Every wind in the last few days had brought traces of snow. And though grief had made Arthur a *roi fainéant* for a while, the wounded impotent who could not act, yet with himself and Gawain at his ears every day, clattering like ravens, *vengeance, vengeance, vengeance,* they must prevail.

Vengeance, yes—

Mordred slowed his steps. His round of the camp was bringing him to Gawain's tent, as it often did. He was on good terms with Gawain now, and laughed to think that he'd ever feared Gawain as a rival for the throne. With a nod to the guard outside, he stepped forward and lifted the flap. Inside, a guttering torch threw a blood-red light on a table, a camp chair, and a great couch heaped with furs. A good rug or two covered the earthen floor, and thick hangings kept out the worst of the cold. In each corner a burning brazier of herb-strewn coals warmed and sweetened the air. Mordred smiled. For a son of the isles, the rough Orkneyan served himself well.

In more ways than one. On a brazier stood a pot of mulled wine, releasing heady vapors of honey, juniper, and spice. And two wooden goblets beside it, ready to drink—

Mordred turned his head to the bed. In the heaps of piled-up furs, some were more rounded than most. As he watched, the mounds stirred, and an arm and a bare shoulder came into view. He saw a tousled mass of hair, a pair of terrible, empty, knowing eyes, and then the wan, pointed face of a girl of—what?—eleven? Thirteen?

Gods above, Gawain, young enough to be your grandchild now! Mordred turned away, his lips and nostrils flaring in disgust. Like all promiscuous men, he drew a clear and self-flattering line between his own normal and natural deeds and those of others, which fell beyond the pale. He knew that camp followers came in all sizes and ages and combinations too, mothers and daughters, twin sisters, what you will. He had seen mothers and fathers and older siblings too energetically trading girls and boys to the bored soldiers sitting out this siege. But he had virtuously held aloof from all of it. Buy a child? No, he would wait for a woman, and one worth the choice. And the harder the waiting, the more welcome the woman would be.

Ignoring the girl, he withdrew. He knew now where Gawain would be. Nodding and smiling, greeting the night watchers as he went, Mordred made for Arthur's tent in the center of the camp. The royal pavilion stood apart from its neighbors, and was crowned with Arthur's flag. But at this time of night the red dragon hung drooping on its staff.

He could see a flurry at the doorway as he approached, and Gawain came out.

"Good night, sir."

"Sir, need an escort to your tent?"

"Mind your business, soldier, or I'll—"

Gawain's thick voice descended into a stream of mumbled oaths. Drunk and truculent then, Mordred noted, like every night, and ready for anything now, including imminent collapse. But not a soul in the camp would think of crossing him. Every knight, squire, and page, down to the lowliest of the donkey women and baggage boys, knew the madness of Sir Gawain after his brothers' death.

"Mordred? That you?"

"Over here. How's the King?"

Gawain's small eyes were red from liquor and grief. "How should he be?" He glared suspiciously at Mordred. Then his mood swung again, as it did so often now. "Never better!" he roared. "An' d'you know why?"

"Tell me," said Mordred easily, with a jovial smile. He could handle Gawain. In the weeks of the big knight's bereavement he had studied him closely and knew that his rival kept no secrets from him. Yet Gawain could still surprise him, he soon learned. For he was not prepared for the news Gawain gave him now.

"Why?" Gawain bellowed. "Because tomorrow I'll have Lancelot on the end of my sword!" Waves of rage shook him from head to foot. "Then he'll pay for my brothers' lives. Then I'll get revenge—"

"What?"

"I'll fight with the King—you'll take the left flank—"

"Gawain—" Mordred could have struck him. "What are you talking about?"

Gawain laughed madly. "The King has agreed—tomorrow we attack!"

TOMORROW THEY ATTACK—

Guenevere woke with a start, seeing the scene glimmering through the dark as clearly as if she were down there on the plain. Through drifting wreaths of sleep she watched messengers slipping silently from tent to tent, waking the huddled sleepers on the ground. She heard the groans and muffled oaths, then the low clatter of arms as each man reached for the weapons that would mean death for others but life and limb to him. Then the sight began to break up and dissolve. The call that had woken her faded into the dark as her mother's voice dropped through the midnight air one last time: *Hear me, little one—tomorrow they attack—*

She slipped from the bed and went in search of Lancelot. She found him on the battlements, staring out over the darkened plain. As he turned, his ravaged look and the lines round his eyes caught at her heart: *Oh my love, these last weeks with me have been the hardest of your life.* But as always his face brightened at the sight of her, and reaching for her hands, he drew her to his side.

His hands were very cold. Feeling her shiver, he extended one long arm and wrapped her in his cloak, gesturing to the campfires below. "Something is stirring. Tomorrow they attack."

"How do you know?"

"A hundred little things. But most of all, they must. No siege can last forever. The men must be hungry for action after all this time."

She nodded. "And you'll counterattack."

She had known this would come. They had discussed it and agreed to it a hundred times, deep in council with Bors and Lionel and the leaders of Lancelot's knights. One in particular, Sir Angres, had been hotly in favor of a bold sally from the first. An arrival from Little Britain, one of hundreds of knights of Benoic who had flocked to Sir Lancelot's side, he had no allegiance to King Arthur, and his one thought was to strike from the castle and drive the besiegers from the plain.

But Lancelot had drawn his breath and shaken his head. There would be no action that might endanger Arthur or his knights. The King must parley or attack; nothing else would do. The honor due to the King demanded that he make the first move.

And afterward—? she did not dare to ask. All this had been debated a hundred times too.

Goddess, Mother, help us. Save my love.

He hugged her hard and kissed the top of her head. "It is coming, I know it," he said quietly. "So, lady, will you help me to arm?"

THE FIRST WAVE rolled forward as dawn broke. Dull and red, the sun peered suspiciously over the horizon at the advancing men. Before they were halfway across the plain, the gates of the castle swung back. Flying out in a silver stream of fluttering pennants and shining mail, Lancelot and his knights rode forward to take the brunt of the attack.

For Arthur must not get as far as the castle, Lancelot had decreed. Once he came under the walls, he could not be protected from above. With stones, spears, and arrows pelting horses and riders alike, and fire and boiling pitch raining down, how could he order the defenders to hold back? Spare the King? Not a chance. Even though Arthur would have the scabbard of the Summer Country to protect him from loss of blood, in a mounted melee like that, no one was safe.

Pacing the battlements, Guenevere felt her hopes dissolve. Her soul rode out with Lancelot, but her life was hanging on the point of Arthur's spear. Lancelot would not fight against the King, and Arthur would try to take Lancelot's life.

So be it. The wheel is turning. Let it begin.

She gripped the rough edge of the stonework and looked down. Shouts and battle cries reached her through the raw, dank air. The front ranks engaged with a dull clashing shock, their lines wavering and mingling in the misty light.

Lancelot rode to and fro, forcing his way through the press. "The King!" he shouted, over and over again. "Spare the King! Any man who encounters King Arthur, spare him on pain of your life!"

"Arthur needs no pity from you, Lancelot!"

And suddenly there he was, the great bearlike form, solid as ever in his saddle and armored from head to foot. There was no mistaking the red plume of Pendragon, the silver-gilt glint of the scabbard, the gold coronet round the helmet, and the threatening mien. Storming through the press, Arthur had come up so fast that he had left the four companion knights trailing in his wake. Lancelot's heart lurched, and he signaled grimly to Bors and Lionel fighting by his side. He knew that they relished fighting against Lucan, Kay, Gawain, and Bedivere every bit as little as he desired to kill the King.

"Traitor!" cried Arthur through gritted teeth, bearing down.

Lancelot raised his sword in defense. "Not so, sire! I could not let the Queen die. I beg you, let me speak—"

His only answer was a violent blow that almost pitched him from the saddle with its force. "Death to you, traitor," Arthur cried. "Defend yourself, or die!"

Lancelot raised his sword in despair. How long could he go on parrying blows like these? Beside him, Bors and Lionel were fighting like madmen to hold the companions back, and losing ground. On the left flank, Mordred was making steady inroads, fighting with a determination beyond his years. Lancelot gave a heartfelt inward groan. Even with the aid of his knights from Little Britain, his side was getting the worst of it. Yet they must not win—

"Jesu have mercy!"

With a wild scream Arthur toppled from his saddle to the ground and lay still.

"À moi, Benoic! À moi!" Appearing from nowhere at Lancelot's side, Sir Angres triumphantly reined in his snorting charger, brandishing his spear.

"I brought him down, sir," he howled above the din, "before he could kill you." He raised his lance over Arthur's prostrate form, aiming for the throat. "Give me leave, lord," he exulted, "and I'll end this war!"

Behind Arthur a cry of agony rolled across the field. "The King," Gawain screamed, "the King's down! Pendragon à moi!"

"No!" Lancelot roared. "Sir Angres, fall back, or leave my service now." He did not wait to see the knight obey. "Bors!" he called. "And Lionel." Pulling up his horse, he threw Bors the reins and leaped to the ground. Careless of the trampling legs and iron hooves, he knelt beside Arthur and tried to raise him up.

But the great body lay in his arms like lead, and when Lancelot pushed up his visor, Arthur's face was gray. Tearing off his mailed gauntlet, Lancelot stroked Arthur's face, kissed his closed eyes, and blew into his mouth. But his skin was as cold as clay, and bloodless too. Neither the sprawled torso nor the slack limbs gave signs of life.

Lancelot rocked back on his heels and began to weep. Suddenly he saw that Arthur's eyes had opened and were staring at him, likewise full of tears. Feebly he waved his hand, and tried to raise his head.

Lancelot dared not speak. He struggled to his feet and, with a mighty effort, helped Arthur up. Beside him the loyal Bors was leaning down to help. Close by, Lionel was steadying Arthur's horse for the King to remount. In front of them rode Sir Angres, still disputing Lancelot's command by his furious face, but strenuously defending the little group from attack.

Staggering, Lancelot shouldered Arthur back onto his horse, offering cupped hands to step the great weight up. Beside him now was Bors, with his own horse. Hastily remounting, he turned back to the King.

Arthur swayed in the saddle, tears pouring down his cheeks. "Ah, Lancelot," he said thickly, "that ever this began!"

"My lord, you can end it!" Lancelot waved his sword wildly round, his eyes filling again at the sight of blood and terror, mangled faces and broken limbs. "See, already too many good knights lie dead who might still be alive. I shall never fight with you, whatever you do. I am no traitor to you, nor is the Queen. I beseech you, sire, make peace!"

"Is that true, Lancelot?" Arthur leaned heavily on the front of his saddle, nodding his head. "God knows you are the truest soul alive. To spare my life, when you could have had my crown——" He laughed in disbelief. "I won't find courtesy like that in another man."

Lancelot closed his eyes. Gods, let him agree!

Mordred!

Across the field Mordred stirred sharply at the buzzing in his head. Like a gnat in a window, it instantly came again. Mordred! Over there! See, Arthur is making peace with Lancelot. Get to Gawain and tell him, then trust to the blood of the Orkneys to deal with this.

Yes, at once.

Mordred never argued with the voice in his head. Tearing round his horse's head, he forced his way through the press till he got within earshot of Gawain's broad back.

"News, Gawain," he cried. He waved his sword. "Over yonder—the King and Lancelot—d'you see?"

In the center of the field, the fighting was already dying down.

"Peace?" Arthur said wonderingly, and Lancelot could see the decision forming in his face. Around them the nearest knights had picked up the word, and hostilities were slowly coming to a halt.

He will agree! Praise and thanks, Goddess, thanks! began to fumble haphazardly through Lancelot's mind. Already he could hear the blessed words "Peace, Lancelot, then——?"

"No!"

Gawain bore down on Arthur, wild with rage. "Blood for our blood," he screamed, "his life for ours! You promised me, sire, he'd dance on the end of my sword. Don't betray me now as he betrayed you."

High above the fray, Guenevere craned forward as the shouts and screams came toward her through the pearly air.

Oh, Arthur, Arthur, don't weaken——

But with her heart in her throat she watched Arthur turn this way and that, and knew with the leaden certainty of thirty years just what he would do. In vain would Lancelot swear that Gawain's brothers had died by mishap in the affray around the stake—that he loved Gaheris and Gareth and would not strike them down.

Blood, blood, blood——

She heard the screams of vengeance and felt it darkening her eyes. She saw blood washing up from the horizon, heard the plain running with great rivers of it down to a roaring sea, drowning the land in great glistening waves. Red stained the clouds, swept the sun from the sky, and rained down on the battlefield where the fight went on.

Only now two figures held the field alone.

"Single combat!" screamed Lancelot as Gawain bore down on him, sword upraised, weeping, cursing, and swearing to drink his blood. "I demand the right to answer this charge myself, and if I lose, no jeopardy to the Queen."

"Grant him, sire!" bellowed Gawain, already loosing off his first stroke.

"Granted!" Arthur called in kingly, stentorian tones.

Oh, Arthur, cried Guenevere again, beginning to weep. For already she could see what lay ahead. And so she paced the battlements for hours as Gawain lashed and thrashed at Lancelot in vain, while the one stroke Lancelot released in self-defense split Gawain's skull.

CHAPTER 51

Crows and ravens were hovering over the plain, and they could see the dead and wounded from far away. Some had been too badly injured to move, and their shuddering cries and groans could clearly be heard. Others, silent and still, were awaiting the attentions of the burial detail with the patience of those who have passed all earthly concerns. Compared with some battlefields he had seen, this was not the worst. But Jesu Maria! The Archbishop wanted to weep. To see knights of the Round Table turned against one another like this!

"One moment, brothers."

At his signal, the little cavalcade of monks drew to a halt. From the crest of the hill where they stood, the path wound down to the plain where the aftermath of the battle unfolded its grisly burden to their view. Ahead of them on its rock, Joyous Garde stood handsome and serene in the pale wintry sun. Some of the dead were being borne up its winding causeway and taken within its gates. Others were being carried in the opposite direction toward the pitched tents and banners of the King's camp.

"Is it over, then, the fighting?" the Archbishop wondered aloud. "Or is this just a truce to bury the dead?"

Riding at his side, Sylvester pricked up his ears. "Let me find out, sir." Without waiting for an assent, he urged his mule into a trot, and set off down the slope. Obedience was not one of Sylvester's monastic virtues these days, the Archbishop reflected grimly. But he knew his deputy needed to feel of use.

For Sylvester had not taken the Archbishop's displeasure well, nor the Pope's reproof. Striking against the enemies of the faith? How could that be wrong? He still smarted under Guenevere's escape from the stake, and did not believe it was better to let her live. If the Holy Father said so from Rome, then it must be. But Sylvester did not have to like the papal decree.

"She's a witch!" he'd insisted to the Archbishop through gritted teeth. "The brothers round the stake saw her leap from the platform and fly by herself through the air! And she's more whore than ever, now that she's been with Sir Lancelot all this time. That's open fornication and adultery too."

"He will say that he merely saved her from the fire," the Archbishop had told Sylvester quietly as they jogged along. "And we will support that too. She must be reconciled with the King if our mission is to thrive." He had frowned sternly at Sylvester and his eternal shadow, Iachimo. "Think, brother! We could still lose Avalon. I see a great abbey rising there in time, with a monastery for the most gifted of our monks. It would be one of the greatest spiritual centers in these isles, a center of pilgrimage for all the world. But now, with the church still unfinished on the Tor, we could still be swept back into the inland sea!"

Never, thought Sylvester scornfully. Avalon is ours, now that the Old Whore who lived there has been driven to her hole. And this whore too would follow, he was sure of that. But there were more ways than one to skin a cat. He would triumph over Guenevere in the end.

What he learned in the King's camp confirmed this view. Returning to the side of the path, he awaited the Archbishop's arrival with a sanguine air. As his superior approached him down the narrow slope, Sylvester greeted him briskly, full of news.

"One battle fought, sir, between the King's men and Sir Lancelot, with no advantage to either side. Then it came to single combat between Sir Lancelot and Sir Gawain, and Sir Gawain was hurt."

The last of the Orkneys—Arthur's first companion knight. "Badly?"

Sylvester nodded. "One blow—but it was to the head."

The Archbishop closed his eyes. If Gawain dies, Arthur will never make peace. Oh God, do you delight in throwing boulders in our way?

Sylvester laughed. "Still, they're saying in the camp that an Orkney head's thicker than most. He's holding his own."

Lord God, let him live. Or else this land will go down in a sea of blood. Heavily the Archbishop clambered down from his mule. "Bring me to the King." And God, Lord God, speed my words, he prayed, for I have much to do with Arthur before night comes.

"OH, MY LADY, never better!"

Chirruping softly with pleasure, the maid put the final touch to Guenevere's headdress and smoothed down her hair. "Your coloring's so clear, my lady—oh and your lovely gown—"

"Thank you." Guenevere smiled resolutely to hide the sadness in her heart. No matter how sweet the maids were here at Joyous Garde, she still missed Ina badly, especially at times like this. Not knowing Ina's fate was a constant source of distress. Like her, the maid must have fallen into Mordred's hands. But after that? If only she knew.

She dismissed the maids and watched them giggling together and rustling happily away. Her heart moved. Had she ever been that young? Tense and restless, she prowled across to her mirror in the gathering gloom. The face staring back wore a strange, haunted look—*older? no, not older, but afraid—* yet luminous too, softer, lit from within. She knew then what Lancelot would see when he came, a woman loved and in love, her every feature molded by love and desire. The time she had had here with him had been the happiest of her life since Amir died. There had been fears and tremblings, many times a day, and deep hurts, for the fire, for Arthur, for herself. But above and beneath all the pain had been the simplest of joys, only time, time spent with the man she loved.

Now she had ears like a bat's, waiting for him, flying across the chamber at the sound of his foot on the stair. But all the joy in her died at the sight of his face. Her stomach lurched: *What is it, what now?* Last night he had wept in her arms for wounding Gawain, while she lay raging inside for the great fool's lust to kill. *But I would not wish him dead—*

She steadied her voice. "Is it Gawain—?"

He came wearily through the door, a bundle in his hand. "No." He shook his head. "Gawain lives, and he's mending, they say."

"Then what?"

He faced her in the center of the room, eye to eye. Already he was withdrawing himself from her, she could tell. When he spoke, an odd formality constricted his tones. "A herald, my lady—with a message, down at the camp."

"Yes?" Her heart clenched and thumped in her chest like a fist.

His voice was completely flat. "King Arthur requires that I return his wife to him."

"What?"

For the first time he looked at her properly, and she could see the pain cracking the shell of his outer calm. "He wants you back." He gave a crooked smile. "I can understand why."

"But why now?"

"His Christians have decreed it."

"A few weeks ago they wanted to burn me alive!"

"That urge has been reversed by a higher court." Bitterly he broke open the bundle in his hands and scattered the contents before her eyes. "Papal bulls, madame. Interdicts from the highest court in Christendom, solemn binding orders to your husband to reconcile with his Queen!"

Your husband— She winced at the flick of cruelty in his tone. Buying time, she knelt down and reached for the great folded sheets of vellum with their spider-black script. The lead seals on their red ribbons were cold in her hands, *like the weights on dead men's eyes*—

She rose to her feet. *Think, Guenevere*—

"They are not sure enough of themselves to kill me yet," she said grimly. "They fear war, and the people rallying against them to fight for the Mother-right if I were dead."

Lancelot nodded. "Whereas by acting as if they care only for peace—"

"—and reconciling the King with his beloved Queen—" Guenevere pulled herself up, disgusted by the savagery in her tone.

Lancelot stood unmoving. "So, Your Majesty, what must we do?"

Your Majesty—he has already decided that I must go back—

Back to Arthur—

Back to being Queen—

She could see him fading, dissolving before her eyes. For a moment she was a child again. "What if I don't go?"

He smiled, looking infinitely sad. "If you do not go, the King will besiege us here, for years if need be, till he starves us out. Many knights will die, and I will die too, for I cannot fight the King and would have to yield. I and Bors and Lionel will meet a traitor's death."

No—

"That I could endure, to save your life," he went on steadily. "But you would be found guilty too."

She nodded stiffly. "I know. As it stands, you only rescued me from the fire. You're my knight, it was your duty to save my life—save me for the King—" Her voice cracked.

"Most of the kingdom would have done the same." His voice was very low. "No one wanted you to die."

"Except Sylvester. And now even his own people are saying he was wrong." She tried to keep the bitterness out of her voice. "You are a hero now for saving me. But if you keep me, and defy the King, all the world will know you wanted me for yourself. And I wanted you!" She cursed and tore her hair. "Goddess, Mother, why can't I acknowledge my love? Why? *Why?*"

"Oh madame—"

He came toward her and took her in her arms. "You ask why? Ask the Great Ones, ask the Old Ones, why fate spins its wheel. We can only give thanks for the sweetness we have had."

Beyond compare—

You brought me to the garden that blooms both night and day, she sent spinning fiercely through the air to drop into his mind. *You made me whole, you answered the cry of my heart, the longing I carried with me from my birth between the worlds.*

As you did mine, came back to her in the soft, steady beating of his heart.

She stood quietly in his arms and let her mind run back over the joyful, blessed, brief love that they had shared, this precious space carved out of two separate lives. Here they had walked the world between the worlds, and here they had come to the place they had to leave.

She lifted her head and looked up into his face. "So many farewells—"

"I shall never leave you, madame—you know that."

She gave him the best smile she could. "I do now."

He closed his eyes to hold down the pain. "So, madame, what would you have me do?"

She made her voice sound as normal as she could. "Say I'll come in the morning, on condition the King stands by the terms of the peace."

He folded her to him again with a tender kiss. "The message is all ready and prepared. It's the only thing of honor we can do. I shall order it sent and then—oh, my love, my little love, we shall have tonight!"

CHAPTER 52

awn was breaking over Lancelot's sleeping face. Her drowsy
eyes traced the beloved line of his long jaw, the dusky eyelashes
lightly kissing the shadowed half-moons beneath his eyes, and the
rich, sweet lines of his mouth. In the gray light, his skin, his hair
were gray, and it came to her, *He will look like this when he dies.* She
slid close to him, trying not to wake him as she laid her body gently against his. The warm comforting smell of the bed rose
around her as she moved. *His bed—our bed—*

Then the next thought was, *No longer.*

We shall never be together like this again.

She wanted to tear her eyes out, to run away. Instead she sought dili-
gently for a grain of comfort in this hill of grief. *He will never leave you, he
has sworn that now. You will see him, you will love again, just not as often and openly as
you do now.*

Outside the window she caught the sound that had woken her up. A few
silver streaks were over the horizon and a dove was calling her heart out in
the glittering dawn. *What, love-bird, singing in winter, when everything has died? Or are
you like me, crying for your love? Never fear, he will come to you again, he has to, that is love.*

Love-birds mated for life, everyone knew that. Apart, they pined but
never changed their love. The dove had been sent to help her, she saw that
now. She reared up on her elbow and leaned over Lancelot's sleeping form.
"Wake up, love," she whispered, "be with me? Love me one last time?"

OUTSIDE GAWAIN'S TENT the air was thick with bad feeling, and worse.
Limping forward, Kay made one last attempt to dispel the unspoken dread.
"Don't do this, Gawain."

Lucan hastened to back Kay up. "Listen to him, Gawain!" he urged.
"You know he's right."

Gawain stood beside his horse, clutching its reins. His face was livid, and
his eyes pinpoints of pain. "I'm not going to miss this, if it's the last thing
I see on earth."

Kay, Bedivere, and Lucan exchanged glances behind Gawain's back. They had all watched helplessly as Gawain had torn off his bandage and forced on his helmet to cover his terrible wound. Now the big knight's head was rolling and his speech was thick and slurred, though all three of them knew that no liquor had passed his lips. That at least we took care of, Lucan mused grimly, by sleeping in his tent and watching him round the clock. But it'll take more than rough nursing like ours to get him through. Gods above, why won't he do what the doctors say?

"You've been ordered to stay in bed," Kay said harshly, covering his fear.

"Not by the King," Gawain muttered. He grasped the pommel of the saddle and crooked his knee. "Leg me up."

"No," Lucan retorted flatly, for all of them. "Let the King handle Lancelot. You need to lie down and rest!"

Gawain turned a look of stark hatred on his fellow knight. "I'll rest in my grave," he said with a terrible laugh. "But only when I've seen Lancelot there too. Darkness and devils!" He loosed off a blood-chilling scream. "He killed my brothers, and he's half-killed me. How can I rest in my bed till I know what's become of him?"

GAWAIN, YES, ALONGSIDE KAY, Lucan, Bedivere, and all the knights, with Arthur and Mordred at the front—Guenevere could see them all drawn up and waiting as she rode down. All the knights were turned out as if for a tournament, and a hundred flags and banners made the scene as bright as May. But looming darkly to one side was a massed gathering of another shade. Rank after black-clad rank of monks stood to Arthur's right. In front of them, proudly horsed like Arthur and his knights, she could see the Archbishop of Canterbury and Father Sylvester, who had brought her to the stake.

So the Christians are out in force with their leaders at their head?

Why?

"Why so many monks?" she muttered to Lancelot through frozen lips. *Another burning?* cried the ever-present terror in her heart.

"A show of strength, Your Majesty, nothing more." Lancelot's heart was suddenly liquid with pain. The love of his life was shaking, almost fainting with fear, and he could offer nothing but hollow platitudes and distant, formal address.

He wanted to weep. But the urge was dispatched before it could be born.

They would put on a good show, the two of them, or die. He did not need to look at Guenevere riding by his side. For all her tragic eyes and pain-washed face, she looked as fine as she ever had done in her life.

He knew because he had dressed her, step by step.

"White and gold," he had insisted, "your white silk gown and gold kirtle, then a white woolen overgown and a gold cloak. Your purity and royalty, madame, need to be blazoned for every man to see. You are Guenevere and you have done nothing wrong. You must wear your jewels too, madame. Come now, you must be every inch a queen!"

She was attended like a queen too, he saw to that. All the women he had hired for her and all his knights, fully armed, rode behind them in a royal train. If Arthur tricks us, he thought, we are well prepared. For one desperate moment he found himself hoping that Mordred would try to spring another trap. Then he and his own knights would fight back, he would wrest Guenevere from Arthur's arms forever and carry her off to France—

But the next thought was, The King would never lend himself to this. Arthur is the soul of honor. He does not betray...

Beside him Guenevere sensed his sharp distress. She was aching to touch him, to turn to him, but the time for that was past. What was he thinking? She did not know. But she knew that he must be in hell, as she was too. Around them were frozen ranks of strangers on all sides. In front of them loomed her fate, a row of hard-eyed men.

They were near enough now to see Arthur's face.

My husband.

Guenevere prodded at the idea like a broken tooth. But there was no pain, only deadness where the pain had been. That life was dead and gone for her now. The man who had been her husband was no more. She no longer knew the lofty figure, still tall but seeming gaunt and suddenly more aged now, who sat between his knights and the monks of his church.

"Halt there!" Mordred's voice rang out across the plain.

So, Mordred. Guenevere returned an aloof acknowledgment to his fulsome bow and looked him coldly in the eye. *Do you have it now, all you wanted, Arthur in your hand and yourself in the seat of power?*

Arthur rode a pace or two forward, with Mordred and Gawain on either side. As Guenevere and Lancelot came to a halt, the Archbishop and Sylvester urged their mounts into a position facing both camps.

As if he were going to marry us again, Guenevere thought inconsequentially. *Perhaps in his mind, he is.*

The Archbishop rolled up his eyes to the heavens and spread wide his hands. A lofty peroration was clearly trembling on his lips. But Lancelot had no intention of waiting for a Christian to speak.

"My lord!" he cried, bowing deeply to Arthur. "You required me to restore your lady, and here she stands. The Queen is no traitor to you, sire, nor am I. I crave peace and pardon for the Queen during all her life, and freedom and good cheer wherever she may go. Give me your royal oath that she will be treated well, and I have my highest desire. That is all I set out to do when I pulled her from the fire."

Arthur paused with a quick sideways glance. Mordred smiled and nodded approvingly.

"Your wish is granted," Arthur rumbled. "I pledge you peace in this land, and full pardon for the Queen."

"I take your royal word." Lancelot leaned down and picked up Guenevere's reins, offering them to Arthur with a bow. "Then, sire, receive Her Majesty from my unworthy hands."

No, Lancelot—wait—

Something was wrong, she knew it.

"A moment, my lords." Guenevere spoke as coolly as she could. She looked Arthur in the eye. "You spoke of peace in the land, sir—peace for all?"

Arthur inclined his head. "All."

She gestured to Lancelot and his two cousins, grim-faced in the rear. "Lancelot and all his people? Sir Bors and Sir Lionel?"

"As far as our kingdom runs," Arthur repeated, "peace for all."

Arthur's eyes were opaque. A bright shaft of panic ran through Guenevere. Why could she not trust Arthur now?

"Your Majesty—?" Despite his mask of cold formality, Lancelot was looking at her with an angry question in his eyes. *Why draw this out, madame? You heard the King. Arthur does not lie.*

Yet still Mordred sits his horse glinting with a secret mirth. Gawain too, his eyes are rolling in his grinning head. He looks like death, but he can hardly sit his horse for some pleasure he sees—it's a trap, Lancelot, it's a trap!

"Once again, Arthur," she pressed on. "Do your swear before all men here that Lancelot may go freely all his life?"

"With our blessing," Arthur said more sharply. "As long as his life may last."

Her nerves were screaming now. "You will not take his castle, his land, or his estates, his knights, his—"

"Enough!" Arthur had risen in the saddle, angry and dangerous. "What, Guenevere, d'you think I'd steal from any man?"

"Madame, you shame us both!"

Lancelot's low-voiced reproof stung her far more than Arthur's hot words. "They are against you, Lancelot," she forced out through stiff lips. "There's a plot—something—beware!"

He leaned toward her. "Lady," he muttered, "have a care yourself!"

Throwing his reins to Bors, he vaulted from the saddle and made a pretense of adjusting the bridle at the side of her horse's head. "We must not betray ourselves at this final hour. All is well, I promise you, this is nothing but your fear." He threw back his head and looked her in the face. "Come, let us make an end."

Taking her reins, he led her toward Arthur and the line of mounted men. "Here is your Queen, sir," he called, bowing and turning away.

Arthur leaned forward. "Welcome, Guenevere. I am glad to see you back." His words and his voice were warm. But why could he not look her in the eye?

"Thank you."

She took up her reins and brought her horse into line with Arthur's, numbly acknowledging the greetings of Mordred and the knights. Facing them, the Archbishop had spread his arms and raised his hands to heaven.

"Thanks be to God!" he proclaimed loudly. "Those whom God hath put together, let no man put asunder!"

Lancelot remounted his horse and came toward them over the frozen grass.

"Farewell, Your Majesties," he cried with a deep bow, "till our next meeting at court." He bowed again to Arthur, with a sweep of his hand. "By your leave, sire, as soon as I have set things in order here at Joyous Garde, I shall follow you to Caerleon and attend you there." He turned his horse's head to move away.

Gawain gave a thick, stupid laugh. "Not so fast, Lancelot," he cried.

Guenevere's hand flew to her mouth. *I knew it—oh my prophetic soul—*

Lancelot stopped in his tracks. "Sir?"

"You're banished, Lancelot," cried Gawain in his strange, thick voice.

Lancelot turned to Arthur, pale to the roots of his hair. "Sire, is this true?"

Arthur lifted his chin. "In recognition of the deaths of my kin," he repeated like a lesson he had learned, "you are banished from these islands, never to return."

"Sire—!"

Mordred leaned forward sorrowfully. "Sir Lancelot, hear the King."

Arthur pressed on. "We would have pardoned you for the death of Agravain—he sought your death, and set on you unarmed. But the deaths of Gaheris and Gareth we cannot forgive. They were unarmed. You still took their lives."

"Not so!" Lancelot's cry of anguish split the plain. "I never saw them at all, I didn't know they were there! But sire, the crowd—the smoke—as I rode through, they fell beneath my sword."

"As you will fall before mine!" Gawain howled. A thin line of spittle edged his mouth.

"Arthur, you gave your word—"

Guenevere could hardly speak for rage. "You promised Lancelot his freedom—"

"—to go as he pleased, yes, I did." Arthur smiled like a schoolboy conscious of having done well. "And he has it! He has perfect freedom to go, all the way back to France!"

"Arthur, that's not what he thought, and you know that!"

Lancelot flushed, though with anger or humiliation she could not tell. "Lady, no more," he cried, "spare yourself!" He gestured at his cousins and the men in his train. "By the laws of chivalry, sire, you will give me safe conduct out of your land. Then I shall leave your country and never return."

"Never in your life," Arthur pronounced with harsh emphasis, "as long as my rule holds sway."

Never?

A short while ago, she had thought things were at their worst. But *never* was a crueler word than them all.

Now Lancelot was fading before her, drifting away. She was in a mist, she could not see his face, only a gray figure on a gray horse. His voice reached her from far away.

"Farewell, then, to the land I have loved so long. The Gods alone know what it has meant to me. Now my quest is ended here, and I must depart. But each dawn and evening I shall remember it."

And I you, sweetheart, always—

"Farewell, King Arthur." His voice was fainter now. "And farewell, my Queen. The Gods go with you wherever you may walk. And at the meeting of the worlds, I shall see you there."

I shall be waiting—

Motionless, she watched him ride away before the riders around her started moving and she had to move too. Blindly she took up the reins, struggling to comprehend. *Banished—? Goddess, Mother, was this the last farewell?*

Suddenly she was conscious of a tall figure at her side, and Arthur's voice came booming in her ear.

"Guenevere, we ride for Caerleon tonight."

Mordred appeared on her other side. "I trust that is acceptable to Your Majesty?" He smiled sympathetically.

Ignoring him, she turned to Arthur as mildly as she could. "Whatever you say, Arthur."

Yes, Arthur, whatever you say . . .

The submissive, wifely phrase made her stomach heave. Then a bitter inward laugh shook her frame. *That's the way things have to be now, Guenevere—for Lancelot and for Arthur, for the country, for yourself—*

"To Caerleon then," Arthur boomed. "Good!"

Mordred raised a hand to signal the troops. "Onward, on the King's orders!" he trumpeted round the plain. "To Caerleon!"

Slowly the great block of mounted men got under way. Without urging, Guenevere's horse began to move off with the rest. Sitting very still, holding her breath made the sharp stabbing round her heart seem less. But there was nothing she could do for the pain in her mind.

Whatever you say, Arthur.

Take my body if you want, for it's quite dead now. My soul has gone out of it, see, there it rides away with Lancelot.

With Lancelot, my love.

Farewell, love.

CHAPTER 53

Night had fallen by the time they reached Caerleon, and there was no moon. A handful of stars encrusted the glittering sky, and the mist from the river veiled everything in white. As they approached the castle, she felt as if she were riding into another world. *Do I know this place? Did I ever live here before?*

The troop of horses and men clattered up the hill and into the narrow streets of the slumbering town. The long hours in the saddle riding through the cold had left her numbed beyond caring, as dead outside as she was within. *Mother, let me fall from my horse and end it all*, came to her in the sadness of a dream. But she knew she would not.

Now the clattering of the horses' hooves had awakened the town. Here and there candles flared in the sleeping dwellings as windows flew open and inquiring heads appeared. Then the townsfolk came eagerly to their doors, crying out with glee.

"It's the Queen! She's back!"

"Praise be! The King has found the Queen!"

"And brought her back alive!"

Knots of joyful people gathered in the streets, laughing, weeping, hailing her return.

"Oh my lady, we have nothing to offer you," called one woman, torn between tears and joy. "We should be lining your way with fires and flowers——"

Guenevere put back her hood, despite the raw, dank cold. "When I left, you threw blessings under my feet," she called. "I need no more goodness than that at your loving hands."

"Oh lady——"

"See, she hasn't changed——"

Laughing and rejoicing, reaching out to touch her stirrup or kiss the hem of her robe, they followed her all the way to the castle gate. As the groom helped her from her horse in the courtyard, she stumbled and almost fell, for she could not feel her feet. But a new and fragile warmth had come to her. *This is how I must live now,* she instructed herself, *taking comfort where I find it and thanking the Great Ones for the love they give.*

In the courtyard, Arthur bade her a formal good night. He was in good spirits, despite the long, weary ride.

"You will find the Queen's apartments all prepared," he said jovially. "Tomorrow in the Great Hall we shall feast your return."

"As you say, Arthur."

At the Queen's apartments she dismissed the hovering attendants with a smile. *Let me be, let me be,* hammered dully through her mind. All she wanted was to be left alone to weep.

The guards threw open the doors and ushered her within.

"Welcome back, my lady."

"Thank you. Good night."

As the door closed behind her she saw an applewood fire on the hearth, glowing banks of candles lighting the room, and a soft chamber robe laid out by the hearth to warm. A moment later a small figure hurtled toward her and fell kneeling at her feet.

"My lady—oh my lady—"

"Ina—"

Weeping, they clung to each other for a long time without words. Then in fits and starts the little maid told her all that had happened while they were apart. For the first time Guenevere heard how Ina had been bound and gagged by Agravain's men, then held again by Mordred till Guenevere had fled. Although set free then, she had been treated as a criminal till the outriders had swept back today with the news that the war was over, and the Queen was coming back.

"But everything will be all right now that you're here!" Ina finished tremulously, beaming through her tears.

Guenevere flinched. *Not everything, Ina.* But she would not say that. She took Ina's hard little hand. "Bless you, Ina. I've never been more glad to see anyone in my life."

THE NIGHT WAS LONG, and a hard, stony road. Weeping and praying, her thoughts went to and fro as she lay curled up inside the shelter of the hangings of the great bed. *Arthur is my husband and I am wedded to the land. Neither of these bonds may I break.*

If we keep the peace, the land and the people thrive.

In time of war, famine and death prevail.

I have my kingdom and I have not lost my love. Lancelot is mine till the worlds meet and mingle and all things are one. Then I shall be with him in the place where true souls meet. Till then I shall have him in my every thought.

For he was with her now, he was within her, deep in her being, coloring her mind and heart. "You will always be with me now, my only love," she whispered into the dark. "If I forget you, let me forget myself. For I have no self that is not given to you."

Toward dawn she slept. When she awoke, it was to a dreary sense of peace.

"We must make a new start," she said to Ina, cold and dry-eyed. "The King is planning a great feast tonight." She forced a smile. "Let's see how fine I can be."

As she picked out a gown, a rich mulberry damask, Lancelot came into her mind with a pang so acute that it made her catch her breath. *You never liked this, my love.* He had found the heavy fabric, in a red so deep that it was almost black, too somber and regal for his taste. Only tonight she was choosing not for herself but for Arthur and for the land. The deep sleeves were trimmed in a queenly golden silk, and the cloak she wore over it was of ermine lined with gold. For her jewels, she turned away from her beloved crystals and moonstones. *I shall wear pearls tonight—pearls are for tears—*

She went down to the Great Hall in time to see the first candles blooming in the chilly night. The vast stone space was warmed with blazing fires, and bright with courtiers come to welcome her home. As she moved through the gathering with Arthur, many of the knights and ladies could not speak, but simply bowed and turned aside to weep. Others pressed forward to kneel and kiss her hand, and she could hear murmured prayers of thanks on all sides.

Outside a high wind lamented, and howling shafts of rain lashed at the roof. But inside a fragile comfort flickered through the night with every candle's rosy glow. On the dais the high table was set with silver and swathed in red and gold. Branches of winter berries, shining plates and goblets, and great bowls of candied fruit all gleamed like jewels in the flaming light. Arthur took her hand to lead her to her place, and a lost familiarity stirred in her heart again. *Perhaps we shall succeed—we may still be friends—*

At the high table Arthur's knights stood waiting beside his place and hers, the two thrones facing each other across the narrow board.

"Majesty!"

The tears in Bedivere's eyes were sincere, she knew. Beside him Kay bowed stiffly, struggling for a smile, but her heart forgave him—he had always loved Arthur, never her. Lucan bowed and kissed her hand as warmly as if she had never been away. Only Gawain, waiting to take his seat on Arthur's right, seemed indifferent, greeting her with his thoughts clearly elsewhere. But she was glad to see that he looked better than before. Some color had returned to his great face, and his eyes were brighter than when he had sat beside Arthur on the plain at Joyous Garde.

"At last!"

With a sigh of satisfaction Arthur took his place and settled himself on his throne. On his left, Mordred leaned forward attentively. "Welcome, madam." He gave her his flashing white smile. "It is good to see you back."

"Thank you." She smiled coldly. *I have to tolerate you, Mordred, I know that. But never ask me to trust you again as long as I live.*

"Well said, my son," cried Arthur heartily. He reached for his goblet. "Come, sirs, a toast to the Queen!"

"The Queen—"

"The Queen—"

Somehow the evening wore on. Brawn followed broth; then wild swan, suckling pig, and roast boar chased one another across the laden board. Guenevere could touch almost nothing except a goblet of the blood-red wine to keep down her stomach and ease the pain in her heart. Around her the knights were eating and drinking without restraint. But still an odd heaviness hung over them and she was visited with a strange, unquiet thought: *It's as if the war they've just fought were still coming, not over and won.*

Again and again she caught Mordred's eyes on her with something incalculable in the depth of his gaze. And Kay was too sharp, while Bedivere was subdued, and Lucan communed mainly with his goblet and the nearest pitcher of wine. Only Gawain was the odd one out again, carousing with growing animation as the night wore away. The first shoot of unease grew till it invaded Guenevere's mind. *Something is happening—something I don't understand—*

At length Arthur set down his goblet and leaned back against his throne. "We must say good night," he announced jovially. "Now that the Queen has returned, we may go about our business with good heart."

What business? She leaned forward. "Arthur, I am ready for—"

"No, no, Guenevere," he said overhastily. "This is not a matter for you."

Mordred's eyes were very bright. "But the Queen will need to know."

Her stomach lurched. Ignoring Mordred, she appealed to Arthur again. "What are you talking about?"

Arthur raised his eyes and gazed out over her head. "A war expedition, nothing more."

Against the Saxons! Her heart leaped with relief. *It must be, we have no other enemies. Strange, they have not troubled us for years.* A raft of memories swept through her mind. *We became High King and Queen, Arthur, fighting off those cruel men. We saved these islands for the Britons, you and I—*

Soft feelings flooded her and she held her breath. "The Saxons," she said quietly to Arthur with a luminous smile. "After all these years? Well, may the Great Ones go with you."

"Not the Saxons," Arthur said loudly. "This is a matter for my kith and kin."

She stared at him. "What?"

Gawain gave a crude guffaw. "Vengeance, madam, for my brothers' deaths!"

Mordred saw her face and leaned forward helpfully. "Gaheris and Gareth, my lady. Gawain is taking war into Little Britain for their murder at Lancelot's hands."

Oh my love—

Goddess, Mother, no!

She struggled to find her voice. "Arthur—"

He raised a hand, cutting her off. "An expedition, Guenevere, no more than that."

She gasped. *Then why won't he look me in the eye?*

"Let's drink to it, lads!" Gawain grabbed wildly for the nearest goblet, and raised it in a savage toast. "Vengeance for the Orkneys, and peace to my brothers' souls!" He drank deeply, then hurled the goblet to the ground. "We're coming after you, Lancelot, make no doubt of that," he cried. "War in your land! Not an inch of Benoic will be safe. We'll make it a wasteland to pay for my brothers' deaths!"

Beside her Lucan let out a groan of pain. Bedivere dropped his head in his hands and wept. Guenevere threw a glance of agony at Arthur, who did not see. "We?" she forced out.

Mordred shook his head sorrowfully. "The King is grieving for the loss of his sister's sons. He will lead the army against Lancelot. It's the biggest force of men these islands have ever seen."

"You're a dead man, Lancelot," Gawain was shouting drunkenly, "you and your cousins too. Hide where you like, we'll chase you through your kingdom and kill you there!"

CHAPTER 54

Guenevere could not breathe. She fixed her eyes on Arthur and saw him turning from Mordred to Gawain as each of them spoke. *Arthur, you have lost your mind, and worse, your soul. You have given yourself into the hands of men in love with death, when you should be choosing life. Nothing can save you from them when you lose yourself.*

At last she found her voice. "So, Arthur, is this your peace and goodwill to all?"

Arthur's eyes widened. "Peace in this land," he repeated self-righteously. He glanced questioningly at Mordred, who gave him a supportive nod. "Those were the stated terms. In this land, I said—not Lancelot's."

She was choking with rage. "And your pledge that he could go free—"

"That was true." Arthur looked up indignantly. "He was free to go all the way back to Benoic." He looked round and laughed.

"So that we could follow him there!" Gawain slammed his fist onto the table triumphantly.

Ye Gods and Great Ones, help me get through this—

Already the knights and ladies farther down the table were throwing them curious glances, attracted by the noise. Guenevere surged to her feet. "Sir, I shall withdraw. Tomorrow, by your leave, I shall have audience with you."

HE WOULD SEE her early, he'd said, before the hunt. Since she could not sleep, it was no hardship to cross the slippery courtyard as dawn broke and pass through the cloisters teeming with busy monks. A copper sun was crawling up a lifeless sky, and the mists of morning lay like dead men's fingers on the clammy earth. Like vengeful spirits from a darker world, the black-clad brethren were already bustling about the offices of the day. The mournful chant from the chapel assailed her ears in the same way as the raw rank vapors of earth choked her throat.

In the King's apartments, Arthur was on his knees. *Praying to your God, Arthur*, she wanted to cry, *for permission to kill Lancelot?* He rose to his feet and approached her jovially enough, but at the sight of her face his expression changed. "Good morning to you," he said quietly.

She moved away from him, prowling round the chamber, unable to stand still. Gods above, with his statues and crucifixes, he'd made his chamber a private chapel now! She turned to face him, digging her nails into her hands.

"Arthur, why are you pursuing Lancelot? Is it because he defied your judgment and saved me from the fire?"

Arthur looked away. "That was an evil thing. The Archbishop has shown me that I should never have agreed to it." He shot her a tentative glance. "I have to beg your forgiveness, the Archbishop says." He broke away, not waiting for her reply. "No, do not blame Lancelot for that. He saved your life, and that is good enough."

The Archbishop says, the Archbishop says—

As he shifted away, it was her turn to follow him. "Then are you seeking vengeance for yourself?" She hesitated, then took her courage in both hands. "Do you think we were traitors to you, he and I?"

She could not bring herself to say *lovers*, but she had vowed one oath. *If Arthur challenges me, I will not lie. If he wants to know, he will have the truth.*

But Arthur was looking at her calmly enough. "No, I knew Lancelot didn't love you when he gave you up. Oh, he loves you as his lady, of course, he is your knight. But the kind of adulterous passion they talked about—" He laughed in bluff embarrassment. "No, that was all in Agravain's mind."

Her nerves were raw. "Why are you pursuing him then?"

Arthur's face hardened. "For Gaheris and Gareth."

She could have torn her hair. "But they died by accident!"

"They died because of him!" He drew a harsh breath. "So because of him, my kin is dying out. They were my sister's sons, and the last of the line."

"Killing Lancelot won't bring them back to life!"

"But it will feed their spirits with his blood."

He was very pale. A raw light like blood shone in his eye.

She started. "Arthur, what is this—?"

Her sight shivered and a face swam back to her through the mists of time. It was Arthur in full battle armor, covered in gore, as he had come to her after the first great battle to reclaim his throne. Dimly she could hear the cries of the fallen enemy, the last curses rattling in their throats, *Beware the Red Ravager—Arthur Pendragon is here—*

She came to herself, the sickness of death in her mouth. "Arthur, you must not do this!"

He gave a brutal laugh. "I have no choice. D'you think I can hold back Gawain? He hates Lancelot now as much as he once loved and honored him."

"But if Lancelot made amends—" she whispered with the last of her strength. "Offered blood-gelt—did whatever Gawain wanted to repay the debt—"

Arthur shook his head. "Gawain has sworn a blood oath to end Lancelot's days. It is the faith of the Orkneys. He can never take it back."

Never—

Gawain will never forgive, and I shall never see Lancelot again.

She bowed her head. "Good hunting then," she murmured through numb lips. "I shall leave you to your war." *And I must leave too. I must go to Camelot, as soon as you have gone.*

She turned to go. But the tone of Arthur's voice stopped her in her tracks.

"One moment, Guenevere," he said authoritatively. "While I am away, I have taken every care of you. I have ordered Mordred to make you his special charge."

A creeping dew of horror broke over her skin. *"Mordred?"*

"I have named Mordred regent in my stead. He will rule as me, and you will remain my Queen."

She could not believe it. "He will rule as you—?"

"I have granted him full royal powers in my place," Arthur pressed on. "He has the royal seal to enact his commands, and my Council have sworn an oath of allegiance to him. The keys to the kingdom are Mordred's until I return."

A darkness descended and she could hardly stand. *Mordred—*

And suddenly he was there, coming through the door from Arthur's inner chamber, and she knew that he must have been there all along. Dressed in hunting green with his daggers through his belt and a heavy scabbard swinging at his side, he cut a handsome figure from head to toe. There was something in his air that she did not like, but he stood at Arthur's side with just the right expression of concern in his large lustrous eyes and gave her his finest smile.

"Your Majesty—"

The depth of his sweeping bow was not courtesy but sheer insolence. *I have you now*, it said.

Mordred—

She had to get out. *Get away to Camelot, escape!*

"One last thing," Arthur's booming voice reached her through the mist. "I want your word, Guenevere, that you'll honor my wish?"

She dragged breath into her lungs to steady herself. "You are asking for my allegiance to Mordred, like all the rest?"

"Not allegiance, Guenevere," Arthur said heartily. "You are the Queen. But I want you to rule with Mordred and support his sway."

She stared out through her window over the winter waste. *If I refuse, he will know I am his enemy. I have no choice—not even time to think—*

"Of course," she said firmly. "I shall honor your will." She made herself smile at Mordred. "You are the King's regent, and must rule as the King."

"God bless you, Guenevere," Arthur roared.

Mordred smiled too. "Thank you, my lady. I shall need your help."

Does Mordred believe me? Who knows?

The question would remain with her, she knew. But when Arthur left, she put it out of her mind. She stood beside Mordred as Arthur made his farewells and took solemn leave of all the knights. She held her place in the courtyard as troop after troop rode out, smiling and waving and wishing them all good speed. She even spoke easily with Mordred about trivial things, exchanging pleasantries as if life went on as before. But nothing could shake the iron message lodged in her heart. *I was wrong to ignore you, Mordred, before this. Well, I shall not make the same mistake again!*

BORS STOOD IN the prow of the ship, his face white with salt, his knuckles blue from gripping the wooden rails on either side. Even now, when the long-hoped-for coastline was looming into view, he did not believe that they had escaped, they were here, they were free!

Gods and Great Ones, bring us safely home!

Gulls swooped around the boat, lamenting like lost souls. Wheeling and diving, the hungry, squabbling birds had first tracked the boat miles out at sea, then escorted her home. Home—Bors rolled the word round his mind and had to hold back his tears. They were here, they were safe, they were *home*...

Guiltily he knuckled the suspicious wetness from his eyes, and reminded himself that nothing was ever as simple as that. Lionel would grieve long and hard at being banished from the islands, he knew. His younger brother loved the misty terrain, the pleasant pastures and fertile meads, the rolling hills and fallows and little chubby farms. It was all he had ever known, and all he wanted now. After the fearful sojourn in the Holy Land, he desired no more than to live out his life in this cool and fragrant place. Bors bit his lip and paced unhappily up and down. Yes, Lionel would need long love and care to recover from this.

And if Lionel would suffer—

Bors closed his mind. He would not, could not think of Lancelot's grief. He would walk with him, talk with him, and watch with him all night long, as he had done ever since they'd left Joyous Garde. But thinking of what Lancelot suffered was too much to bear. To lose Guenevere just when he had her in his arms— For a fleeting moment Bors wondered what it must be like to love another so much that leaving them was a kind of death. He did not know that this was how he loved Lancelot.

"Hoy there! Look lively! Throw us a rope."

"Aye, aye!"

Below him the sailors were making ready to land. He had not noticed how near they were to the quay. Now Lionel had appeared behind him on deck, and Lancelot too was making his way to the prow.

Bors nodded ahead. He did not trust himself to speak.

It fell to Lancelot to break the silence that gripped them all. "Home and safe," he said with a watery smile. "We'll be back in Benoic tonight."

Lionel nodded. "We have much to be thankful for."

Lancelot turned his back on the land and frowned. "And much to beware."

Bors stiffened. "What do you mean?"

Lancelot gestured back toward the open sea. "We have not left our enemies behind. Whatever is driving Mordred, he is not done. And Gawain will never give up his blood-feud till he dies." He paused. "Or brings about my death."

Bors and Lionel locked eyes. At last Bors spoke again. "So they will pursue us here, is that what you mean?"

"They must." Calmly Lancelot looked out on the stone-gray sea. "But knowing that, we shall be ready for them." He switched his gaze back to the land. "As we ride, we shall set every town, every castle, on a war footing now. They will not catch us unprepared."

A deep silence fell. Together the three cousins watched as the ship drew in. Behind the little port, the high cliffs and slumbering hills rolled away out of sight. Beyond them lay miles of eternal forests, broad rivers, and shining lakes, and the long, strong mountain backbone of the land.

Home.

Suddenly Bors knew that he did not care if Arthur came after them. He cared nothing too if he lost his life here now, fighting beside Lancelot. There was no better place to die than the place he was born, no better rest than in the arms of mother earth.

He raised his eyes to the heavens with a heart at peace. Let them come. Let them do what they will. We are here, we are safe, we are *home*.

CHAPTER 55

I t was the peace he had been craving for all his life. All his many lives, as demon child, bard, Druid, wizard, and Lord of Light. It was a blessed state. Merlin sighed. And that was why he knew it could not last.

Prostrate on his velvet couch, his ring of candles breathing round his head, Merlin closed his eyes so that he could see. *ArthurArthurArthur* throbbed through his mind. Grimly he clung to the precious thought. Love was the only defense against the cold.

And the cold was coming, he had felt it from far away. Already the air in his cell was growing chill. The thousand million tiny crystals round his walls were shivering and looking sad and dull.

"Don't be frightened, my dears," he encouraged them. But the fear was coming, it was growing; he felt it himself.

Now his limbs were cold and his flesh was juddering on his bones. When his thumbs started pricking, he knew that she was here.

"Welcome, spirit," he called as warmly as he could. But he knew that she was beyond such blandishments now.

And now she was here, dissolving space and time. He felt the walls of his crystal cell melt and fade away, and then he was spinning through glittering infinity. On a hundred horizons around him, stars were burning out, and galaxies racing to swallow one another in their flaming embrace. This was her universe, this liquid cascading world, forever ablaze with her hot desires and bubbling with her weeping, quivering hurts.

Then the velvet curtain of night came down and she brought him to a softer, safer place. The glorious rank smell of her womanhood reached him through the warm indigo darkness, and he felt her sharp breasts rub against him, then her lean writhing flanks. Her nipples scorched his fingers, but how good they were—

Now her eyes were glowing and glaring through the gloom. "Have you forgotten me, Merlin?" her hot voice breathed.

He laughed fondly. He would have known her touch, her stench any-where. "Forget you, Morgan? What man could do that?"

"You could, Merlin," she spat, "with your eternal games!" A howl of fury rattled from her lips. "Or rather, with your one great game above all. But where is your mighty house of Pendragon now?"

She flew at him, snarling and spitting, tearing at his gown, his hair, his flesh. He felt his garments rending, and the molten lava of her fury scalded his skin. He gasped with pain, but still his muscles leaped at her touch and his old loins sprang to life. She was the only woman who could move him, after all...

But he must not go down to that darkness, that despair. *ArthurArthur Arthur* surged back into his mind. Bravely he mastered his ancient, quivering flesh. She may have stripped him naked, but he still had his singing robes. *You have passed through the veil*, he reminded himself furiously, *you pierced the cloud of unknowing, you unsealed the seventh seal, you are a bard!*

In the far, calm regions of his mind he reached for his great cloak of black and white feathers, part raven, part swan, and his gown of gold flakes, shining fragments of the sun and the moon. Sending his spirit through the air, he called back his singing voice from the mountain torrent where it played, roaring from the crags and whispering into silent, hidden lakes.

Now he was ready. "Ah, Morgan," he sang up and down the scale. "Will you never be free?"

A blinding flash hit his eyes and blistered his skin. "Free of what, old fool?" she hissed.

Gamely he hung on to his resolve. "Free from yourself."

"Words! Words!" screeched the phantom, flaring across the sky. "You may tie up the winds, old man, and make the waters run away from the sea, but don't try to fool me! Speak to me plainly, Merlin, or not at all!"

She was in agony, he knew, and his pain was nothing in comparison. He crushed his tortured thumbs into his hands and made his voice sound as sweet and low as a woodland stream on a sunlit day. "Morgan, Morgan, when will you give up your revenge?"

A hissing, howling explosion was the only response. Now he saw stars colliding and worlds falling into fire as she tore the veil and raged unchecked through the astral plane. Above her, he knew, the Old Ones would be shak-ing their heads, while the Star Children ran to hide. On earth, women would miscarry and men run mad.

Gods, give me strength, he prayed. He sent his voice winging round the spheres. "It is true that the crimes against you are very great. Arthur was born of a primeval wrong. His father took your mother to create a Pendragon child. Your father, your mother, your sister were scattered to the winds. Your life was broken in pieces to pay for this."

Wronged, wronged, yesssssssssss, I wasssssssssss!

And now she was with him again, straddling his shrunken old frame. "Give up my revenge?" her wonderful lips spat and snarled. "Not while Arthur lives!"

Merlin's eyes dazzled. What a rare creature she was. Straining, he held on to the task he had to do. "Then Arthur had your love, and he gave it away." Thirty years and more, he knew, had not touched that terrible hurt. His heart yearned for her endless pain, and he held out his hands. "But Morgan, lovely Morgan, does that not tell you how green and foolish Arthur was?"

Her teeth on his fingers cut through to the bone. "The more fool he! Such fools deserve to die."

Fear and anger ambushed him unaware. "Lady, it was another time, another life! All the world knows he wronged you now. But who cares if you make him pay?" Almost sardonically he ticked off the words on his bleeding fingers, scattering his life's liquor as he went. "Attend, Great Ones, to Arthur Pendragon's crimes, and see the punishment Queen Morgan exacts." Then he changed his tone. "Morgan, my Morgan, *it is time to give up your revenge!*"

"*NEVER!*"

He felt her mount him, tearing at his flanks, but he did not care. He raised his voice and sent it booming round the stars. "So now you will set Mordred against him, and make Gawain mad. You will break the Round Table and send all its knights to the everlasting dark. You will pull down the heavens on Caerleon and bury Camelot in the bowels of the earth. And this will show the world how wronged you were? You will be hated, Morgan, hated. Give up your revenge!"

"*Hetriedtokillmyssonnnnnnnnnnnn—*"

Screeching and spitting she laid into him.

"But he loves Mordred now!" Merlin cried wildly. "Mordred will inherit Arthur's throne. Guenevere's too, there is no other heir. Only wait, Morgan, and it will all come to him!"

"Merlin, you are the greatest fool of them all." Her voice was deadly now. "It is not enough that Mordred wins the throne. Arthur and all the rest must suffer as I did!"

"If you bring Arthur down, your suffering will never end. You and he are one, flesh of one flesh. When you end Arthur's life, you must die too!"

"*No!*"

Her scream split the great spaces of the astral plane. The clouds fled, and the stars in their tracks bucked and heaved. Groaning, he felt her open his flesh with her fangs. In a mist of blood and pain it came to him. *She will tear me to pieces and scatter me through the dark. Well then, peace at last, freedom from the eternal wheel.*

ArthurArthurArthur was his only thought now. For Arthur's sake he had to accept what was coming; there was no turning back. Suddenly he knew he must not lose her, even though it meant the ending of the world.

"Morgan!" he screeched.

No sound but the roaring of the skies.

"Come to me!" he implored.

And suddenly he wished she could be sweet and soft against him as she sometimes was, her flesh plump and forgiving, no longer bony and harsh. Sobbing, he reached out for her, and with a practiced touch drew her down to his side. In the silken gloom, light hands fluttered over his body, dainty kisses brushed his eyes, his flanks, his sex. Then he knew that she had heard his mind, reading his every thought as she always had. Gods, how he loved this woman! How many ages had she been his pride, his bane?

"It is determined then?" he asked hollowly. "You mean to draw them to a battle on the Great Plain?"

"*Yessssss!*" she purred, biting at his ear.

"You could still turn back the tide."

The spirit froze. "Why should you care?" She laughed scornfully. "You'll be safe enough here in your crystal cave."

Merlin paused. His love for this dark-souled creature made his own soul ache. *Great Ones and Lords of Light,* he prayed humbly, *speed my thoughts like arrows and let my words fall like sun and rain—*

"Beloved Morgan," he said softly, "safety comes from love. You love Arthur, and he is your flesh. He is your brother, your lover, your chosen one, and the father of your son."

Her screaming and wailing was splitting the astral plane. "He killed our love! He abandoned me to his hate!"

Merlin made one last desperate throw. "But you love him!"

She was raving now, spinning out of control. *"And I hate him more!"* Spitting sulfur, spraying like a polecat, she drew herself into a frozen, shuddering ball. "Arthur will die. They will all die. I, Morgan Le Fay, have written it in the stars!"

"THE KING HAS embarked, you say?"

Mordred paced excitedly away, then composed himself: a king does not pace.

He turned. Before him stood the fastest of his gallopers, the knight he had trusted to bring him this very word. "They sailed on the morning tide." The knight grinned. "He'll be halfway to France by now."

Smile, Mordred, came the voice in his head. He smiled. "A fair wind, was it?"

"Blowing a gale."

Praise the Gods! Mordred wanted to leap up and punch the air. Arthur gone! And Gawain too. And before they came back—

If they came back—

He leaned forward and clapped the mailed shoulder with a kingly hand. "I shall remember this."

The knight bowed. "Sir, I am yours to command." His eyes were full of meaning as he withdrew.

Mordred stood still. *Sire?* Did he say "Sir" or "Sire"? His heart surged. "Sire" it must be, yes! He saw me as King, as the King I was born to be! He and thousands of others will turn their faces to me. He laughed aloud. Arthur's star is fading into the west. I am the rising sun.

Alone now, he paced at will, roaming through the King's apartments, in an ecstasy of glee. Arthur gone with Gawain to make war on Lancelot meant that all those who stood in his way were pitched against one another in a rage to destroy—could anything be more fitting, more fine? Mordred crowed with delight. And what an inspiration it had been to take Arthur's scabbard when the King had placed him in the inner chamber to overhear Guenevere! It had been no more than the work of a moment to step over to the chest where he knew it was concealed and slip it inside the heavier scabbard he wore. He had walked out with the precious thing swinging innocently at his side, right under the noses of Arthur and Guenevere. Now when Arthur went to arm himself for battle against Lancelot, he would know at once that his sheath of power was gone. And whichever way the battle between them went, Mordred could not lose! Truly his Gods were fighting for him now.

"Great Ones, thanks!" he cried. The way ahead lay clear and shining in his mind. Lancelot would defeat Arthur and Gawain. Then Lancelot would take Guenevere to Little Britain and he would be King at last.

"King Mordred!" he exulted, raising his arms in the air. His whole body shook with the passion he had nurtured all his life.

The air shivered and turned cold.

Be careful, said the voice in his head.

Mordred threw back his head. "Why?" he cried fretfully. "I have it all now! I am King, I have the kingdom—and Guenevere too, if I want!"

Guenevere? For a moment he checked himself in fear. Why should he think of her? And in that way?

And suddenly, without warning the demon was back in his mind. Take her, Mordred, the hissing voice began. You are King now, she is Queen, she's yours.

Take her? Mordred started violently. It was all he could do not to cry out. But she's——! he protested silently.

A burst of bitter laughter rang round his head. But she's married, you mean? That did not stop Uther Pendragon from taking Queen Igraine. He killed her husband and gave her children away. Women like Igraine and Guenevere only come once.

Mordred clutched his head. But there was no silencing the unseen voice. She's your father's wife, is that what you fear? Oh, my son, in all the old faiths as far back as the land of Egypt, men and women of one flesh ruled together for the good of the land. Couples like these shared the finest love.

The finest love—

Mordred flushed. Yes, love with Guenevere would be fine indeed—

The air shifted and the voice began again on another tack. To the victor the spoils; she's yours if you succeed. But you've not won yet, my son. Be bold and swift but, above all, be careful, take heed!

"Yes, yes!" Mordred cried aloud.

There was a knock on the door, and Mordred's chief knight came in.

"Welcome, Vullian!" Mordred cried in unnatural tones.

Vullian's face changed, and he looked around. "Are you alone, my lord?"

"Of course, of course." Mordred waved a dismissive hand. "What news?"

Vullian came forward. His pale face wore its habitual bitter gleam, the look that had never left him since Ozark died. Vullian would never forgive himself, Mordred knew, for missing the ambush in the Queen's chamber when his friend and fellow knight had fallen beneath Lancelot's sword. Revenge had become the one thought of his life. For now, at least, Lancelot was out of range. But Mordred had found him more than ready to keep watch on Guenevere.

"The Queen keeps to her chamber, my lord, and will not stir," Vullian reported. "But you may be sure she's not asleep in there."

Mordred felt a strange crackle of delight. "You think she's plotting, then?"

"Who knows what women do? She'll be plotting or planning something, that's for sure." Vullian leaned forward earnestly. "You can't trust her, sir. She still thinks she's Queen. But you're the King here now. You'll have to teach her that."

Morded gave a long, slow, luxurious smile. "Show her who's master? Let her feel the spur?"

Vullian made a gesture of crude brutality. "Like a bad mare."

In shared silence both men pictured it, drawing out the process in their minds. Mordred was the first to collect himself. "We must be careful," he said.

"Why, sir?"

"She's still a force to be reckoned with. The people love her. We'd be fools not to treat her with respect."

Vullian gave a hostile grin. "One of these days she'll get the respect she deserves."

Mordred paused. "Tonight I hold my first audience in Arthur's place. Suppose I invite the Queen to sit with me—"

"What could be more gracious, lord?" Vullian's wolfish smile gave him all the support he craved.

"And afterward to a private dinner to—discuss the state of the realm?"

"Discuss the state of the realm?" Vullian repeated, savoring the phrase. He grinned. "How could she refuse?"

"See to it, then." Mordred swung away, overtaken by a feeling he could not name. "Get the Queen here tonight!"

CHAPTER 56

"**W**hat does he want, Ina?"

Standing behind Guenevere, Ina studied her mistress carefully in the mirror as she adjusted her headdress and put the final touches to her hair. "Perhaps he only means to show respect."

Guenevere gave a watery smile. Ina tried, the Gods knew how she tried, but they had to do better than that. "Well," she said, "we shall soon find out."

Carefully she scrutinized her image in the glass. *What does Mordred want?* was reflected in her hollow, wary gaze. *Why has he asked me to attend the audience tonight? And to feast with him afterward? Goddess, Mother, sharpen my wits, keep me on my guard!*

"Make me fine, but forbidding," she had told Ina earlier. "Whatever Mordred wants, I must resist." Now her purple-black gown and severe headdress said, *Mordred, you'll get nothing from me.* She wore no jewels, and no colors warmed her cold, unhappy face: she had no need to allure. *I look like a widow,* floated across her mind.

A plain veil binding up her hair was the final touch. She nodded. "That will do."

Ina's hands hovered over the pots on the dressing table. "Lady, you're too pale."

Guenevere shook her head. "Ina, I'm feasting with my enemy." *And my husband no longer loves me, and my lover is a world away. I shall never be lovely again.* She straightened her back. "I must go."

The pale image in the mirror nodded back. Nothing must keep her from the Audience Chamber at the destined hour.

"Her Majesty the Queen!"

"Make way for the Queen!"

The guards in the antechamber greeted her as they always did. But through the great bronze double doors, the world had changed. The Audience Chamber was seething with faces she hardly knew. And high above them all, in pride of place on the dais where she and Arthur used to sit, Mordred sat ensconced on Arthur's throne.

Mordred—

He tried to kill me. And now he takes Arthur's throne!

Black curses filled her brain. *Mordred, may the Dark Ones take you to themselves, may the*—

"This way, Majesty."

The hard-faced Sir Vullian was instantly at her side, seizing her arm to lead her to the dais. As they moved through the crowded chamber, never had she entered to more fulsome acclaim.

"Queen Guenevere—"

"Your Majesty!"

Bowing and groveling greeted her on all sides. Forced forward through a sea of sycophants, her head spun. *Who are all these people? Where are all our faithful knights and former friends?*

Immediately the answer came. *Many died in the quest for the Grail and the siege of Joyous Garde. The rest are with Arthur, over the sea in France. Now Mordred is King, he must have a court. Arthur left him the keys to the kingdom, and there are many souls for hire.*

"My lady Guenevere—"

Mordred reached down from the dais to help her up to the throne. He was magnificently clad in Pendragon red and royal blue, but his fingers were as cold as iron, and it came to her: *Is he afraid?* She almost laughed. *Come, Mordred, surely you have no fear of me?*

"My lords and ladies—" boomed the Chamberlain.

The audience was beginning. Bowing and scraping, the first of the new courtiers approached the throne. Guenevere sat at Mordred's side, watching in disbelief as the hours dragged on. To her surprise, she even felt a twinge of compassion for the dismal show. *Toads and creeping things, Mordred—not much of a court.*

At last the final obsequious bow and servile, hopeful smile had gone. Only Mordred and his knights remained.

Mordred turned to Guenevere with a charming smile "Now, madam, I am yours to command."

Do you think I am so cheaply bought? Coldly she gave him her hand. "You asked me to dine with you, to discuss matters of state."

Bowing, he led her from the dais and out of the room. "This way, madam."

Now her senses were suddenly alert. *Why this small dining chamber, when we have so many bigger rooms? Why the low light, instead of the glittering bank of candles that should greet a Queen?*

But as they entered, a consort of minstrels struck up, and a dozen of Mordred's knights were standing round the walls. Suddenly her fears seemed ridiculous, even gross. *What, did you think Mordred had designs on you?*

In the center of the room stood a table set for two, laden with dainties to tempt a lady's appetite. In place of the brawn and beef, the greasy pork and dripping lamb of feasts at court, Mordred had commanded tiny gleaming dishes of quail and whitebait, fruit and berries and cheese. Silver goblets stood beside golden plates, and a lamp of rock crystal shone beside her place.

You're a clever man, Mordred. You know how to treat a Queen.

Mordred saw her smile and pounced. "This pleases you, lady?"

Her face froze. "As you say."

She busied herself with taking her place at the table, deliberately ignoring him as she arranged her gown, her sleeves, her veil. Mordred watched covertly as she settled herself, noting the graceful flutter of her hands, the poise of her head. Even sorrow became her, he marveled, in the poignant shadows round her mouth, and the indefinable air of something lost. But above all he felt her distance, her conscious defense. Vullian was right, he swore furiously to himself, she is plotting something—

An attendant was at his elbow, plying him with wine. Smile, Mordred, he told himself. After all, what could Guenevere do? He lifted his goblet to his lips and looked around, taking comfort from what he saw. The fire was roaring up the chimney, the minstrels were singing like a wilderness of birds, his knights looked fine and handsome along the walls, and the food was fit for a king.

King Mordred, said the voice inside his head.

Yes! he cried, exulting silently. He took a heartfelt swallow of his wine. King Mordred, dining with Queen Guenevere! Again he found himself watching her closely, absorbing her every move. Why had he never noticed before the beauty of her small, birdlike movements, the depths of her twilight eyes?

"More wine, my lord?"

Nodding, he thrust forward his goblet. They were good fellows, these, no need to tell them to take care of the Queen. Appreciatively he took in her white neck, her full bosom and shapely waist. His soul expanded. What a woman she was!

As most of them were not. For no reason, the last woman he had bedded came into his mind, and the full-blooded wine turned sour and cold in his mouth. Trembling, he fought down the memory of the woman's grinning face, her fat, white, all-enfolding flesh, and fixed his gaze on Guenevere. Why had he lowered himself to another's loose embrace when he could have lain in arms like these?

He reached for his wine again and gulped it down, swilling the blood-red liquor round his mouth. Furiously he chased away the vision of splayed legs and bare breasts, a parade of sweating bodies and long-forgotten names. Against Guenevere, all these paramours had been like water to red wine. No wonder Lancelot loved her, and Arthur thought of her as forever his. Well, a woman like Guenevere must be missing Lancelot now—

Speculatively he eyed her over the top of his goblet, taking in her creamy skin, her full body, her flowing hair, and his resolution stirred. She was his, yes, he had known it all along. Tonight he would stake his claim and make it good. Laughing to himself, he began to shape the scene in his mind. Yes, Guenevere, yes. His flesh thickened and began to throb.

Glancing up, Guenevere caught Mordred's gaze fixed on her, and there was no mistaking the look in his eye. Her stomach heaved. With a huge effort of will she took control of herself and the conversation. "So, Prince, you and I are in charge of the kingdom till Arthur returns. You wanted to talk to me about affairs of state?"

Mordred laughed, refusing to relinquish his dream. Already he could feel his fingers luxuriously tracing her white neck, see her heavy breasts released from the confines of her gown, her hips in his hands, her body beneath his—

He raised a hand, and the music stopped. The minstrels took up their instruments and disappeared. One by one, the servants faded away behind the scenes, and the last of the knights slipped quietly through the door. They were alone. Guenevere braced herself. The small chamber seemed like a prison now.

Mordred leaned forward smiling, and Guenevere met his gaze. *Goddess, Mother,* she prayed, *let me keep my wits about me, be with me now!*

"It's getting late," she said, keeping her voice as natural as she could. "And it's been a tiring day." Leaning back in her chair, she passed a hand across her eyes. "I think we'll do better to meet another time." She pushed back her chair and unhurriedly rose to her feet. "I shall bid you good night then, Prince."

Still clutching his wine, Mordred struggled up too. But he made no move to escort her to the door. "Before you go, lady," he said invitingly, "think what ruling with me will mean."

She forced a careless laugh. "I rule with Arthur, Mordred. You are only the King's regent till he returns."

He fixed his eyes on her. "If he returns——"

"What d'you mean?"

Mordred shrugged. "He's making war on the best fighter in the world. And even if he returns, will he be fit to rule?"

Oh, that would suit you, Mordred. She lifted her chin. "Arthur is King, Mordred, whatever you think."

Mordred tried to sound concerned. "My father is failing, madam, you must have seen that. He's feeding on dreams, suspicions, fantasies. It will harm us all to have an aged king." He gave a modest smile. "Many people tell me that they'd welcome a new ruler—a younger man."

Guenevere held back her rage. "That's for the King to decide!"

"Or the Queen."

"What?"

He came toward her, speaking with a peculiar intensity. "You are the Queen, and the living spirit of the land, its sovereignty, its soul. You owe it to your people to be partnered with a younger man." He was nearer to her now, and she could smell his scent. "And more, lady—you owe it to yourself."

Her stomach lurched. "Mordred, beware——"

Emboldened, he stepped in her path. "The Goddess Herself takes a new lover every year, at the feast of Beltain. You are the Queen and Goddess of this land. Use your power! Take a new consort, a younger man—take me!"

It was out in the open; there was no avoiding it now. Guenevere reached for the last shreds of her authority. "Mordred, I beg you, think again. I am your father's wife——"

"—but no kin to me!" he laughed triumphantly.

"—old enough to be your mother——"

"Lady, nothing surpasses the bed fellowship of an older woman and a younger man." He grinned lasciviously. "And you are the Throne Woman, the sovereign lady beyond compare."

Fury came to her aid. "But the Throne Woman chooses her own lovers!"

She tried to move away, but his hand shot out and gripped her wrist. His voice was urgent, seething, and very low. "And you will choose me! I'll do for you what Arthur never could, I'll drive these stinking Christians from the land! My knights will sweep through their cloisters and put their monks and nuns squealing to the sword. The Goddess will be supreme again and we'll revive the old rites and make fruitful the earth." He took a greedy gulp of his wine and raised his glass. "Come, lady, what d'you say?"

She was choking with anger and terror. "Mordred, I shall never love you, you will always be my enemy. *You are Morgan's son!* She stole my husband and took my child from me! You are her revenge!" She cast around madly, half crazed with fear. "She's probably here now, rejoicing in all this! Are you there, Morgan? Morgan, are you there?"

A wild laugh burst from her throat and died.

She's laughing at me—

Black fury flooded Mordred's brain, and a howl of protest began inside his head. Shaking from head to foot, he threw the contents of his goblet over Guenevere, splashing her white neck and veil with spots like blood, while the wine ran down her bodice and stained her lap.

"Laugh at me, and it will be your last sound on earth!" he heard himself hissing in a voice not his own. He sent the goblet crashing against the wall. "I rule here now. Arthur is dead, d'you hear? And willy-nilly, you will marry me!"

CHAPTER 57

rthur dead?

He's lying, it can't be true!

But how can I know?

Think, Guenevere, think! she berated herself. Aloud she cried, "Arthur dead?"

Mordred waved a lordly hand. "My men are everywhere," he said with a grandiose air. He cocked his head on one side with a strange smile. "A little bird told me that I am King these days."

Then it came to her like the chiming of a bell: *Poor soul, he's mad.* So she knew she must not argue or question what he said, but smile and agree.

"You honor me, Prince, to speak of marriage now," she said as easily as she could. "And I take back anything I said that gave offense." Pointing to her gown, she mimed a rueful air. "I beg your leave to change. We can talk tomorrow when I am more fittingly clad."

In an instant Mordred was himself again. "Till tomorrow then." Tossing back his blue-black hair, he gave her a winning smile. Her resistance and harsh words only moments before had been forgotten.

She smiled back, with a hint of seduction playing on her lips. "I hope we shall dine alone again tomorrow night. We have much to"—she gave a breathy pause—"to discuss." She dropped her eyes. "But for now, I must rest."

She's mine! Mordred crowed to himself. Triumphantly he extended his hand. "Allow me, lady." With a bow he escorted her to the door. "See the Queen to her quarters," he ordered the knights outside. "And guard her well. She is the precious sovereign of this land."

"We shall, sir."

Vullian! Guenevere recognized the knight's knowing leer. When would she escape the scrutiny of these men?

Back in her chamber she unburdened her soul to Ina, weeping with rage and pacing the floor as they talked.

"He said the King was *dead?*" Ina stammered. "It's not true?"

Guenevere shook her head. "Mordred wants it to be, that's all. And if people believe it, he'll be King in Arthur's stead."

Ina's eyes were haunted with fear. "Then he'll need you, lady, as his Queen, to make good his claim."

"Yes. We must get to Camelot....Camelot," she repeated like a prayer, "that's the only place now."

But she knew it would be hours before they could leave. To take flight under cover of darkness, when Vullian and his knights were on guard, would be to run the risk of being brought back in chains. Yet to stay would only allow Mordred to increase his hold. And if he spread the rumor that Arthur was dead—

THINK, GUENEVERE, THINK! Through the long sleepless night, she hammered out what they must do.

At last her aching eyes spied the first signs of dawn. Thin clouds like prison bars darkened the breaking day, but the time had come. Gritting her teeth, she summoned Vullian, treating him like her own trusted knight. "Sir Vullian, may I entreat you to take my morning greetings to my lord, Prince Mordred, and tell him I shall be riding out with my maid." With a becoming hint of modesty, she dropped her gaze. "The Prince is welcome to ride with us if he desires. But above all I beg the favor of his company tonight."

Vullian gave an unpleasant leer. "Lady, I shall tell him so." *And the rest of your game,* he added to himself. Grinning, he ran his instructions through his head.

"She'll make a break for it, Vullian, or she's not Guenevere," Mordred had said with a cruel glint. "When she does, be sure to let her run. She'll head for her own kingdom, and then we can follow her and take Camelot too." Yes, the Prince was a smart one, and no mistake. Let Guenevere think she was ahead of the game. But Mordred would have her and Camelot and all. He grinned again.

Why does Vullian look like that? went through Guenevere's mind. But there was no time to dwell on misgivings now. The only hope was to be clear and strong. They would only have one chance to get away.

But would Mordred come swooping down with a troop of men? Would he not suspect she was planning to escape? At the stables Guenevere's heart was in her mouth, and Ina's mobile face was pale and set. Even outside the gates, with no one following, they dared not set out at a gallop as they were craving to do.

"Smile, Ina, act as you normally would," Guenevere instructed through gritted teeth. "They can see us from the battlements. They could still send the guards in pursuit."

But once inside the forest, they gave their horses free rein. Panting, they drew up at the first parting of the ways.

"We have a few hours, no more, till Mordred knows we've gone!" Guenevere gasped to Ina, her elation rising in spite of her fears. "Ride to the shore, find out what has happened to Arthur, and tell him he's been betrayed. Then, if you can, come to me in Camelot. But take care. Mordred will raise an army and follow us. He'll probably have the country in his grip for miles around!"

"Lady, I will," Ina cried with her Otherwordly gleam, before turning tail and flying off down the dry woodland path as if a hundred Mordreds were on her heels. Sooner or later, she knew, Ina would reach Arthur if he was still alive. Then whatever happened, Arthur would learn the truth. There was comfort in that.

But what could Arthur do? Mordred held Caerleon and had the treasury at his command. He would be sending for mercenaries even now, knowing that all Arthur's lords had sworn their allegiance to him. Once he had the country in his power, he could wrest the throne from Arthur, even have him killed.

And if Arthur won—

On she rode and on, trapped in unhappy thoughts. Swaying in the saddle, she wished she had slept even a little the night before. Hour followed hour, till at last the dusk came down and night fell in a shower of glittering stars. She thought she saw a great star plunging down the sky, but her eyes dazzled and she could not be sure. By the time the white towers of Camelot came into sight, she was almost too tired to see. Clinging to the horse's mane, she rode over the causeway and up to the postern gate.

"Open up!" she cried hoarsely. "A weary traveler craves your assistance here."

From inside the gatehouse a rough voice cursed and spat. "Be off with you! This is Camelot. We take no late travelers or benighted beggars here."

She burst out laughing. "Why, soldier, don't you know your Queen?"

❖　◆

BUT EVEN THEN she could not get to her bed to sleep. When the wretched gatekeeper had been forgiven and the guard called up, she still had to order the whole castle made ready for siege or war.

"Who knows how soon Mordred may be here?" she demanded of her Council as the bleary-eyed lords stumbled, blinking, out of their beds. "He's ruling for Arthur, and he thinks he is the King. He can raise or hire the biggest army he likes."

The oldest of her knights smiled sagely. "True, madam, but he can never buy what we have here."

She paused. "What's that?"

"Men who will die for you and the Mother-right."

She pressed his wrinkled hand, ambushed by sudden tears. "Thank you, sir." *And with knights like this, tell me, how can we fail?*

As she fell into bed she could hear the trysting horn ringing round the valley and knew that it was sounding far and wide. An hour or two later she woke to the rumble of cart wheels as the first of the loaded wagons rolled in to provision the palace for a siege. Water, at least, was never short in a land blessed with underground lakes. As she followed the Captain of the Guard on his round of inspection of the castle's ancient wells and subterranean springs, a random thought came into her mind: *All waters lead to Avalon in the end.*

The thought was as sharp as a pain. Had Avalon gone from the Island in the Lake? Was it already somewhere else by now—perhaps even where Arthur was, far across the sea? That was what the Lady had promised him, years ago. *At the last crossing of the water, I shall see you there.*

"Madam, you're looking pale." The Captain was at her elbow, his honest face frowning with distress. "Let me bring you back up to the fresh air."

In the Queen's apartments, she gave thanks for the white-walled calm and peace. "No callers, no messengers," she told the attendants, "for an hour at least." Mordred would soon be here, she was certain of that. And she had to be rested for the battle ahead.

Wearily she let the chamber women bathe her forehead and help her into a loose chamber gown before shooing them away. "Call me in an hour," she said with a tired smile.

But no sooner had they trooped bobbing and blushing through the door than the leader was flying back in again. Guenevere saw the woman's startled face and caught her breath. But nothing could have prepared her for what she heard.

"It's the King," the attendant gasped, "the King!"

Gods above, Mordred had been quicker than she thought! *The King?* Don't dare to call Mordred that! Gods above, you all know he's our enemy now." She cast madly round the apartment for her mother's sword. "Call the men to arms!" Furiously she checked the sudden onrush of tears. "There's only one King of the Summer Country, and he's far away."

"Not so, Guenevere," came a somber voice from the anteroom.

What——?

She flew to the doorway, blinking back her tears. The first face she saw was Ina's, full of love and relief. Beside Ina were Lucan, Kay, and Bedivere. And in the center of the chamber, tall and terrible, stood Arthur, looming like avenging fate.

"*Arthur!*"

"Lady, lady——" Crooning words of comfort, Ina flew forward and helped her to a chair.

Guenevere passed a bewildered hand over her eyes. "Arthur," she said wonderingly. "I thought you were in France."

"Ah, Guenevere——"

Arthur stepped forward with a heavy sigh. "We've just disembarked; we're camped on the edge of the Great Plain. I can't stay long. I have to get back to Gawain." For the first time she noticed the grave concern on his face and saw that the three companion knights all shared the same stricken look. "Gawain's worse—much worse. When we set sail, he told us he was well enough to go. But his wound—the motion of the ship—we had to turn back."

Tears sprang into his eyes. Guenevere found herself moving forward to take his hand. "I'm so sorry, Arthur."

He nodded and cleared his throat. "Well, we have a doctor for him now. We've left him in his tent, with the best of care. He's safe enough there, at least till we get back." His face darkened, and a new, unfathomable grief appeared in his eyes. "Unlike Mordred, if all I hear is true." He gave a savage grin. "You know what Mordred has also done to me?"

Guenevere's stomach contracted. "No, Arthur, I have no idea."

"He's taken the scabbard you gave me. He must have stolen it when he was in my chamber that time." He threw back his head and howled. "Mordred! My son, my only son!"

Guenevere could hardly bear to witness such pain. And she knew she could not tell him, *He said you were dead and tried to marry me.*

"Speak to him, Arthur," she said steadily. "At least try to parley before you go to war. He'll be coming with his army to take Camelot. He will soon be here."

THE ORANGE EYE of sunset, the treeless hills, the miles of gray stone, and above it all, the gannet's wailing cry—yes, it was good to be home. Gawain's eyes drifted across the long-loved landscape of his boyhood, and he knew that he was blessed. Gods and Great Ones, he prayed humbly, how favored we were to call the Orkneys our own. And now as the sun sets, what better place of rest for the warrior, the seafarer, the hunter home from the hill?

Except that he had not yet reached home. The glimmering landscape faded, and he saw in the corner of the tent the Druid whose task it was to keep him here on earth. Every time his spirit made ready to depart, the healer had some potion, some powerful remedy. Gawain laughed, despite the killing pain in his head. By the look of him, this Druid had been a doughty warrior before he turned to the life of prophet and bard. He would fight for Gawain's life with all the vigor that the invalid lacked to save himself.

Strange, Gawain mused, how ready he was to die. But Arthur and the Druid were determined that he should live. So were Lucan and Bedivere, and strange again, even Kay. For the little, limping knight was not jealous, as Gawain had always thought, that he claimed to be Arthur's first companion and had sworn to be the last. Well, he'd been wrong about that too. It would fall to one of the others to hold Arthur as his life ebbed away, and close his wounded eyes.

And here they were now, entering the tent. How long had they been away? Owlishly Gawain watched the faces of Lucan, Kay, and Bedivere as they swam into his ken. Why did they all look sorrowful? Everything was well enough now that they were here.

"How is he, Doctor?" he thought he heard someone say. But that didn't matter now. He had to speak to Arthur before he went home. And it had to be soon, as he did not have much longer now.

He rallied his strength and felt the blood surging through his veins. "My lord," he said clearly.

The next moment Arthur was kneeling by his bed. "I can hear you," he said urgently. "Speak."

Gawain opened his eyes upon a world of blood. "My brother Agravain worked with Prince Mordred to take the life of the Queen, and died himself. Then Gaheris and Gareth were killed, so I turned against Lancelot. This blood-feud has cost me my life, and all the Orkneys will go down to the Otherworld." He felt for Arthur's hand and found it already gripping his own. "Enough bloodshed, sire. Make peace with your son, I beg."

The sound of grief mingled with rage came to Gawain's ears. "I have no son!"

"And with Sir Lancelot," Gawain went on.

"Never!"

"My lord—"

"Sire—"

Above Arthur's tears, Gawain could hear Lucan protesting and Bedivere's low murmur of distress. Slowly he shook his great head. "Make peace," he said clearly, "make peace!"

Now the waves were louder on that eternal shore. The clouds parted, and the sun brightened in the west. He saw Gaheris coming toward him with the wind in his bright hair, and Gareth smiling his unfading smile. Behind them came Agravain as he used to be, and now here, suddenly, her arms warm and enfolding him, his mother, Morgause—

His blinded eyes saw the light of the world where the sun never set. The pale blond air he loved brushed his skin, and the sea cried and called his spirit to come. Sighing deeply, he prepared his soul for the last great leap.

"Peace," he said clearly, and died.

Joyfully, like a bird, he took wing for the astral plane. The stars leaped up to greet him and his spirit sang. Roaming the skies and riding on the winds, he did not look behind. Freed at last from his earthly shell and soaring to the islands of the west, he was not to know that his final prayer had fallen on deaf ears. In his pavilion in the war camp with his army on full alert, Arthur was lying prostrate on Gawain's corpse, weeping, cursing, vowing vengeance, and swearing to smooth his soul's path to Avalon with Mordred's blood.

CHAPTER 58

"See for yourselves, my lords." Leaning back in his chair, Mordred tossed the heavy scroll down onto the table with a careless hand. "The war challenge from the King!"

The air inside the pavilion was thick with apprehension and something worse. Twenty pairs of eyes around the narrow board fastened on the flaring red dragon with the black lettering marching away underneath, "I, Arthur, son of Uther of the House of Pendragon, Lord of the Middle Kingdom and her City of Legions, High King of Britain and Dragon King of these isles—"

Not a soul stirred. Even the attendant beside the brazier warming the pot of mulled wine stood as if made of stone. At last Vullian broke the silence from his place at Mordred's side. "When does he call us forth to battle, lord?"

"Tomorrow at dawn."

Still no one moved. The torches in their rough sconces guttered over a dozen or so faces made sallow by fear, while others showed naked calculation or the crude delight of war. What a low, foxy, ferrety bunch they are, thought Mordred, raging with disgust. Yet these had been the best that money could buy!

Darkness and devils! His fingers flew to his temples to silence the storm in his head. When Guenevere had fled, he had laughed to hear the news. Pursuing her had amused him, and storming Camelot was a war game he was glad to play. Guenevere was his, there was no doubt of that, and her resistance only added zest to the conquest that had to come. But what evil of the Old Ones had brought Arthur back from France?

He raised a shaking hand. "More wine!"

Swiftly the attendant scurried round the tent, replenishing the wooden goblets one by one. Mordred downed the contents of his beaker in one draught, and rapped it loudly on the table for more.

"Come, lords," he said with sinister emphasis, "the King's army lies waiting for us across the plain. I did not buy your silence. Let me hear your thoughts."

Halfway down the table, a hard-eyed man leaned forward, raising a scarred finger to emphasize his words. "Sir, it's true that the King has a mighty force. And he got here before us, so he has the better ground. But our men have not had to make a forced march from the coast. So our army is fresher, and we outnumber them too."

His neighbor nodded, warming to the theme. "It's true the King has the high ground with the hills at his back. But we're well deployed across the heart of the plain. With the forest behind us, we can hold our ground."

Mordred frowned. "Arthur's men are loyal. Ours fight for hire."

"I think you'll find the Saxons are worth their gold," Vullian put in with an admiring grin. "They're the finest mercenaries in the land. How long have they been raiding our coast, after all?" *And how long have you had them in readiness for this, my lord?* he was longing to know, but did not dare ask.

There was a judicious cough from Mordred's left. "Sir—if the King will parley—and if he agrees to your just demands—"

Mordred covered an angry sneer. This man would do anything to avoid a fight, he knew. Yet even a coward and a timeserver could be useful too. "Yes?" he prompted, glancing around.

Vullian nodded. "Sir, you have asked no more than is rightfully yours— the rule of the kingdom now that the King is growing old. And if the King yields—"

Mordred summoned up a confident smile. "He must." He heard his own words and paused. Did he believe this? He did not know.

"As you say, sir." The toady hastened to pick up the cue. "Surely the King will not risk the lives of his beloved subjects to kill his only son?"

"No." Mordred released a hissing breath. "But say—"

But say that you venture everything now to kill him! the spirit sang inside his head. And now she was no longer in his mind but outside it, shimmering round the edges of the tent, dancing in and out of the candles' flame, and hovering in the hollows where the night wind flapped the canvas and rattled the poles. That was all he could see, but he knew she was there.

"No!" The low moan fell out of his mouth before he could check himself. He started, and threw a hasty glance around the tent. From the faces around him, he had not betrayed himself. But if she was here—Gods above, in here!—he had to draw the war council to an end before he did.

"Tomorrow before dawn, we shall meet, my lords," he announced, surging to his feet. "We'll agree on a parley and decide the battle positions for yourselves and your troops. Till then, good night."

"Good night, my lord."

He could tell that most of them were as eager to go as he was to see them leave. Only Vullian wanted to remain, hovering at the entrance to the tent with a question in his eyes. But Vullian had seen too much, and guessed a lot more. He may have sensed how the spirit haunted his master night and day. Mordred sighed. There could be no better reason to get rid of him now.

Firmly Mordred swept his close crony toward the doorway and waved him through the hangings, into the night outside.

"Attend me before the others in the morning, Vullian," he ordered, turning away.

"Good night, sir." With a bow, the knight disappeared into the darkness of the forest of tightly packed tents.

"Good night."

Mordred paused, one hand on the pole at the entrance, to steady himself before going inside. Then he strode boldly back in, dropping the hanging to close up the doorway and dismissing the attendant to face the spirit alone.

But the demon had gone. The pavilion lay as silent as a tomb. Trembling with relief, Mordred hurried into the inner chamber of the tent and fell to his knees, burrowing into the camp bed. Groping under the straw of the mattress, his hand encountered something cold and hard. Gods and Great Ones, thanks! No need to draw it forth, he knew what it was.

All the breath left his body in a heartfelt sigh. Kneeling beside the bed, he laid down his head, fighting the impulse to weep. But a moment later he was on his feet again. What weakness was this? Did he think anyone could have stolen the precious scabbard from under his very nose? Taken it from a royal pavilion, surrounded by armed men?

He returned to the main chamber and crossed to warm himself at the brazier, struggling to keep the chill of the night at bay. "You're a fool, Mordred!" he told himself furiously, reaching for the wine. "A weakling and a fool. The scabbard's safe, and you have nothing to fear. Wear it tomorrow, and nothing can touch your life!"

✦   ✦

FROM HERE, ALL the world was spread out before her like a dream. When she had been too young to leave the castle, her nurse would bring her up to these ancient battlements to take the air, and it was still one of the places she loved best. In those days she had thought the sturdy manors and little wattled farms lying so far below were not real, but toys for her delight. Even now she could still have named every whitewashed cottage, every hovel, every cattle pen scattered about the patchwork of forests, fields, and hills rolling out from the foot of the castle as far as the eye could see.

But not on a night as dark as the inside of a tomb, when the dead of the year had curdled the wintry air. All round her, a freezing mist clung to the old stones, and clammy wisps of fog curled round the flagpoles, where Camelot's bright banners drooped on their gilded staves. Guenevere shivered, and huddled deeper inside her wrap.

Tomorrow at dawn the place would be alive with soldiers of the garrison, armed and ready to repel Mordred if he came on. But for now she was alone, but for the lookouts in the watchtowers—halfway between earth and sky. In the distance she could see the fires of the two armies camped on the Great Plain. A hundred pinpoints of rosy light bloomed on either side, with a great river of darkness in between. Tomorrow the armies would close that gap with blood, unless Arthur would parley and Mordred would concede.

If—

She shuddered. Never had she seen Arthur more implacable. He would not parley now that Gawain was dead. And with Camelot's forces added to his own, he was set on driving Mordred from the face of the earth.

"I'll hunt the bastard down and drain his blood!" he ground out, his eyes glittering. "That'll be for Gawain. Then I'll go back to France and kill Lancelot too!"

Kill—kill—kill—

Her head was splitting. *Peace, Mother,* she prayed, *grant us peace, not death.* Below her she could hear the castle seething with preparations for war. To be alone up here, like a bird on its crag, was the last chance she had to be quiet in a place that was pure and clean.

She strained her eyes through the black and bitter air. If only she could part the darkness like a curtain and see what lay ahead. *Tomorrow will be the ending of our world, I know. Goddess, Great One, let me know what is coming, draw aside the veil.* But the darkness only deepened, mocking her attempts.

And suddenly it was colder than before. The mist thickened, weaving its way round the walls, and a raven croaked faintly from the distant wood. Guenevere stood still, possessed by a black thought: *This is the end—the end— the end—*

Ahead of her the darkness shivered and took shape. Writhing through the gloom came a tall, lean form swathed from head to foot in black, with a long white face and purple mouth. Blue-black and lustrous, her angry eyes glared like an owl's bearing down on its prey; they were everything Guenevere remembered, and more.

"Morgan," she said.

The figure shuddered, coming daintily to the ground. Impatiently she put back her voluminous hood and shook her head, braving the midnight air. "Afraid, Guenevere?"

Her voice was as rusty and harsh as a nail in a door. She gave a savage laugh. "D' you think your wretched life is in danger from me? I could have killed you anytime in the last thirty years! In your countinghouse, in your chamber, seated on your throne, I was the mouse behind the wainscot, the cat rubbing round your legs." The great eyes flared. "I have walked with you, talked with you, slept with you in your bed. You are only alive now because of me."

Guenevere felt a sorrow beyond words. *Mad and bereft as ever—oh, Morgan, will it ever change?*

But she had to remember that Morgan could hear her thoughts. "After all these years," she said gently, "why are you here?" Then in the silence between them, she heard the answer grow. "Arthur?" she said.

Morgan made a sound halfway between a laugh and a howl. "Yes!" she cried. From beneath her midnight wraps she produced a long, thin shape that glimmered and shone even in the starless night.

Guenevere felt the blood rush to her head. "It's—"

"*Yes!*" Morgan cried scornfully. "What else?"

Guenevere could not speak. In a trance she moved forward and took the object from Morgan's hands. It throbbed between her palms like a living thing, and suddenly she was warm in spite of the freezing cold. Ecstatically she traced the woven silver and gold and counted the ancient jewels up and down the sheath. A handful of runic charms were emblazoned on the shaft, and it sang to itself strange tunes from long ago. *My mother's scabbard, the gift of the King of the Fair Ones to the first Queen.* How long since she had called this magical thing her own?

Morgan overheard her thought. "You gave it to Arthur on your wedding day," she said ferociously, "and he gave it to me."

Morgan, you stole it when he wronged you, but no matter for that. Guenevere was not inclined to quarrel now. "Then you gave it to Mordred," she said intently, staring into Morgan's eyes. "You wanted it for your son. But now you've taken it from him and left a substitute?"

"Yes!"

"But why? Why have you taken it away from him now?"

Morgan turned her face away. "You know why!"

For Arthur? Guenevere shook her head. "But you've hated Arthur madly all these years."

"Not anymore."

"Does that mean you've given up your revenge?"

"No!" Morgan howled. "He killed my father!"

A huge pity welled up in Guenevere's heart. "Not Arthur, Morgan—that was his father, and King Uther is long gone."

"Yes, yes, I know!" hissed Morgan feverishly. "D'you think I am a fool?" Her great eyes were very bright.

"No." Guenevere drew a breath. "But I think—" *Oh Morgan, now I know, if I never did before.* "I think you love Arthur—"

"No!"

"—more than anything in the world," Guenevere pressed on. She dared not look at the ravaged face opposite weeping its grief, the tortured purple mouth like a smashed fig. "And more than your son," she said with terrible emphasis, "if you take the scabbard from Mordred to save Arthur's life."

"Yes!" Morgan's scream bounced round the battlements and split the frozen sky. "Mordred betrayed me when he thought to marry you! I did all this so that he could rule alone."

"Pity him, Morgan—he's mad."

"Not mad!" Morgan screeched. "But not mine! As a child, he was my flesh, my son, all mine. But when I sent him to Arthur, his nature split like a rotten reed. He tried to live like me, fulfilling his desires, and yet be like Arthur, respected and admired."

She broke away and raged round the battlements like a streak of flame. "I tried to teach him!" she lamented. "I have whispered in his ear—"

"Morgan—" Guenevere wrung her hands. She wanted to tear her hair. "Look there!" She gestured toward the armies on the plain. "Tomorrow your son and his father will do battle to the death. You have brought them here. What have you decided? How will this battle end?"

"I don't know!"

A scream louder than all the rest rang round the battlements and split the frozen sky. Morgan's cartwheel eyes lit up and spun. "Oh, Guenevere, don't you see? Whatever will happen was written when the world was born. The Old Ones have already set this in the stars. And we latter creatures may not know till our world ends!"

CHAPTER 59

t was still dark when she rode down to Arthur's camp. But the night was as full of noise and light as day. Beside every flaring campfire, men were intently sharpening their swords and preparing their armor for the battle ahead. A few recognized Guenevere and greeted her as she went by. But most were too intent on what they were doing to take notice of a passing chariot with one woman on board, heavily muffled up against the cold.

Guenevere felt for the scabbard hanging at her side. All around her, she felt the onset of war. She had left Ina behind with firm orders to take charge of the castle and raise the guard at the sign of any alarm. Yet perhaps there might still be peace, now that things had changed—

In Arthur's pavilion, the candles were burning low. Their guttering light played on Lucan, Kay, and Bedivere seated round the table, with Arthur at their head. Arthur's face was pale but burning with purpose, and his eyes were bright and clear. The three companion knights wore the same look of exaltation and a sense of fate approaching, bringing resolution at last.

"Guenevere—"

Arthur rose to his feet and came forward to take her hands. Clad in a rich tunic of Pendragon red, he seemed to flame in the confined space. Gold glowed at his neck, wrists, and waist, and Excalibur hummed softly to itself at his side.

"My lord." She returned his greeting, and bowed to the knights as they stood up. "I'm sorry to disturb your council of war."

Arthur smiled at his companions with unconscious love. "We've made our plans. We were about to part."

Kay moved to the door, with Lucan and Bedivere not far behind. "Good night, sire—and my lady." They bowed and were gone.

On the brazier a pot of mulled wine stood almost untouched, its rich spicy odor filling the tent. Beside it lay a neglected plate of meat and cheese. "You should eat something, Arthur," Guenevere said, noting the lavender shadows under his eyes. "You'll need your strength."

He gave her a tender smile. "I shall do well enough today, whatever comes."

"I believe you will." She took off her cloak and unbuckled the scabbard from her side. Stepping forward, she laid it in his hands, feeling the power pulsing through the shaft. "The Great Ones themselves are fighting for you now. They have sent you this."

The warm glow from the scabbard filled the room. Arthur stood trans-fixed, his face alight with awe. "Where did it come from, Guenevere?" he whispered through pale lips. "How did you get it back?"

"Morgan brought it to me." She had resolved to tell him every word of the encounter on the battlements. "She was here tonight."

"Morgan?" His hands, his whole body shook.

"Just now."

"When?"

"An hour ago."

She could see him struggling to come to terms with it. Then he shook his head and handed the scabbard back. "You must have it, Guenevere. You'll be at the battle, you may need it yourself. And it was your mother's before Morgan took it away."

Guenevere shook her head, refusing to take it from his hands. "Arthur, I'll only be watching the battle from the nearest hill. You are the one in danger of attack. Morgan brought it back to save you, not me. And it's yours, Arthur, it always was." She moved closer and placed her hand on his fore-arm, feeling a deep, abiding love welling through her veins. "Remember our wedding, all those years ago? I gave it to you then, and now I give it to you again."

"Guenevere—" His eyes were full of tears. "You are good to me."

And bad, Arthur, came into her mind. *We have hurt each other. But there must be no more pain.*

"Morgan brought me this?" He clasped the scabbard and clutched it to his chest. "She must have wanted to save me." A laugh of disbelief cracked his baffled face. "Guenevere—can it mean that she's given up her revenge?"

"I think it must."

He threw back his head and passed a hand over his eyes. "Then it's over! God be praised, we'll be free at last!"

Hope leaped up in her heart. "Will you parley with Mordred then and avoid the war?"

There was a long, somber pause. Then he folded her to his chest. "I shall try."

In the shelter of his cloak, she was warm and safe. With her arms round the great bearlike body, she stood quite still and let the years drift away. He had held her like this when he asked her to marry him—whenever they came together to make love—when he last rode away. His broad shoulders and muscular flanks, his strong legs and confident thighs had been as familiar to her then as her own. Some of the old comfort returned with the feel of his tunic against her cheek and the warmth of his arms. "You're a good man, Arthur. You have done great things."

"But there is more ahead."

She saw his face set like marble with a new regard. "What do you mean?"

He gestured to the scabbard. "Mordred offered battle, believing that he would win. But as long as I have this, he must surely lose."

She stood back and put all her soul into her eyes. "Then he must not fight. You gave him life. You do not want to kill your only son."

"He betrayed us both, Guenevere," Arthur said somberly. "And I do not trust him now. But I shall offer parley, I'll send Kay and the others to take the message straightaway. And unless he betrays us again, I will make peace."

Goddess, Mother, thanks—

She moved forward and put her arms round his waist. "And with Morgan too?"

Arthur caught his breath. "Oh, Guenevere, d'you know what you're asking me to do?"

Guenevere took her courage in both hands. "She loves you, Arthur. She always did. The scabbard is a peace offering from her. Can you forgive her and make peace with her now?"

"Peace?" Above her head came a sigh like the last wind from Avalon. "Yes, I must. We must all hope for forgiveness in the end."

They stood for a long while without speaking, full of thoughts and tears. Then Arthur raised his great hand to her chin and turned up her face to his. "Do you remember when I wore your favor at every tournament and proclaimed my lady the fairest in the land?"

She smiled through her tears. "Of course I do."

"Then will you arm me now? Dawn will soon be here."

Bringing Mordred with it, she thought, but did not need to say. She crossed to the stand where his armor stood waiting, the gleaming silver pieces embossed with gold. "Those were golden days, Arthur," she said softly. "And the world will not forget. Together we dreamed a golden dream, and it will never die."

He stood braced as she buckled on the shining breastplate over his silver mail. "Even though we shall die when our time comes?" But he spoke without fear. Tall and remote, he seemed to have passed beyond fear to a better place.

"We must. All life ends in the rhythm of rise and fall." She found herself oddly transcended, too. "But whatever happens, we have seen the days of gold."

She buckled her mother's scabbard firmly to his sword belt at the back and felt the warmth of its protection surround him like a shield. At last he was armed from head to foot, his silver helmet with its gold coronet in the crook of his arm, and Excalibur swinging lightly by his side. They stood alone together one last time.

"Kiss me, Guenevere," he said.

And she kissed him with all her heart.

THE SUN ROSE over the horizon, streaked in angry red. Low in the sky, black clouds were threatening foul weather before nightfall. On the plain far below, two small groups of mounted men made their way slowly toward each other across the expanse of grass.

Under the banner of Pendragon, Arthur rode out at the head of his band of knights. Watching Mordred and his knights approach, with the dark mass of his army drawn up behind, Arthur knew he had been right to confine the parley to a small band of men. With two hostile forces facing each other and keyed up for battle, it would not take much for fighting to break out. Once launched, it was hard to stop a bloody conflict from running its course. And Arthur was now praying to his God for peace.

But the wise man hoped for peace, and prepared for war. Arthur did not need to look back to know that his army was ready, like Mordred's, to swing into action at his lightest word. On the ground behind him, rising toward the hills, all his troops stood waiting in battle array. If the parley failed, Mordred would attack, he knew. But a show of force should convince him that the talks should succeed.

"Have every man armed and on the field, keep nothing in reserve," he had ordered all his captains before he left. "And don't take your eye off Mordred's party when we meet. If you see swords drawn, attack at once." He laughed grimly. "It'll mean that Mordred is up to his tricks again. If that happens, my life is in your hands."

A hundred heads nodded as his loyal captains took the order and laid it to their hearts. Now Arthur rode out across the level plain secure in the knowledge that every soldier at his back was ready to obey it too. But they should not need to, he reminded himself with a great surge of relief. His hand traveled to the scabbard at his side, and his fingertips joyfully picked up its secret pulse. Now that Morgan had relented, everything had changed. Her revenge was over, thank God. Now he could surely be generous with his son.

So he and Mordred would parley and make peace. Then he would give up his pursuit of Lancelot and devote himself to Guenevere again. A smile of long-ago sweetness curved his lips. This morning had been like the old days, when they were young. How could he have forgotten how much love they had shared in Camelot in those springtimes of long ago? He would give his life to learning to love her again.

And before long, winter would give way to spring. They would ride out together, and go Maying as they used to do. They would dance again in the Great Hall at night, and even hold tournaments, though now he would have to learn to give way to younger knights. Then again, he knew he still fought with most of his old fire. His right arm had lost little of its strength, and his mighty, bearlike body was still unbowed. Arthur chuckled to himself. Yes, he would take some beating for an old man. Hoping, remembering, forgetting, Arthur rode on, allowing himself to dream.

Across the plain, Mordred and his knights watched with barely suppressed tension as Arthur approached. Mordred's hand rested on the scabbard at his side, and a deep sense of comfort ran through his veins. The familiar silver and gold had looked dull this morning when he'd strapped it on in the sullen dawn. But as soon as the battle began, it would come to life, he knew. And he alone on the battlefield would not lose blood. A smile of hungry satisfaction curved his lips. Yes, I am invincible. Death to my enemies; I shall not die.

Beside him Vullian leaned forward intently on his horse. "The King looks pleased with himself."

Mordred nodded. "Yes," he said slowly. The next instant a worm of fear bored into his brain. Why? Arthur knows something. What? Is it a trap?

Trembling, Mordred surveyed Arthur's forces drawn up behind him, ready to attack. What was there to fear? His own men were in place, straining for action, a solid wall of comfort at his back. There was no danger of an ambush, no chance of foul play. But Mordred was impelled to make doubly sure.

"Vullian," he said quietly under his breath, "ride back to the lines, and order all the captains to watch the parley like hawks. If they see any sign of a weapon, we've been betrayed. Tell them not to wait for further orders, but attack at once."

Vullian stared. "But surely the King would never stoop to that?"

Mordred jerked his head. "Do it!" he hissed.

Vullian's galloping hooves faded away behind. Hurry, Vullian, pounded through Mordred's mind, my father hates me and my life is in your hands.

But still he bowed and offered a respectful smile when Arthur, Kay, Lucan, and Bedivere drew up before him with the rest of the knights. In silence all the riders dismounted and faced one another across the scrubby grass.

Arthur's face was a mask of anger and contempt. "Mordred," he ground out. It sounded like a curse.

Mordred's head went back. "I beg you," he cried, "hear me, Father—"

Arthur howled with rage. "Traitor, I will not take that name from you!"

"I am no traitor! I claimed no more than I believed was mine."

"What, the rule of the kingdom while I was still alive?" Arthur snarled. "You insolent cub!"

Mordred fought to hold his anger down. "I only wanted to keep the country safe until you came back."

"If I came back—"

"True, Father, I did fear for your life." His large eyes filled with tears.

"Feared I might live, you mean, not that I might die!"

Mordred took a step forward and fell to his knees. "I beg you to forgive me!" he cried. "And show the world that I am your son."

Arthur gave a scornful laugh. "And how may I do that?"

"Give me my right and my due!" Mordred sprang to his feet. "Proclaim me through the islands as your heir. Then let me sit in audience with you, so that all the world may see that I am your choice."

Arthur paused. "Is that all?"

"One more thing, sire." Mordred gathered his strength. "The time has come for me to have land of my own. Give me one of your lesser kingdoms to rule as your vassal king—the Humberlands, say, or Gore, wherever you will."

"And if I do," Arthur forced out, emphasizing every word, "will you give up this war, disband your army, and make peace?"

Mordred could not restrain a triumphant gleam. "I will!"

Arthur closed his eyes. Clasping his hands, he stood for a long moment in prayer. Then he turned back with a war-weary smile. "All this you shall have and more, as long as you will reconcile yourself with me and behave like my son."

He opened his arms. Mordred stumbled forward into his embrace. As he threw his arms around his father's back, his hand encountered the scabbard at Arthur's waist. With a thrill of terror, his fingers brushed its distinctive tracery and felt its glow. He has the scabbard! overwhelmed his mind. How—? Who—? He wanted to scream, to weep.

But then came a wisp of comfort—we shall not fight! Slowly the life trickled back into Mordred's heart. Arthur has forgiven me. Perhaps he even loves me. All will yet be well. "Father!" he cried, and wept on Arthur's shoulder without restraint.

Kay exchanged heartfelt glances with Lucan and Bedivere. Thank the Gods, peace! What celebrations the two armies would keep tonight!

Weeping openly, Arthur threw his arm round Mordred's shoulder and drew him to his side. "Send for a scrivener," he called to Kay. "We shall have all this set down before we leave."

As he spoke, the struggling sun broke through the clouds. Pale rays of watery light poured down on the scene. Bedivere turned up his face to let the sunbeams dry his tears. "It's an omen," he murmured. "The Mother is smiling on us."

At the back of Mordred's followers, two young knights were keenly digesting the news.

"So our Prince has got what he wanted?" grinned one, his eyes fixed on Arthur and Mordred ahead.

The other laughed. "Mark my words, it'll be King Mordred before long!"

He punched his fellow's shoulder in boyish glee. As he moved, there was a rustling in the grass, and an adder hissed and slid away beneath his foot. Without thinking, the knight reached instantly for his sword. It was bad to disturb a snake in its winter bed. Better kill it now before it struck out again.

His sword flashed from its sheath, and the sun caught its blade. It fell on the snake, severing its spitting head. But the body went on wriggling, refusing to die. And a dreadful life began to stir in the two armies at the sides of the plain.

Distant cries and the harsh call of the war horns began to fill the plain. Arthur looked up in horror. "What's that?"

Mordred turned and saw his knight with his sword drawn. "No, man!" he screamed. "Put your sword away!"

But already he could see it was too late. From the center of the field, his army was on the march. He could see Vullian's standard with the leaders in the van, urging the soldiers on to the attack. The knight had carried out his orders all too faithfully, it was clear.

"No!" Mordred howled.

Arthur turned to him, aghast. "Mordred, have you betrayed me again? Oh, evil day!"

"Sire!" Lucan cried, frenzied with alarm. "Mount up and ride! We have to get back to our lines!"

"Oh, Mordred!" Arthur howled. "Treacherous to the last! You wanted my death. Well, sir, you shall buy it dear!"

He vaulted onto his horse and drew his sword. Excalibur howled in his hand, hungry for blood. Behind him came the war cries of a hundred thousand throats, moving forward to the beat of a thousand drums as his men too, inflamed by the sight of the sword, went onto the attack. Already those in the front ranks were hurtling downhill, furious for the fray.

"Pendragon!" Arthur cried, waving his sword round his head. "Pendragon à moi, and death to my bastard son!"

He tore his horse's head round and galloped away.

"No man calls me a bastard!" Mordred screamed. He stood in the center of the field shaking his head at Arthur's fast-retreating form. "With those words, Arthur, you doomed your own death!"

CHAPTER 60

igh on her hill, Guenevere saw it all. In one slow eternity of
time she watched Arthur folding Mordred into his arms, then
seconds later came the flashing of the sword. The peace she
prayed for had been born and died in the same breath. A hollow
roar rose up from the plain. The horror had begun.

A dim red dawn bathed all the scene in blood. The two
armies were moving inexorably toward each other across the field.
She saw men like toy soldiers, rushing toward their doom. Overhead the
rooks and ravens wheeled and cawed, startled from their roosts by the wild
battle cries from below and the sound of clashing steel. Above it all rose the
wailing of the war trumpets and the roaring of the drums.

The two heavy masses of fighting men came together in the center of
the plain. Howling their defiance, the front ranks engaged with an impact she
could feel. Her stomach turned at the unmistakable shock of sharpened
metal striking quivering flesh—how long since she had been at a battlefield
like this? Already she could hear the screams of dying men.

In the thick of the action she could see Arthur's banner fluttering above
the fray, with its great snarling red dragon spitting war. Beneath it rode
Arthur, surrounded by his knights, with Lucan, Kay, and Bedivere bringing
up the rear.

"Pendragon! For Pendragon!" reached her through the misty air.

"For the Prince! For the Prince!" rang back from Mordred's men.

Before long it was clear that the battle was equal on both sides. Arthur's
army was strong and well drilled, moving with the ease of long-serving fighting men. But Mordred's forces were fresher and younger too, powered by a
savage impulse and engaging with deadly zest. On their flank, the Saxon mercenaries were fighting a war of their own. Hacking, thrusting, driving forward as one, they chose their own targets and moved to destroy them with a
terrible joy.

The day wore on. Now she saw battle-weary knights dragged off their
horses and losing the fight on foot, as they went down in a sea of gore.

Horses too staggered with fatigue and lost their footing on the pitted grass, rolling over, wallowing in mud and all the carnage on the ground. Others ran riderless, trampling those below, screaming like humans from their terrible wounds. High overhead the ravens circled and cawed, attracted by the thick, sour smell of blood.

The sun crawled up the sky, reaching its zenith without losing its sickening shade of red. Whipped by the wind, the black clouds drifted sullenly to and fro, casting ominous shadows on the struggling hordes beneath. Guenevere stood without moving, above and beyond the fray, aloof like a God. But did the Great Ones, she wondered, even the Mother of them all, ever feel for Her suffering offspring as she did now?

A light dew was falling over the plain. Guenevere watched as it crept up the foothills and slowly enveloped the knoll on which she stood. Now the chilly fingers of mist were caressing her face and feeling their way damply down her neck. The battlefield was fading from her sight, and the position of the two armies was hard to see. A dull fear seized her to her bones. The fighting should have been over by now, if Arthur was going to win.

A strange stillness descended on the hill. In the silence she could hear the writhing mist whispering to itself. The harsh cawing of the rooks fell silent, and in its place came the sound of a fairy horn. Behind it came a flutter of high plangent notes and a thousand little plaintive twangling sighs. A gust of wind brushed her face with a frozen kiss, and the air grew cold. Then the breeze lifted the mist like a curtain and she saw an unearthly glow.

Across the hillside stood a great bronze chariot with three tall, queenly figures looking down on the battle below. Each was dressed from head to foot in black, with a black veil held in place by a golden crown. Their pale faces and large eyes gave them the air of beings from the Otherworld. Yet each was intensely present and alive.

In the forefront stood Morgan, leaning forward to look down on the fighting, in the grip of a passionate grief. From below rose a deep primeval groan, as if the whole battlefield were lamenting its burden of pain and death. Suddenly Mordred appeared through the blood-soaked gloom, locked in close combat with an enemy knight. He was fighting with vigor and zest, free-swinging, invincible. With one tremendous stroke, he had his opponent down. But as he fell, the knight thrust wildly upward, and the point of his blade found a chink in Mordred's armor under the arm. It could be no more than a flesh wound, a feeble stroke by a dying man, but Mordred stood frozen in disbelief as the red blood ran down. Then he tore the scabbard from his belt, threw back his head, and howled like a soul betrayed. Leaning out of her chariot, Morgan raised her hands to her temples and cried out in an answering lament. Watching Mordred's anguish was a killing grief to her, Guenevere could see.

At Morgan's shoulder stood a woman of great age, her hair like snowflakes clustering round her brow. She had Morgan's face, and her large eyes too expressed a life of glory mingled with grief. Her austere air was that of a queen born to command, but her features were softened by a beauty that had outlasted time. For thirty years Guenevere had known her as Morgan's mother but Arthur's too, the Queen of Cornwall, once the fair Igraine. Her heart froze. There was only one reason why Igraine would be here to greet her son.

The third occupant of the chariot was the tallest, though Morgan and Igraine would make other women look small. Her black robes had a richness not of this world, and her draperies moved with her like living things. The crown round her brows shone with crystal and gold and a gauzy veil covered her face. But Guenevere could still trace within the outlines of her Otherworldly face, her thousand-year-old smile. And once again she heard a voice from long-ago Avalon when the Lady had first wished Arthur farewell, and given him a pledge to take with him to the end of his days: *We shall meet again, King Arthur, never fear. At the last crossing of the water, I shall see you there.*

Guenevere gripped her chariot wheel and stared dry-eyed in the mist. Morgan, Arthur's mother Queen Igraine, and the Lady herself—a chariot of queens come from Avalon to bring Arthur home.

Morgan sobbed, the weeping of a lost soul crying for the moon, the lament of a mother keening for her young. Queen Igraine reached to take her daughter in her arms and folded her to her breast. "Hush, little one," she said tenderly. But her eyes were full of tears.

The Lady held up her arms above them both, and raised her face to the sky. The sun was fading into a bloodstained horizon, and the first star of evening had appeared in the west. Her low, musical voice chimed like the stroke of doom. "It is time."

The ghostly chariot moved off down the hill, gathering up the last rays of light as it went. The Lady turned as it disappeared from view. "Come, Guenevere," she called, "follow. You are with us too."

❖   ❖

"KAY, KAY!" LUCAN screamed, pulling up his horse and gesturing with his sword. "Over there! Get to the King!"

Kay reined in his own charger and pushed up his visor in answer to Lucan's cry. Blood and sweat had made a nightmare of his face, and his eyes held nothing but despair. "I've been trying for the best part of an hour!" he howled back. "But that band of Saxons has been too much for me."

"Me too," Lucan cried grimly, looking round the terrible scene. On all sides, armored figures swung and slashed with the slow, uncontrolled action of men beyond fatigue. Kay was swaying in the saddle and trembling in every limb. The day's fighting would have taken a terrible toll on Kay, Lucan knew. Left to himself, the little knight would soon fall prey to a stronger enemy or the pain of his damaged leg.

"Get behind me, then," Lucan shouted, "stay with me, we'll get through to him."

Not far away they could see Arthur, fighting on the ground. He had long since lost his horse, as most of the knights had by now, the poor beasts going down under the enemy's long lances or slashed to ribbons with the Saxons' short stabbing swords. Like the horses, the Pendragon standard too was long gone. Near to where it lay trampled underfoot, Arthur was engaged in furious combat with a troop of Saxons, fighting back to back with Bedivere.

Lucan plunged back into the fray and Kay followed. They had to get to the King. Never before, Lucan wept inwardly, had they been cut off from Arthur in the thick of battle, and many times they had saved the King's life by being at his side. Had Arthur ever gone to war, he mourned, without the three companions at his back?

But the battle today had been like none they had fought before. It seemed like a war to end the world. Lucan shook his head in an agony of bewilderment. From the first the onslaught had been so heavy that they had lost their formation at once, and it had been all that each man could do to stay alive. Mordred's troops had proved far more ferocious than they had thought. They were everywhere too, with fresh reinforcements pouring in all the time—the Prince had plainly squandered Arthur's treasury on fighting men. Now, Lucan brooded, for every one of Mordred's troops killed, ten more sprang up to take their place. Hack and maim as he could, Lucan had the deadly sense of fighting an enemy that flourished the more it was struck down.

Meanwhile the Saxons, whispering to their weapons and shrieking to summon up their Gods of war, had cut swath after swath through Arthur's loyal ranks. Many an honest man, once a devoted father or loving son, had left the world to walk the astral plane with no more warning than a sound like a lover's kiss, when a fatal Saxon battle-ax had parted his head from his shoulders without remorse. To the men from the North, war was their religion and killing their holy rite. Tonight, Lucan knew, these warriors would lie down either in sleep or in death, rejoicing that their ancient Gods of blood and bone would revel in the feast they had had today. And now that they had tasted slaughter, who would hold them back?

"The King!" Lucan encouraged both Kay and himself, as they fought their way forward. Time enough to cleanse the land of the Northern killers when this battle was won. *If it is won* was the thought increasingly knocking at the back of his mind. But he would not admit it as long as he had breath in his body and the use of his sword. "Pendragon!" he bellowed.

He threw a glance over his shoulder and was reassured to see Kay coming up behind. Ahead of them Arthur battled his opponent to the ground, dispatching the Saxon with one blow.

Now the fighting was dwindling as the light faded and the overweary troops could do no more. But Lucan knew this was the most dangerous time of all. The horses now were resisting their commands, refusing to go forward when every step meant treading on a corpse or a screaming face. But with a ruthless use of his spurs, Lucan forced his way on.

And suddenly he was by Arthur's side. Breathlessly Lucan dropped from his horse and leaped forward to take Arthur by the arm. "Sire!" he gasped, pushing his visor back. "Here, take the bridle, you must remount at once."

"Lucan?"

Arthur turned toward him, his face a mask of blood. His helmet was split in two across the brow, and the visor had long gone. In the glaring red features, his eyes were a startling white, milk-blind with exhaustion and pain. Great slashes on his armor showed where battle-axes and broadswords had pierced the metal to the bone. But his flesh was intact. The scabbard at his belt had kept the wounds whole.

That meant the blood on his face came from other veins. Lucan felt a surge of fear. It was just such a look as this that had earned Arthur the nickname of the Red Ravager in his youth. And from the pile of dead lying around his feet, it seemed he had lost little of the strength of his killing arm.

"Mount, sire!" Lucan howled into his ear. Arthur's face changed, and he swung up into the saddle, roaring heartfelt thanks. He turned the horse's head into the fray with Bedivere fighting on foot at his side. Lucan clapped the horse on the rump to speed it on its way, and stepped back with an over-whelming rush of relief. His only thought was for Arthur—Goddess, Mother, save the King!

So he did not see the blood-crazed Saxon moving up from behind. The first he knew of the attack was a scream of dismay from Kay as the little knight drove forward to protect Arthur's flank. Gasping with triumph, Kay hurled himself into the breach. As he did so, the blow meant for Arthur swept Kay from his horse.

Ahead of him Arthur pressed on forward without alarm, unaware of Kay reeling at his back. The Saxon delivered a final thrust to bring down Kay's horse, then turned to other prey.

"Kay!"

Lucan leaped toward the small figure already slipping off his charger into the melee of bodies and horses writhing on the ground. He was just in time to see Kay's mount let out its dying scream, rear up, then buckle and collapse on the ground.

"Goddess, Mother!"

Lucan stumbled forward to catch up Kay's body in his arms, pushing up his visor to see his old friend's face. Kay favored him with the shadow of his old sardonic smile. But lost in tears, Lucan watched the light fading from Kay's eyes and knew that the little knight was making a drowsy farewell.

Lucan bowed his head. "Wait awhile, brother, in the Otherworld," he vowed hoarsely. "I'll either send you the villain who dared to take your life, or join you there myself."

"Go then!" screamed a guttural Saxon voice. Before Lucan could look up, a venomous stabbing spear pierced his neck. A brilliant shaft of light filled his brain, and he knew no more.

"GODDESS, MOTHER, THANKS!"

Following Arthur closely and, like him, unaware of what had happened behind, Bedivere cried with relief. It seemed like hours since he had last seen Kay and Lucan in the fray. Never had he felt more hopeless, more alone. Now, praise the Gods, they were all here again.

Furiously Bedivere fought onward through the press. Must not lose the King, he told himself fearfully for the thousandth time. A sick sense of failure was invading him to the heart. From the start, the day had not gone as it should. They had no room for maneuver, not enough horses, too many men. Yet was this enough to explain a battle where dead men were lying six deep and neither side could win? How would they account for it in ages yet to come?

Already the dead outnumbered the living on the battlefield. The fighting was coming to an end, and only the hardiest souls were still on their feet. It was not long before he saw Arthur lose his second horse, then scramble to his feet and battle on. Through the blood-misted gloom Bedivere saw Arthur strike his opponent down, then pause, resting heavily on his sword. There was time to push forward through the carnage to Arthur's side.

"Sire!" he cried.

Arthur cocked his head with a strange, mad air. "Who are you?" he said hoarsely, his eyes very bright.

"It's Bedivere, sire." He cast round the rapidly thinning battlefield, where the survivors were starting to limp off as twilight fell. "It's over, sire. I've come to take you home."

"Not yet."

Bedivere followed Arthur's pointing hand. Across the battlefield, Mordred stood like Arthur, leaning on his sword. His visor was up to allow him to catch his breath, and he was gasping and bleeding heavily, but alive.

Bedivere caught at Arthur's arm. "Come away, sire!" he cried. "You can have your revenge tomorrow, if you wish. Prince Mordred cannot escape now. There's nowhere in all the islands he can hide from your wrath."

But Arthur had already kissed Excalibur and swung it singing around his head. Weeping, cursing, swearing death, he waded toward Mordred through a sea of blood. "Turn, traitor!" he cried. "Defend yourself, or die!"

Mordred raised his head and saw who called to him. A smile of terrible beauty curved his lips. "Father," he said exultantly. "It is your turn to die!"

CHAPTER 61

n a trance, Guenevere followed the queens' chariot down the hill. She drove without feeling or thought, drawn onward by the strangeness of the vision and the sense of events still hanging in the stars. Dusk was descending in a fresh fall of dew, and the mist grew thicker as they came down to the plain. But the ghostly carriage with its three queenly occupants pressed forward unerringly through the gloom.

In the distance Guenevere could hear the cries from the battlefield, the shrill clash of weapons, and the groans, prayers, and curses of dying men. But the noises grew fainter as they passed, and for a while they traveled in silence, the quiet humming of their wheels the only sound.

Then the mist thinned, and a light breeze moved the air. Now a low wind sighed through unseen trees, rustling the leafless branches as the silver fingers of willows brushed against the bark of old oaks, and the aspens quivered as if their hearts would break. And now the soft, steady purl of running water came toward her, and the fresh moist smell of watercress and weeds.

They had come to the bank of the river beyond the plain. Morgan dismounted from the chariot and helped Igraine down. The Lady stepped forward, beckoning through the dusk. "Come, Guenevere." Guenevere followed the three tall shining forms. The mist moved with them as they went, now deepening, now drifting aside to show other landscapes from the one they trod. They came to the water's edge, then turned downstream. A little way down, the Lady raised her hand again, pointing toward a star-hung coppice overhanging the running stream. Her low voice rang like music through the night. "There!"

A long black barge was waiting beside the bank. Its stately sides were hung with funeral wreaths, and within it stood a royal bier shaped like a fighting dragon, with dragon's feet. A tall canopy shielded it from above, and the whole vessel was furnished and swathed in black.

A black-clad boatman stood ready in the prow—one of the Lake villagers, judging by the bright eyes peering from beneath his shaggy hair and the damp garments fashioned out of otters' pelts. Guenevere gasped. *A boatman from the Sacred Isle, waiting for us here——?* With a deep intake of breath, she steadied herself. *All rivers lead to Avalon in the end.*

Silently the queens stepped down from the riverbank into the barge. One by one they took their places round the bier.

"Come, Guenevere," the Lady called again.

Guenevere moved forward to the water's edge. The long, low vessel lay at her feet, and the Lady stood waiting, holding out her hand. There was no mistaking the light in the Lady's eyes, shining through the folds of her midnight veil, and the warmth of her smile. Guenevere could not move. Her mother had smiled like this when she'd said good-bye. All Guenevere had of her now was that undying farewell. Every night she had prayed to see her mother again. And it came to her like a shower of winter rain: *I thought they had come for Arthur—have they come for me——?*

The damp of the river was chilling her to the bone. She hovered on the bank.

Is this my hour?

"Guenevere——" came the Lady's voice, soft and low, but commanding too.

"Yes, Lady."

She took a deep breath and stepped into the barge.

THE SUN WAS dying in a blaze of red. Crouched like dragon lamps on the far horizon, the westering stars were beginning to appear. Starkly lit in tones of sky and blood, the two men faced each other on the twilight plain.

Arthur swung Excalibur joyfully in his hand. Tired as he was, a rare power warmed his veins. "Come on, sir!" he cried.

Mordred squared his back, his face transfigured too. He had been preparing for this all his life. Confidently he hefted his sword and drew his dagger from his back. Arthur had the scabbard, but youth and skill could beat down an old man.

And Mordred himself was still fresh and strong, he knew. All day long, even in the thick of the fighting, his Gods had been shielding his back and riding on the point of his sword. He had suffered blows, but not much loss of blood. And he had thirty years' advantage on the King. Arthur must surely be nearing the end of his tether now.

For there was no disguising the lines on Arthur's forehead, the deep grooves carving his battle-marked face from nose to chin. His eyes wore an odd, exalted look, and he was clearly so weary that he could hardly stand. Mordred saw Arthur's upraised arm shake, and his heart leaped up.

"Come on, then!" he cried.

In answer Arthur swung Excalibur in a clean, shining arc. Mordred parried swiftly and slipped to one side. But the singing sword had anticipated his move. Already it was flashing down to meet him again.

"So!" Mordred chuckled. His nerves tightened, and the blood sang in his veins. Every muscle and sinew tensed to fight to the death. Ducking, weaving, and treading lightly to and fro, he slashed back at Arthur with ferocious power and struck his slow-moving target more often than not.

"Goddess, Mother, save the King!"

Standing to the side, Bedivere watched in an agony of fear. Arthur's great body had fought too much today. Against the younger, lighter man, he seemed chained to the ground, nipped and tormented like a bear at the stake. Yet Excalibur was weaving its spell, and the scabbard he wore meant that none of his wounds had bled. Above all, Arthur's undaunted spirit shone through like a flame, and his dogged endurance was wearing Mordred down.

At last one swinging blow sent Mordred to his knees. For the first time, fear showed in the younger man's eyes. Winded, groveling, he reared up, scrambling to his feet. But Arthur was ahead of him, with his sword at Mordred's throat.

"Oh Mordred," he groaned. "You were the bastard of my own black lust, and God has justly punished me for my sin. But no traitor can hope to live. Make your peace with your Gods, and prepare to die!"

Bastard—

He called me bastard—

Mordred's brain was bursting. He could bear no more. In one animal move he sprang up from his knees, slipped his dagger under Arthur's breastplate and drove it deep into his side and up toward his heart.

Of its own volition, Excalibur found his throat and with it a vein. Mordred screamed and staggered back, clutching his neck, vainly trying to stem the bright red torrent gushing from the wound. Then his voice was choked by a bubbling rush of blood, and he fell to his knees. Moments later he lay on the ground, his life's liquor pouring away into the earth.

"Mordred!"

With a howl of despair, Arthur threw down Excalibur and ran to Mordred's side. Weeping, he took Mordred in his arms. Mordred's eyelids fluttered, and he tried to smile. Arthur tore off his battered helmet, covered the cold face with kisses, and stroked his hair.

"Sire—" Bedivere stood by in hopeless grief as Arthur lamented over his dying son. The young man's breath had grown shallower, and his flesh had the pallor of the damned. A febrile pulse was throbbing in the hollow at the base of his neck. Bedivere locked his hands together and began to pray. Mordred's heart was failing. It would soon be over now.

Then Arthur stiffened, struck with a new thought. His hand moved to the sacred scabbard and tore it from his belt. Arthur brought it to his lips with a prayer and laid it on Mordred's chest. At once the gaping wound in Mordred's throat changed color and the blood ceased to flow. His breathing eased, and some fragile signs of life came back to his face.

But without the precious scabbard, blood spouted from Arthur's side. At the same time, all his other wounds began to run. He rose to his feet, a look of triumph and fulfillment in his eyes. Bedivere saw his spirit withdrawing from life. Ahead of him lay only the road to death.

"No, sire!" he cried, shaking in every limb.

"It has to be, Bedivere," Arthur replied.

His smile was very sweet. Stooping to pick up Excalibur, he kissed the blade and thrust it through his belt. Then he laid a farewell hand on Mordred's head. A great light of love shone in his fading eyes. "Farewell, my son."

Turning, he beckoned Bedivere to his side. "Help me a little farther, if you will. I shall not call on you much longer."

"Sire, let me get you back to Camelot—we can still save you and the Prince—"

"No—never again. It is finished. We are all shadows now, creatures of the dark." Arthur's smile transcended the sorrow of his words. He threw a heavy arm round his knight's shoulder and pointed a faltering hand into the mist. "To the river, Bedivere. They are waiting for us there."

CHAPTER 62

The dark barge glided onward through the dusk. High overhead the bright stars glittered and sang. Guenevere stood in the prow, her eyes vainly trying to pierce the mist ahead. Behind her in the boat, not a soul stirred.

Afloat on the dark running river, she was at one with time. Now she saw her life, her loves, her losses, and her joys lost in another world an eternity ago. Lancelot came briefly into her mind. Then *Arthur—oh, Arthur* came to sweep him away.

On either side of the river the trees arched and met, leaning out to reach one another like lovers divided by fate. In the warmth of the summer sun, they would have formed a living corridor of vivid green. Now they stood blasted by winter's creeping rage, the leafless branches no more than stark black bones.

The barge was gliding into the bank. In the depth of the wood she could see a rough brake of ancient holm oak, the low evergreen offering some shelter from the night. As they watched, two figures came into view, one staggering under the other man's weight. Guenevere gasped. Assisted by Bedivere, Arthur was answering the unseen call.

"No farther!" Arthur cried.

"Here, sire?"

Their voices carried clearly through the trees. From within the barge, she could hear every word.

"Lay me down," Arthur gasped.

Bedivere hastened to obey. He knew every word was costing Arthur pain. He had half-carried, half-dragged his King all the way from the battlefield, watching the trail of blood marking every step. Now he knew they had come to the end of the strength they shared. And he feared they had also come to the end of the world.

Fighting back his dread, he laid Arthur tenderly in the shelter of the brake. With a sigh, Arthur settled back and closed his eyes. His great face was ravaged with a thousand lines of pain. But a kind of peace was coming to him at last.

"Hear me, Bedivere," he said hoarsely. "My day is done. The fellowship of the Round Table is at an end. Caerleon will crumble and Camelot is no more. My journey now lies west with the setting sun."

"No!" Bedivere cried.

"Do not grieve," Arthur said gently. "We were the noblest band the world has known. Our story will live when countless men have died. Our names will bring boys and men to knighthood in ages yet unknown."

"Don't leave us, sire!" Sobbing, Bedivere saw himself a castaway and alone, a wandering knight without a master or a home, forlorn forever, pining like a seabird on some unknown shore. "You are our lord, we have nothing without you."

Arthur pressed his hand. "Seek out Lancelot, and take service with him. He will gladly accept your sword." He gave a ghostly smile. "Bear him my loving greetings and beg his forgiveness for my lack of faith. Say I shall meet him in the Otherworld."

Bedivere shook his head wildly. "But sire, let me get a doctor, and you will live! Prince Mordred too, you must have saved his life. We'll have Kay and Lucan, we'll restore the Round Table again. And then—"

"No, Bedivere." Arthur's voice chimed like a passing bell. "I gave my life for Mordred's when I gave him the scabbard to stanch his wounds, but the Gods will decide if they wish to accept the gift. Only they can say whether we live or die. No human hand can turn back the great wheel. Now take Excalibur and go to the water's edge. Then make a prayer to the Mother, and cast it in."

The great sword was keening at Arthur's side. Bedivere hurriedly drew it from Arthur's belt. Then his mind misgave what he had just heard. He gasped. "Throw Excalibur in the water?"

"Yes!" Arthur winced with pain. "Do it now, go, don't delay!"

Bedivere pushed through the undergrowth clutching the mighty sword, blind with confusion and dread. The long silver shaft danced before his eyes, and every one of the ancient, lustrous jewels on the hilt seemed a living reproach to the thought of casting it away. All down the blade, the ancient runes danced in the dying light like living things.

She Who Is and Was, Made Me for Your Hand

Bedivere did not need to read them now. He could remember as well as yesterday when Arthur had pulled the great sword from the waters of the Lake. "Your hand, sire!" he agonized to the empty air, "not mine!"

Throw Excalibur in the river? How could he do such a thing?

Before he reached the bank, he already knew that he could not obey the King. Arthur was not himself. He would recover, he would need Excalibur again. Then Kay and Lucan would not forgive him; he would never forgive himself.

He did not hear the silver sword crooning with excitement as the water drew near. Instead he buried it carefully in the lank grass, heaping up dead leaves to cover its shining blade.

"What did you see?" Arthur demanded huskily as he returned.

Goddess, Mother, forgive me—Bedivere drew a breath and launched into his first lie. "I saw the river running, and the willows weep."

"Oh, Bedivere," Arthur groaned. "Would you play me false? Go back and do as I ordered you."

"Sire, why?" Bedivere cried in desperation.

"For only so can my soul leave the world! Only by this is our story finished, and Arthur, Guenevere, and the Round Table set in the stars for all time!" He raised a trembling hand. "Now go!"

Bedivere stumbled away, weeping like a child. Bring an end to the Round Table, an end to Arthur's life? At the place where he had hidden the sword he sat down on the ground, hugging his knees and pouring forth his grief. "I am his knight!" he wept. "I swore to save his life. How can I bring about his ending now?"

At last he collected himself and got to his feet. When he came back to Arthur, he was prepared.

"So?" Arthur's eyes glittered harshly in the gloom.

"I saw the water lapping and the waves grow dark."

Arthur's eyes darkened. "Bedivere," he cried, "you have betrayed me twice! Is it all for Excalibur's jeweled hilt? Or do you mean to be king with it when I am gone?"

Bedivere flung himself sobbing at Arthur's feet. "Sire, it is none of these things! But I don't want to be the one to end your life!"

"End my life?" Arthur's voice was scarcely more than a harsh croak.

"Bedivere, you will bring me to eternal peace!" He closed his eyes. "Or condemn my soul to wander the world without the worlds. When I had the sword from the Lady of the Lake, I swore to return the gift to the Goddess when the time came. Only so will I enter Avalon—if it is not too late—"

"Forgive me, lord!" Sick with shame, Bedivere took to his heels. At the river's edge he pulled out Excalibur from its hiding place, then took up a place on the farthest reach of the bank.

"Goddess, Mother," he cried, "hear my prayer! My lord King Arthur offers his sword to you, and with it his soul to bear away to rest. Accept this gift, if it please you, for it is all he has to give. But his spirit will grace any heaven and walk shining with the stars!"

Reverently he kissed Excalibur's singing blade. Then he swung the great sword three times round his head. On the third count, he let go of the stone-encrusted hilt. The weapon spun away through the night.

It flew in a shining arc through the misty air, then fell in a graceful curve to the blackness below. But before it could enter the water, a hand broke the surface, then a white arm. The unseen creature caught the sword as it came flashing down, and held it upright quivering through the mist. Then it solemnly returned Bedivere's salute, circling once, twice, three times through the air. With a final flourish it sank below the waves and the water boiled above it, and then was still.

This time Arthur greeted him before he had a chance to speak. "It is finished."

Bedivere nodded humbly. "Sire, it is."

"Lay me by the water, and I shall go no more."

At the water's edge, Arthur lay smiling but deathly pale. A light shone round him, and the lines of pain and age were gone from his face. He turned to Bedivere. "No tears," he said gently. "You have served me well." Then his smile became even sweeter, and the light about him deepened to a glow. "Farewell," he said.

"Oh, my lord—" Bedivere thought he would go mad with grief. "Will you leave me here alone among my enemies?"

"All our great enemies will die with us. The world we knew is gone."

Bedivere wailed aloud and tore his hair. "Alas, lord, then what will become of me?"

"Comfort yourself," came the last husks of Arthur's voice. "For I am only going to the valley of Avalon to heal my grievous wound. There I shall rest with my knights until I return."

He closed his eyes. The air shimmered and a chill settled on the earth. Before Bedivere's eyes, Arthur's features became more noble, more cold, more set. His face took on a marble purity, and his body relaxed into its eternal sleep.

There was no place for him now on earth. Bedivere leaped to his feet. "Goddess, Mother," he howled, "where are you?"

FARTHER UP THE RIVER, the willows shivered at the grief in Bedivere's cry. The Lady nodded to the boatman. "It is time."

The stately barge glided forward and into the bank. Bedivere fell to his knees and raised his hands in prayer. His eyes roved in wonderment over the four queenly figures all dressed in black, but Guenevere could see that he knew none of them. The mist hanging over the river had clouded his eyes.

In silence the boatman lifted Arthur onto the bier. Weeping, Morgan and Igraine settled him tenderly among the black draperies and began to attend to him, one on either side.

The Lady stepped toward Arthur and took his hand. "Welcome, my lord." Her voice had all the music of a waterfall and the depth of a standing mere. "It is the last crossing of the water, King Arthur. I shall bring you there." She raised her arm and pointed down the fast-flowing stream. "To Avalon!"

The barge moved off. Guenevere gripped the prow and stared out into the night.

CHAPTER 63

A valon, Avalon, *mystic island, home*—

The black waters pulsed steadily, bearing them along. Here and there an owl lamented, and she heard a heron cry. Arthur lay on the bier, his breathing steady, his eyes closed in sleep. His face had softened, and all signs of battle had faded from his dress. Watching from the prow, Guenevere traced the outlines of the face she had loved so well, the broad forehead and strong chin, the open, fearless contours of truth and trust. Arthur's noble features had shaken off conflict and pain, and she could see once more the high ambition of their youth, the will to do good, the visionary gleam. Even now, the thick fair hair was not much streaked with gray but silver-gilt, curling onto his shoulders as it always had.

Seated by his side, Morgan was feeding her eyes on the sleeping form, her huge, hungry gaze starlit with famished love. She clung to Arthur's hand, cradling it between hers, reaching up in wonderment every now and then to stroke his face or hair. Behind her Igraine stood guard over them both, one hand on Morgan's shoulder, the other resting lightly on Arthur's head. At the back of the barge the Lady stood tall as a lily shining through the night.

On they went, and on, moving downstream, westering into the night. But as they went the swirling mists lightened as if toward day, and each dancing, gleaming particle of air took on a silvery light. They floated onward into a golden dawn, passing through smiling meadows and well-kept fields. An endless summer sun shone on leafy groves of oak and ash, and the banks were white with hawthorn, the tree of the Goddess, eternally in bloom.

The sun passed over the meridian and began its descent. The waiting mists rose from the waters and blotted out the banks, and the stream ran slower as the river broadened out. Now Guenevere could hear the call of wildfowl from the mere, the soft weeping of curlews and the bitterns' sorrowful cry. The faint air of spring, the pink-and-white scent of apple blossom reached her from far away. She shook her head. *The apple trees are all gone,* the Lady had said. *The Christians have stopped the streams, and the Lake is no more.* Yet her every sense told her that Avalon was near. *Avalon, Avalon, mystic island, home.*

They glided onward into the setting sun, floating down a river of red and gold. Through the mist she could see the outline of the Tor, the great hill shaped like the Mother lying asleep, hiding the secrets of the world within her grassy flanks. As far as she could see, the streams and rivers ran into the Lake, and the Lake lapped round the island as it always had. But in truth now she could not tell the sweet waters from the mists of memory. All she knew was that the great island still rose majestically over the smiling, eternal water as green as glass.

The sun was sinking into the west as they entered the Lake. All Avalon lay open to them like a dream, reaching out, calling to them through the blossom-laden air. At the far edge of hearing, she picked up faint sounds of building work, the ring of trowel against stone, a volley of monkish commands, and the shouts of men. Through the mist she could see a great church rising on the Tor served by a mighty abbey, home to a thousand black-clad creatures with raw, shaven heads. She saw their fishponds, their bread ovens, and their dovecotes, their rich treasures, their alms for the poor. But all this was in another time and place.

The barge floated silently into the Lake. The island opened to meet them, and they glided over the glassy water and into the hollow hill, into the land of eternal summer in the heart of the Tor. Before them spread groves of shining trees, each bearing silver leaves and golden fruit. In the distance she could see the white hawthorn tree blowing on the hillside above Merlin's crystal cave. And waiting at the water's edge to greet them were Nemue and Merlin himself.

The Chief Maiden was robed in gleaming green, her silky gown falling like water to her small sandaled feet. As always her arms and neck were open to the air, and her head was veiled with a green gauze as soft as the mist on the Tor. She looked at Guenevere with loving eyes. "You are welcome here. And King Arthur most of all."

Beside her stood Merlin, his golden eyes alight. Like Nemue, he was finely dressed in woodland green, his velvet gown and trailing sleeves woven about with glossy ivy and wild bryony. His familiar rings adorned his hands with blue and yellow stones as big as blackbirds' eggs, and his hair was held back by a wide gold coronet with the Pendragon crest. Leaning on his wand of polished yew, he looked every inch a king, and he greeted Guenevere like the queen she was. There was a true warmth in the depths of his agate eyes as he reached out to welcome her to the shore and bowed to kiss her hand. But when his gaze switched to Arthur, there was no mistaking his deep and hungry love.

Behind Merlin and Nemue clustered a bevy of the Lake Maidens all in white, crowned with moons of gold. Singing, they moved forward to lift Arthur from the barge. With Morgan and Igraine on either side, they carried the bier through the grove and up to Merlin's hill. But the disc of white stone at the entrance to his cave had gone. Drifts of white hawthorn covered all the hillside, and there was no opening to be seen.

The small procession came quietly to a halt. Standing at its head, the old enchanter lifted his wand and breathed the words of power. As the spell deepened, the hawthorn blossom shimmered and the earth parted on command. Two massive doors appeared in the hillside, paneled with carvings depicting the deeds of the knights of the Round Table, scene by scene.

Merlin clasped his wand, and whispered to it again. Slowly the doors opened on the space within.

"Goddess, Lady—" Guenevere caught her breath and tears rushed to her eyes. There could be no better place to lay Arthur to rest.

Within the hillside was a lofty cavern, a great hall formed by nature but finer than the highest work of any human hand. Its shapely roof soared like the vaulted chambers of Camelot, and its walls were tapestried in crystals shining white and red. The high domed space was a place of healing, bringing rest after strife and peace after battle's wounds. And with rising joy, she saw that Arthur would not be alone.

Within the chamber stood a stone table, crowned by a massive throne. All around were carved stone sieges for Arthur's knights, each topped by a canopy bearing the occupant's name. With a leap of her heart, Guenevere saw that each seat was filled with a ghostly, sleeping form. The Round Table was united again as it had been in life, the fellowship resting for all eternity as one.

On Arthur's right hand sat Mordred, his eyes closed, his handsome face almost too beautiful to be borne. To Arthur's left was Kay, his slumbering face unmarked as Guenevere remembered before the long-ago wound to his leg had crippled him for life and left him in endless pain. Next to Kay, Lucan too looked his old self again. His red-gold hair sprang from an unlined forehead, the gold torque of knighthood gleamed at his neck, and his mouth curved again in the shadow of his youthful smile.

The warm domed space was lit by dragon lamps, peeping out of niches in the walls and ceiling like stars waiting to be born. Transfixed, Guenevere looked round the table at the enchanted forms. Sagramore, Griflet, and Tor, Ladinas, Helin, Erec, Balin and his brother Balan—they were all there, just as they had been in life. Pale and transcendent, Sir Galahad had come to the end of his quest. Opposite him, serene as he had never been in life, Gawain reposed with his brothers at his side. Gaheris and Gareth had a new dignity in death, but of all the four Orkney princes, Agravain was the most changed. In his pale face, Guenevere saw the man he was meant to be, before jealousy and fear had eaten his soul alive. Now all the darkness had left his strong-featured face, and he was a son of whom any mother might be proud.

His mother—yes, Guenevere was sure that Morgause must be here too. And all the mothers of all Arthur's knights gathered together with him for their last sleep. For here were old Sir Niamh, she saw now, and his long-ago rival Sir Lovell, along with King Pellinore and Arthur's foster-father, Sir Ector, the father of Sir Kay. Ancient as they were, they had had mothers once. And the women who bore these heroes would be with them now.

Merlin looked at Guenevere and smiled. "They are all here, every one." He gestured with his wand at the empty throne. "We were lacking only the King."

Morgan, Igraine, and the Maidens gathered round. Arthur was reverently set at the head of the table, seated on his throne, with the dragon crown of Pendragon on his head. The Maidens placed his orb and scepter in his hands, and fixed his battle standard above his head.

Merlin turned to Guenevere. "Now is the time for you to say farewell. Arthur will remain here with us, to sleep in peace. He has all that he needs now that the Old Ones have given him his knights and his son. But your race is not run. You must return to the upper world."

She had known all along that this moment must come. But now that it was here, she was shivering and afraid. Under the scrutiny of the Lady, Morgan, and Igraine, she moved round the table toward Arthur and kissed his sleeping brow. "Farewell, my husband and my love," she whispered. "May your God keep you till we meet again." She turned back to Merlin, her voice breaking. "What will become of him?"

"He will rest until the time when he comes again."

"He will come again?"

Merlin's golden gaze played over Arthur, full of love. "He will recover from his grievous wound. He will rest here, deep in his hollow hill, till the time comes when there is danger to the land. Then the trysting horn will sound, and he and his knights will ride out."

Her soul revived. "Then his name will live on in these islands—?"

"For all time." Merlin's smile was wonderful now. "Why, Guenevere," he said softly. "The very thought of Arthur guarding the land will hearten our people through ordeals yet to come. There will come evils greater than any yet, but in the darkest hour the spirit of Arthur will reign. When the last enemy beats against our shores, the King and his knights will meet them at the flood and turn back the tide."

"Glory to the King." A haunting chant began around the throne. In tones like the pulse of the earth itself, the Maidens sang of Arthur's greatness in battle and his glory in peace. The Lady stepped forward and laid Excalibur on the table before him, the hilt toward his hand, its jewels gleaming in the silver light.

"Farewell, King Arthur!" she cried.

The mystic chant went on. Now the Maidens' song remembered the days of his youth, when Arthur was strong and fair. When the widow and orphan were safe at his hand, and rogue knights and land-hungry lords dared not do ill for fear of the reach of his sword. Now soaring, now dipping, the sound brought back all the years at Camelot, all the sunlit days and secret, joyful nights. Looking at the noble, sleeping form, Guenevere lived again her love for Arthur, man and king, down the long span of time since their first fateful day.

And now she saw her life with Arthur becoming one with the story of the islands, that which had passed, and all that was to come. In their hands a dozen tiny kingdoms, scattered in forest clearings, lashed by wind and rain, had come together into something greater than them all. A fledgling nation had been brought to life under their rule as High King and Queen. Arthur had fought his last battle, but the story would go on. These gallant islands, tiny outcrops of rock on the edge of the earth, would roll bravely down the ages, beating onward, ever onward into the shining mist of the world still to be.

Her vision grew and spread. The walls of the cave dissolved, and she saw the gardens of Avalon, green fields bright with daisies, meadows gilded with buttercups and merry with little ones at play, children in woodland tunics with stars in their hair. One of these Star Children was Amir, she knew. *Wait for me, my son. One day I shall be here with you again.*

Beyond the gardens she could see the Lady's grotto, the cavern of the white spring and the red, lying deep below her house. On the distant altar, radiant in the dark, were four mighty golden objects seen only in dreams, the Goddess's loving cup, Her dish of plenty, Her sword of justice, and spear of defense. Guenevere cried out in joy and fear. "The Hallows! How did they come here?"

The Lady smiled her thousand-year-old smile. "Look, Guenevere." She gestured back into the cave of knights. Leaning over Arthur, Morgan was watching him with adoration. "Morgan brought them. They are her gift to Avalon, to ensure her admittance here."

"She took them from Lancelot when he was asleep," Guenevere cried. "She had them all along!"

The Lady nodded. "She was waiting for him in King Pelles's castle that night. She tricked him in the shape of old Dame Brisein. But she kept the Hallows safe from the Christians to preserve them for us. Now they are back on Avalon, where they belong."

Reverently Guenevere feasted her eyes on the sacred objects. Time out of mind, with these the Mother had fed and comforted all who came to Her, righted their wrongs, and championed their rights. Now they gleamed through the dark like the burning light of faith. Guenevere's soul trembled with a new vision, a new faith. Wherever women lived and loved, the Hallows would be with them, working out their way. In the glory of women's love for men, for their children, and for one another, these things would never die.

The Lady read her thought. "My work is over. The Hallows are safe now till the end of time. I must go."

Guenevere started with fear. "But if you leave us—what will become of Avalon?"

The Lady turned and smiled. "Look again, Guenevere."

In the body of the hall, Morgan was moving round each of the recumbent knights with a soft caress or a whispered word. Like the sleeping heroes, she was not as she had been. Her black eyes were full and bright, and her suffering face was transfigured with a humble joy. Taking care of others, forgetful of herself, Morgan was beautiful as she had never been in her life.

Guenevere looked, and understanding dawned. "This is Morgan's fate. At last she is with the only man she ever loved."

The Lady nodded. "Morgan's path here has been long and hard. She should have come to Avalon as a child. Queen Igraine knew that Morgan had special gifts. But King Uther sent her to the Christians instead. Now at last she is where she was destined to be."

Guenevere knew what was to come. "Morgan will be the Lady here when you have gone."

"As she was born to be. The Old Ones decreed it when the world was young. Have no fear, Guenevere, she will never be your enemy again. Now that she has Arthur, her life is fulfilled." She sighed. "Just as my work here is. I am free to go."

Panic ran through Guenevere. "Where are you going?" she cried.

"I am called to join the Shining Ones."

The Lady unveiled her face. It was like staring into the rising of the sun. Guenevere could hardly bear the radiance flooding the cave.

But already the Lady was fading before her eyes. "Farewell, Guenevere."

Behind her Guenevere could see rank upon rank of glowing points of light, each one a luminous being, a living entity of love. In their midst she thought she could see her mother's face, smiling at her with starlight in her eyes. Agony seared her, and she held up her arms. "Lady, take me with you! Don't leave me here!"

The Lady's words dropped through the air like pearls. "Arthur's struggle is over. Yours is not yet done. There are many miles to Camelot. But your place is there."

Already the air was shivering before her eyes. The hall was dissolving, the silver groves of golden apples melting into the air. Before her drifted the wall of white hawthorn above Merlin's cave, and she found herself out on the sleeping hillside. Night was falling, and the world was bare and chill.

The Lady's last words came chiming like the music of the stars.

"Your time will come, Guenevere. When your sun sets, we shall be waiting for you. But your day is not done. You must return to Camelot."

CHAPTER 64

Dawn was breaking as she came back to Camelot. Weary beyond words, she drew up on the edge of the Great Plain. In the center of the battlefield, a lone figure was wandering hopelessly among those aiding the wounded and burying the dead. Weeping, he would stoop every now and again to examine one of the fallen, then weep again when he saw that his search was in vain.

Guenevere's heart wept too. "Bedivere!" she called.

He came toward her with the end of the world written in his face. She leaned toward him. "You are looking for Kay and Lucan," she said gently.

"Yes, madam." He was blue with cold, and his teeth were chattering so violently that he could hardly speak.

"They are at peace. They are with the King."

"So—" He did not ask how she knew. His chin went up. "Then my task is done. I only wanted to give them a decent burial. Now I must obey the King's last command to seek out Sir Lancelot and take service with him."

"Sir Lancelot—"

The sound of his name stabbed her like a knife. She struggled to keep calm. "Sir Lancelot will surely welcome the offer of your sword." Her voice sounded strange even to her own ears. She tried again. "He will be glad to have a knight from these islands with him in Little Britain to remind him of former times—"

—since he has sworn a solemn oath and may never return—

She could not go on.

Bedivere saw her distress. Stepping forward, he took her hand and brought it to his lips. "May the Mother go with you, Majesty, wherever you go," he breathed, the lilt of his voice rising as he spoke. "And wherever I go, I shall pray for you."

She gathered the remains of her voice. "The Great One bless you, Bedivere, and speed you on your way. You were loyal to the King's last wish, you fulfilled his command, and so shall the world report you in after days."

❖   ❖

IN THE PALACE she found Ina white and strained, but everything in order and the household under control. "You left me to take charge, madam," she said as soon as the tremulous greetings were over and done. "And all has been well. We know that the fighting was deadly on the Great Plain. But up here at Camelot we have been at peace."

Will I ever be at peace?

Guenevere forced a smile. "I am glad to hear it."

Ina frowned. "Except for——"

"What?"

Ina made a gesture of furious distaste. "It's the Christians, lady. They've been here ever since you went away. They'll be demanding to see you any minute now."

"The Christians?"

But there was no good time to deal with men like this. She looked at her travel-stained gown, and resolutely forgot her aching bones. "Come, Ina, help me change. Then let us see them and send them on their way."

IN THE ANTEROOM, Sylvester and Iachimo sat stolidly on a bench while the Archbishop paced the flagstones to and fro. Furious, he felt it should be the other way round. Though the Pope was aware of their troubles as far away as Rome, the Archbishop had no doubt that His Holiness was not walking the floor for them. A superior should delegate such distresses, not feel them himself. Yet there was no way to avoid the pain of this.

Arthur dead! Lord God, is this Your will, or the Devil's work? For the hundredth time, the Archbishop clasped his hands in anxious prayer. The King had been a good Christian, and the loss of that noble soul would cost them dear. But Arthur had been more; he had been a friend. The Archbishop was shocked and saddened to be reminded of how few in his life had held such a place in his heart. He would dearly miss Arthur's magnanimous spirit, his gentle grace.

Now he was wrestling with a sorrow so deep he knew it must be a sin. Well, he would chastise himself for that later on. And it was a further sin, to be sure, that somehow or other he should have stopped this war. How could he ever explain this away in Rome? He knew with clear-eyed certainty and loss of hope that this was the end of his ministry in the islands here. To fail was to thwart God's purpose, and Rome did not forgive. A penitent's cell awaited him now, he knew. But on top of that, to see the concubine ruling the land! After all they'd done, God's victory so nearly won, to be in the hands of a whore they had almost burned?

And he'd committed yet another grave error, he arraigned himself bleakly, in letting her live. When Sylvester had wanted to burn her, had even brought her to the stake, he had known better, he had saved her life. And for what? To see God's will defeated, and the Great Whore restored again?

His pale lips tightened. Guenevere must not bring back Goddess worship in the land. He must convince her that the Christians did Arthur's will. Then perhaps she would let them continue the work they had begun. His soul revolted at having to beg like this. But the woman was Queen here now, and with Arthur and Mordred gone, of Caerleon too. What else could he do?

"Sir?"

He became aware of the cat-faced creature who served the Queen, curtsying to him with an insolent air. His fingers itched. Under the rightful rule of men, she and her kind would be the first to feel the whip.

Ina read his mind, and gave him a level stare. "Her Majesty Queen Guenevere will see you now."

In the Audience Chamber, Guenevere sat alone on her throne. Empty at her side, the other throne cried out for Arthur's familiar great body and larger-than-life presence. In the hall itself, a subdued clutch of courtiers attended quietly, anxious for life to begin again. Guenevere clasped the cold bronze arms of the great chair and felt the chill in the depths of her heart. *From now on, it will always be like this.*

The Chamberlain struck his staff upon the floor. "The Archbishop of Canterbury, Father Sylvester, and Brother Iachimo!" came the cry.

Gown flapping, the Archbishop strode down the center of the room. "Your Majesty—"

The bow he made her would have graced any court. Why was she so sure that he came in hate?

"Our deepest condolences to Your Majesty," the Archbishop began, "on your husband's death. The late King—"

"A moment, sir—" Guenevere leaned forward. "Arthur is not dead. He is merely sleeping till he comes again."

"Madam, to Christians there is no such sleep." The Archbishop drew himself up. "And King Arthur believed, with us, that there was one way, one truth, one life."

These ignorant men, with their little, little minds— Guenevere smiled. "King Arthur lives. He will never die."

It was not going well. Standing behind the Archbishop, Sylvester stared straight ahead and tried to keep calm. He had counseled against this visit from the start. The woman was their enemy. They would never prevail. But the Archbishop had insisted that they should try, and listen to him now, losing ground with every word and still floundering on. Well, thank God it's his job, not mine. Suppressing a savage grin, Sylvester clasped his hands behind his back, and set himself to enjoy his superior's discomfiture.

"Either way, madam, as the King's widow, or relict, as we might say, you would surely wish to carry out his will," the Archbishop was saying firmly. "And King Arthur had promised us—"

"Excuse me, sir, did you say that my husband was dead?"

The Archbishop paused. They had dealt with this already—was she mocking him? Or perhaps she was simply slow in seeing the truth, as most women were. "Yes indeed, my lady," he said with all the authority at his command. "The King was killed in battle. We know he is dead."

"Then death cancels all promises, does it not? Therefore I am not bound by what Arthur promised to do."

Cunning whore! The Archbishop caught his breath. "But the King would not wish to leave you alone and unguided in the world. The Church will be a second husband to you, the Holy Father will be the father you lost long ago—"

Guenevere held up her hand. "In my country, priest, women do not turn to husbands and fathers to run their lives. Whatever seems good to me in my soul, I will do."

Holy God, will she tear down our churches, drive us from the land? For the first time the Archbishop knew despair. She could despoil our treasures, set a mob to have us killed—

"Never fear, priest. You are safe from us." Guenevere tracked his fearful thoughts and did not bother to hide her contempt. "Your God destroys others; we have faith in love. Do not judge us by your miserable selves."

"Hear me, madam!"

"No, priest: in my court you hear me." Guenevere rose to her feet, gathering strength with every word. "Go about your business. Your churches and your lives will be spared. But for your part, do not think to destroy the

Mother-right. Learn to honor women, and you will be welcome back when you do. Till then, leave my court, and do not think to return."

She signaled to the guards. White with fury, the Archbishop was escorted out. He would not be silenced forever, she knew. But for now at least, she had given him pause for thought.

But would every encounter leave her drained and alone like this? Tersely she brought the audience to an end. Returning through the palace she met a hundred calls on her time, as well as tears, some of the people weeping for Arthur, some fearful for their own lives. Was the war over, would the King be back? These and a thousand questions detained her weary steps.

At last she gained the shelter of her quarters, where Ina was waiting, full of love and care. Swiftly the maid assisted her off with her robes and wrapped her in a soft chamber gown. Then she chafed her temples and wrists with patchouli and settled her on a great couch by the fire. "Rest now, lady. I shall call you in time for dinner in the Great Hall."

Dinner in the Great Hall—yes, she would have to be there; she had to be King and Queen to the people now. "Very well, Ina." She laid down her head.

As the maid moved away, there came a knock at the door. She lay back on the sofa as Ina went to see what it was. Weariness gripped her. She had no more tears, and felt she would never weep again. She needed to collect her strength and think of others now.

The door closed as Ina came back in again. She heard uncertain footsteps crossing the floor. Then they came to rest at the side of her couch and someone took her hand. And she heard again the voice she never thought to hear.

"Madame?"

CHAPTER 65

She was in his arms before she could open her eyes. The roughness of his cloak was sweet against her face, and his beloved body was strong and hard and warm. She could not speak. But at last she could weep, and her burdened heart overflowed.

"Hush, hush," he soothed her, and at last her tears grew less. But it was a long time before her soul grew still. She clung to him, afraid to let him go, plucking at his tunic, gripping his hand. "I thought you were gone—and I'd never see you again," she gasped out, winded with pain.

"*Never* is too long a word to say."

"But Arthur banished you—never to return." Her eyes opened on new vistas of pain. "You will lose your honor. You are breaking your oath—"

He laid a finger on her lips. "Not so. Remember what the King said."

"What was said when you left? Yes." She could hear it still.

"*Lancelot, you are banished from these islands, never to return.*"

"*Arthur, you gave your word—you promised Lancelot his freedom——*"

"*And he has it! Freedom to go all the way back to France!*"

"*Sire, I shall leave your country and never return.*"

"*Never in your life—as long as my rule holds sway.*"

Her eyes widened. "'As long as my rule holds sway—'?"

Lancelot nodded. "The King himself said that my exile should last only as long as he ruled."

"And now he's gone—fallen in battle—" She could hardly speak for pain.

"Hush," he said softly, and she could see his eyes bright with unshed tears. "Lady, come——"

He drew her to her feet and led her to the bed. Gently he laid her down and stroked her face, kissing her eyes until she had no more tears. Then his mouth found hers in a dozen kisses, sweet but starved, like winter fruit. So she wept again, and he held her till it passed.

Then with gentle persistence he began to caress her flank, circling her hip and lightly brushing her breast. Little by little she grew comforted, like a lost child returning to its mother's hand. Quiescent, she watched the dancing candles till she felt at one with the flickering flames. Then slowly the golden warmth invaded her too.

His kisses fed a hunger she had carried all her life. Now the old, sweet rhythm was building in her veins, as her gentle languor gave way to a deeper need. His touch, his every breath, were wonderful to her now, kindling her to a new anguish of desire. His familiar body, as dear to her as her own, stirred her as it never had before. Something rare and strange unfolded between them, and their spirits soared hand in hand to a different place.

Yet there was a sadness, a desperation about it too. His love, her need, split her to the core. *Never* beat through her mind with the pulse of doom. Every fear only made her reach for him more hungrily again. Then he would pause and soothe her, slowing her down, refusing to hurry on, no matter how she moaned for him and wept. When at last he took her, she was open to him as never before. He came into her body and possessed her soul.

Afterward they lay without speaking, watching a wintry sun dying in the sky. In the antechamber, she knew, Ina would be busy lighting the candles and making up the fire. Soon it would be the dinner hour, and the world outside would be knocking at the door. The enchanted moment was over, it was almost gone. And the grief ahead was almost too much to bear.

In the gloaming she studied his beloved profile, weeping inside. How many times had she tried to capture him like this, fix his image in her mind to take with her through the long days alone? How would she bear what she had to do? She knew she must speak, but she could not breathe a word. *Just a little longer—a moment more—*

"Madame?" Lancelot stretched sleepily, then gathered her back into his arms.

"I must get up."

He felt the stiffness in her body and smiled. "Lady, you can rest now. From now on, I shall always be at your side. I shall take you to my kingdom, and we shall rule there as king and queen. You are my lady—now I may be your lord."

It was the hardest word in all her life. "No, Lancelot."

He started. "No?"

"I cannot go with you." A wave of bitterness racked her from head to foot. "Arthur may sleep in Avalon in eternal peace. But he has left two shattered kingdoms crying to be restored. The dead, six deep, are clogging Camelot's plain. Caerleon has lost its barons and its knights. The vassal kingdoms look to me for sway. Who will heal the wounded country if I leave?"

He flushed, angry with himself and her. "I did not mean to advance my country over yours. Of course there is a great task here. I shall honor that. I shall be with you every step of the way."

That word, that pain again. "No, Lancelot."

"What do you mean?" he cried furiously. "Are you saying that I may not be at your side?"

She closed her eyes. *Goddess, Mother*— "Yes. We cannot be together. You must go."

"Look at me!" He reared up and seized her shoulders, wild with pain. "Do you mean this—?"

"Lancelot, I—" She could not go on.

He shook her frantically. "Talk to me, madame!"

"I have no choice. It simply has to be."

He threw her from him in a passion of rage. "A queen will always have a choice!" Gasping, he ran his hands madly through his hair. "You do not love me!"

She shook her head. "We have known the moment at the heart of love when two hearts beat as one."

His face was blind with shock and disbelief. "And you will still do this—?"

"Oh Lancelot—" She drew herself up in the bed and pulled away. "Even now, I am not free. All the world knows that Arthur is in Avalon— that he is not dead but sleeping till he comes again. How will it be if I am living here in open adultery with his knight—his friend?"

He seized her hands. "It needn't be open—we could take care—"

"All those around us would know. How could I command the allegiance of his men?"

"I shall give you battalions of my men, knights of Benoic, sworn to you to the death!"

She shook her head. "I have to rebuild the Round Table, and make new knights of my own—men of these islands, who would lay down their life for the land."

"The land?" he repeated savagely. His eyes were very bright. "Is that my rival, then, your beloved land?"

She rose from the bed and paced away over the floor. Through the window the bright hills and twilight valleys roamed away as far as she could see. The dark green landscape shimmered before her sight, and she saw the Fair Ones coming from their hollow hills and valleys at the misty dawn of time. Their task then had been to make the land as fair as themselves, and how they had succeeded, all the world knew. Then came the first dwellers in the silver skein of sea-girt islands, the dark children of the Old Ones, slipping silently through the marshes like otters, taking to their secret hides as the Romans marched by. Then after them came the warriors, the horned men from the North, then new invaders, bringing fire and blood. Wave after wave broke on the battered shore, and still the land lived on.

The land—never would she tire of each season's mystic dance, the soft blooming of spring into summer, autumn's ripening and winter's decay. The primrose by the path would always whisper to her heart in the same voice as the oak trees' mighty roar. The sweet rivers and shining mists would call to her, the high winds and glittering frosts would warm her spirit on the coldest day.

The land—its waters are the lifeblood of my soul, its sunlit fields and upland forests my flesh and bone. My sisters are the white doves in the trees, my brothers the bright-eyed lynx, the fox, the bear. Like the Druids now I can hear the ants chiding as they set about their work, the damselflies purring to their dragon mates, and the ladybirds hastening home. All the offspring of the Mother are kin to me now, all the kingdoms of the Gods are open to me through Her love.

So I crave no more than to live at one with this beloved land, her mountain spine my own cage of bones, her flowers my crown, her stones my bread, her growing things my food. And after me will come others, men and women who will love and serve this land and give their lives to cherish her green acres and fight against her enemies to the last syllable of human breath.

And so it will be till the end of time.

"The land, yes," she repeated in a dull trance. "Before you, before Arthur, I was wedded to the land. It is a mystic marriage none may break."

She turned toward him and held out her hands. One bore the ancient ring of the Queens of the Summer Country from time out of mind. On the other she wore the moonstone Lancelot had given her in the morning of their love. One by one she brought them to her lips, stroking the moonstone, reading its weeping depths.

She looked up to see his eyes fixed on her, burning with grief. "You are the love of my life," she said simply. "But I am the Mother of the land."

Now he felt the merciless power of her love, felt it penetrating his every fiber, stripping nerve from bone. Yet he knew he was fated to love her through every ravishment and anguish their hearts could conspire. A shaft of pain zigzagged across his face. Leaving you is an old wound of this war, he wanted to say. The war of love. But he could not add to the suffering he saw in her eyes.

"So be it!" He threw back his tangled hair with a reckless laugh. "Then lady, if I have to leave, give me something to remember you by." He held out his arms. "Come to me," he commanded with a fragile calm, "and let me love you once again before I go."

EPILOGUE

$\mathcal{A}$nd there the story might have ended, and some say it did. But the Old Ones are too wise to leave such things in mortal hands. Fate spins as it will, and nothing can hold back the wheel.

The night passed in flights of whispered memories, transcendent kisses, and a thousand shining tears. All night long the moon smiled on their deep embraces, and then Lancelot took his horse and rode away. The lovers parted weeping in a lifeless dawn, the world turned, and a bleaker day began.

Then Guenevere rode down to the Great Plain to see all those who had fallen in the King's last battle honorably interred and all Arthur's knights mourned, as was their due. And likewise were the remains of the Round Table also committed to the earth, for that great fellowship of knights was no more.

Then the Queen turned from the dead to the living and summoned all the followers of Mordred before the throne. There she gave them a month to quit the land, or else look for no mercy at her hands in the new realm.

Now the earth ran down to the dead of the year and a great cold locked the land in ice. Snow and frost bound all the roads and rivers, and the hills and valleys slumbered under banks of snow. Storms lashed the Narrow Sea, and no ship could sail. Men and beasts huddled together for warmth, the fires roared up the chimneys, and all the world slept an enchanted sleep.

But alone in the land the Queen girded up her forces and took to the road. The days were short, the ways drear and cold, but the love of Sir Lancelot was with her wherever she went. That night of parting, their two souls had kissed in a higher union than their bodies had ever known. "Tonight the Mother is with us," she had breathed in Lancelot's ear, and he had loved her again and whispered, "Yes."

Now she rode through snow and hail and sleet throughout the land, taking in all the kingdoms one by one. At each Great Hall of every petty king, she told of Arthur sleeping in Avalon, and everywhere she was acclaimed as sole ruler and High Queen. The vassal kings hastened to kneel to her and swear allegiance to her dying day. And everywhere their sons offered her their swords, and those who were worthy she enrolled in a new Round Table, her own band of knights.

Then slowly the Mother came back again to the earth. Day by day, Her pale unseen fingers warmed the trees and awoke the wayside flowers, and by night Her great healing light shone down. The birds played and sang in every tree, and the season was ripe for the land to be renewed.

Now as she traveled, Guenevere forsook the Great Halls where the wine and mead went round and royal bards sang to knights and kings and queens of battles long ago. Now she sought out yeomen and farmers, small-holders and lowly peasants, no matter how poor, to urge them to plant their crops and feed the land. At every snug-kept farm or straggling field, every orchard, byre, or barn, she stopped to put heart into those whose work must hearten the land. And they returned her love and set to work, tilling and sowing and planting as never before.

So she made her way back to Camelot in a world of burgeoning green, the tender shoots of the crops sweetening the starved earth. And reveling in the sweet leafy wonder and glory of spring, one day it came to Guenevere that the Mother's love was not for the land alone. Truly the Goddess had been with her that night. A new life was springing underneath her heart.

She was with child, the child of Lancelot. And as spring turned to summer and the seasons wore on, she grew full and blossomed like the land. When autumn *came, she labored long and hard and came near to death, but the Mother blessed her pains and she bore fruit. "We have a princess, lady," Ina murmured with shining eyes. And all knew that there could be no other name for the new lady of the Summer Country but Maire Macha, Battle Raven, after her mother's mother in the line of Queens.*

A child should know its father, and a father his daughter, the unexpected gift the Great One had sent. So then, as soon as spring unlocks the waters of the Narrow Sea, Guenevere will take ship to France. Lancelot has never failed to send to her since he left, greetings of love and longing she has gladly returned. Now she has a message for him that may not be entrusted to pen and ink.

So when Beltain comes round, bringing its fires and flowers, and the hawthorn drifts again on every hill, she will go to him. The country lies quiet, all the kingdoms are at peace, and all the islands know her as their High Queen. A queen may always make a visit to a neighboring king in pursuit of peace. And in furtherance of love and laughter and the joy of hearts united, nevermore to part.

In time another child will come to them, maybe more. But timeless lovers now, they will wander forever in the world beyond the worlds. She will never notice the gray hairs in the thick chestnut brown of his ever-handsome head, and he will not see the silver in the clustering mane of the lady who is to him all gold. Enchanted with each other, they have found the secret way into the house of love and will never leave it now. And always the blossom will blow for them on Avalon, and all true lovers will find peace there.

And in spring, when the woodland ways lie open again and the mountains are clad in their aching, misty green, Merlin will awake in the depths of his hollow cave. He will call his white mule and take to the roads again, searching, watching, guarding, for that is what Merlin does. He will voyage to Lyonesse and then to the Island of the West, anywhere, everywhere they keep the Old Faith. He will never fail in his eternal task: through him Pendragon will live forever, and Arthur will never die. And wherever Merlin goes, all the bards and Druids, all the dream weavers of the world and all the servants of the Great Ones wherever they roam, will tell tales of Arthur and Lancelot and Queen Guenevere. For together these lovers dreamed a golden dream, and it will never die.

HERE ENDS THE STORY WHICH HAS
NO BEGINNING AND NO END.
ANNO DOMINAE MAGNA MATER MM

LIST OF CHARACTERS

Abbot, the Father Head of the Abbey in London where
Arthur was proclaimed, leader of the Christian monks in
Britain, implacably opposed to the worship of the Great
Mother and the Lady of the Lake, later Archbishop
of Canterbury, highest Christian office in Britain

Agravain Second son of King Lot, brother of Gawain,
Gaheris, and Gareth, nephew and knight to Arthur, banished
for the murder of Sir Lamorak, his mother's champion and
chosen one

Almain, Sir Knight to Arthur, lost on the Quest for the Holy
Grail

Amir "The Beloved One," only son of Arthur and Guenevere,
killed in battle at the age of seven when Arthur took him
to war

Anselmo Monk of the Abbey in London, scholar and spiritual
authority on the Scriptures

Arthur Pendragon High King of Britain, son of Uther
Pendragon and Queen Igraine of Cornwall, husband to
Guenevere and father of Amir

Balan, Sir Knight to Arthur, twin brother of Balin, lost on the
Quest for the Holy Grail

Balin, Sir Knight to Arthur, twin brother of Balan, lost on the
Quest for the Holy Grail

Ban, King Former king of Benoic in Little Britain, father of
Lancelot, brother of King Bors, ally to Arthur in the Battle of
Kings

Bedivere, Sir Knight to Arthur, one of his first three companion knights

Blithil, Sir Knight of the Round Table, supporter and crony of Mordred

Boniface Once monk of the Abbey in London and an emissary to the Lady of the Lake on Avalon, later Cardinal and close adviser to the Pope at the Vatican in Rome

Bors, King Former king of Benoic in Little Britain, father of Bors and Lionel, brother of Ban, ally to Arthur in the Battle of Kings

Bors, Sir Son of King Bors, brother of Lionel, cousin of Lancelot, and knight to Guenevere

Brisein, Dame Former nurse and later waiting-gentlewoman to Princess Elaine of Corbenic, whose body is usurped by Morgan Le Fay

Brunor de Gretise, Sir Lord of a large estate who hosts Gawain, Gaheris, and Gareth on the Quest for the Holy Grail

Dinant, Sir Knight to Arthur, lost on the Quest for the Holy Grail

Domenico of Tuscany Papal envoy from Rome to the Father Abbot in London, and supporter of his crusade against Avalon

Ector, Sir Foster-father to Arthur on his estate in Gore, father of Sir Kay, knight to Arthur

Elaine Princess of the Castle of Corbenic, daughter of King Pelles of Terre Foraine, lover of Lancelot, and mother of Sir Galahad, the Child of the Holy Grail

Erec, Sir Knight of the Round Table, lost on the Quest for the Holy Grail

Excalibur Sword of power given to Arthur by the Lady of the Lake, which must be returned before his soul can find peace

Fair Maid of Astolat, the Elaine, daughter of Sir Bernard of Astolat, unjustly suspected by Guenevere of having a love affair with Lancelot, who died of unrequited love for him

Gaheris Third son of King Lot, brother of Gawain, Agravain, and Gareth, nephew and knight to Arthur

Galahad, Sir The Child of the Holy Grail, son of Elaine of Corbenic and Sir Lancelot through the trickery of Morgan Le Fay, in fulfillment of a prophecy made to his grandfather King Pelles of Terre Foraine

Gareth Fourth son of King Lot, brother of Gawain, Agravain, and Gaheris, nephew and knight to Arthur

Gawain, Sir Eldest son of King Lot, Arthur's first companion knight at the drawing of the sword from the stone and his nearest kin as the son of his half-sister Morgause, and brother of Agravain, Gaheris, and Gareth

Giorgio Once a monk sent from Rome to work with Boniface in the first Christian onslaught on Avalon, later choirmaster at the Vatican in the service of the Pope

Gorlois, Duke Champion and chosen one of Queen Igraine of Cornwall, father of Morgause and Morgan, murdered by Uther and Merlin

Griflet, Sir Knight of the Round Table feared lost on the Quest for the Holy Grail, who finally returns

Guenevere Queen of the Summer Country, daughter of Queen Maire Macha and King Leogrance, wife of Arthur, lover of Sir Lancelot, and mother of Amir

Helin, Sir Knight of the Round Table, lost on the Quest for the Holy Grail

Iachimo Monk sent with Brother Sylvester to Avalon to support the Christians' attempt to claim the Hallows for their own use, later deputy to Sylvester when he becomes the Abbot of the London Abbey

Igraine, Queen Queen of Cornwall, wife of Duke Gorlois and beloved of King Uther Pendragon, mother of Arthur, Morgause, and Morgan le Fay

Ina Maid to Guenevere

Kay, Sir   Son of Sir Ector, foster-brother of Arthur, and knight of the Round Table, one of Arthur's first three companion knights

Ladinas, Sir   Knight of the Round Table feared lost on the Quest for the Holy Grail, who finally returns

Lady of the Lake   Ruler of Avalon, priestess of the Great Goddess

Lamorak, Sir   Son of Sir Pellinore, knighted by Arthur after the Battle of Kings, where his father killed King Lot, later knight and chosen one to Queen Morgause of the Orkneys, murdered by Agravain

Lancelot, Sir   Son of King Ban of Benoic and Queen Elaine, knight of the Round Table, and lover of Queen Guenevere

Lionel, Sir   Second son of King Bors, brother of Sir Bors, cousin of Sir Lancelot, and knight to Guenevere

Lot, King   King of Lothian and the Orkneys, onetime ally of King Uther Pendragon, husband of Morgause, father of Gawain, Agravain, Gaheris, and Gareth, and later usurper of the Middle Kingdom and enemy of Arthur, killed at the Battle of Kings

Lovell the Bold, Sir   Ancient knight of the Round Table, and onetime champion to Guenevere's mother, Queen Maire Macha

Lucan, Sir   Former champion to Guenevere's mother and her chosen one, later one of Arthur's companion knights

Mador of the Meads, Sir   Former knight of the Round Table in love with Guenevere, who left court and returned to his estate after the death of his brother, Patrise

Maire Macha, Queen   Guenevere's mother, Queen of the Summer Country, wife to King Leogrance, and lover of Sir Lucan

Merlin   Welsh Druid and bard, illegitimate offspring of the house of Pendragon, son of a Pendragon princess and a spirit from the Otherworld, adviser to Uther and Arthur

Mordred   Son of Arthur and his half-sister Morgan Le Fay, cast adrift as an infant off the coast of Gore, later found by Merlin and restored to Arthur as his heir

Morgan Le Fay   Younger daughter of Queen Igraine and Duke Gorlois of Cornwall, placed in a Christian convent as a child by her stepfather, King Uther, Arthur's half-sister and onetime lover, mother of Mordred, once married to King Ursien of Gore

Morgause   Elder daughter of Queen Igraine and Duke Gorlois, given as wife to King Lot by King Uther, Arthur's half-sister, mother of Gawain, Agravain, Gaheris, and Gareth, and lover of Sir Lamorak

Nemue   Chief priestess to the Lady of the Lake, once courted by Merlin, who heals him in Avalon's crystal cave

Niamh, Sir   Ancient knight of the Round Table, early champion of Guenevere's mother and defender of the Mother-right, killed when Morgan Le Fay usurps his body at the knight-making of Mordred

Patrise, Sir   Knight of the Meads, brother of Sir Mador, poisoned by Agravain

Pelles, King   Fanatical Christian king of Terre Foraine and the Castle of Corbenic, father of Elaine and grandfather of Galahad, possessed of the belief that his daughter was fated to bear the peerless knight who would win the Holy Grail

Pellinore, King   King of Listinoise, father of Sir Lamorak, ally of Arthur

Pope, the   Leader of the Christians in Rome, Supreme Pontiff of the Church

Roddri   Monk of the Abbey in London, pupil of the scholar Anselmo, ambitious for advancement in the Church

Rutger, Sir   Knight of the Round Table, supporter and crony of Mordred

Sagramore, Sir   Knight of the Round Table, lost on the Quest for the Holy Grail

Saracens   Inhabitants of the Holy Land, valiant Arab warriors, and knights fighting against Christian invasions of their land

Sylvester   Monk sent with Brother Iachimo to replace Boniface and Giorgio on Avalon to wrest the Hallows from the Lady of the Lake, later the Abbot of the Abbey in London

Theophilus   Monk in the service of King Pelles of Terre Foraine

Tor, Sir   Knight to King Arthur, defender of the Saxon shore

Ursien, King   King of Gore, overlord of Sir Ector—the foster-father of Arthur—and husband of Morgan Le Fay

Uther Pendragon   Former king of the Middle Kingdom, High King of Britain, lover of Queen Igraine of Cornwall, and father of Arthur

Yvain, Sir   Eldest son of King Ursien of Gore, knight of the Round Table, lost on the Quest for the Holy Grail

LIST OF PLACES

Avalon   Sacred island in a lake in the Summer Country, the center of Goddess worship, modern Glastonbury in Somerset

Caerleon   Arthur's seat and the capital of the Middle Kingdom, formerly the City of the Legions during the Roman occupation, seized by King Lot after the death of King Uther, reclaimed by Arthur in a surprise attack, modern Caerleon in South Wales

Camelot   Capital of the Summer Country and ancient stronghold of its line of Queens, home of the Round Table, modern Cadbury in Somerset

Canterbury   Base of the Roman Church in the British Isles, and site of the first archbishopric in England

Cornwall   Kingdom of Arthur's mother, Queen Igraine

Dolorous Garde   See Joyous Garde

Druid's Isle, the   Mona, off the north coast of Wales, modern Anglesey

Gore   Christian kingdom of King Ursien in the northwest of England where Arthur and Kay were raised, modern West Lancashire and Cumberland

Hill of Stones   Ancient burial site of the Queens of the Summer Country, location of ritual queen-making, and site of the feast of Beltain

Iona   Island off the northwest coast of Scotland, site of the first settlement of Celtic Christianity in Britain

Island of the West   Modern Ireland

Joyous Garde   Sir Lancelot's castle, once known as Dolorous Garde when it belonged to Guenevere's kinsman, Prince Malgaunt, won by Lancelot in battle and the refuge to which he takes Guenevere

Listinoise   Kingdom of King Pellinore and his son, Sir Lamorak, modern East Riding of Yorkshire

Little Britain   Territory in France, location of the kingdom of Benoic, home of King Ban and King Bors, modern Brittany

London   Major city in ancient Britain, center of Christian colonization of the British Isles

Lothian   Ancient kingdom that was once part of the lands of the kings and queens of the Orkney Islands, located around modern Edinburgh

Middle Kingdom   Arthur's ancestral kingdom lying between the Summer Country and Wales, modern Gwent, Glamorgan, and Herefordshire

Orkney, Islands of   Cluster of most northerly islands of the British Isles, and site of King Lot's kingdom, later ruled by his widow, Queen Morgause

Rome   Capital of Italy, early center of Christianity, seat of the Pope, and the mother city of the Roman faith

Saxon shore, the   Site of invasions by tribes called the Norsemen, raiders from Norway, Denmark, and east Germany

Severn Water, the   The Bristol Channel, estuary of the River Severn, dividing the Middle Kingdom from the Summer Country

Summer Country, the   Guenevere's kingdom, ancient center of Goddess worship, modern Somerset

Terrabil   Castle of Queen Igraine of Cornwall, defended by Duke Gorlois, taken by King Uther in the siege where Gorlois lost his life

Terre Foraine   Kingdom of King Pelles in northern England, modern Northumberland

Tintagel Castle of Queen Igraine of Cornwall, capital of her kingdom

Welshlands Home to Merlin, modern Wales

York Second most powerful center for the Christian colonization of the British Isles after Canterbury, and the second most senior archbishopric

The Celtic Wheel of the Year

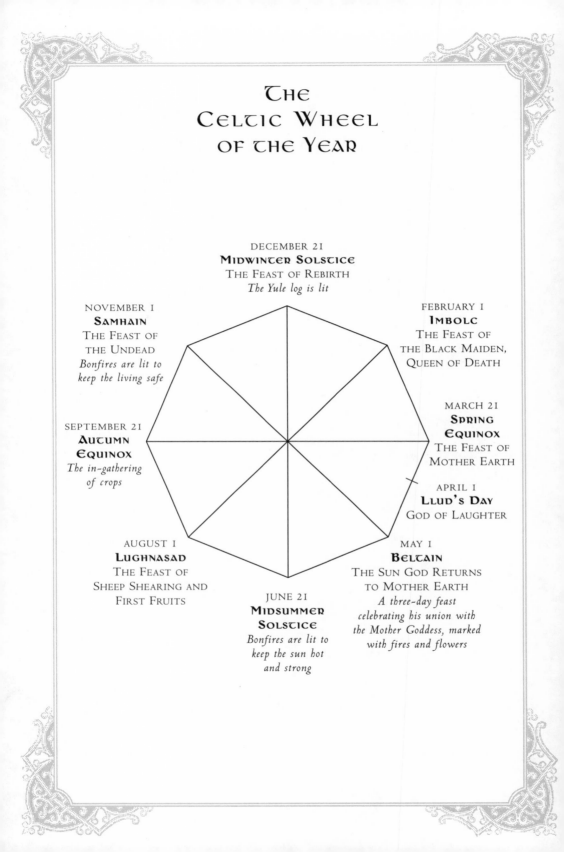

DECEMBER 21
MIDWINTER SOLSTICE
THE FEAST OF REBIRTH
The Yule log is lit

NOVEMBER 1
SAMHAIN
THE FEAST OF
THE UNDEAD
*Bonfires are lit to
keep the living safe*

FEBRUARY 1
IMBOLC
THE FEAST OF
THE BLACK MAIDEN,
QUEEN OF DEATH

SEPTEMBER 21
**AUTUMN
EQUINOX**
*The in-gathering
of crops*

MARCH 21
**SPRING
EQUINOX**
THE FEAST OF
MOTHER EARTH

APRIL 1
LLUD'S DAY
GOD OF LAUGHTER

AUGUST 1
LUGHNASAD
THE FEAST OF
SHEEP SHEARING AND
FIRST FRUITS

JUNE 21
**MIDSUMMER
SOLSTICE**
*Bonfires are lit to
keep the sun hot
and strong*

MAY 1
BELTAIN
THE SUN GOD RETURNS
TO MOTHER EARTH
*A three-day feast
celebrating his union with
the Mother Goddess, marked
with fires and flowers*

The
Christian Wheel
of the Year

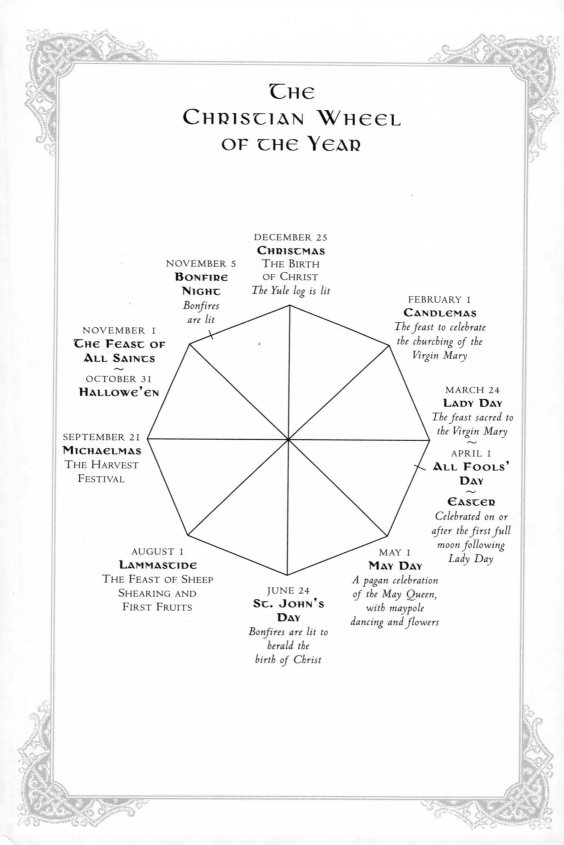

DECEMBER 25
Christmas
The Birth
of Christ
The Yule log is lit

NOVEMBER 5
**Bonfire
Night**
*Bonfires
are lit*

FEBRUARY I
Candlemas
*The feast to celebrate
the churching of the
Virgin Mary*

NOVEMBER I
**The Feast of
All Saints**
~
OCTOBER 31
Hallowe'en

MARCH 24
Lady Day
*The feast sacred to
the Virgin Mary*
~
APRIL I
**All Fools'
Day**
~
Easter
*Celebrated on or
after the first full
moon following
Lady Day*

SEPTEMBER 21
Michaelmas
The Harvest
Festival

AUGUST I
Lammastide
The Feast of Sheep
Shearing and
First Fruits

JUNE 24
**St. John's
Day**
*Bonfires are lit to
herald the
birth of Christ*

MAY I
May Day
*A pagan celebration
of the May Queen,
with maypole
dancing and flowers*

ABOUT THE AUTHOR

Rosalind Miles is a well-known and critically acclaimed English writer and broadcaster. Her novels, including *Guenevere: Queen of the Summer Country* and *I, Elizabeth,* have been international best-sellers. A native of Warwickshire, she lives in California and in Kent, England.